DISARMING
Dakota

DISARMING
Dakota

SUMEYA ABDI ALI

wattpad books

wattpad books

An imprint of Wattpad WEBTOON Book Group

Copyright© 2024 Sumeya Abdi Ali

All rights reserved.

No portion of this publication may be reproduced or transmitted, in any form or by any means, without the express written permission of the copyright holders.

Published in Canada by Wattpad WEBTOON Book Group, a division of Wattpad WEBTOON Studios, Inc.

36 Wellington Street E., Suite 200, Toronto, ON M5E 1C7 Canada

www.wattpad.com

First Wattpad Books edition: December 2024

ISBN 978-1-99025-900-5 (Trade Paperback edition)
ISBN 978-1-99025-901-2 (eBook edition)

Names, characters, places, and incidents featured in this publication are either the product of the author's imagination or are used fictitiously. Any resemblance to actual persons (living or dead), events, institutions, or locales, without satiric intent, is coincidental.

Wattpad Books, W by Wattpad Books, Wattpad WEBTOON Book Group, and associated logos are trademarks and/or registered trademarks of Wattpad WEBTOON Studios, Inc. and/or its affiliates. Wattpad and associated logos are trademarks and/or registered trademarks of Wattpad Corp.

Library and Archives Canada Cataloguing in Publication information is available upon request.

151302999

Cover design by Amelia Schiffer

I dedicate this book to my *hooya* (mother).

Thank you so much for encouraging me to read at a young age.

Because of your advice, and my desire to improve, my dyslexia became more manageable.

I cannot thank you enough for the world you opened up to me.

Part I
The Good

There was a beauty in our loveless lore.

A beauty that only the eyes of the wounded could admire and desire for.

A beauty that appeared to be,

To the watchful eyes,

Underneath me,

Growing beyond its seams.

I had met him on accident,

Could you believe?

An accident that almost destroyed me.

—Sylvia Ellington

Chapter One

West Coast

In mid-July, my mom woke up from her self-induced intoxication long enough to realize something was wrong with me. For most of the spring term, she'd dismissed my actions as teen angst. She'd thought she could avoid addressing the problem, and I'd simmer down after my birthday.

My mood didn't change. When summer break started coming to an end, she concluded that I needed help, and the only help that would suffice had to be financed by my dad.

For the first time since their separation, I would be living with my father in the golden state of California. If it were up to me, I'd still be in Maine, sleeping until two o'clock in the afternoon and inhaling cheese puffs for breakfast.

There was something else that had led up to that major decision, but I'd prefer to skip that part like an overindulgent opening credit to a movie. First impressions are key. And by ditching that portion, I get to be semi-normal for once in my life.

"Sylvia, at least smile a little more," Mom said as she loaded the last of my stuff into the back of her beat-up minivan. "I know this trip isn't what you want, but it's for the best. I'll miss you every second. You know that."

That wasn't what she really said.

It was what I'd like for her to have said to me—you know, being my mother and all. In reality, she stood there silently, smoking a cigarette until it turned into a stub. For unknown reasons, she had a habit of ripping off the filter before starting a cigarette. It was almost as if she wanted to be one breath closer to death.

White smoke streamed out of her mouth like a chimney as she exhaled the last puff and tilted her head up to the sky. Mom glanced down at me and smiled weakly. For a moment, no longer than a heartbeat, I could see why Dad had once found her pretty.

She used to be a model, or so she'd told me countless times growing up, reliving the heyday that lived frozen in her portfolios. I was the spitting image of her in her youth, and a lot her former friends had pointed that out. She'd done some photo shoots up in New York City for a few years while taking classes at a local college.

Not NYU, if that's what you're thinking. Some state college or something. None of that mattered in the end, because she never got her degree. She did, however, meet my father in an economics class that always let out late in the afternoon.

They loved to tell me the story. One day after lecture, when the sun was low on the horizon, he'd offered to walk her to her bus stop. Soon enough, it became a pattern. A pattern they both found comfort in, sharing conversations across the twinkling city.

Mom got pregnant with me the very same year. When my dad completed undergrad, the three of us relocated more inland for his law degree. My parents' divorce unfolded over the beginning of junior high, dominating my life and altering my sense of normalcy from the ages of ten to thirteen. Mom moved us to Portland, Maine, soon after the finalization of their strenuous split.

"You've got your plane ticket, right?" she asked, opening the driver's side door. "I don't want to have to do a U-turn halfway—"

"I printed it out yesterday."

She popped her chewing gum, loud. "Don't get snappy with me."

I bit my tongue.

Here I was, minutes from leaving my mother behind for the first time in over five years, and there wasn't an ounce of sadness in me. Leading up to this flight, I'd struggled to hide my smile at every turn, praying she didn't notice.

"I hope you ate breakfast," she said, "because I'm not stopping for food."

"That's fine by me. I've got a bit of cash for food when I get to the airport."

Mom hesitated at the open driver's door, hand on the handle.

"Can I see how much you got?"

"No," I stated. "I only have enough for myself."

She grumbled incoherently under her breath, jumping inside the car with a frown she didn't bother hiding from me. "Get the hell in and put on your seat belt, then. I don't have forever. I've got to pick up Kevin from work."

"I thought you broke up with him."

Or he broke up with you, I thought.

Kevin was her deadbeat boyfriend. He drank at a faster rate than my mother, pounding a six-pack of beer within an hour, and he appeared twice as old as anyone else in their social circle even though he was younger than my mom. My thoughts on his whereabouts were based on a hunch, a solid hunch that had developed more depth the longer he avoided my mother. For two years, Kevin had mooched off the small amount of child support we got from my dad—emphasis on had. Once I'd turned eighteen this month, and the checks stopped showing up, Kevin disappeared just as fast.

The only person who hadn't caught on was my mom.

"We're okay," she said firmly. "I'm thinking, with you out of the house, he can move in. Probably change your room into a storage area, too, while I'm at it."

"How old is Kevin again? Thirty-two?" I asked without waiting for an answer. "Why doesn't he figure out his own driving arrangements? Or take the damn bus for all I care."

I murmured the last part, but clearly not quietly enough.

"Hey, I heard you. You can't talk about Kevin like that. He's going to be your stepfather one of these days."

That man is closer to an early grave than he is to marrying you.

I didn't say that out loud. I had wanted to, though, for weeks now. But whenever I spewed honesty to my mother, she would give me the scariest look known to man. It was too early in the morning for me to take her infamous glare, so I let this one drop.

Mom stuck the key into the ignition. "You better at least have some gas money."

"The tank is full. I filled it up last night," I added before she could argue with me, slipping into the passenger seat.

She scoffed, buckling herself in. "Do you even know what kind of gas I use? I told you—I hate when you mess with my car."

"I wasn't messing with it. You wanted gas in the car. I figured I might as well put it in before our drive to the airport." I fastened my seat belt with shaky hands. Keeping myself calm around my mother was a task that even eighteen years couldn't train me for. Even if I was in the right, no amount of convincing would get an apology out of her. Her stubborn pride wouldn't allow it.

"Since my flight is so early," I said, "I knew we had to beat the traffic."

I hoped to let the conversation drop.

But Mom had to throw in the last word.

"You could've left it at that. I don't like being late to a flight either. I get it. Next time, ask if you're gonna take my car to fill it up, though."

That right there, ladies and gentlemen, was my mother's form of saying, "Thank you." I liked to pretend she was a typical mom sometimes. Like the ones I saw on TV and in movies. The kind of mom who made cookies in the kitchen, not cocktails at midnight. The kind who talked about boys with her daughter and snuck a quarter under the pillow, pretending to be the Tooth Fairy. Instead, I'd been gifted a mother who took my money if she was given the chance.

To comfort myself, I would constantly make up scenarios about how it would feel to have a mother that cared.

During the long drive toward the airport, a light drizzle began to coat the outside of the car. My gaze landed on the populated sidewalks and crowded storefronts.

I wondered how much of an effect this move was going to have on the people I knew in Maine. Would they miss me? Would they notice I'd left? Would they care?

I didn't really need to answer that last one.

Of course, without a doubt, they wouldn't care.

The alarming number of death threats I'd received was one way of knowing. People would be glad to see me go. They'd be happy, pleased, elated, overjoyed, enthusiastic, relieved . . .

I was running out of adjectives.

There wouldn't be a single soul who'd miss me.

I pulled out my phone and started deleting every contact I had saved, every text message I had, and every voicemail I'd ever received. I'd already changed my number earlier that week. The only person I'd given my new one to was my mother. And that wasn't by choice.

As the car eased onto the highway ramp, I counted each individual reason why I was glad to leave my home state. But the main reason, and the only one to give me real joy, was how ecstatic I was to retire from the debilitating job of babysitting my mother.

Chapter Two

Ghosts

There were no tears when I got out of my mother's car at the airport. She didn't bother putting the car in park to step out, not even to help me with my things or to hug me goodbye. I entered the building the same way I'd done most of the important things in my life: alone.

Pausing before I stepped fully inside, I turned around slowly to see her drive off. I'd like to say that I was heartbroken by her inability to show any care for me, but that would be a complete lie.

I lost my mother the same day I lost my father. He'd stolen her sanity and her peace as he swept up a second woman, leaving us in the dust the moment the divorce was finalized. I'd rushed to reattach my mother's heart to her chest, but there wasn't much I could do for the unrecognizable monster he'd created.

In the years that followed, Dad returned to his old stomping grounds, finding joy in the same town he had desperately tried to run away from after graduating high school. Back then, he couldn't stand the way time stood still there, but now he longed for it. My mother's words—of course—on why he'd left and then returned.

Based on what the map on my phone said, Harper Falls was twenty minutes from a beach. Dad had showed me photos of his hometown a few times when I was a kid, and Mom had spoken about their wedding there. She still, to this day, bragged about how elegant and costly it had been. Other than those primary-school stories, I was clueless about the place I'd be calling home. Mom said it had small-town vibes, bordered by barren valleys. Harper Falls was over an hour from San Francisco, where I'd be landing, making it closer to the state capital.

The reunion between my father and me after my plane landed was nothing to sob over. There was a lot of restrained tension in the beginning. And when we did decide to talk, we kept interrupting each other. This happened twelve times. Yes, I counted. I have a tendency to count. Backward and forward; words and numbers.

You name it, I've counted it.

"How was the flight?" Dad inquired while turning down the smooth jazz playing on the radio. His world was so calm compared to mine; I could tell from his choice of music and the shiny four-door SUV he drove, with its minimal scratches. It was nothing like my mom's dusty minivan—the only thing she had, other than the set of purple bags under her eyes, that identified her as a mother.

"Well, I slept for the most part," I said, yawning into my hands. "So, I guess it was all right. No screaming babies."

His laughter filled up the space. "That's good. Did your mother buy any school supplies for you?"

I was the one laughing now.

"I'll take that as a no then," he noted. "I know Hanan and Malik are ready for school. I can have Tara take you shopping before classes next Monday."

"Which grade are they in? I forgot."

"They're going to be in the same grade as you."

"Oh." I sat back in my seat, slightly disappointed at the fact that they were going to be seniors. "Are they eighteen yet?"

"No, they're seventeen just like you."

"I'm eighteen."

"Oh," he said with a cough, realizing that he didn't know my birth year. Because of moving at the tender age of five, I'd ended up going to school a little bit later than the kids I knew.

Hanan and Malik Pejman were my twin stepbrothers. I'd planned on meeting them two years ago at my dad's wedding to their mother. Mom had refused to let me take a plane cross-country—even after Dad had paid for the ticket.

My mother had no interest in meeting the woman who had stolen her husband. Tara had also been married when she met my father. The twins and I were ten when the affair started, far too young to understand the gravity of it. Divorce wasn't a word I understood, not fully at least, until it happened to my parents. Us kids, for the most part, were protected from the details of the separation process. The result ultimately pushed my mother off the deep end.

There wasn't a way for us to intervene. I was a child, and so were the twins. None of us knew what was happening. The only thing for certain was that our families would never be the same. I didn't know how my father had met Tara in the first place, but I knew—because of my mother—that their relationship had been going on for six months before taking a serious turn. On the eve of my parents' ten-year anniversary, he put a dagger to their union, freeing himself from his vows.

"You'll love Harper Falls," Dad said with a smile. "There're a lot of good people here. I'm sure you'll love Tara and the boys too. She's going to be taking you back-to-school shopping."

I shifted in my seat, not making direct eye contact. "I don't know if it would be a good idea if I go on a shopping trip with her. Can't you take me?"

"Don't be silly. She won't mind going with you."

Dad had entirely missed my point.

Heaving a sigh, I agreed.

Red-brick homes with gorgeous, well-manicured front lawns lined the street around me. Dad's tires crunched over gravel, easing into the driveway as he circled a fountain in his front yard.

I hadn't noticed the way my nails were clawing the leather seat as we neared my father's house, but I did notice my pulse pounding louder and louder. My stomach began churning, bubbling up from its sheer emptiness, and my mouth popped open as we got closer and closer to the front door.

Breathe, I told myself. They're already family. It's no big deal.

Dad walked ahead of me, lugging one of my two suitcases. I hadn't brought much from Maine, and Dad was shocked at my lack of clothes. He insisted that I needed to get new clothes after we got school supplies.

Even though I wanted to minimize my time with Tara, I merely nodded. But that was all I did. That was the only thing I wanted to do from now on—just nod to any of the questions, statements, or complaints anyone directed at me.

Dad used one hand to unlock the door. It creaked open, and he stepped in. I followed him quickly, hiking my duffel bag higher on my stiff shoulder. I swept my narrowed eyes over the large foyer, absorbing my surroundings. Caught up in the high ceilings, I found myself walking into the spacious living room.

A thin TV was mounted in a way that gave the illusion of floating perfectly in midair. Abstract paintings dotted the tall mint-green walls. Sculptures—some appearing to be fertility statues—were placed on glass shelves leading to the dining area.

What struck me as odd, beyond the interior design, was the

most mundane thing in that living room. Family portraits and photos from outings were intermingled with my dad's collection of art. We'd never had that in our old house when he lived with us. Mom had to drag him out of bed to do the bare minimum.

I guess he wants to be better for Tara.

Spinning around, I took in the house in one glance, realizing the stillness between the walls and the silence throughout the hallways. I finally came to a stop and asked, "Where is everyone?"

"Oh, Tara is out with the boys at the country club. They'll be back any moment," Dad assured me, dropping my suitcase at his feet and motioning to the stairs. "Do you want me to show you up to your bedroom?"

I nodded and followed him to the second floor. He paused, heaving, shortly before the last room on the left and opened the door. I stepped over the threshold on my own. He stayed behind. It was twice as large as my last room, lightening my mood at the sheer size of it.

It was a fleeting feeling, though, fading fast as I eyed the gross piss-yellow shade.

Tolerable, I thought, weighing back and forth the idea of painting over it.

For the time being, I went against it.

Tara will probably beg you to move out the moment you graduate.

Hushing my mind, I shifted to the task of unpacking. I flung the duffel bag on the bed and pulled out my camera. Out of everything I owned and had worked hard to pay for, this was the most valuable thing that I'd taken from home and brought with me.

Dad cleared his throat as I went over to the nightstand.

"What?" I asked, sneaking a look over my shoulder.

"Can you not do this? I thought you promised you were coming to California so things could be different. You swore to me."

I stood back and narrowed my eyes at him. Was he kidding me? Did he think what had gotten me expelled was all my own fault? Sure, I'd played a big role in finishing things the way I had, but I didn't start it. I wasn't the one who'd betrayed someone. If you asked my mom, even she understood that I was only trying to make things even. Sadly, it had blown up in my face.

I picked the camera back up and clutched it in my hands. "Why can't I have it?"

"I don't want it here."

"I'm your daughter. I don't know if you've forgotten, but if there's anyone's side you should be on, it should be mine. Not anyone else's. Why don't you trust me?"

He stepped in my direction, holding his palm out to me. "I do, I do. It's just that I think...in everyone's best interest, you shouldn't pick up that hobby of yours again. I don't want a repeat of what happened earlier this year. Give it to me, and I'll put it somewhere safe for you."

"Safe? There's nowhere safer than my room."

"Not until you can show me that you have that level of responsibility," he said, moving in closer to snatch the camera. "We're not there yet."

"Dad—"

"Sylvia."

"You wouldn't be acting like this if you knew why I did it," I muttered. "If you actually cared about me, you'd be saying something else."

"I'm fully aware. I was informed the moment you proceeded to make a spectacle out of yourself. That's precisely why you won't be granted permission to use your camera."

I scrambled to find something to say. "I want to keep it." The sharp tone I'd used prior dropped down to a whisper. "It's not like you asked for permission to bring that woman into our family."

Oh, no. You weren't supposed to say the quiet part out loud.

Dad clapped his hands together, gradually placing a single finger over his mouth. The act looked painful, almost as though to stop himself from spewing out every obscenity he could imagine for insulting his marvelous, magnificent mistress-turned-missus.

"You could get away with an attitude like that in Maine, but things are different around here. You will respect my rules and show respect to the adults in this house," he roared, rushing to snatch the camera. My reflexes were too quick, meeting him in the middle and pulling with all my might on the strap. In a matter of seconds, a harsh snap rattled throughout the room, followed by the sight of my camera sailing across the room and shattering in half.

Running to one of the halves, I picked it up, grazing my fingers over the lens. Abrasive material tugged at my skin, revealing the state my camera was in. I almost cut myself in the act of touching the surface, hissing at the heap before me.

That was it.

The lens was done for.

A tremble flowed through me, consuming me. Everything before me turned a shade of crimson as I registered what he'd done to my beloved camera.

Peeking over my shoulder, I saw my father hadn't left yet.

I'm so sorry, Sylvia were the only words I wanted him to say. It wasn't much to ask for, but when it came to both my parents, they shared the common struggle of never finding the right words to apologize—or outright refusing to do it. Didn't matter if they were in the wrong or right, they were blind to their own faults. He understood that he'd never wanted it to get this far. And yet, there he was in my room, silent as a mouse about what he'd done.

"This wouldn't have happened if you had just let me keep it in storage," he finally said.

"For what?"

"You need more supervision in your life." He sighed, pinching the bridge of his nose.

Something unexpected happened next.

Dad opened his mouth and said, "That was my fault."

Yeah, I know. The camera didn't break itself.

This time, I kept the comment to myself.

"Next time I say to do something," he warned, "you do what I say."

There it is. The predictable tone of my father.

I only nodded.

My mouth refused to produce any words.

Quickly and quietly, Dad went to the door. "I'm sorry for yelling."

I lowered myself to the floor, wrapping my arms around myself. "It's okay."

But it wasn't okay.

It looks like you haven't changed, I thought as he exited.

After his footsteps were hardly audible, I retrieved the memory chip from the debris. There were a lot of important photos I wanted to transfer over to my laptop. I tucked the chip back into my duffel bag and carefully cleaned up the mess Dad had left behind.

Like I always did.

Chapter Three

I.F.H.Y. (I Fucking Hate You)

When three o'clock came around, a car pulled into the driveway. It drew my attention from across the room. Through the window, I saw two very tall boys around my age leaped out from the vehicle, along with a woman who had to be Tara. I didn't know which boy was Hanan and which one was Malik. They were twins, but one had a buzz cut.

"Sylvia," my father called. Before I knew it, my dad was opening my door wide enough to stick his head in. "Everyone's here. Come down and meet them."

I'd rather play on a turnpike than hang out with them, was what I was thinking, but I kept to that dark remark to myself.

Exhaling, I rose off the bed and walked out of my room to the staircase. With my hand gripping the railing, I strolled down. My nerves started acting up midway. Counting each step, I paused for a full second every now and then, just to kill time.

A loud conversation had broken out between the twins, asking about a party one of their good friends was throwing nearby. The party was tomorrow, and their mother didn't seem thrilled, losing confidence in letting them go with every question.

"I don't like the idea of you two staying out when school is so soon. Staying up that late at night could mess up your circadian rhythm," Tara said worriedly, knitting her brows together in a scowl. She took off her trench coat and flattened it over the white couch. "Who's going to be there? Do you have a list of the names of those attending?"

"Mom, it's a regular party—not a wedding. We don't have a list," the buzz-cut boy groaned, flopping right onto the trench coat. His mother hissed at him until he rolled off it. He still had his shoes on, and I found that unsettling. "You know his parents. His parents know you. I don't see why you'd mind us going."

"Malik, she said no. You asked her last week. The answer is the same," my dad said, coming down the stairs ahead of me.

Everyone's eyes followed the sound of his voice. They finally looked up at where I was, now frozen on the steps.

Dad cleared his throat, sidestepping and folding his hands behind his back. "Tara." He faced his wife. "Malik, Hanan. I'd like you to meet my daughter, Sylvia."

Malik gave a brief greeting before making his way to the kitchen. I waved sheepishly at my stepbrothers, mustering a smile—but it wasn't reciprocated. When I started to speak, I was instantly cut off by Malik yelling from the kitchen about dinner.

Dad didn't respond to any of this awkwardness.

Looking at the floor, I pretended like I wasn't embarrassed at how my entire existence was ignored.

You didn't need to tell me twice. We were two separate families, forcefully merged through infidelity. I understood there were first-time jitters when meeting new people. What I needed was patience and a whole lot of courage.

Dad turned to Tara, asking her if she was free to take me shopping for school supplies.

Tara lit up like a skyscraper. "I'd love to!"

After hearing the news that we were going out to shop, Malik headed back to the living room with new interest. Finding something worth his while in the conversation, he said, "I need to pick up some things too. Can I tag along?"

"You most certainly can."

"Are you going right now?"

"Yup," Tara said, slipping into her shoes. "I'll be in the car."

The plan was set, and I rushed upstairs to get ready. Since it had been a while since I'd arrived from the airport, I'd already changed into more comfortable clothing. Swiftly, I switched out of my soft, pink sweats and threw on the same jeans I had worn during the flight. Barely looking at what I was grabbing, I fished out the first piece of fabric that felt like a shirt from my bag. After one glance at the mirror, I knew I had to do something with my wild mane of curly hair.

"Today is a beanie day," I concluded and shoved my head into the blue beanie I'd worn on my flight to California. Once I felt satisfied with how my hair was covered, I put on socks and my black shoes.

Tara and Malik were waiting for me, both already in the car, by the time I got downstairs.

"I bought extra classroom supplies for the boys when I went shopping last week," Tara announced as she started the car. "We're only going clothes shopping."

I clicked on my seat belt. "That's cool with me."

"I know a place we should stop by first," Malik offered. "Can I drive? It would be good practice for me. My test is coming up next month."

Tara agreed, happily swapping spots with her son.

After driving for less than ten minutes, we pulled up to a

strip mall. Many of the storefronts—which weren't many to begin with—had the same cheap design above their doors. On the store ahead of us, two birds' nests had been constructed inside the big, green letters forming the words BETTER BARGAIN CENTER. The G was totally messed up, blinking on and off.

"This place must be the spot," I said, adding a slight whistle at the end.

No one reacted—once again cementing the feeling of discomfort that had been floating in the air. I decided to reduce my attempts to speak.

That was a challenge after seeing the clothes inside. The apparel the store carried made my stepmom gasp at almost everything.

"Look at this." She held up a button-down shirt plastered with a loud animal print. "Wouldn't this be cute?"

"Yeah, on a carpet," I muttered. "Or perhaps a divorcee."

"What's wrong with it?"

She put her hands on her hips, waiting for my answer.

"Too . . ." I pointed at the whole shirt, trying very hard not to hurt her in the process. "Chaotic."

She looked back at the rack of clothes. "How about this?" She pulled out a purposely tattered flannel. "Edgy, huh?"

"No, thanks."

I walked away and looked at another rack. I found a pile of activewear that wasn't that bad, and I started rummaging through it.

From behind me, I could hear Tara sighing.

I turned around. "What?"

"We're going back-to-school shopping."

"I know."

"This is the workout section, though. Don't you want a cute new shirt or a jacket instead?"

"Isn't there a uniform policy at the school?"

"That's true."

"I checked online about the school dress code before I got here, and the guidelines on what the uniform entails. I saw that the only area that gives real options to the students—other than free dress days—is during gym class."

She sighed again and, to my surprise, disappeared after saying, "I'm sorry for bothering you. Pick whatever you want."

"Thanks," I said. "Much appreciated."

A second later, I heard someone speaking to me.

"Moms, huh?"

To my right, I saw an employee putting prices on mugs. He was on a ladder with his back to me. From what I could see (which wasn't a lot), he was considerably taller than me and had pitch-black hair. The uniform he had on didn't do him any justice. Either he'd accidentally been given a size too large or he favored looking like he was drowning in his clothes. His jeans hung low off the edges of his shoes, appearing worn out and white at the hems. The company shirt, red and bearing no name tag, draped on him like a kid trying out his parent's wardrobe for the first time.

"Oh, she's not my mom," I revealed. "I met her literally a few minutes ago."

"Well, that's one nosy stranger."

No part of me felt an urge to correct him by saying that she was my stepmother and not a total stranger.

I heard him step off the ladder. For a brief second, I stole a glance up. When I did, I had to do a double take. I couldn't quite see his eyes, and for some reason that bothered me. Loose, liquid black curls covered his eyes while he gazed down. No part of me felt shame for checking him out. He looked to be around my age. He moved his hand over his blemish-free forehead and stared at me like I had just said something awful to him.

"Do you need help?"

My cheeks felt warm.

"No, I'm fine."

It was then, and only then, that I realized I had been gawking at him. I grabbed the shirt I'd momentarily admired and moved as fast as I could away from him.

Bumping into a cement column, I whispered a sorry, too busy wondering where Tara and Malik were to realize how dumb I looked apologizing to an inanimate object.

Truth be told, I hadn't gone that far when I heard a raised voice.

"You can't keep ignoring me for the rest of your life."

"No," said a second voice. "But I can try my hardest to."

"You don't mean that."

Peering from behind a rack of clothes, I tried to pinpoint the source of the argument. To the left of me, Malik stood with his hands closed into fists at his sides. "Trust me when I say I didn't want things to end up this way. It wasn't my intention. One thing led to another . . ."

I had to strain my neck a little to see who Malik was talking to, getting a glimpse of the price tag boy from a few minutes ago standing with his arms crossed over his chest.

"Lie to me all you want," the boy urged, "but it's not going to change the outcome."

Outcome? Outcome of what?

"You don't have to go down this path. Aren't we friends? How long have we known each other? Years, no?" Malik asked, but the boy was losing patience faster and faster with each importunate question he tacked on. "There's no reason you should be thinking like this. Reconsider, Dakota, please."

"Don't say that when you're the one who's forcing my hand," the boy snapped. "You started this all when you set me up to go to juvie."

Whoa, what had Malik gotten mixed up in?

"I did everything I could to stop that from happening. You've gotta believe me. It wasn't me pushing the narrative that you were acting alone."

Dakota raised his hand. "Quit it. You and I both know that you had the power to stop everything. You could've stepped up and done the right thing. But, of course, you couldn't stand up to your dad."

"He's not my dad. Elijah is my stepdad," Malik said as though each word was dipped in snake venom. Had he been given the opportunity, I bet he would have spat on the ground for dramatic effect, hoping to wash away my father's name from his mouth. "I'm doing the morally right thing by apologizing."

"It's a little too late."

"I'm not even supposed to be talking to you—"

"Then don't," Dakota interrupted, lifting the hand holding the price gun. "I need to head back to work. Please, just leave me alone. I don't want to get fired because of you."

"Dakota, I'd never—"

"Stop coming back here. I mean it," he warned, hovering the end of the price gun at Malik's temple as though it were a loaded pistol. "I'm not joking, Malik. Quit showing up. The friendship we had is over. Anything and everything coming to you is karma, and I hope it makes your life a living hell. I wish you the worst."

"You don't mean that. You can't be serious."

"As serious as a death sentence." He tilted his head. "I'm eighteen already. I can't be as reckless as you."

Malik turned at the sound of his name.

His mother was in another aisle, calling for him. By the time he turned around to speak to Dakota again, he was gone.

Instead, Malik locked eyes with me.

The softness around his brown eyes hardened at the mere appearance of me. "What the hell are you looking at? Were you eavesdropping on me?"

"I...I..."

"Malik!" his mother called out again.

He wanted to say something more, something harsh and hurtful, but nothing came out of his mouth. Malik's lips were pressed into a fine line, trapping whatever he had been about the say on the tip of his tongue.

Spinning around on the balls off his feet, he went in the opposite direction. For sure, I thought he was ready to blow. But thankfully, it seemed like I had dodged the bullet.

Not knowing what else to do, I followed him to see where his mother was. I dropped the two items I'd found into the shopping cart. "I need to use the restroom. Is there one in here?" I asked.

"There should be one by the back," Tara said, motioning with her hands to where she thought it would be in the store. "I'll go check out while you go to the restroom."

I nodded and walked away. When I was done, they weren't anywhere near the front of the store, so I assumed they had finished paying. Exiting the building, I saw them loading the bags into the trunk of the car. Before entering the car, Tara turned to Malik.

"I thought I told you to not talk to him anymore." She laughed to herself. "If I'd known he worked here, then I would've never let you recommend this place."

"Huh?" Malik raised a brow.

"You're not fooling me. You set this up."

"I didn't know Dakota worked here. It was a coincidence."

She refused to believe it. "What were you talking about?"

"The weather."

"Don't play dumb with me."

"I'm not."

"I saw you standing there for an awfully long time, talking up a storm." She shook her head. "I thought your father and I told you not to speak to him—"

"He's not my father. You marrying him doesn't make him my dad," Malik quickly clarified. "I already have that role taken care of. He did a damn good job raising me."

"Debatable," I whispered, but low enough so no one would hear.

"You didn't answer my question," Tara noted, waiting patiently for Malik to reply. Her brow lifted, reading the reaction of her son. "What were you talking about?"

"I don't have to tell you."

She laughed. "You know what? Then you don't have to go to that party you were raving about earlier either. Sylvia, dear?" She faced me. "Are you in the mood to go to a party with Hanan? I think that would be a nice way for you to meet the kids at your new school."

"Mom!" Malik exploded.

"Hush, I've made up my mind. You're cleaning the garage tomorrow night while Hanan and Sylvia enjoy a pleasant time at the Greers' house."

"I, uh." I struggled to find words. "Thank you for letting me go, but ... I have a lot of unpacking to do."

The reality was I had no interest in meeting anyone at a party.

Tara smiled at me, not reading my expression properly and probably chalking it up to social anxiety. "Oh, don't be silly, you'll have enough time to unpack later. You'll love the kids at Crescent Hart Academy."

It was settled. No amount of persuasion would stop her. She probably felt like stepmother of the year, rewarding me while punishing her own child.

•••

The next day, I was ready around 8:40. Dressed in a wool sweater and dark jeans, I was satisfied with my reflection after I applied my makeup and found jewelry to match. There were two silver rings I never left home without, which I'd paired tonight with gold hoop earrings.

For a girl who didn't want to go to this party, I hadn't dressed like I didn't care. That had to do with my perfectionist nature, wanting to look good when it came to first impressions. However, at one point I had contemplated showing up at the party in my sweatpants and sweatshirt.

It was a little past nine o'clock when I saw Hanan go up to his room, saying he would start getting ready. Ten minutes later, he was wearing a different shirt that was identical to the last one, only in a slightly darker shade.

Hanan bounced his car keys back and forth in his hands, heading for the door. "We can go now." He spoke in a soft whisper. I had to crane my neck to catch the words.

I shot to my feet and clasped my hands together. "Okay," I said a little too loudly. "Can't wait."

He glanced at me, brown eyes peering right into my soul.

Or whatever was left of it. I was pretty sure I'd sold it back in the fourth grade for some light-up sneakers or better parents. I didn't care what I got. Whichever came first.

"Well, aren't you cheery? I thought you didn't want to go."

"I thought you wanted to leave at nine."

He peeked at the phone in his hands. "It's nine-thirteen. Close enough." He opened the front door wide enough to let me exit first. I headed toward his car in the driveway. It was a gorgeous pearl-white drop-top convertible. "Besides, it's not like we're missing anything. It's the same old fake people going to the same old house, doing the same old crap."

"Why do you want to go then? You sound tired of the whole routine."

He unlocked the car from the porch. The headlights blinked as he did so. "I am tired of it, but there's nothing else to do here. The only thing we've got going for us are those dumb parties. Even if I have to deal with the same old bullshit and annoying people, it's better than being stuck at home."

"Or forced to clean the garage," I noted, and he cracked a genuine smile. For the first time, I was happy. Happy I didn't have to see any familiar faces at the party.

We piled into the car and headed to the Greers' place. It wasn't a long drive, probably ten minutes. Hanan's beauty of a car swerved into a busy street. Vehicles were lined up, bumper to bumper, for a couple of blocks.

People poured outside, laughing and chatting amongst themselves. Green pastures surrounded the last house on the street, looking like a sea of muted emerald beyond the strong party lights. I wondered what this place had been before; I could see the outlines of a silo in the distance. We were definitely on former farming land. You wouldn't have known that from the air, though. It didn't smell like fertilizer. The night air was crisp, and the stars were out, twinkling far more than they did back home.

I went to grab the door handle, but Hanan's words stopped me. "Hey, uh."

I darted my eyes at him. "Yeah?"

"I know this is weird coming from someone you don't know, but make sure you don't take any drinks from anyone."

"I never do. I've been making wise decisions since I got out of diapers."

He chuckled. It was a nice chuckle. One that made you want to join in. "It's just that ... some of these guys are bad news. I don't want anything to happen to you that I can prevent."

I shook my head at his choice of words. "You can't predict crime."

"I didn't say that—I just want to add safeguards. For starters..." He brought out his phone and handed it to me. It was open to the screen where you add new contacts. "In case you feel dizzy or scared, text me. If you can't text, then just shoot me a call."

I couldn't help fighting back a grin. Was that weird? I didn't know. Shielding my smile, I began typing out my information. I wasn't smiling in the hopes of something tragic happening to me. I was smiling at this person I didn't even know caring about my safety. That was something I'd never experienced. Ever.

Sad but true.

I didn't understand why he cared.

He probably doesn't want to get in trouble with your dad if something happens to you.

That was plausible, but something deep within told me it was more than that. Somehow, it seemed as though it would bother him, keep him up at night even, if he didn't give me his number. A glimpse of his conscience was visible in that moment. He wasn't lying about these partygoers.

After putting in my info, he texted me, and I saved it to my contacts. I thanked him softly and ducked out of the car.

I was about to say goodbye to Hanan when a bright blue Corvette swerved into the area ahead of us, boxing us in. Girls spilled out of it, one by one, like a clown car. Out of the four I'd counted, only two walked toward us.

I stepped out onto the grass and slammed the car door shut. A short, stocky girl was glaring daggers at me as I moved away. I hadn't said a word, and she already looked like she wanted to rip my throat out. Keeping my eyes low, I started toward the house.

"Hey!" the girl barked. "Who is she, Hanan!?"

Chapter Four

Who's Afraid of Little Old Me?

Turning my head toward a very angry, very noisy girl, I began considering if I was supposed to speak first or if Hanan would cut in. She was still giving me a nasty look. Hanan went to her side, saving me the act of talking, and explained to her that I was his stepsister who had recently flown into town. He placed his hand on the small of her back, detailing to her that I would be attending the same school as they did.

Her anger melted, and whatever else he had whispered into her ear made her blush. I had a feeling she'd caught him with other girls in the past from the way she'd reacted. And I wouldn't be shocked. Hanan was an attractive guy. His sharp features could cut glass.

"I'm Carmen." She introduced herself, stretching out her arm to me while simultaneously flipping her stiff, jet-black hair with the opposite hand. I approached and took her hand in mine, shaking it.

"Sorry about that. I didn't mean to scare you there or anything." Carmen tried brushing the obviously awkward encounter under the rug, chuckling so forcefully that it came off affected. I laughed along with her to help, hoping it would ease the tension that was still lingering in the air like a fart no one wanted to claim.

"Hanan, do you know if Malik is coming?" one of the other girls asked.

Hanan shrugged. "He's stuck cleaning the garage. If he can sneak out, maybe he might make it. I wouldn't get my hopes up."

The girl whimpered. "Oh, okay then. I was hoping he'd make it before midnight."

"Uh, he's not into you," another one of the girls said. Moments ago, she'd been standing by the car, but she had now decided to join our conversation. "Chill for a bit and quit being so hung up on everything he's doing. He's got a girlfriend."

"Last time I checked, I wasn't talking to you," the previous girl countered. "So why don't you stay out of my business, huh?"

I figured this was my cue to jump out of the discussion and try to find shelter. With the way those two girls were glaring at each other, I knew a fight would be starting soon.

No one batted an eye as I walked away. And I was kind of glad about that the closer I got to the house.

People rushed in and out of the house, carrying those mysterious red cups that made you curious about what was inside. I watched my surroundings attentively, wondering whether I should leave now. Everything about this party felt different from the parties back home.

One thing was similar, though: there were drunk people.

And I mean everywhere.

Drunk guys dancing on the wooden coffee table. A drunk girl swaying in the arms of a boy, holding on to him for dear life. Drunk couples kissing in the corner, giggling to themselves . . .

Maybe they weren't just drunk.

Smoke billowed up to the ceiling, creating a thick, gray cloud above our heads. Kids drank until they collapsed on the floor and sprawled against the couches. Others rushed to the bedrooms upstairs, but I doubted that they were going there to sleep.

I cut through the dense crowd and went to the kitchen. Recalling what Hanan had said about being safe around the guys at these parties, I searched for a drink. It took time, but I located a closed soda can inside the fridge.

Popping the lid open, I felt eyes zeroing in on me. I peered around.

A girl was staring at me.

She was dressed in a knee-length tie-dyed shirt that damn near swallowed her petite frame. Her long rainbow socks and headband didn't make her look any better. She had bone-straight black hair. You could tell her natural hair was probably wavy, though, and she went the extra length to straighten it.

"How do I know you?" she asked, tapping her chin. "I feel like I know you." She shut both her eyes and grabbed my shoulder as if she was trying to read something off me by simply touching me. Her eyes fluttered back open, and a sad look painted her face. "I don't know you."

"Uh . . . no, no you don't. Or at least I don't think you should. I'm from Maine. I just flew into Cali yesterday."

"Cali? Oh, yeah. You're definitely not from around here."

"Sorry?"

"Oh, don't apologize!" she rushed to say. "It's just that I could've sworn I knew you. I was reading your aura—"

"My what?" I arched a brow.

"God, Beth, where did you go? Ugh, there you are." A boy practically fell over his own feet running up to her, storming in from the sliding back door. He faced the girl, combing through his bright blue bangs, and then turned to me. His hair color had caught me off guard; it was vibrant in the dimly lit space.

His eyes were scanning me like a hawk.

Respectfully, I stretched my hand out.

And waited.

Then waited even longer as the silence became more obvious. At once, he lost total interest in me, angling himself toward his friend. "What were you doing? I've been looking for you."

"I was getting drinks, but then I felt this . . . this sudden urge," the girl said, waving at the room between us. She patted my arm, but then her grip tightened like she was gaining stability. "I swear I wasn't bothering her. Was I?"

"No," I answered, taking another sip of my Coke. "She was, however, going to tell me what my aura was giving off."

"Beth," the boy cried out. "I told you to drop that. We didn't throw this party for you to bring up that nonsense again. As your best friend, I'm not going to let you drag this into our senior year. We're past that."

"But it's not nonsense." She pouted. "I really can read auras."

"Yeah, yeah. You say that all the time, but you can't even read at a seventh-grade level. Baby steps, Beth, baby steps."

Jeez, I can't believe they're friends.

"You live here?" I asked.

She nodded. "Yup. I'm Bethany Francesca Greer."

"You go by Beth now. Stop telling people your full government name," the boy ordered. "You don't know who she is . . . wait. I don't even know who you are." He ran his fingers through his chemically damaged hair, altered from countless bleaching treatments, as his eyes narrowed on me. "Who are you?"

"She's from Maine!" Beth sang.

"Last time I checked, I didn't send invitations to anyone in Maine."

He maintained his cold stare.

"She can stay," Beth told him. "She's okay in my book."

"I don't like walk-ins."

What was this? A hair salon?

Beth rolled her eyes. "Most of the people here are walk-ins."

"I came here with my stepbrother," I said, sloshing around the remaining liquid in my can. "Maybe you know him."

"I didn't ask to hear your family tree," he noted. "You weren't invited."

"I'm sorry—"

"Save the apology," he snarled. "I want you out of here."

Beth touched his arm, raising both her brows. "That's not needed."

"We didn't plan for this many randos to show up. There's not going to be enough pizza for everyone. It's on the way."

Who in their right mind ordered food to a party without assuming some strangers might snag a slice or two? He was delusional.

"I'm lactose intolerant. I don't like pizza," I lied—mostly about the second part. All milk-based products messed with my guts. That didn't mean I couldn't ignore that grim reality for a good pizza. Smiling to them both, I rattled the soda can in my hand. "You don't have to worry about me. I'm fine with this."

"I wasn't talking to you," the boy said, peering at me as though I'd just run over his grandmother with an electric scooter. "I want you gone."

"I came with Hanan Pejman," I informed them, ignoring his demand. "If that rings a bell."

Both of their mouths widened, gaping at me in a new way.

Beth slapped my shoulder. "Ohmigod, I didn't know they had a stepsister!"

Relief washed over me. Them not knowing I existed was the best possible thing to happen to me since I got here. "My dad married his mom two years ago. I'm Sylvia Ellington, Elijah Ellington's daughter. I got into town not that long ago."

"Wow, that's crazy. What a small world. I'm glad you got here safely. How was your flight? Did you have a layover, or did you go straight to California? I bet you're jet-lagged," the boy rambled, instantly shifting from a defined frown to a growing grin. He linked my hand in his as though I weren't a stranger whom he'd had no interest in moments ago. "Sorry about earlier. I get cranky when it comes to food."

Brushing it off, I shrugged.

"I'm Alexander Wallenberg, by the way. You can call me Alex for short."

"I'll call you Xander for short," I said, not really shaking his hand back.

"Oh, that's not really my nickname—"

"I like the name Xander, though."

"Yeah, it's got a nice ring to it," Beth agreed.

He beamed, clearly forcing the expression for my benefit. "Uh, Xander it is then."

Such a suck-up.

• • •

Two hours into the party, Beth had introduced me to everyone in her circle. People hardly acknowledged her presence as she bounced around from person to person, shouting their name at the top of her lungs, dragging me along behind her. Not many of their names lingered on my tongue longer than a brief greeting. I sucked at remembering names.

One thing that did stick, though, was that I recalled the exact number of names they'd told me. I'd counted twenty-five people, not including Beth and Xander.

Beth wasn't shy in telling me how popular my twin stepbrothers were—which was no surprise to me.

It was then that I decided I quite liked Beth, or at least her level of honesty and excitement toward the world. In the few short hours since we'd met, I knew, for a fact, that I liked her more than I liked Xander.

"And that concludes my tour." She fell into one of the only empty seats in the living room. "On Monday, when we go to school, I can tell you all of our hangout spots and how to sneak off campus."

"How fun." Xander grimaced, rubbing his sleepy eyes. "I can't wait."

"Oh . . . okay, if you don't want to go with us, you don't have to," Beth replied.

"No, I will. Who else is going to stop you from doing idiotic, reckless things?"

"I don't get myself in idiotic, reckless situations," she roared, causing a couple of heads to turn. "Idiotic, reckless situations happen all on their own without me doing anything."

While they argued, I zoned out, relaxing against the wall. To distract myself, I let my gaze drift around the poorly lit room, scanning the sea of faces and bobbing heads. An annoying lamp pouring out bright red light blinked on and off in the corner.

In that brief second, as it flickered on to illuminate his face, I saw him.

The crimson light sank deep into his eyes. With the red glazing over his pupils, it gave them an eerie, almost inhuman look. For a moment, I didn't recognize him. But when the recognition struck me, it was hard to stop staring.

It was the boy from the store the day before.

Why was he here?

He was the last person I'd expected to see. Something about how Malik and Dakota had interacted had made me assume they weren't in the same social circle. Given how willing Tara had been to let me come, I doubted she'd known Dakota would be here.

He spotted me, noticing my attentive eyes studying his movements from across the room. I shook my head, creating a curtain around my face, and did my best to act like I hadn't seen him meet my gaze. Opening my eyes, I eased off the wall and focused on him again.

He wasn't there.

Playing it cool, I tugged at the sleeves of my wool sweater, becoming hyper-focused on how my caramel skin looked against the white material. Why wasn't I moving anymore? I'd gone still, confused as to what I should do.

Deep down, I knew I had promised myself to be on my very best behavior and not dive headfirst into trouble. As much as I wanted to stay true to that vow, a primal part of me lit up when I found Dakota again, closer to me now than before and beginning to approach me.

"Sylvia," a heavy voice cooed in my ear from behind me. Out of nowhere, someone sidestepped and got in my way. My view of Dakota was blocked by a large figure.

I looked up, coming eye to eye with one of the football players Beth had introduced me to an hour ago. I'd taken note then of how he'd peeked down my top the whole time and attempted to flirt, standing out from the rest. And not for any good reasons. Emphasis on attempted to hit on me—and failed miserably.

"Hey," I said. What was his name again? Fred? Finn? Future Inmate . . . 1389? I just couldn't remember which one it was. Dang it. "I'm kind of busy right now."

"Yeah, you're busy dancing with me." He grabbed my wrist. "That's why I ran up to you. You wanna dance?"

If I say no, will you promise to disappear into oblivion?

"I don't dance."

"One dance."

"I'm not a good dancer."

"Oh, it's not that hard." He wrapped his hand around my waist and slammed his body into mine. This guy really wasn't planning on winning the Nice Guy Award this year.

The song playing was slow, and the guy took full advantage of the opportunity. Nearing the third verse, he slipped his palm lower and lower until his hand cupped my butt.

I pushed on his chest. "Hey. That's not okay."

Shushing me, he pulled on my arms to bring me in close once more, smoothing his hands down my back to an appropriate level. "Chill, I'm only messing around. I'll stop."

His grin told me otherwise.

"No." I pushed my palm against his chest again, harder this time, and added more space between us. "I think that's enough dancing. I'm going to get some fresh air."

He snatched my arm, holding me in place. "C'mon, I said I wasn't going to do it again. At least finish the song with me."

"Leave my sister alone," a voice demanded. Hanan's words made the guy before me falter in his steps, bumping into the couple dancing behind us. "Franklin, I thought I told you to calm down. How much have you had to drink tonight?"

Hanan's question left Franklin pale as a ghost. It seemed like there was a hidden threat looming in the air that I couldn't decipher. "I didn't know she was your sister, bro. I'm sorry."

"I could've handled that on my own," I hissed, shuffling past them both. Chugging down the last of my second soda, I headed to the kitchen to toss the can out. In the act of dropping it into the trash can, one of my rings fell inside.

Muttering a string of profanities under my breath, I popped open the trash.

"Want some help?"

Dakota stood to my right, offering to grab the trash from my hands. "You look too nice in that sweater to be rummaging through garbage."

This time, I let a guy cut in to do the dirty work. "I dropped my ring in there. It's silver."

He flipped on the flashlight on his phone, handing it to me. The kitchen itself wasn't lit very well. Carefully placed fake candles, some red and others white, littered the counter (and the rest of the house), giving the space an intimate and sensual vibe that seemed too mature for high schoolers.

"Found it," Dakota announced, rushing to the sink to wash both his hands and my ring. "There you go."

I slipped it back on. "Thank you."

Dakota asked if I wanted to step outside. After I nodded my head, he led us to the backyard. "I saw you at the store yesterday," he said before I could say anything. "I didn't catch your name. What is it?"

"Sylvia," I answered. "What's yours?"

"Dakota Ridgewood."

I acted as though this was news to me. "I like your last name."

"In the eighteen years I've lived in this town, that would be the first compliment I've gotten on my name." He chuckled. "Most people don't have that reaction when they hear Ridgewood..."

The corners of his eyes softened for an instant, but they hardened again once he remembered I was there. He flashed a smile, but more to convince himself than to fool me.

I was about to ask him how he was enjoying his summer break when something stopped me. Dakota lazily put his arm on my shoulder as we walked, then he spoke in a manner that made my heart skip a beat.

"I wasn't going to come tonight," he said, "but now, I'm glad did."

Biting my cheek, I fought the impulse to smile.

The moment didn't last.

Because, truth be told, you can't have much privacy at a party.

A lot of stares shot our way. There were a few whispered remarks and gestures in our direction too. I refrained from giving them the bird.

"Ignore them."

"I'm sorry, I can't. I hate people who stare."

He touched the back of his hand to my cheek, stunning me at the contact. I was more shocked by what he said next. "They'll do that for the rest of the night."

"Why are they staring at us?"

"Not us. Me. They're staring at me."

"Well, aren't you a little cocky," I joked. "Are you some TV star I don't know about?"

He grinned. "I wish."

He left it at that, and I didn't press him. I had no right to pick and pry into anyone's past. Especially given the kinds of demons I had running loose in my life.

We stopped beside an aging oak tree. Dakota leaned his shoulder into the bark and looked at me again. I was fully aware of our proximity, waiting for him to do something besides stand there with his impenetrable stare.

He cleared his throat. "So, you know my name."

"I do."

"Which means it's only natural to ask for your name in return."

"I told you. It's Sylvia."

"I mean your full name."

"Ah, did you want to stalk me online?" I asked but didn't wait for an answer. "I should tell you now that I deleted all of that a month ago."

"I don't believe that."

I brought my phone out, showing him the lack of applications. "I have no reason to lie."

"That doesn't mean you can't tell me your name."

"Hmm." I scrunched up my nose. "I want to give off a mysterious allure. At least until school starts on Monday."

"Trust me, I can learn your name faster than that. Harper Falls has a tiny population. The school is even smaller. You can't hide anything for too long. I'd advise you to enjoy the mysterious allure for the next twenty-four hours."

I puffed out a long breath. "No way. You guys still have secrets."

"Hardly. Secrets don't stay secret very long. Any time you step outside your house, no joke, it feels like you're being watched by every gossip-loving aunt and uncle, reporting back to their group chats about where you're going and who you're talking to."

"That must get obnoxious."

He sighed. "It's like I can't do anything without the entire street knowing."

I was about to respond, but my phone's beeping caught me by surprise. It was a new text message from Hanan. I squinted at my phone, perplexed.

HANAN: What are you doing?
ME: Nothing.
HANAN: It doesn't look like nothing. Step away from Ridgewood. I hear you guys are hanging out outside.
ME: Is he one of the "bad guys" you were mentioning in the car?
HANAN: He's worse. Much worse. If he knew who you were, he wouldn't be nice to you. Crazy he's even talking to you.

I didn't reply. What did that mean? Based on what had happened, Dakota seemed like the only guy I liked here. He wasn't rude. He hadn't forced himself on me. Those were two things I couldn't say about my lovely interaction with Franklin.

What did Hanan mean by crazy he's even talking to you, though? I wondered.

Instead of asking, I dove into a new conversation with Dakota, blabbering about our favorite movies and TV shows we'd recently watched. But still, in the back of my thoughts, I was stuck on the last words Hanan had texted me.

"I don't believe you," I said. "You can't be serious. I've seen that movie ten times, and you're telling me you've never even heard of it?"

"We still have a video store that rents out VHSs. This whole place feels like it's stuck in the year 2003."

"No, you have no excuse. Ghost World came out in 2001."

Dakota shrugged. "Okay, so maybe we're stuck in the nineties then. That's more likely when you listen to half of the adults who live here."

A tug at my shoulder stopped me from replying. Dakota eased back from me, groaning at whoever it was he saw from the corner of his eye. Craning my head to the left, I saw a sweaty, shaky Beth and Xander behind me.

"Um, Sylvia . . . we need . . . to talk to you," Beth said, dragging each word out, "over . . . there. All the way . . . over there . . . in a different part of the house."

I was guessing Dakota was another one of the walk-ins Xander didn't want. But, unlike with me, Xander didn't rush to yell at him or try to kick him out.

"That's my cue," Dakota said, combing his fingers through his hair. "Well, it was nice meeting you, Sylvia. I hope next time I see you I can get your last name."

"It's Ellington," Xander spat out.

Dakota's brows met together in the middle, hardening his expression.

"That's not funny."

"No, really. Her name is Sylvia Ellington, and she's from Maine. Her stepbrothers are Hanan and Malik Pejman." Xander spewed all of this in one breath.

My body went rigid. I was positive he'd give away my social security number and underwear color to Dakota if he knew that too.

"Told you I'd find out." Dakota frowned, balling up his hands into fists.

I reached out to grab him as he walked past us, but he flinched from my touch.

He was long gone before I could stop him. People split apart to let him get through, trying to not get in his path.

"Whoa, are you okay?" Beth's question snapped my eyes away

from Dakota. She inspected my arm and face in search of . . . I wasn't sure. Scratches? "Did he hurt you?"

"What?" I asked. "Why would you think that?"

"Because you were talking to Dakota. Dakota Ridgewood."

"Yeah, I know," I said. "What's the big deal?"

"The big deal is that he's a ticking time bomb. He just got out of juvie," Xander informed me. "I didn't know he was back in town until tonight."

"I don't care about that," I snapped. That wasn't my problem right now, and certainly wasn't what I was mad about. I turned to Xander, not holding back any of my anger. "Why did you have to go out of your way to tell him my last name? I didn't appreciate it."

"I'm sorry." He bit down on his lip. "I had to. He wouldn't have left if I didn't."

"What the hell is that supposed to mean?" I almost screamed.

"You don't know?" the two of them said at once.

"No. If I did, I wouldn't be asking, now, would I?"

Beth sighed. "The Ridgewood family kind of . . . somewhat . . . don't like the twins . . . or your dad."

"That's a nice way of putting it." Xander snorted. "Your dad ruined their lives. They hate your family."

"Don't say that," Beth retorted. "That's a little far."

"What did he do?" I inquired.

"Elijah Ellington's the reason Dakota's dad is serving a life sentence in prison. He was the lawyer that helped make it happen."

"What did his father do?"

"He set his own house on fire," Xander said, "with his wife and her sister still inside."

What does that have to do with my dad? was what I wanted to ask. But more importantly, why would any of this matter to me when I barely liked the man to begin with? "If Dakota's dad harmed people, then my dad was doing his job—"

"That's the thing, though," Beth interjected, shrugging her shoulders. "We don't know if his dad did it. Sure, he's serving the time for it, but most of the people in town don't think he was capable of doing it."

"And a lot of other folks," Xander trailed on, "think he was framed."

Chapter Five

Dakota

In that moment, three questions sprang to mind, my thoughts a single stream of consciousness.

Why did they say Dakota hated the twins?

How come scratches were the first thing Beth searched for on my body?

Was there any evidence to prove Dakota's dad was framed, or was it hearsay?

Beth totally gave off the vibe that she spent too much time watching true crime documentaries, daydreaming of being a detective and itching to solve a cold case.

"Your dad is only the tip of the iceberg," Beth said.

"Beth." Xander tugged at her shirt. "There's no reason we should bring up old stuff."

"What old stuff?"

They fell silent.

"Nothing," Xander said with a tight-lipped smile.

Beth hesitated, tripping up on what she should say next. But with Xander glaring at her, she shrank in her tattered Converse shoes and held her tongue. Reading her expression, I could tell she wasn't going to dismiss the demands of her best friend. Shitty friend or not.

•••

The party flew past in a blur.

When Hanan texted me, saying he was waiting for me in his car, I was still arguing with myself regarding if I should or shouldn't bring up what had unfolded between Dakota and me.

After I'd slid into the seat and clicked on my seat belt, Hanan didn't waste any time. "You're unharmed? Ridgewood usually doesn't leave anyone without a mark."

"I find that difficult to believe." I switched on the radio. Hanan turned it off instantly, waiting for me to keep talking. "He's a lot nicer than some of the guys I came across."

"Oh, really? Was he all nice and fun to be around after he found out who you were?"

I kept my mouth sealed.

"I thought so." Hanan snapped his fingers, getting his answer. "I don't know one person who genuinely likes the guy."

"I'm sure Franklin has a tiny fan club too."

"Franklin isn't that bad." He hit the brake. A red hue briefly brushed across his copper-toned skin as we waited for the light to change to green. "Franklin has never gotten in trouble with the law. That's something Ridgewood can't say."

I scoffed. "Simply because someone has a criminal record doesn't make them a bad person. You don't know what kind of obstacles he had to overcome."

He moved the car onto another street, pivoting sharply. "You're giving him a lot more credit than he deserves. You don't know the guy. And trust me, you don't want to."

"What's his problem? Tell me."

"It's an endless litany of excuses." Hanan barely paused at the stop sign. "Sylvia, my advice to you is to drop this before you get caught up in a mess older than the both of us."

"How about this?"

"What?"

"I'll stop asking about him if you tell me why he doesn't like my dad."

"He doesn't like any of us."

"So, start explaining, chop chop."

Hanan released a slight puff of air, finding humor in my tone. "He hates Malik and me just as much as he hates your dad. Possibly more."

"What did you guys do?"

His hand went up to the back of his neck, rubbing it, probably to buy him time to rack his brain for a good response. With one swift motion, he turned on the radio, blasting a pop song that was midway through its hook.

Twisting the volume knob, I repeated my question. "What was it? It can't be that bad."

"That's not something I want to talk about. How about you ask your dad?"

At the mention of that idea, I returned the volume to its previous level.

There was no way my dad would tell me anything. How the hell was I supposed to get information out of him? He held his secrets close to his chest, like he was playing poker and holding his best cards until the right moment.

Or, in the case of the fallout of his first marriage, he'd waited until it blew up in his face.

Easing my seat backward, I linked my fingers together on my lap.

There was a new task at hand.

I began counting how many weeks there were in a semester, the number of months from now to graduation, and, more importantly, the numerous ways I could get my father to slip up.

Before Hanan got to our house, I'd come up with ten tactics.

Chapter Six

Only a Matter of Time

Monday came along, and the cloud above my head that had followed me from Maine, gray and thundering up a storm, remained intact as I got ready for school. Tara had offered to drive the three of us to school, thinking that I could get a full tour from one of my stepbrothers. Over breakfast, they'd agreed and said they would be fine with not driving their own cars to campus the first day, like they did most days.

When my dad had gone here, Crescent Hart Academy had gone by another name. Before becoming a charter school, Crescent Hart Academy was a public school that simply went by Crescent High.

The drive that morning was quiet. Malik hummed to himself as he stared out the window from the passenger seat, simultaneously twiddling his fingers in his lap. I sat in the back.

The day before, my dad had taken me to school since the campus was open to register the incoming freshmen and transfer students. One of the office workers had informed me that I was the only transfer student this term. Learning that made me a little more scared.

"Did you get your schedule and the school map?" Malik asked.

I stayed silent, unsure if he was talking to me or not.

He glared at me, confirming that he had indeed asked me a question.

"Uh, yeah. I did." I showed him my binder with my schedule and map on the front cover.

He pointed at the notes I'd added onto the margins of the map. "What's all that?"

"I've been thinking of good routes to get to school without having to pass the cafeteria."

No one likes cafeterias—or at least I didn't. To me, everyone had their eyes shifted to judgmental mode, waiting for me to humiliate myself.

A smile formed on his face, startling me. Malik perpetually looked upset. Even the way he stomped throughout the house, loudly making his presence known, made me think smiling was a task he reserved only for picture day. He shook his head. "There's no chance you can get on campus without passing the cafeteria."

Tara found a parking spot near the back of the lot.

Malik rocketed out the door when we came to a complete stop, waving to us as he threw his backpack over his shoulder. "Bye!"

Hanan disappeared into the masses soon after that, leaving me to walk in solo.

I guess they forgot about their promise to give me a tour, I realized with a deep sigh, clicking off my seat belt and exiting the car. The campus looked bigger than the last time I'd visited. Probably because being alone made it feel ten times more intimidating. There were four different buildings surrounding a wide, spacious courtyard.

Looking up from the map, I saw people jump out of cars and dash up the front steps. I'd have to endure the unbearable walk through the cafeteria, appearing lost and confused the whole time like most of the incoming freshmen.

Readjusting the binder and notebooks in my arms, I went through the corridor to the main dining area. One of the office workers had told me to go by the library after school to get my books. I made a mental note to remember that. I had bought a backpack, but I'd stupidly forgotten to bring it with me, thinking I could handle carrying everything for the short walk to my locker, where I'd throw everything in.

Stumbling into the noisy cafeteria, I watched people skirt past me, admiring the laughing, smiling students who filled the place.

My heart leaped into my throat when my eyes settled on a classmate sitting all on his own at a table. There were ten empty seats around him.

Hanan was right about one thing. Dakota wasn't popular.

A few people ran from his table, rushing out of his way to the other side of the room. I noticed a huddled group of girls at a table across from him pointing at him and glaring.

What was up with everyone? He didn't seem like that bad of a guy.

I took a step toward his table, going against everyone's advice. As I lowered my binder and notebooks, a soft whisper began down the table from us. I sat in front of Dakota.

His mop of hair bobbed as his head went up. He was drawing with charcoal, working fast on a loose-leaf piece of paper. The tips of his fingers were black, and he was clearly using the pad of his thumb to smudge the page and create shadows. Quickly, right as I started to sit, he flipped the page around so that I couldn't sneak a peek.

"You shouldn't be here," he grumbled, returning to his drawing. He put one hand in front of the paper, creating a wall so I couldn't see what it was.

I smirked. "It's school. I think I'm supposed to be here."

"That's not what I meant . . . I meant here. Sitting with me. Do yourself a favor and go sit somewhere else."

"I'm sorry. Am I bothering you by sitting here?"

"You're bothering me by simply existing. Now leave."

I didn't rush to get up out of my seat. "I don't think there's any rule that states I can't sit here."

"There is. It's called common sense."

Just to be annoying, and always wanting to have the last word, I said, "I guess I don't have any of that because here I am. Sitting here. With you."

"You clearly don't."

He stopped drawing and straightened his back, folding the paper up, causing his arms to flex. His clear blue eyes met mine, shimmering behind long black lashes. "Look, Sandra—"

"My name is Sylvia."

"I don't care. Like I was saying, you shouldn't be here. I'm trying to put it nicely . . . Clearly you and your entire family don't know what 'leave me alone' means." He paused, tilting his head. "Don't you have anything better to do with your life?"

The lightness in my tone had evaporated. No one spoke to me like that. "That was you trying to be nice?" I faked a gasp, flattening a hand on my chest. "Oh, I'm sorry then. I must've been mistaken. Because all you've been since I sat down is rude."

"You're lucky that's all you think of me." He sighed. "Now, for the one hundredth time, I'll ask you to get the hell out of my face."

"You're not asking me; you're clearly telling me."

"Seriously." His voice was strained. "Leave me alone."

I was having a little too much fun with this. "Or what?"

He snorted, but I could tell he wasn't the slightest bit amused.

"Fine, I'll leave then," he said and got out of his seat, stuffing the drawing in his notebook and dropping everything in his backpack.

"Have you lost your mind?" Beth asked, crashing into the empty seat Dakota had previously occupied. Xander was hot on her tail, taking the seat next to her and carrying his textbooks in one hand. He had such long fingers that he could grasp them all, unlike Beth, who had her books pinned to her chest. Xander's off-putting blue hair, spiked up with gel, looked even brighter than it had at the party.

"Why would you think that?" I questioned after they settled in. It took a second to get what they were trying to tell me. "Oh, with Dakota. We were only talking. Long story short, he's either playing hard to get or—"

"I think you're delusional," Beth concluded. "That looked intense, even without knowing what you were saying. You need to raise your standards if you think that's boyfriend material."

"I was kidding," I tacked on. "None of that was serious."

"I could tell you were joking. You're not dumb." Xander came to my rescue. "And it's a shame. Man, if you subtract all his issues and his rude attitude, I'm sure he'd have every girl going for him. Oh, well. No one's stupid enough to try with him . . . or at least no one anymore."

Considering how Xander had reacted at the party, forcing Beth to go silent, I decided there was no reason to ask Xander to elaborate on what he meant.

Yawning, I combed my hair. "I regret trying to communicate with him." I motioned to the people blatantly looking over at us and obviously gossiping about me. "It seems like I've got everyone talking about what just happened."

"That's not what's on everyone's mind." Xander covered his mouth, a smile slipping out between his fingers. "They're talking about your wild night with Franklin Simmons."

Chapter Seven

Caught Up On You

My heart was in my throat.

Banging my hand flat on the table, I gawked at Beth like she'd sprouted a second head. "Excuse me. Franklin said what?"

"You hooked up with him."

"No, I didn't. I barely danced with him. He tried to cop a feel, but Hanan stepped in and got him away from me. That's what happened. I did a lot of the work on my own, though, and pushed him off me."

"Well, that's not what Franklin is saying," Beth revealed. "In fact, that's the opposite of what he's telling people. He said that Dakota was groping you, drunk as hell. You were trying to get away from him, but he wouldn't let you go. Franklin supposedly hopped in and saved you."

"And afterward, he led you upstairs, and you apparently 'thanked' him for being your savior." Xander moved his fist up and down, suggestively raising one of his brows. "If you know what I mean."

"Good thing is he said you were great at it. A little nervous at first, but he talked you through it," Beth announced, and I wanted to sob.

"What the . . ." I buried my head in my hands. "He's lying! I didn't talk to Dakota until I was in the kitchen, and then outside after. There were lots of people around us. That can't be the story everyone's going with. I know there had to be witnesses."

"Lots of stoned and drunk people," Xander recalled. "And the few people who were okay enough to remember say you were seen with Franklin. You just said you were with him . . . and Beth and I both saw you with Dakota at one point also."

"Those were two different times that didn't overlap. He's lying," I repeated.

Xander shrugged. "He's popular. Highly don't think anyone is going to say he was lying."

Beth reached out and rested her hand on mine. "I don't believe the rumors. Franklin has done this before with other girls. Honestly, wait two weeks. This will all blow over, and there will be bigger drama taking over the school."

"Beth is right." Xander nodded. "He does this after every party. You're not the first, and you won't be the last."

"I should talk to him," I declared. "No, I need to talk to him."

"Oh, not a good idea," Xander said rapidly, stopping me in my tracks as I got up from my seat and picked up my belongings. "He's sitting with the other jocks. The second you walk up to them, no doubt he'll be cracking jokes about you. It'd be better if you got him when he's far from his posse of deranged buffoons."

I refused, drifting away from them and shaking my head. "No, I'm going to do it now. Are either of you coming with me?"

"Nope," Xander said. "I feel perfectly fine witnessing your social suicide from this seat right here."

"Beth?" I turned to her.

"I'll be there in spirit," she said softly, "cheering you on."

I'm doing this on my own. That's cool. That's fine. I don't need them.

I rested my binder on my hip and shuffled up to the "jock table" Xander had pointed toward.

Their area was a fire hazard.

Someone had pushed two tables together, making it extend a lot more than it should. They also occupied the last three sets of tables. Anyone who didn't have a seat circled around them (blocking one of the exits) and craned their necks in the direction of the current debate taking over the conversation. A good fifteen to twenty people were there, give or take.

Franklin spotted me when I got close enough, and a sly, devious grin spread on his face. It took every ounce of self-restraint in my body to not run over and slap it off him.

"Oh, look who came back for seconds," Franklin shouted, leaning back in his seat, knitting his hands together and wrapping them around the back of his thick neck. "Sorry, babe, but I don't do repeats."

"Shut up and stop making stuff up, Franklin," a voice bellowed. "Everyone at this table knows the last time you even got close to doing anything worth mentioning was back in freshman year. And it was with your second cousin."

The whole table darted their eyes over at the person who had spoken. Hanan was sitting at the end of the table, cuddling up to his girlfriend. I hadn't expected him to join in with such a quick response. And I was even more shocked when Carmen put in her two cents.

"Yeah," Carmen mused, "and from what your cousin said at summer school, you were very inadequate and hardly lasted longer than two minutes . . . then again, she did mention that there wasn't much you could do with your lack of equipment." She wiggled her little pinky finger, and with that, the entire table burst into laughter. They threw in their own jokes. The noise got louder and louder.

Franklin's face turned beet red. I opened my mouth, having prepared my own comeback, but he vanished before the words could leap off the tip of my tongue.

I rushed a thank you to Carmen and Hanan. He waved his hand, shrugging.

Carmen plastered a tight lip smile on her face. "Anytime, Canada."

I arched a dark brow. "Canada?"

"Yeah." She pointed to Hanan. "Isn't that where you said she was born?"

"I said she was from the New England area, Carmen," Hanan reminded her.

She inhaled sharply, glancing up at me like this was the first time she'd ever seen me. "Wait . . . you're British? That's so cool. I couldn't even tell."

I narrowed my eyes at her. Was she really asking that? Wait. Wrong question. Was she really that stupid? I contemplated saying something in an English accent, simply to mess with her.

"I was born in the state of Maine," I said instead.

"Maine is like basically Canada," she said, rolling her eyes.

"But it's basically not. Have you seen a U.S. map before? Maine is like totally there." I mimicked her airhead voice.

"Maine is the same thing as Canada, right?" She gazed around the table looking for sympathy and for someone to tell her she was indeed correct.

"Yes, Maine is very close to Canada, but last time I checked, my birth certificate says I was born in America."

"Canada is America's hat, so like yeah, it is the same thing," she pressed on. "It doesn't matter. You're welcome and whatever for what I did. Franklin won't be bothering you."

Nothing about her "you're welcome" sounded sincere.

"Thanks."

"Hanan said you speak like three languages. How did you learn so many?"

My back stiffened.

How much of my identity had Hanan shared with Carmen? What was the context, if any at all, as to why I was the subject of one of their discussions?

"I'm Somali from my mom," I revealed. "Somalia is in East Africa. My mom's parents grew up there and learned Arabic as well, so she passed it down to me, along with her mother tongue, Somali."

"That's so cool. Is Somali one of those clicking African languages?" She looked around the table, seeking confirmation but gaining averted gazes in return. "That's not offensive. My nanny is South African. And she used to sing lullabies that were..."

To be fair, I began drowning out her explanation, waiting for a cue to slip out of her line of sight.

The bell rang, cutting into my thoughts on an escape route and stealing my attention from the stupidity coming out of Carmen's mouth. Going to the hallway, I raced up the mostly empty staircase, beating the rush. I had to get to room B103 for homeroom. My map said it was in a different building. Peeking down at the map, I came to an abrupt halt when someone called out: "And she's alive!"

It was Xander.

Beth was right behind him. "Oh, my. She's breathing and walking still. How is this possible?"

Hiding my hurt feelings over them abandoning me, I gave a short recap of what had transpired, repeating the exact words Carmen had used about Franklin and his "lack of equipment."

"For about a second, I did feel a tad bit sad about what they said," I admitted as we went down the crowded hallway. "But then I remembered how badly I wanted to admit it was true, all of it, only so that I could say Franklin moans like a possessed goat."

Beth snorted. "The guy is wrong to have done that to you—and to other girls. Karma came knocking. I wouldn't feel sorry. It was meant to happen."

"I bet if it was Pierson spreading rumors like that about you, then you wouldn't care. You wouldn't say the rumors weren't true," Xander said, wiggling his brows. "Isn't that right?"

"Shut up!" She pinched him. "Pierson wouldn't say things like that about anyone."

"Who's Pierson?" I asked, curious. "Are you dating him?"

"Oh, yeah. She's totally dating him—in her wet dreams." Xander hooted.

Beth prodded him with her elbow. "Let's talk about something else. Who wants to talk about something else? I do. I really, really, really do."

"Tell me who this guy is," I said to Xander, ignoring her request.

"Pierson Bowen is possibly the most adored person here at Crescent Hart Academy." Xander leaned in. "He's super internet famous, and you know that counts way more in a boring town like this."

"Ooh, and how long have you had a thing for him?" I poked Beth.

Her blush didn't disappear. "I have more than a thing for him."

"It's more in line with an obsession," Xander said softly. Beth, unsurprisingly, heard him and pinched his arm again. "What? It's true! Are you telling me if he came over here right now, you wouldn't melt into a puddle and let him do anything to you?"

"Alex, you've heard me say this a million times. If he gave me the time of day, I'd let him screw me backward, upside down, on the ground, up a tree, in a house, on a couch—"

"Whoa, calm down there. You sound like a hormonal Doctor Seuss," I joked. "We get it. We get it. You'd let him do just about anything, anywhere."

"Sadly, that'll probably never happen." Xander sighed. "Rumor has it he only sleeps with older women."

I chuckled. "What kind of momma trauma does he have?"

"It's a stupid, untrue rumor! A rumor has no value," Beth roared. "And people have no evidence to back it up. He's had girlfriends our age before."

"Yeah, in Ireland. Who knows how true that is?" Xander rolled his eyes. When he noticed my confused look, he went on to explain. "The guy transferred here back in our freshman year. His granddad lived up in Boulder Valley. Pierson's aunts came, too, bringing their kids. There's three girl cousins and one guy. Two of the girls go here as a sophomore and a freshman."

"His granddad got sick, so they moved into town," Beth filled in. "They're from Sligo."

"Mmm, I like your taste, Beth." I nudged her. "Why don't you make a move on him?"

She slowed her steps, slumped her shoulders, and gestured at her own body. "Have you looked at me long enough to notice why I would never get with him?"

"We're all in uniforms," I noted. "I don't get what you mean."

She sighed. "It's not about the clothes. It's like I only ever have a thing for guys I have no chance with. Something's wrong with me."

Putting a hand on her shoulder, I told her, "That's how it is for all humans. You can't blame yourself. Someone much smarter than me once said that a crush is only ever developed on people you don't know very well."

"I refuse to subscribe to that belief."

"I don't know why you try so hard to impress boys. Most function like a single-celled organism," Xander said, butting into our somewhat serious moment and causing us to laugh.

At the stair landing, entering the mouth of the hallway, we split apart and went our separate ways for homeroom. Xander and I shared the same one, plus two other classes.

Inhaling deeply, I yanked the door open first. I scoped the room for an empty seat and clocked one near the window. Dropping my things on the desk, I sat down and tried not to make eye contact with anyone. The teacher was already at his desk, waiting for the classroom to fill up. After the two-minute warning bell rang, he got to his feet and paced in front of the white board.

"Oh, God," the girl next to me groaned, crumbling into her seat. "I forgot this was Mr. Huang's class. Please, someone save me now."

"Wait, why? It's only homeroom," I whispered to her.

"He gives assigned seating," she answered. "Doesn't matter if it's homeroom."

"That's not so bad."

She flinched at my words, almost like she was insulted. "Assigned seating has no purpose in my book. By next week, I'm going to sit wherever I want. Watch. Everyone else will, too."

The door flew open right at the bell. My eyes, along with the rest of the class's, checked to see who had stumbled in.

Hunching, with a backpack low on his shoulder, Dakota stood at the entrance of the room.

Chapter Eight

Birthday

"Do you have a reason for nearly being tardy, Dakota?" Mr. Huang asked, staring over at Dakota from in front of his desk.

"I wasn't aware I had to give you a reason for nearly being late. I only need a reason if I'm actually late. Which I'm not."

"Just don't make it a habit." Mr. Huang slid his thick, red-rimmed glasses up the bridge of his nose. Dakota only found humor in the teacher's warning, laughing at him. "Don't take a seat just yet. I'm about to do a seating chart."

The class groaned in response, clearly displeased with this announcement. I didn't care if he made a seating chart. If he did it by last names, I wouldn't be seated next to Dakota. If he did it by first names, I still wouldn't be forced to sit next to him. I was safe either way. But if he did it randomly, I was totally screwed.

A boy at the front of the class asked, "Why can't we just sit where we're sitting now, sir?"

Mr. Huang hushed him. "Stop being so negative about it. It's only the first day. Also, I'm trying something new with you guys. This year the seats will be arranged by birthdays. Isn't that fun?"

The class was not amused.

"You haven't heard the actual fun part yet. You have to find out whose birthday goes first by yourselves. Without talking! Only use your hands. Don't write anything down—that's the most vital restriction. Nod or shake your head. But no speaking whatsoever. And don't think you can trick me. I've already written out the chart, so I will be checking to see if you're right or not."

Before anyone could voice their opinions on the matter, he instructed us to get up out of our seats. I collected my things and waited for people to start moving around. I knew I'd be somewhere midway to the far end. My birthday was August 10.

The only downfall with this little activity was that I didn't know what Dakota's birthday was, so I didn't know where he'd be in the room. I discreetly tried to watch the signs he showed people. There were way too many students moving around, shifting to different rows. I couldn't get a clear view. He wrote his birthday down on his hand, showing people.

Dakota was breaking the main rule, taking the words of the instructor as a gentle suggestion.

A few people started showing me their birthdays by using their fingers. I got to the back of the class, making my way through all the birthdays before mine. I planted myself in my chair and searched the room, finding my heart in my stomach when I saw Dakota strolling up to me.

He was gradually getting closer to the row where I was.

Oh, God. Please don't have a summer birthday. Be a winter child. Please.

My prayers were useless. He was in front of me in no time. I held up the numbers eight, and then ten. It matched the numbers he had written on his palm: 8/10

He scowled at me. "You've gotta be kidding me."

"No talking!" Mr. Huang called out.

"There must be a mistake."

"What is it?" Mr. Huang walked to us. "What's wrong?"

"She's lying. That's what it is," he accused. "She's put up the same numbers as my birthday. I bet she's only doing it so she can sit with me."

I snorted. "Get over yourself. You're nothing special. No one in their right mind would want to deliberately sit with you." I faced Mr. Huang and pointed at Dakota. "Is there somewhere else you can seat him?"

"Is there somewhere else you can seat her?" Dakota shouted back.

"Now, kids. You can settle this in a much calmer way." Mr. Huang double-checked the chart in his hands. "What's your name, young lady?"

"Sylvia Ellington," I answered.

"Hmm, that's interesting. You two have the same birthday. You're in the right place. You're supposed to sit next to him."

Dakota didn't move.

"Can't you sit down?" Mr. Huang's tone was getting rough.

"I'd rather break my own two arms before even considering sitting there." Dakota paused momentarily. "In simpler terms . . . no."

Mr. Huang took a slow intake of air. Needing a solution, he called a girl two rows down to sit in between us.

"Is that better?" Mr. Huang asked Dakota.

He sat and plastered a grin on his face. "Much, much better."

"Drama queen," the other girl snarled.

"I heard that," Dakota grumbled.

"You were supposed to, dumbass." A threatening glare brewed behind her stare.

It looked so strange on her. Even stranger, from the sound of it, she might be the only one who wasn't afraid of Dakota.

Chapter Nine

Everybody's Watching Me

The rest of the class was uneventful.

Dakota, for the most part, kept his head low. A sketch had captured his imagination, and he was drawing on the same sheet of paper he'd had in the cafeteria. Everyone else was preoccupied with socializing—twisting in their chairs or leaning over to the person beside them. Chatter filled the room as students talked about their summer vacations—where they'd gone, what they'd eaten—and which teachers they had this year.

I was interested in only one individual.

At some point, Dakota brought out a bulky sketchbook and started doodling in there instead. He was completely focused, letting his hair fall around his face. With each stroke added to the drawing, he drowned out the rest of the world.

I'd be lying if I said I didn't try to peek at his art. From my seat, I didn't have a decent view. Faye, the girl sitting between us, leaned so far forward in her seat that it blocked me from seeing Dakota's desk area or even his profile.

Without a doubt, it felt spiteful.

When the bell rang, Dakota grabbed his sketchbook off the

desk and stuffed it into his backpack. In the process, the loose-leaf piece of paper he'd been drawing on earlier fell off his desk, hitting the floor.

As students went for the exit, talking amongst themselves and discussing which class they were heading to next, I stayed in my seat, hesitating as to what I should do.

I don't know why I care about that drawing, my thoughts piped in. He's annoying.

Dismissing my internal battle over what was right and what was undoubtedly wrong, I collected the folded-up paper. The words To Diana were written in beautiful handwriting, almost like calligraphy. Just as I started unfolding it, it was snatched from my hands.

"That's not yours," Dakota seethed, stuffing the paper into his fitted jeans.

"I, uh ... uh ... "

"Spit it out," he demanded. "Actually, from what Franklin says, you're not much of a spitter."

I gasped. "You know that's not true. You were there."

He shrugged. "I may or may not have been there. Either way, that doesn't mean I'll waste my breath trying to save your reputation by telling people I was anywhere near you that night. I'd rather pretend I was never there to begin with."

In that split second, I could've sworn someone had punched me, knocking the wind right out of me. My cheeks burned as he smirked.

I squinted. "Go to hell."

"I'll see you there, doll. I'll make sure to save an extra special spot for you." He winked and walked off.

●●●

Replaying the events of homeroom later, I thought about what I should've said as a comeback. That was something I hated after leaving a moment like that. After Dakota headed out the door, I had the most perfect response. But the moment was gone. I'd missed my opportunity.

The rest of the day wasn't as crazy as the morning. I noticed Dakota in my PE and AP US History classes, but he was in the back of the room for each. Because of that, I didn't have to see that stupid, gorgeous face.

What I hated more than wasting an insult because you had no one to use it on was the fact that I found Dakota attractive even after what that had occurred in Mr. Huang's homeroom.

My mind dwelt on the girl's name he'd written on the sheet of paper. At the party, I'd seen a tattoo with the name Diana on his arm. Even in the middle of our talk, I'd been curious about who she was. I hadn't been bold enough to prod, and now it was the focal point of the chatter in my head.

I bet she's pretty. I bet she doesn't have a family he hates. She probably drives one of those cute Volkswagen Beetles—

I shook my head, pulling myself out of my own mind before I got any further. This wasn't the time to hate on a fictional girlfriend he might or might not have.

Maybe Beth was right. I was being delusional.

●●●

"Your stepbrother does voodoo," Beth concluded during lunch that next day.

"I have no clue what you're talking about," I said.

"I'm talking about Hanan. After yesterday, when Hanan and Carmen made fun of Franklin, I haven't heard anyone talk about you."

"Everyone's quoting Carmen now and talking about Franklin's you-know-what," Xander said, twitching his little finger. "I think he ruined his own rep by messing with you."

"How'd you do that?" Beth stared at me like I had all the answers in the world at my fingertips. "How'd you convince Hanan Pejman to defend you like that? The guy doesn't stand up for his own brother half the time."

"I don't know. Your guess is as good as mine," I said. "It's not like I bribed him. He did it all on his own."

"He could feel sorry for you," Xander guessed, forcing a pout. "I'm not even related to you, and I feel sorry. You're like a sad, lost puppy. You know, if puppies weren't as cute. So that just leaves you with sad and lost. Who wouldn't feel bad for you?"

I held back a mean retort.

Xander wasn't worth the effort.

Lunch ended with Xander heading to English while Beth and I went to Physiology together. It was our second to last class. We had a block schedule, meaning each day we only did half of the classes we were enrolled in. I kept the dialogue between us light for the most part. But deep inside, I knew what I wanted to do. After Xander left, I gained the courage to ask Beth something.

"Do you know who Diana might be?" I paused. "In relation to Dakota, I mean."

She came to a standstill, gripping her textbook a little tighter. I'd struck a nerve.

Jackpot.

"What do you want to know?"

"Well. I don't know a thing about her, that's the problem."

Her tense shoulders relaxed, and she went back to her normal pace. "Good."

I cleared my throat. "Is she Dakota's girlfriend?"

She snickered. "No. Not even close. It's his sister."

I exhaled a little bit easier after hearing that. But I'd never admit that in front of a judge. "Oh, okay. It's his much younger or older sister, I'm assuming? Because I haven't seen her around here."

That same pained expression graced Beth's face. "By saying she's his sister, I mean she was his sister. She died last summer. She was a year older than him."

Chapter Ten

White Teeth Teens

"She's d-dead?" I stammered.

I had a hard time speaking about death.

Despite not knowing her, a part of my heart went out to Diana. No one deserved to die that young. Death was ugly and menacing as it taunted you at your bedside.

Death had almost met me three months ago, although I didn't have much memory of the ordeal. Babbling alone on the edge of a building, walking without supervision, I'd lost sense of reality. At the time, my conscious mind was on a different plane. There wasn't any rational thinking going on. When someone called the authorities to get me down, I snapped out of my trance and realized what I was doing.

Something had pulled me out of the unbearable currents of depression, though, lifting my head from the roaring tidal waves. My mother tried to help in any way she could. But she was at war with her own personal demons and only found herself sinking deep into the water with me at each attempt to pull me out. It made sense that the water finally took her under. She was never the same after my father left, and she never would be.

She should've known by that time in her adult life, though; everyone knows that you can't help the dying when you're already dead on the inside. She was more dead on the inside than anyone in my family would like to admit. I think that was what made me worse off in the end.

My heart grew heavy, thinking of my mother in those first weeks after the divorce. Heaving a deep breath, I threw myself back into the conversation with Beth. Back to this world. Back to the present, not trapped in the past. The past was never a pleasant place to be.

"I don't know much about what happened before her suicide. Honestly, I don't," she emphasized. The way she forced the words out made me skeptical. It was hard to believe her when she spoke in such an overdramatic way.

"I wasn't close with her or anything. Their older brother, Dion, was overprotective of them both and didn't really let them go out to parties and stuff, so I only ever saw her at school. It wasn't until the year before she died that I started noticing her showing up at my brother Adam's parties."

I hummed, intrigued by the fact that Diana had made such a jump in the social food chain. She'd gone from seldom attending parties to being invited to them—and coincidentally so close to when she took her own life. Even having only been at Crescent Hart Academy for two days, I knew that the lacrosse team was looked at highly around here. Both of my stepbrothers had been on the team last year.

Out of curiosity, I went on to ask, "Did she hang out with anyone on the lacrosse team?"

Beth nodded, tilting her head a little. "She did. How'd you know?"

"Lucky guess."

In my head, the wheels were turning, trying to connect the

dots between Malik and Dakota. It wasn't a solid link, but I was sure there would be more if I kept digging. The bell rang. We piled into the classroom and found empty seats. The teacher wasn't there yet, but they'd left the door unlocked for the students to come in. At my old school, that had been against the rules. And for good reason too.

"Hey, now that I think about it," Beth began, "I don't think Dakota liked it all that much that she was close with some of the popular guys on campus, which is odd, if you ask me."

"Why is that?"

"Because—" She caught herself. "Never mind."

I didn't bother to ask her to elaborate. It was clear enough.

Something was up with that lacrosse team. I didn't have any solid proof about them, but there had to be a connection with Diana's party phase right before her suicide. I wouldn't pry into a dead girl's life, though. This didn't involve me. If anyone cared, it would be Dakota. He was probably doing his own little investigation, piecing together what had caused her to commit suicide. It was none of my business.

Was it tempting to investigate the meaning behind the conversation Malik and Dakota had had? Yes. Very much so. Holding me back and subduing my excitement was the fact that I knew there would be no prize for finding the missing puzzle pieces. What would I gain? Most likely nothing at all. It wasn't like Dakota would stop hating me or would start being nice to me. He'd be the same. I would be the same.

"You know what I never asked?" Beth chirped out of nowhere.

"What?" My head snapped up, looking perplexed.

"Why'd you move to California? I was meaning to ask you at the party, but it slipped my mind. The only thing you said that night, at least from what I remember, was that your mom wanted you to come here. Is that all?"

Something happened. Me ending up on a rooftop scared my mom back to sobriety for a bit. I did some things I probably shouldn't admit to without an attorney at my side. To my mom, I became a "handful," and she didn't want to deal with that anymore. Wanna know how it feels when your habitually inebriated mom thinks you've got issues? It feels awful. I turned into more of a mess than her—and I didn't need to use a substance to do it.

Each cell in my body wanted those words to leap off my tongue and dive into Beth's eardrums. I was itching to say that to her. There was a blockage in the way, though, stopping me from telling her the truth. The desire to confide in Beth wasn't powerful enough to push that out of the way . . . so I settled for the more appealing option: a lie.

"She thought it would be a good way to get some father-daughter time with my dad before I go off to college." I balled my hands into fists in my pockets, hoping she couldn't see them starting to tremble. "My grandma lives not too far from here, and they wanted me to visit her more too."

"That's kind of your mom."

"Yeah, real nice."

I fell back in my seat.

Lying was exhausting. But telling her the full truth—something I hadn't done in a long time—seemed to be more exhausting. There was too much I had to unravel for anyone to understand what I'd done and why I'd done it. People would never understand me. Against my better judgment, I kept my true feelings inside, waiting for a moment of bravery to spit them out.

I was hoping that someone would pull them out for me, or I

just might drown in my own thoughts like my mother had. The mind was a wicked thing, evoking feelings and repeating the past behind your sealed eyes at any hour. I could stay strong in front of anyone's vicious attacks, but I crumbled in an instant at my own thoughts.

My biggest fear, more than dying young, was morphing into a carbon copy of my mother. Without addressing the past or what had forged me into this person, I knew I'd eventually snap at the worst time possible.

And pay for it for the rest of eternity.

Chapter Eleven
Lousy Reputation

One thing dominated the exchanges I had whenever I met someone new. Everyone thought I was Canadian. And annoyingly, they started calling me "Canada" as a joke.

Carmen was kind enough to go around and tell people I was Hanan and Malik's Canadian stepsister, and soon enough, it stuck like glue.

I felt like I was in Mean Girls. If she had labeled me "Africa," like they did in the movie with Lindsay Lohan, I would've protested, considering it a micro-aggression.

By Thursday, most of the school population referred to me as Canada—including people I had met at the party who had heard my real name. In the past, I'd been called some nasty things, and this was the only one that wasn't mean. I figured I'd stop correcting people one of these days.

When Friday arrived, I realized the unnatural divide within the town of Harper Falls. The teens who came from more privilege neighborhoods—like Beth and my stepbrothers—followed their parents to the country club up in Fox Hills. The students who came from less fortunate households went to the plaza near Main Street for a cheap slice of pizza, affordable attire, and a decent place to buy a secondhand book.

But the two groups had one thing in common: they both went to the Smell.

The Smell was an all-ages club that showcased indie bands and served vegan food. It was located closer to Boulder Valley, so the terrain was dry, flat land, more barren than what you'd see in Harper Falls' leafy streets.

"That sounds disgusting," was what I said when I first heard the name. "Who in their right mind thought it would be a good idea to call it the Smell?"

"It's a cool name," Beth assured me.

"No. The Bronze is a cool club name."

"The fact that you hate the name is more of a reason why you should come tomorrow." She grabbed both my shoulders, shaking me. "Please, you have to join us."

"I'm with Sylvia on this one," Xander chimed in. "I don't like going there. There's always a lot of drama, and there's always a fight near closing time."

"But what if you find a hot guy there?"

He flipped his hair. "You and I have different definitions of hot. You think Ted Bundy was attractive."

I cringed, staring at Beth as though she was a stranger to me now. "You think that psycho was hot?" I didn't wait for an answer. "The only time Ted Bundy was ever considered hot was when they were pulling him off that damn electric chair."

Beth swatted me. "It was a phase."

"Please, keep those phases to yourself next time. No one wants to hear about your attraction to mediocre, murderous men," Xander proclaimed. "Going back to that terrible idea of yours, I'm not interested in going. Beth, did you forget what I said last year? I want to work on us becoming popular. Do you know what it'll do to my reputation at this school if I get caught stepping in there? Going to the Smell after the first week is going to tarnish my social life."

"Alex, you have a social life? Since when?" Beth inquired comically.

"Yeah, where did you get this so-called social life of yours?" I played along. "Can I buy one online?"

"Ha ha," he laughed dryly. "You two aren't cute."

In the end, Beth convinced Xander and I both to come on Saturday.

•••

It didn't take much convincing to get my dad to let me go out. From his point of view, any activity that meant I wasn't left alone to my own devices was something he was all for.

"Could I speak to you about something personal?" Dad asked me before I could run back upstairs. "I was thinking about some ways to improve your time here."

"I've been getting along with the kids at my school."

"Hanan told me." He smiled at the floor, getting up from his spot on the couch. "And that's amazing to hear. But I was talking about what happened the first day you were here." The smile dissolved. "I'm genuinely sorry for how I acted that day."

Stunned, I hit my spine to the railing. "Thanks . . . thank you for saying that."

"When I shared what I did with Tara," he revealed, raking a hand over his balding scalp, "she suggested an idea I know would benefit you."

"Which is?"

"A therapist."

"Er—no. I tried that out when I was younger," I said without fully thinking about it, facing my palms at him and rushing into the living room. "I don't need another shrink."

"A shrink isn't interchangeable with a therapist, Sylvia."

"Who cares? I don't want one."

"You need help, Sylvia." He lowered himself to the armrest. Dad was sitting on the exact spot that would cause my mother to roar in anger, saying that I was damaging the structure of the furniture. "Tara said . . ."

Oh, please, tell me what the woman who isn't my parent said to do.

". . . it would be important and vital to incorporate a hobby into your daily routine."

"A hobby?" I echoed. "Taking pictures was a hobby."

He took a painfully slow breath through his nostrils. "I mean a new hobby that won't get you in trouble. Tara said there's a poetry club starting up for high schoolers at the local community center."

"I'm not into poetry."

"You should give it a try before you say no."

I yawned. "My writing isn't any good."

"Give it another shot. Maybe this instructor will spark some inspiration in you," he said, disappearing into the kitchen and returning with a pamphlet about the community center.

Seems less like a suggestion and more like an order.

I mustered a grin. "I'll think about it."

He clasped his hands together under his chin. "That's what I want to hear!"

●●●

While getting ready, I grabbed my "safety purse." The bag had always made a special appearance in Maine as I lugged it on outings. I hadn't brought it with me when I went to the Greers' party because I didn't think I'd need it. But in case someone like Franklin (or Franklin himself) tried to pull the same crap that had happened at the party, I knew this time I'd be prepared.

An hour or so after the sun disappeared from my window, Beth's car pulled into my driveway. A guy with curly red hair was seated in the back. He gave me a short wave and told me his name was Doug. I vaguely recalled him being in one of my classes.

"Hey," Xander greeted me from the passenger seat. "Did you bring a fake ID for tonight? I'm trying to get drunk."

I tensed up in my seat. "Wait. What? Why? Was I supposed to?"

"Chill." Doug chuckled. "He was kidding. This guy gets dizzy after taking Nyquil or Advil. There's no way he'd ever take anything stronger than that. None of us have fakes."

I exhaled and eased back in my seat. "Oh. I, uh, knew that."

"Doug, do you have any new cheesy pickup lines?" Beth asked.

I checked the rearview mirror, and Beth gave me a quick grin. With that one look, I could tell she was purposely changing the topic. She was a good friend.

"I have a few new ones of my own," Beth added.

"Oh, really? Try me," Doug demanded. "Mine are always better than yours."

"You try pickup lines on girls?" I asked, raising my brow. "You know that rarely works, right?"

"It's less about me getting the girl and more about me finding something ridiculously funny to make the girl laugh. Listen to this one." He cleared his throat and shifted his body closer to mine, taking my hand in his to shake it. "Hi. I'm Doug. It's God spelled backward with a little you in it." He finished the joke with a wink, which only made me laugh even harder. It wasn't the joke itself but the way he'd said it, like he believed he was the greatest gift God ever made and a pleasure to be in the presence of. The confidence was sexy.

"That was a cornier one," Doug said with a defeated appearance, thinking it hadn't worked. "The dirty ones are funny too but could easily blow up in your face."

I shrugged. "Try a dirty one."

"Babe, I'm like a firefighter. I find them hot and leave them wet."

"That's the best you got? I have a better one." Xander snorted. "Babe, I'm like a Rubik's Cube. The more you play with me, the harder I get."

"Ew, I'm driving. Stop that. I don't like this anymore," Beth groaned. "Shut up before I ram this car into a pole. I can actually taste my dinner in my mouth."

Xander prodded her with his elbow. "Oh, shut it. It was funny."

"Yeah, I'm positive it would be funny in an alternate universe where you're not Alex."

We pulled into a large parking lot in front of the Smell. The place was swarming with people, and the lot was packed. Once we were inside, Xander and Doug hurried to find us a table while Beth sprinted to the opposite corner, greeting some friends as if she hadn't just seen them a few hours ago at school.

Doug found us a round table with tall black stools. We all sat down and were joined by one of Beth's friends. I learned that her name was Natalie and that she was in the grade below ours.

"I'm new in town," I said after introducing myself. "First time coming here to the Smell."

"Oh, wow, really? I've been here a million times. My brother works as a server."

She waved at a cute brunet wiping down the counters. Xander must've noticed him too because he whipped out a mirror in a nanosecond. Before I knew it, he was touching up his gloss and checking his teeth.

Xander tapped Natalie. "Do you think if I walked up to him and asked for his number, that he'd feel confident and comfortable enough to give it to me while he's still working?"

Quite done with the conversation, I scoped the room and spotted Malik. He was sitting near the back of the club, chatting up some girl with long blond hair. She was laughing so hard that she had to hold on to his arm for stability, leaning forward and bracing herself.

It was a total flirting move.

The look on his face told me he knew exactly what she was doing, and he was eating it up.

"I'm assuming that's Malik's girlfriend," I commented, nudging Beth to get her attention. "That blond over there."

She looked where I was pointing at. "No, that's not his girlfriend. He's dating Faye Daniels."

"Wait." I grabbed the crook of her arm and stared back at her, hard. "Are you sure? The only Faye I know doesn't . . ."

"Seem to be the same social status as him? Yeah, I know," Xander finished, gaining interest in our conversation. No part of me was going to make a comment like that, but I let him think that was where my mind had gone. "They started dating over the summer."

"I hear he started dating her as a joke," Natalie said. "And honestly, I believe it. I mean, c'mon. Why else would he go for a girl like her?"

I furrowed my brow. "And what's that supposed to mean? A 'girl like her'?" I reiterated her words. I was hoping she wasn't going to say what I thought she was going to say.

"Well, you know." She turned to me. "She's always around other guys. I doubt she's ever had a stable boyfriend."

"Get to your point," I ordered, snapping my fingers. "What's wrong with that? She's probably only seventeen or eighteen like me. Having a stable boyfriend is easier said than done. Do you have a boyfriend?"

"No, but that's not what I was hinting at. She sleeps around," Natalie spat out. "Like a lot. I'm sure she's been with half the football team or something." She turned to Beth, giggling, but Beth wasn't amused.

"I don't get the problem here." I scowled. "Are you her doctor? No? Then you shouldn't care whether if she's sexually active or not. It's her damn body. Not yours. So that means you shouldn't be judging her for doing whatever she pleases with it." I leaned in a little closer, spewing out my words in hot anger. It wasn't entirely directed toward her. All the pent-up thoughts I had about girls like her at my previous school had overshadowed the more sensible thing to do. "How often does Malik sleep around? More? Less?"

Natalie made a face that I could only describe as what pretending to think might look like.

"I don't know." She shrugged.

"Then why do you believe it's acceptable to judge her for sleeping around but not even acknowledge how much he does? Is it because he's a guy?"

"What the hell is wrong with you?" She inched away from me. "You don't need to take this so seriously."

"I think it would be best if you sat somewhere else, Natalie,"

Beth announced. "I don't like the energy you're giving this group. Negativity like that isn't good for the soul."

"I'm not liking the rudeness," Xander commented.

"The tribe has spoken," I said, making a reference to one of my favorite shows growing up. "It's time for you to go."

"Fine," Natalie grumbled, snatching up her purse. "I was going to leave anyway."

Xander grabbed my hand. I resisted snatching it away. "What you just did took guts. I don't know if I told you this before, but I really like you, Sylvia."

"I don't know if I told you this before, but I really don't like you, Xander." I beamed.

He laughed.

Aw. He thinks I'm joking. How cute.

As if my night couldn't get any worse, I watched the front door open and found the star of my daydreams—and the cause of most of my headaches—walk in. The one and only Dakota freaking Ridgewood.

He had on the same ratty black boots he'd worn at school today. The only difference was that he'd exchanged his uniform for a dark jean jacket and deep maroon corduroy pants. It pained me to admit it, but I was sure he looked great in just about anything.

And most likely better in nothing at all.

Chapter Twelve

Jump Into the Fog

"Ugh. Why does he have to be here?" I grimaced, covering my eyes with my fingers. There was no chance tonight would end well.

Xander, Beth, and Doug searched the area with newfound interest, trying to pinpoint who had walked into the Smell that was pissing me off. What had I done to deserve this? Having Malik here was bad enough. I regretted coming here. This night was going to be a nightmare, and I just knew it.

"Oh, you're not a big fan of Dakota, I'm guessing," Doug observed.

"Tell me one person who is."

"You should ask Carmen. She used to date him," Dough revealed, making me choke on my own breath. "You didn't know? Isn't Hanan your brother?"

"That doesn't mean I know his whole dating history."

"They broke up pretty soon after your brothers moved into town." Doug pointed at the small group of people Dakota was heading toward. The circle of teens clapped their hands together and cheered when he arrived, patting him on the back and greeting him with big smiles. "And those people seem to like him."

"I don't recognize any of them," I said and elbowed Beth. "Do they go to our school?"

The corners of her mouth fell downward. "They go to Boulder Valley High. Dakota gets along with them better than the kids at Crescent Hart. Mainly because they probably don't know half the stuff about his family."

Doug let out a cough. "Or he hangs out with them because none of the girls are scared of him there. I don't think I've seen one girl go after him since Carmen dated him in freshman year."

Beth nodded. "I hear he's dating a girl who goes to Boulder Valley."

My frown deepened unknowingly. "He could just transfer if he likes it there so much," I said, and everyone looked at me a little weird.

Beth scoffed, almost like I should know why he couldn't transfer schools. I gave her a curious look. "There's no way he could transfer schools. The parents need to sign off and go up to the school. And his mom—"

Xander nudged her, hard.

As tempting as it was to ask Beth what she'd been about to say, I understood she wouldn't tell me anything worth mentioning about Dakota. Especially with her best friend here, stopping her at every turn.

Doug got up from his stool and offered to buy us a side of fries. When he left, Xander reprimanded Beth. I didn't like how he constantly threw negativity her way. Xander was always telling her what was acceptable and what was "cool." I wouldn't take guidance from him. No one should take advice from a person who still dressed in a matching pair of jeans and a denim jacket like Britney Spears and Justin Timberlake in 2001. It was okay then. In this climate, though, it was ridiculous.

"You've hardly talked to Doug all night," Xander reminded her. "At least try, Beth."

"The night is young," she explained. "Give me time to work up some courage."

"Ask him to dance when he comes back."

I tilted my head. "Wait. Is this a date?"

Beth stayed silent, blushing.

"Beth! Why did you invite us on your date?"

"That's what I asked her!" Xander said. "I didn't know until we were getting ready at her place."

Now it made sense why she'd been so insistent about bringing Xander and me with her. I'd noticed that Doug appeared sad even before I got in the car. Xander and Beth were extremely close. I wouldn't be surprised if Beth had forced Doug to sit in the back seat.

To Beth, there was no way any guy could compete with the infamous Pierson Bowen. I hadn't met him yet—usually, I was too busy glaring at Dakota from across the cafeteria to pay attention to any other people around me.

On Friday, I'd discovered that Pierson had missed the first week of classes because he was in Ireland for the funeral of his grandad. The old man had lost his battle to cancer the weekend before school started, leading to a speedy burial in his homeland. Because Pierson was a senior, too, Beth said he was able to convince his parents to let him finish the school year here in California before they moved back to Ireland.

"You got Doug Lewis to ask you out," Xander said, rattling Beth's stool by kicking it. "That's almost as amazing as getting a date with James Dean."

Beth cringed. "By James Dean, I hope you mean the fifties actor and not the porn star."

"Are we going to ignore the fact that James Dean the actor is dead?" I inquired.

"That's not the point!" Xander shouted before composing himself when he saw Doug coming back to our table. "He's almost back. Smile. Sit up. Why are you slouching?"

"I'm slouching because my lifelong dream is to be the hunchback of Notre Dame." She hunched further forward, but it only annoyed Xander, so she sat up quickly.

I scooted closer to Beth, whispering, "I feel like this is more of a date to Xander than it is for you."

"Oh, yeah. Definitely. You should've seen him earlier when I was getting dressed," she whispered back to me. "He's only acting this way because Doug is friends with the other athletes on campus."

"Oh. I see. He's using you as a ladder to get higher up the social food chain." I released a pent-up breath. Xander wasn't earning any brownie points for his selfishness. "That's a nice little tactic. He's too sweet."

She bumped shoulders with me. "Hey, since you think it's a 'nice little tactic,' why don't you start going after one of the athletes? Two girls going after the same goal is a hell of a lot better than one."

"Hunting for an athlete to date is like the first step toward becoming a lonely trophy wife. I have better things to do than to walk into school on Monday trying to find a brainless jock worth speaking to. Let alone worth dating." I nudged her. "We'll be graduating in a few months. I don't know why popularity still seems so important at this point."

That statement caught Xander's attention. "Did you just say that? What could be better than being popular?"

I snorted. "Don't get me started. I could write a well-structured essay, paired with a PowerPoint, breaking down what's better than striving for popularity . . . in your senior year, no less. Use your brain power on something that'll last longer than a school year. Maybe if you were running for class president, I'd support you. But all you want to do is get invited to lame parties and chill with people who won't remember your name in a decade."

Beth and Doug chuckled, and Xander awkwardly joined in, trying to make it appear he wasn't affected by what I'd said.

There were fewer kids from Crescent Hart Academy here than I'd expected. Facing Beth, I asked her why that was, and she said, "After last year, fewer and fewer Crescent Hart students were coming here. I almost never see kids from our school anymore. I mean, other than the occasional sighting of Dakota and Malik. For the most part, it's Boulder Valley kids. It's kind of their turf now, if you know what I mean."

"They don't mind if a few of us hang out," Doug went on to add. "The only reason a lot of people from our school would come here all together was to start up trouble with the Boulder varsity football or lacrosse teams."

"There's an issue with their sports team?" I asked.

Silence fell, and then at last, Doug answered. "There's more than an issue between Boulder Valley and Crescent Hart kids."

"Boulder Valley is literally the closest high school to us. It's only natural they're our rivals when it comes to sports stuff," Beth said.

"It's a lot deeper than that, Beth," Doug said. "It started off as a friendly rivalry, but it got a lot more serious back when my dad and mom went there. Because of the class of '98, things have only gotten worse. That was when the rivalry really started."

I counted back, thinking how old his parents must be now. I came up with the same age as my father. Was this connected to what my father had done to Dakota's family? Had he caused this? I didn't know ... not yet, at least.

I began to ask Doug another question, hoping that he'd tell me more about this rivalry, but the loud bang of the doors swinging open silenced the entire room. The music cut off as a group of Crescent Hart Academy kids stormed into the club. I spotted my stepbrother Hanan in the crowd, glaring daggers at the Boulder Valley kids. Malik walked up to the group and stood beside them, but far away from his own brother.

Hanan stood beside an ungodly tall student right in the middle who was obviously the leader. His dirty blond hair fell over his forehead, curling over bright green eyes. Anger boiled behind his narrowed gaze, growing deeper the longer he stood there, peering at us all as if we were the cause of his bad mood.

Beth shrieked loudly when she saw him.

"Pierson?" I guessed, and she nodded. I completely understood why she had a huge crush on him. He was breathtakingly handsome in his burgundy letterman jacket and black shirt. He scowled and held his clenched hands at his sides, ready to swing them at the first person who crossed him.

Pierson scoped the area from left to right. A few Boulder Valley kids sprang up from their seats, standing their ground. There were at least ten students from Crescent. I spotted Adam, Beth's twin brother, standing to the left of Hanan. My stepbrothers were clearly outnumbered, but that didn't seem to frighten them with Pierson on their team.

Everyone was waiting for his move.

"You know why I'm here," Pierson barked.

I took note of the thick Irish accent. I had forgotten about that.

Pierson cleared his throat. "Jiménez."

A guy who had been sitting with Dakota stood up, pushing past the kids who wrapped around his table. It had to be Jiménez.

A cool look radiated off his face as he pulled a toothpick out of his mouth. Dakota grabbed his arm and started to whisper something in his ear. They shared a few words, and two other guys, followed Dakota and Jiménez to where Pierson and his guys stood.

"I told you not to come back after last time," Jiménez cooed, pushing the toothpick back into his mouth. He had hair that fell to his waist, curling at the ends. Dressed in white, he looked angelic next to Dakota, who was practically melting into the shadows in his dark attire. "You Crescent idiots don't know what's good for you. We had a deal."

"Deal's off, Jiménez. You broke the one rule," Malik pipped in. Pierson lifted his hand, pushing my stepbrother back before he jumped right at Jiménez.

"Handle your dogs, Pierson," Dakota warned. "Or I will."

"You couldn't even keep a hold of your sister, Ridgewood." Malik smiled wickedly, stepping closer to Jiménez and his friends. "And look where she ended up. Do you want to join her six feet under? Because I can gladly arrange that."

Dakota was a blur as he crashed into Malik, tackling him to the tiled floor. He landed punch after punch on his unresponsive body, helpless on the ground.

That was all it took.

A war was raging within the Smell. Both sides raced at each other, swinging fists and kicking their way into the crowd. Someone went for Doug, who was sitting calmly in his chair. They put him in a chokehold, dragging him out of his seat.

I was right: The night didn't go well, but not in the way I thought it would.

Chapter Thirteen

Magnets

Pierson dodged the fists aimed at him, swiftly moving out of the way and then swinging a powerful punch at his opponent. He had to be a hated guy from the way countless people went after him first.

He happily took them on. For a moment, I saw a slight smile on his lips when he saw the number of people he was up against. His reaction was contrary to how I would've responded in his place. I'd be panicking if I were him, frantically looking for the exit.

Doug, on the other hand, wasn't as lucky. He didn't move as gracefully. If anything, he struggled with the guy who held him around the neck. I reached into my purse and retrieved one of the many things I'd put in there for safety reasons.

Who would've known it would be useful tonight?

Drawing out my pepper spray, I popped the top off, pointed it at Doug's attacker, and pressed the bottom, hard. Dark orange mist shot out, hitting the guy in the face and inside his mouth.

Thankfully, Doug had closed his eyes and placed his hand over his face before I'd started pepper spraying his attacker. A pungent scent lingered in the air around us as the guy tumbled backward, holding his face and crying out in pain.

Beth went to Doug's side, hugging him. "Are you okay?"

He nodded, wiping the backs of his hands on his jeans. "Yeah, I'll live," he croaked, holding his neck as he turned to me. "Thanks, Sylvia."

"No problem."

"What the hell was that?" Xander squirmed in his seat. "Where did you get that?"

Oh, this old thing? It was my last gift from my mother.

Even though that was true, it wasn't what I said out loud. Searching my bag, I pulled out another can of pepper spray and a pocketknife. Handing the pepper sprays to Xander and Beth, I kept the pocketknife for myself.

"I lived in a tough part of town. I took the city buses at night." I wasn't completely lying; my neighborhood wasn't the nicest.

"Stay behind me," I instructed. "Don't use the whole thing. And point it in the right direction, not at yourself. Check before you press." I gestured at the guy I had sprayed, who was now moaning on the floor next to us. "Or you'll end up like him."

Xander was shocked when he saw me flip the pocketknife out. Light caught the tip of the blade as I waved it from side to side. I rolled my eyes at his expression and turned to the roaring chaos around us. I had better things to do than comfort a scared Xander.

"Do you know how to use that thing?" Xander gulped, extending a finger to the knife.

I've used it in the past. I'll be fine, I thought. I was glad I'd recently cleaned it.

Switching the knife from hand to hand, I kept it low enough that people didn't see it right away.

"I can manage."

I didn't want to use it, but a primal part of me had been awakened at the sight of this fight. A hidden section of my mind told me

I'd do anything to get out of here. I'd breathe a lot easier if I could just get outside and away from this madness.

Doug created his own weapon, like many of the kids from Boulder had. Getting a glass bottle then slamming it into a table corner, they threatened to place it below someone's chin. Five other students had identical glass weapons in their hands, jabbing them into the air.

I counted.

The four of us moved as one. I led them forward, keeping my guard up as we skirted past the fights erupting around us. A boy wearing a Boulder Valley sweater came running right at us, holding a piece of wood over his head.

I didn't pause or hesitate. Sticking my leg out, I lodged a knee right into his stomach. The plank of wood fell to the floor, along with his body as he held on to his midsection.

"Didn't your mother tell you to never hit a lady? Ugh, men!" Beth yelled, holding up my pepper spray to the guy's face.

Where the hell did that come from? I pushed her hand away, stopping her.

"Whoa, rule number one: Don't hurt someone when they're already down. He's done for. Let's go." I straightened my shirt and smoothed out the wrinkles. As I stepped over him, I switched the knife to my left hand.

It wasn't until we were closer to the front of the Smell that I saw the number of guys Pierson had knocked to the ground. He wasn't even out of breath. That same dazzling smile was still on his lips, taunting his opponents.

"C'mon, give it another shot," Pierson teased. "Your mum was more fun than this last night. You're making this way too easy for me."

God, he was so damn cocky about it. He was dancing circles around a Valley student like he was the predator and the other was the prey. The kid was no match for someone like Pierson Bowen.

"Go on. Hit me. Try." Pierson egged him on. "I might let you get in a punch or two."

His bruised and battered opponent lamely took another swing at him but caught only air. "Aw, that was close."

Winding back, Pierson jabbed him with an upper cut. When the boy collapsed with the others, Pierson wiped his knuckles on his shirt.

"Too bad. I didn't think you would tap out that early. Your mum lasted longer than you." He smirked down at the guy. "You should get some pointers from her on how to get me out of breath." He winked.

I blinked in befuddlement. Was he serious?

While watching Pierson, I had lost focus on my surroundings. From the corner of my eye, I saw someone coming right for me with a bottle in their hand, swinging it like a madman. A figure bounced in front of me, stopping them with a quick push against the chest.

The person who had saved me spun around.

It was Hanan.

Fear shone through his brown eyes. "You need to get the hell out of here, Sylvia." He spotted Xander and Beth next to me. "Take your friends with you. Just get out of h—"

His last words were interrupted by a barstool. A much shorter Valley guy had knocked Hanan out. Doug inched toward the culprit, but the noise of police sirens stopped all of us in our tracks. The entire place went into hysterics, and everyone began racing for the exits.

I reached for my stepbrother, pulling him up to his feet. Xander had to help me.

"Get Hanan to the back exit," Pierson told us, remaining calm and composed in a time of chaos. "I'm going to get my car."

We dragged Hanan's body out back.

• • •

"Keep him awake."

This demand came from Pierson, who was driving.

"I'm trying. But he's not responding," Beth said from the back seat, using the jacket she had taken off as a blanket around Hanan. Xander, Doug, and Beth all sat in the back with Hanan lying awkwardly over them. He groaned and moaned incoherently. "Go to the nearest hospital. I think he has a concussion."

"No," murmured Hanan.

"You need a doctor."

"We can't go to a doctor," Pierson said firmly. "If we do, we'll have to get his parents involved. He's still seventeen. No one can know we were here tonight. It's the last thing I need in my life right now."

"Then why'd you come here in the first place?" Doug asked, something we were all wondering.

Pierson allowed the question to hang in the air, leaving us waiting to hear his answer.

"That doesn't matter anymore," Pierson replied, gripping the steering wheel until his knuckles whitened. "Hey, don't worry. I know a guy we can go to."

"He needs a real doctor," Beth pressed on.

"My guy is a real doctor," Pierson confirmed. "He's a good

doctor at that; I go to him myself. I'll pay for it. You guys need to be quiet. It'll be handled."

The argument ended sooner than I thought it would. Beth didn't have much fight left in her after that. No one went as far as to argue with Pierson. They didn't care what was right. They cared about what Pierson thought was right.

I cleared my throat. I was going to do either the stupidest thing ever or the bravest. Possibly both. "How do you know if that's best for him or not?"

His brow got closer, glancing at me. "Look, I'm doing exactly what Hanan would want if he were conscious. He knows I can't take him to a hospital."

I said nothing. He was the one driving the car, not me. I didn't have any power.

• • •

At one in the morning, hours since we'd pulled up to an apartment building, I got the news that Hanan would be fine. It would be another hour until he could join us. From what Pierson said, they wanted to check his vitals for a bit longer. Back in Maine, I didn't know any teens who had those kinds of connections, calling on a doctor like we were in the fifties. Later, Beth would tell me Pierson's family had the means to make the unimaginable (for a middle-class person) their daily reality.

None of us wanted to go home while we waited for Hanan. We piled back into the car to drive to a nearby diner for breakfast. It was one of the few things open at this hour.

We stayed silent in the vehicle, keeping our thoughts to

ourselves. There was an unacknowledged tension building, and it was eating my insides alive, setting my skin on fire.

Doug said he wasn't hungry, so he stayed in Pierson's car. Beth and Xander sat at a different table, saying they needed to be alone. I knew it was because being this close to Pierson probably freaked Beth out, and she wasn't in the mood or the right mindset to have Pierson speak to her.

Great, I grumbled to myself after ordering a hash brown and coffee. Just leave me with the killing machine. That's not weird or awkward at all, guys.

Chapter Fourteen

L$D

Unlike Doug, I was hungry.

After scarfing down the hash brown, I ordered myself a stack of pancakes to help the uneasy feeling in my stomach. My nerves were clouding my thoughts when I remembered what had happened to Hanan. What was I supposed to say to Tara and my dad? They knew I was at the Smell tonight. I didn't know if Hanan had told them he'd be there, but if he did, I knew Tara would come to me for my side of the story.

Pierson had made it clear that he didn't want any of us to talk about what had happened. Whenever it was mentioned, he shut it down. He was the kind of guy you didn't want to disappoint—even I had realized that after knowing him for only a few hours.

His large frame struggled to fit in our tiny booth. I fidgeted and played with the spoon and fork before me, trying my best not to make direct eye contact. I was anxious. Why couldn't Xander and Beth have sat with us?

"You're bleeding."

The words ripped me out of my chattering mind. "Huh?"

I squinted up at him.

"You. Are. Bleeding," he said slower, gesturing to my arm. I looked at my forearm, finding a large gash above my elbow. I hadn't noticed it during the fight. Pierson pulled out napkins from the dispenser and handed them to me. "Didn't you feel that? It's fairly deep."

I dabbed the tissue against my flesh, shaking my head. In the most serious voice I could muster, I said, "I guess I'm immune to pain."

"As great as that sounds, I know that's not true."

"Unless I have congenital insensitivity to pain."

He popped up a brow. "Can you say that again, but not in medical mumbo jumbo?"

"It's a genetic disorder where you can't feel pain. It's rare, super rare."

He nodded. "Oh. Okay. I think I've heard of that before in a Grey's Anatomy episode."

"There's a House one, too," I mentioned. "That's where I first saw it."

"Do you have that?"

"No. I wish I did, though."

"No, you don't."

"Yes, I do."

"There's always a downfall to everything. Even if you don't feel physical pain, that doesn't mean you can't feel emotional pain. I think that's more damaging. See my hand?" He waved it around. "If I broke it, it'd heal in due time. But there's nothing that can easily heal something messed up inside my head."

"Quit deep for a guy who was making yo mama jokes an hour ago."

"I'm full of surprises." He laughed and relaxed against the seat. The waitress came to our table and refilled both our coffees. Pouring in the cream and sugar, I could feel Pierson's eyes observing every move I made.

"Who are you?" he asked with a half-smile.

"I should be asking you that."

"Why?"

"I don't know many teens who know doctors who take house calls."

"Oh, my secrets aren't that mysterious." His eyes dropped to the table. "They're a friend of my granddad's. Well, were. I lost my granddad this month."

"I'm sorry for your loss."

He picked up his coffee, black with no sugar, and took a sip. "Did you just move here? I don't remember you here last year."

"Is that so?"

"Believe me, I would've known if you were a student."

I dismissed the remark, and how my stomach flipped when he said it. Instead, I pulled the spoon out of my cup, setting the hot metal on my tongue until it cooled down.

"Maybe you heard about me. I'm Canada."

His nose scrunched up, bemusement swimming in his sage eyes. "What?"

"Canada. Like the country. The country above—"

"I know where Canada is. I've seen a map before." He cut me off. "No offense, but were your parents on LSD when they named you Canada?"

I refrained from chuckling. "No, it's not my name. It's how Carmen has been introducing me ... as Canada. My name is Sylvia Ellington."

"Oh. Now that makes more sense. She called me Scotland when I first met her."

I cocked a brow. "Seriously?"

"Seriously." He brought the rim of his coffee cup to his lips. "Someone really needs to give that girl a globe."

"And a new brain."

"I propose we start a GoFundMe for her to get a better brain and a personality that's not so annoying." He grinned, flashing a dimple. My heartbeat picked up for a second. I made sure I wasn't smiling like a fool.

He went on. "I swear, it's like her parents told her she could be anything in life, and she decided to be a disappointment."

On cue, almost like she knew she was being talked about, Carmen stormed into the diner. Malik and a few of the people Pierson had brought to the Smell were behind her.

"Speak of the devil," I announced.

"I'll deal with her." Raising his hand, Pierson got up from his seat. "Are you stalking me? Carmen, we've talked about this. It isn't healthy. I don't want you."

He was smirking the entire time.

She pointed her finger, and her usual tan complexion paled as she glared at him. "I'm not here for you. Where is he?"

"Who?"

"My boyfriend."

"Hanan is safe. He's in good hands. You don't need to stress."

She exhaled a breath. But she tensed up again when she saw me sitting in the booth. "What the hell is she doing here? You know, I heard how it all happened." She put her hands on her hips. "If you hadn't been a distraction, then he wouldn't have gotten hurt!"

"I didn't do anything," I said. "This isn't my fault."

"He jumped in there and saved your ass. That's when someone struck him from behind. Because of you!" she shouted, going right for me. One of the guys stepped forward and held her back, but she only shrugged him off. "Why did you even have to be there? This is your damn fault!"

Pierson yanked her into his arms, saving me from her wrath. "Whoa there, Carmen. Your crazy is showing." A few of the guys around us laughed, but that only seemed to piss her off more from the look of it. "Look, Carmen. I don't think Sylvia wanted Hanan to get hurt tonight. He's the one who decided to come with me to the Smell. He knew the risks. You can't put that on her."

"It is her fault, though," she insisted and nearly lunged at me, but Pierson was quick to grab her before she got close.

Holding her still, he blinked down at her with disdain. "You are not starting a fight. I've seen enough of that tonight." He turned to Malik. "She can't stay here. Go take her back to the car."

"Make sure to crack the window open," I mumbled to myself.

Pierson grinned at me, and we exchanged a look of amusement.

After Carmen was escorted out, Pierson had a discussion with the other guys. They were near the entrance of the diner, talking in low whispers. I caught some small snippets. "The deal" and "Jiménez" were uttered more than once. I recalled them starting the fight about a deal, and how one of the rules had been broken by the Boulder Valley High kids. When I'd asked Beth about the boy, she'd disclosed only that Jiménez was his last name. He never went by his first.

By the time Pierson and his friends were done speaking, I'd finished my coffee and the pancakes the waitress gave me. We paid and collected Xander and Beth from their seats in the corner. Pierson drove back to the Smell, sure that the cops had left. When we got there, he was right. There was no sign of the police.

We split into two different cars. Since Doug, Pierson, and I lived nearest to each other, Pierson drove us home. Xander said he lived closer to Beth, so he went with her instead. Doug was the first to get dropped off. When he got out, I didn't waste any time.

"Thanks," I chirped.

"For what?" Pierson inquired, easing back onto the road.

"For not letting Carmen rip my throat out."

He smirked. "I highly doubt she'd do that."

"You don't think she's vicious enough to do it?"

"Oh, no. That girl is gone in the head. She's very capable of ripping someone's throat out." He nodded. "But I've got a feeling you wouldn't let her get that far. I saw you kick that guy in the stomach and pepper spray another one at the Smell. And you were walking around with a pocketknife so casually—almost like you've held it a million times. If anything, she's the one who should be scared."

I tried to shield my smile. "I'm not scary."

"Where'd you get all that stuff? Most girls don't have that just lying around in their purses."

I shrugged. "Maybe you don't know many girls."

"Maybe," he continued, smiling to himself. For the second time tonight, he asked, "Who are you, Sylvia Ellington? I mean honestly, who are you?"

We pulled up next to my house, stopping right before the driveway. I clicked off my seat belt and hopped out of the car, shutting the door behind me. When I leaned back in through the open window, I said, "I guess you'll have to find out."

"Trust me, I will," he said with a determined look. "I'm very persistent when it comes to things I want."

"You can try all you want, Pierson, but it won't be easy," I said cheerfully. Without another word, I turned on my heels. Silently, I made my way to the front porch, fishing the house keys from my purse. The entire time, I made sure not to look back at him and feed into his games. It was only after the rumbling of his car had faded away that I glanced over my shoulder, watching his red taillights shimmer in the fog.

The confidence behind his words hadn't brought joy to my heart. Only fear. It wouldn't take much digging to learn what I'd done back in Maine. I wasn't hiding behind a false name or fake identity. I was myself, open like a book, constantly fearing the wrong person would find what was lurking inside.

Chapter Fifteen

Trouble

Monday hit us like a tidal wave, unexpected and certainly unwanted. The school was buzzing like crazy about what had happened at the Smell, and how Hanan hadn't shown up today. Hanan was still under Pierson's care. Beth and I had gone to see him on Sunday, to make sure he was okay. He said he was fine, but the guy Pierson got to take care of him said it would be best if he rested another day for good measure. Not once did Malik bother to visit his twin brother.

Tara received a call from Hanan assuring her that he was okay but would be staying with Pierson for a few days. From what Pierson had told me in the car, this wasn't unusual and was something they did monthly since they enjoyed working out together. Carmen and I both aided the lie, insisting that it was true.

That morning, I'd gotten my class schedule changed. I told the counselor about the repeat classes he'd given me and the Spanish 2 he'd put me in. I'd already finished that class back in Maine, so they advanced me to Spanish 3 instead. Which, thankfully, meant I didn't have any classes with Xander—other than homeroom.

It was weird in a way, but I was looking forward to my PE class. Back in Maine, I used to be on the cross-country team before . . . well, before everything happened. I enjoyed the feeling of running, slamming my feet against the pavement, racing, and reaching that finish line before anyone else.

When Coach Walker said we'd be running on the track for most of class, I was the only student who was happy about it. After I finished my required number of laps, Coach Walker caught up with me at the water fountain.

"Ellington," he called, coming to a stop behind me.

"Yes, sir?" I asked, rising from my bent position.

"Do you know how fast you were going?" He didn't stop to let me speak, showing me the timer in his hands. "That's incredible."

I frowned. "I've slowed down."

He was taken aback. "Are you kidding me? You're faster than most of the students on my cross-country team. Have you ever thought about joining the team?"

"No." I wiped the water from my chin. "And I don't think I want to."

I'd been on the cross-country team in Maine for a solid two years. Nowadays, I ran when I felt like pushing my thoughts away, focusing only on the blood pumping through my veins and the oxygen going into my body. Nothing else mattered in that moment. I ran for myself . . . and to get away from problems.

Coach Walker narrowed his thick brows. "Well, before you make up your mind, at least sleep on it. We're having our tryouts at the end of September. I know we'd love to have you."

•••

Beth and Xander met me at my locker before lunch. Xander was beaming like he was hiding a secret that I'd want to know. Beth was gnawing on her lower lip, ignoring my greeting.

"What is it?" I asked Xander.

"Oh, nothing." His lips curled upward. "One thing did come to mind. I can't help but think how cute a couple you and Pierson would make." The tone in his voice gave him away. I knew he was only saying it to piss off Beth. And just like a charm, it worked.

Beth's eyes nearly fell out of their sockets, and she slugged him in the arm. He winced in response, holding the spot where she'd hit him. "Why did you have to bring Pierson up?"

"What?" he yelled. "The whole school already knows about their little date in the diner."

"It wasn't a date," Beth and I said in unison.

"No one is talking about that, Alex," Beth supplied. "It can't be a date. We were there with them at the diner."

"Yeah, we were there, but we were at a different table, Beth," he reminded her. "I told you; you should've made your move the other night."

"It doesn't matter if I did or didn't make a move. She doesn't like Pierson." Beth hesitated, then faced me. "You don't like him like that, right?"

I chuckled for her benefit. Hoping she could see that I wasn't interested in her crush, I deepened the laugh, but it didn't help melt the lines forming on her face. I let out a cough, resting a hand on her shoulder. "No, I don't like him like that."

Frankly, I didn't know how I felt about Pierson. He was funny and easygoing, which were two qualities I needed in a friend. But I didn't need a boyfriend. At least, not at this moment. A relationship would only complicate my life. My senior year would be a lot better if I didn't have to think about holding onto a guy.

Beth smiled for the first time that day. "Good. That's good news."

"I bet everyone else thinks differently." Xander gestured to the bustling hallway of students. As he did, the crowd parted as Pierson, Doug, and a guy I had seen at the Smell came our way. "Ooh, lookie here. It's the man of the hour."

"Beth!" Doug shouted, rushing up to her, smiling more than ever. Man, he liked her a lot more than she realized. You had to be blind to not see it. "Good morning. How are you? You look nice today."

"Thanks, Doug. I'm fine," she said, gazing at Pierson, breathless and dopey-eyed. "Hello, Pierson."

"Oh, uh, hi." Pierson blinked in her direction, then he saw me and flashed a genuine smile. "Sylvia. You're just the person I was looking for."

"Well, I'm not that hard to find." I shut my locker. "What did you want to talk about?"

"Coach Walker told me—"

"Let me guess. He asked you to talk to me about joining the cross-country team, right?" I interrupted. "I told him my answer. I don't want to join. From the way he talked about the team, it sounds like they suck."

Pierson laughed. "They do suck. They need all the help they can get. That's why I think you should join."

Doug rammed his shoulder into him. "Don't lie. You only want her to join because the soccer team practices on the field the track loops around." Doug leaned forward. "He simply wants an excuse to watch you stretch." Doug bent down excessively to demonstrate. In my peripheral vision, I saw a frown creep onto Beth's face as the boys continued to tease Pierson.

Pierson slapped Doug's neck. "Shut up. That's not true. And how many times do I have to tell you? It's football. Not soccer."

"If you don't recall, you're in America. Which means I'll call it soccer like the rest of the country does," Doug replied.

"And I'll call it what the rest of the world calls it. Football," Pierson said.

They bickered back and forth for the next couple of minutes until Beth cut in and asked, "Is that all you guys have to say? Or is there something else?"

"Oh, yeah," Doug chimed. "I was going to ask you a question, Beth. Are you doing anything after school next Wednesday? They're having soccer tryouts, and I wanted you to be there to see me kick Pierson's butt."

Pierson moved against the lockers and grabbed my hand. "Sylvia, are you doing anything after school next Wednesday? I want you to be there to witness me kick Doug's butt while playing football."

Once again, an upset look flashed onto Beth's face. Each time, the frown wasn't directed toward Pierson, it was toward me. Like I was the one in the wrong here.

We quickly decided we'd meet up to watch. Pierson and Doug invited us to sit with them at lunch, which got Xander's attention. Pierson and Doug were part of the in-crowd. This was one small step for mankind and one giant leap toward popularity for Xander.

Beth grabbed hold of my wrist and slowed her step. The guys went on ahead of us, and we ended up near the back of the group walking to the cafeteria.

"What is it?" I asked.

"Pierson never goes to the cafeteria."

"What are you trying to say? He just invited us to the cafeteria."

"He never goes to the cafeteria. Like never. Why would he offer to go there with us?" she questioned. "He usually goes to the weight room with the other guys to work out, or he heads to the gym to play basketball. Sometimes he goes out onto the field to eat his lunch."

"I have no clue where you're going with this."

"He hates the cafeteria."

I arched an eyebrow. "And you know this for a fact?"

"Uh, he's been my crush since freshman year. It's kind of mandatory to know your crush's routine."

"Sounds more like stalking, but okay," I joked, but she didn't laugh like I'd thought she would. "Look, maybe he wants to hang out with us."

"Or hang out with you." She emphasized the you a little too much.

Her eyes raked me with disdain. I knew exactly what she was thinking: What does he see in her? I could see it all over her face. In Maine, it was a look I'd seen often.

"I thought I told you, Beth. I'm not into him. You don't need to freak out. I bet he feels the same about me. He hardly knows me. We only met a couple days ago."

"I know, I know." She dropped her grip on my wrist. "I guess my emotions got the best of me. I'm sorry."

"It's no big deal." I shrugged. "Believe me when I say this, though: he's not into me."

Soon enough, I would be eating my words.

Chapter Sixteen

My Type

Every day for the following week and a half, I spent my lunchtime at Pierson's table. Letting my eyes wander the space, taking interest in a new group every so often, I began to realize that the twins dated two girls who hated each other. Because of that, whenever Carmen sat with us, Faye and Malik were nowhere in sight. The total opposite happened if we saw Malik first, beating Carmen there for lunch.

For a while, I hadn't seen Dakota in my classes or roaming through the halls. Now, as I sat in the busy cafeteria, he wasn't sitting in his usual seat. He was normally doodling in his sketchbook, never eating or talking to anyone. Where was he today?

"Hey, Beth." I cleared my throat. "Have you seen Dakota? Or has he finally transferred like the rest of the school wants him to?" I threw in the last question so she wouldn't think I was hung up on his whereabouts. It wasn't like I was anyway.

Pierson overheard my question and answered for her. "No, he didn't transfer. He got arrested the other night at the Smell—along with some other kids who weren't fast enough getting out."

I sat back, taking in what he had just told me. "Are you serious? That was a long time ago."

"Think he got out-of-school suspension," another kid added. "At least, that's what I've heard."

"His older brother, Dion, had to drive here from Oakland to get him out," Adam said, folding a French fry into his mouth. "Hope that teaches him a lesson not to side with the Boulder kids again."

"Wait." I shook my head in confusion. "Why couldn't his mom get him out?"

That got everyone's eyes on me. At first, only a few people had joined the conversation, but now the entire table was looking at me like I was some wacko for even mentioning Dakota's parents. This wasn't a rare occurrence. I'd gotten weird looks for talking about them prior. But Xander had stopped Beth from telling me anything worth remembering.

"Sylvia," Pierson said softly. "Let's be logical here. Dakota's mom didn't even go to her own daughter's funeral. Why would she drive to the police station to pick up her son?"

"She hasn't left that house in years," Doug pointed out. "Why would she start doing that now?"

"Dion—the only normal Ridgewood—has been stepping in to help out longer than I can recall," Adam told me. "Ever since their dad got locked up, Dion has been the primary caretaker. At parent-teacher conferences, Dion comes in. Whenever Dakota is in trouble, Dion shows up. He works down in the Bay most of the time."

Blinking, I paused to let everything sink in. I was baffled. How could a mother just abandon her kids like that? I knew my mom wasn't perfect, but at least she'd attempted to throw in some form of parental guidance back when she wasn't so broken.

"Someone needs to talk to her," I announced. "This is unacceptable."

The table erupted. I sank deeper in my seat, letting the laughter wash over my ears. I was unsure what it was they were laughing at. Nothing about what I'd said seemed funny.

"Sylvia, no one has seen his mom in six years," Doug said, wiping the corner of his eye from laughing so hard. "Like, at all."

"Is she dead?" I asked, and the group fell silent.

"She's not dead," Pierson supplied. Pierson was the only one who wasn't laughing, not even a little. And in this moment, he wasn't wearing his familiar warm smile. "No one has seen her for the past six years because she's never left her damn house. She's the town shut-in."

"Nothing will get that woman out of her house. It's like she's trapped in there," Beth explained. "When I was younger, my brother and I would sneak up really close to the house to see if we could get a glimpse of Dona Ridgewood. It kind of became a game with the kids in the neighborhood. Whoever could get a good look at her got a buck."

"I hear she doesn't have a left eye," someone at the table said. "Her husband caused it, apparently."

"No, that's not true. I hear she doesn't have a left leg. That's what John Ridgewood did," another person stated.

Adam shook his head. "I bet neither of you are right. My guess is she gained a crazy amount of weight. That's why she won't leave. She can't get out of her bed. It has nothing to do with Dakota's psycho of a dad."

That reminded me of What's Eating Gilbert Grape or To Kill a Mockingbird. Boo Radley was the character who never set foot out of his house. Kids would race up to the house to see how close they could get. From the sounds of it, Dakota's mom was like Boo. Everyone was fascinated by, but also scared of, this person. At our table, I could see the same fascination and amazement spark in everyone's expressions as they made up theories on why Dona hadn't left her home in all those years.

I was still hung up on what Doug had said about Dakota's dad, John Ridgewood, but the table didn't seem all that comfortable when I tried to ask about him. Swiftly, they went back to creating stories about how Dona got where she was today.

•••

Spanish 3 started with me being relieved since it was my last class. Today was Friday. Each day I'd gone to class this week, I'd sat in a new seat, not really deciding yet where I wanted to stay for the rest of the semester.

Doug was a constant fixture next to Beth, sitting wherever she did. Today, Pierson waved me over to take the seat beside him. Beth was behind him. She was displeased by him moving his backpack from the vacant seat for me.

"I didn't know you were in this class." Pierson flashed a dimple. "Are you stalking me? If so, I highly approve of it. In fact, I'm flattered."

"You're so full of yourself. You know that?" I couldn't suppress my smile. "I got transferred into this class earlier this week. I've been here for days."

"To be fair," he inched closer to whisper, "I ditch my last period sometimes . . . so I see why I didn't notice you sooner." He winked. "More reasons to stop ditching."

On the back of my neck, I could almost feel the air leaving Beth's mouth. She was livid.

"You're not her type," Beth practically yelled. "She's into guys more like Dakota. She was all over him at my party. I think you'll have to get a damaged past before she'll be into you."

I twisted in my seat, peering at Beth. What was up with her? I'd repeated my lack of interest in her silly crush, hoping to calm her jealous tendencies. None of it had worked. If she wanted to play dirty, I'd gladly join in and make her day hell. Throwing around information like that wasn't necessary. Maybe she was used to terrible friends like Xander—but that stuff didn't fly with me.

"Is that true?" Pierson asked. "Do you like Dakota?"

I inched closer to Pierson, winning a dark look from Beth.

Perfect.

"No, not remotely true," I said in a smooth voice. "I like how you are. Wouldn't change a thing."

His hungry gaze darted down to my lips and then back to my eyes. I felt the world melt out of focus as he leaned in a little closer.

Someone in the front of the class cleared their throat loudly. It was the teacher, Ms. Diez. She kindly asked us to not interrupt her class again and told Pierson to read the instructions for our class project.

He grumbled while he opened his textbook and did as he was told.

Inhaling sharply, I tucked my hands under the table, hoping that no one noticed them trembling. My mind was still racing at how close we'd been. The crazy thing was that I wouldn't have objected if he'd erased the space between us.

You're being stupid, my inner voice snapped. You don't want what happened in Maine to happen here. This is only the first month of school, and you've already got enemies. Carmen doesn't like you, and neither does Dakota. Do you want to add a third?

As much as I hated to admit it, my recurring thoughts held some truth. I didn't want to add Beth to the growing list of people who hated my guts.

Chapter Seventeen

Only Happy When It Rains

After class let out, I took it upon myself to find Beth and give her the apology I knew I owed her. Sure, she was wrong for throwing Dakota in the mix. But I should've been the mature one. Flirting with Pierson in front of her was low. Once the apology was over, Beth admitted that she'd crossed the line as well.

I shook my head and put my hand on her shoulder. "No, it's okay."

"No. It's not. I was in the wrong. Sorry about that. I shouldn't have dragged Dakota into it. I knew better. And it's not like you've got a thing for him or anything. You're not into him."

"Yeaaah," I said slowly. "I'm not."

Could anyone blame me if I did find him attractive? I was one of those people who liked playing with fire, knowing it would only burn me if I got too close. I never knew what was good for me. When I was in Maine, I was always attracted to the wrong kinds of guys. It was almost second nature to do the same thing here.

Beth yawned, relaxing back against the pale walls. "Hey, what are you doing a week and a half from now?"

"You mean a week next Tuesday?"

She squinted. "No, wait, I mean a week Thursday."

"I don't know what I'm doing. Probably nothing too serious. What's happening then?"

"Well, soccer tryouts are coming up soon. It's kind of Pierson's thing to throw a celebration for getting on the team. It's at his house."

"He knows he's going to be on the team? That's a little cocky."

"He's the team captain. All he has to do is defend his spot and make sure none of the newcomers are going to take it."

"Is he any good?"

"Is he any good?" She echoed my words with a snicker. "He's the best. He's the reason they've won so many trophies. Coach Walker heard about what he did at his last school when he first moved here, and he saw him practice against members of the team during PE. He literally recruited him without having him try out."

"But isn't that unfair to the guys who tried out and didn't get in?"

We went to the exit, moving along with the throng of students. "Yeah, of course, there were some pissed-off kids and parents. But no one was complaining after he made us state champions."

Beth might have been dazzled by his skills and his looks, but all during Spanish class, I'd seen lots of girls practically drooling at the sight of him. Despite understanding the appeal, I wasn't in the same trance as those girls. In the end, his numerous fans were the reason I could never be with someone like him. I was a jealous person. Pierson looked like the kind of guy who would flirt with anyone who tried, making women believe they had a chance so that it could boost his ego. That didn't vibe well with me.

"What I was trying to say, though," Beth said, "is that there's going to be a party at his place. It's a huge house. I think you should go."

I arched a brow. "You're okay with that? I don't want to be the one who ruins your night."

She snorted. "No, I want you to be there. Besides, I think Pierson will ask you anyway when we get closer to the date. The only reason he invited me was because he and my brother are best friends, and he felt obligated to ask me."

"Hey now, you don't know that." I nudged her. We neared the doors, and I saw my stepmother's car out front. I turned to Beth. "I have to go. Tara's here already."

"Wait." Beth's voice stopped me from walking away. "What about the party?"

"Oh, right. Uh, I'll think about it," I said quickly and dashed down the steps. I didn't want to give her a clear answer yet. I needed to weigh the pros and cons of attending and not attending. As much as I liked Beth, I wasn't keen on the person she became when boys were added to the equation. I wanted to think before I made a choice.

• • •

On Monday, Tara wasn't feeling well. During the drive home on Friday, she'd seemed to be coming down with a cold, and she wasn't any better the following week. Malik and Hanan were already out of the house when she told me to take her car to school.

Rain had started pouring down last night and into the early morning. Tara reminded me to be careful. I waved her words away. I'd lived in New England my entire life. I could take a little rain. I loved the rain and had missed it since I'd moved to this dry town. The rest of the state of California was in hysterics, though.

Kids shrieked, running to the front doors of the school without umbrellas. I'd gone through my suitcase to retrieve my raincoat, rain boots, and umbrella before I'd left the house.

After pulling into a parking space, I yanked out my umbrella but didn't bother to open it. The rain was coming down in soft droplets now. I pulled up the hood of my raincoat and locked the doors. Stomping my boots against the carpet inside the school, I shook the rain off and slipped out of the coat.

"You look like a fisherman." Carmen chuckled. "Have you got any fish, or do you only smell like one?"

"No, no fish, but I got a bird." I flipped her off.

She wasn't done. "Why are you dressed like the kid from IT? There's barely any rain."

"Obviously, it was raining more when I left my house, genius."

She rolled her eyes and walked down the hallway, no longer entertained by picking on me.

"School hasn't even started yet, and you've already got people insulting you," a voice chimed in from behind me. "That's got to be a skill or something."

I twirled halfway, caught off guard. Dakota stood there, soaking wet from the storm. His T-shirt clung to his body, outlining his sculpted chest and abdomen. If I didn't dislike him, I would've instantly turned into one of those puddles around his feet at the sight.

"Oh, I know you can't be the one talking about insults," I said pointedly. "You get insulted like it's a freaking pastime around here."

"And do you think I'm affected by it? Having a brainless jock make fun of me for a few moments in a day isn't going to hurt me. But you? You're getting insulted by a girl who might become your sister-in-law. I get to go home and leave these jerks. You won't."

"You're saying that like you've got something better to go

home to," another person said. Hanan came into view from my left, stepping in front of me. I turned and saw Pierson and Doug next to him. "Tell us, Dakota. What was your mom doing that was so important that she couldn't attend her own daughter's funeral?"

Ugh, did he have to come with a gang of people?

"Stop that, Hanan," I snapped and stepped forward. "You don't need to bring his mom or sister into this."

"Why not? We're not lying. We're telling the truth," Doug said.

"Honestly. Stop it," I ordered.

"No," Dakota barked. "Go on, say whatever the hell you want to say. You want to join in, too, Sandra?"

I closed my eyes. "My name is not Sandra. It's Sylvia." I opened my eyes, inhaling slowly. "I'm not one to throw low blows like that."

"Oh, really? Your brothers seem to do things differently then." Dakota glared at Hanan. "You guys get a real kick out of it, don't you?"

Before any of us could add fuel to the fire, Dakota stormed off. A sickening feeling washed through me like a chill as he walked away and merged into the bustling hallways. I wasn't one to bring up family members as if it were some game. People back in Maine knew about my family situation. They teased me about it. I wouldn't feed into the sick cycle of torment by doing the same thing to someone else.

I started to head toward Dakota, but a hand closed around my arm. "What are you doing?" It was Pierson. "He's not worth your time."

I wiggled away. "You know I didn't ask you guys to step up for me. I was fine all on my own. I don't need you to gang up on him."

"He's bad news, Sylvia," Pierson warned. "What we just did was a favor."

"A favor that wasn't asked for," I seethed.

Sucking up my pride, I followed Dakota. He was at his locker, jamming things inside it and seeing how many he could fit without them falling out. He didn't have to face me to know I was there.

"If you have some more insults to throw at me—"

"I'm not here to insult you." I stepped up. "I think you jumped to the conclusion that I'm like my family."

"Maybe because you are."

"But I'm not," I countered. Why was I trying with this jerk? All he ever did was snap at me and call me the wrong name. "If anything, I strive to not be my father. You don't know the first thing about me. And frankly, I don't know a thing about you."

"You could've learned all you needed to know about me by now."

"I'm not talking about gossip," I said. "Everyone has their own personal demons. That's a given. And I'm the last person to make fun of someone's family."

Slamming his locker shut, he angled his body, studying me up and down with an air of contempt. "What do you know about demons, princess? You're an Ellington. Your daddy's a well-connected lawyer, and you live in one of the nicest houses in town. Your grandparents live in one of the wealthiest neighborhoods in the entire state of California. So don't be shocked that I don't believe you've got any demons. Demons aren't in your vocabulary. Spoiled, on the other hand, certainly is."

My mind was spinning, lost on where to call him out first for his inaccurate depiction of my life. He thought my dad was decent enough to have safeguarded my childhood. Should I laugh? Would that be too much?

"My last name might be Ellington," I started, "but that's the only lasting thing my dad gave me. I lived with my mom in a one-bedroom apartment, living off government checks and sometimes waking up with nothing in the fridge because she spent all the money on—" I cut myself off, holding back the urge to cry. "My dad doesn't even know my birthday. You couldn't pay him to remember. My grandma hasn't bothered to see me in years . . . is that what you'd consider spoiled?"

Why did I say that? Why did I spill all that out?

Stupid. Stupid. Stupid.

Take it back!

I began wishing I could swallow the words I'd let fall. Dakota's hard demeanor faded. His scowl dissolved. In its place, confusion settled in as he watched me closely like he had only recently noticed I was there.

"I didn't know that. I'm s—"

"Save your pity," I snapped and went into the crowd. I bit back the real response I had for him. My trip to his locker had pushed us further into the realm of not tolerating each other. There wasn't any progress.

Getting myself lost in the stream of students, I pushed myself toward first period. Repeatedly, I gave myself a mental kick for giving away personal info to Dakota. I couldn't pinpoint what it was, but something in me was frequently provoked when I was near him. The worst part of me was drawn out. I was never nice. But then again, he never was either.

•••

When PE came around, Coach Walker tried to convince me to join the cross-country team again, but I told him I still needed more time to think about it. I said I'd give him an answer before tryouts.

We were playing basketball in the gym. Rain was still falling, heavier now than when I'd arrived. We couldn't go out into the field. Coach Walker was a bit more laid back this time and let people sit out if they didn't feel like participating.

The whole time, I sensed eyes on me. I went to shoot the ball into the hoop. Someone was watching me. I went to stop and tie my laces. Someone was looking at me from behind. I darted a glance over my shoulder and saw Dakota. He was hesitating beside the bleachers with his arms crossed, acting like he was reading the scoreboard when our eyes met.

In AP US History, Dakota had tried to say a word or two to me, but I'd completely tuned him out. I was embarrassed for telling Dakota about the kind of life I'd lived in Maine. I hadn't even told Beth about what I'd gone through.

Combing a hand through my hair, I exhaled and cleared my thoughts. After playing for more than half an hour, I'd worked up a thirst. I made my way to the water fountains in the hallway connected to the gym. The hall was empty, and the water fountains were down at the end, tucked into a little corner.

I was thirstier than I thought, lapping up the lukewarm water for a minute. When I was done, I rose up to a normal standing position.

"Where are you heading?"

I turned to see who it was who'd spoken to me, but a sharp kick in my shin prohibited me from doing so. Air hitched in my throat as my body jerked down, and I felt a jolt in my lower back this time. Disoriented by the pain spreading across my body, I fell to my knees, hitting the cold tile floors as a third blow was sent to my head.

"Get up. It's no fun if you're on the floor," a familiar voice snickered.

I blinked up at the shadowy figure. "Carmen?"

"Get up," a girl beside her barked. It was one of her friends I'd seen at Beth's party, leaving the car. "Listen to her."

Using the wall to help me, I got to my feet.

My hand shot up, tapping my temple. "What the hell is up with you?"

That was the last thing I said before a kick went into my stomach.

Chapter Eighteen

Carmen

Carmen hovered over me like a menacing vulture. "Since you got here, bad things have been happening to me. Left and right. I keep having the worst luck with you around."

"Yeah! Lots of bad things," her friend chimed. Bit by bit, I began to recognize her from one of my classes. To save my life, I couldn't remember her name.

I cleared the phlegm building up. "I don't know what you're talking about, Carmen. I've done—"

"Silence." She shut me up.

"Yeah, shush," her friend demanded. "Don't talk to her, you peasant."

"Peasant?" I echoed and got back to my feet again. "We're in high school, not Camelot. Please remember that for future reference."

Carmen didn't enjoy that comment. "I said s—"

Her foot went right for me again, but I grabbed it midair, twisting my wrist around. She lost her footing and started to tumble. That was too easy. I dropped her leg and sailed my own swing into her stomach, just like she'd done to me moments ago. I went to kick her once more, but a different voice pulled me out of my blind anger.

"You can't blame her for anything." The door connected to the gym swung closed, showing Dakota at the end of the hall. I wondered how long he'd been standing there, watching us.

What was up with everyone today? The rain made people feel like jumping into my conversations was normal. I liked it better when people didn't try to defend me. I could handle this on my own.

I touched the back of my head where I'd been struck, feeling a bump slowly forming. I couldn't believe she'd resorted to violence. And for what? I knew she was a crazy person, but the other time she'd lunged at me, she'd had reasons. She must have found new reasons now.

Her nameless sidekick darted out the other end of the hallway when she spotted Dakota.

"Rosemary!" Carmen shouted after her, but she was long gone. She grinned up at her ex. "Glad you could join us, Dakota. I'll hold her down, and you can get some punches in."

He held her gaze. "What for? She's done nothing to me."

"Oh, don't start acting like that now," she proclaimed, flailing her arms around. "You've been bad-mouthing her since she got here. I know you have."

A pang of emotion slammed me in my chest, hitting me harder than any kick Carmen had sent my way today.

To my relief, Dakota only rolled his eyes and said, "I'm not like you and your friends. I have a sense of security in my day-to-day life, and my happiness doesn't depend on breaking people down."

That's a lie, I considered saying. This morning, he'd been as mean as Carmen with his little comments.

"What are you lying for?" She took a step toward me, but Dakota was quicker than her, wedging himself between us. "Move. Move before I make you."

"You should get out of here, Carmen," he warned. "You can't get in trouble at school this year. We're seniors. You have too many privileges that you can lose. If you leave, I'll pretend like this didn't happen. Leave before I regret it."

Regardless of how much she was scowling at him, she obeyed and went to class.

Dakota brought a gentle hand up to my face, frowning at my cheek. "I think you banged your face on something."

Why did he care?

I touched my left cheek, feeling moisture on my fingertips. I recalled banging my face on the water fountain when they hit me the first time.

"I have some alcohol wipes and bandages in my locker."

I gave him a strange look.

"Why do you have alcohol wipes and bandages in your locker?"

"I eat them for lunch, of course—why else would I need them?" he said sarcastically. "I have them for times like these. God, you ask some stupid questions."

"Whoa, there's no such thing as a stupid question. No need to be a grumpy cat," I said, trailing after him. "I didn't ask for your help back there. Carmen was on the ground by the time you came along. I would've gotten her friend, too, if you hadn't broken up the fight."

"That wasn't a fight. That was an ambush," he corrected, proving that he had been watching us a lot longer than I'd thought. He probably saw the whole thing. "Also, may I add, Rosemary isn't much of a fighter."

"She's feral. You sure she doesn't fight?"

"Her name is Rosemary. Please don't tell me you're afraid of a girl named after a damn herb. She doesn't do anything. Carmen only ever brings her along to pump up her ego and cheer her on."

I popped up a brow. "She brings a hype man?"

"Basically." He smirked. But it was short-lived. He replaced it with a stoic expression at breakneck speed. Dakota walked ahead of me and led us to the lockers in the main building. "I don't think I've ever seen Rosemary lay a finger on anyone. She's all talk."

I found myself smiling. This was the most we'd talked since the party. "How d—"

"I think that's enough speaking for now," he interrupted me while turning a corner.

My smile fell as quickly as it had formed.

"I was only going to ask a harmless question."

"I think you ask a lot of damn questions, Sandra."

"You say 'I think' a lot," I said, "but you don't hear me complaining about that, Mister Sassy Pants."

"Mister Sassy Pants?" he reiterated, looking at me with wide eyes. "Never call me that again. Matter of fact, don't call anyone that. Forever. Especially a man."

"A man!" I busted out.

"I'm eighteen. I'd consider myself a man."

I hummed, holding back another laugh. We got to his locker, and I stopped next to him, waiting for him to pull out the bandage and alcohol wipes he'd promised. He pulled out a first aid kit. Across the top, it had "Dakota Ridgewood" written in beautiful handwriting.

His penmanship made me truly envious. My handwriting was only slightly better than what I could produce with my left hand. Basically, they were both equally awful. One was just more legible.

Flipping the first aid kit open, he retrieved the things he'd said he'd get for me. I wiped off the blood myself with the wipes, crying out from the stinging pain.

When I was done, he stood there with a scowl painted over his usual bored look. His hands rested on my shoulders as he tried to steady me. "Don't move."

I couldn't move even if I'd wanted to. It was physically impossible.

I was in a trance, following his hands and watching where they landed. I felt my throat tighten and my lungs contract, wishing he would move his hands a little bit lower.

He was a lot taller than me, so he leaned forward, making sure we were at eye level. A sweet bubblegum scent left his mouth as he moved in closer to apply a bandage over my left cheek.

The corner of his mouth twisted upward.

"What's so funny?" I asked.

"Nothing."

Dakota shook his head, smiling harder.

He was irking me again. "What is it?"

"You look like Nelly."

"Nelly Furtado?"

"No." He brought his thumb to the bandage, outlining the edges. A jolting sensation shuddered up my spine from the contact. Unsurprisingly, his fingers were cold, just like the rest of his personality. "I mean Nelly, the rapper."

"Oh," was the singular thing that came out of my lips. I hadn't paid attention to the last thing he'd said. I was paralyzed by the hand on my face as he trailed it down my cheek and brushed his thumb over my jawline. I was hyperaware of the distance between us, praying it would decrease.

A door opening down the hall snapped me back to the real world. He jerked his hand away from my face—as if it burned him—and forced the first aid kit into his locker. He whispered to himself, but it was too low for me to hear a thing. I swore, for a brief millisecond, that he had said, "Beautiful."

That could've been my ears playing a sick trick on me.

"What did you say?"

"Nothing," he hissed, averting his eyes from me as he rearranged the things in his locker. He stopped before slamming it shut and stunned me. "Why do you try so much?"

"I-I don't get what you mean," I stammered. "What am I doing?"

"Trying," he filled in. "You're trying to talk to me, trying to be... I don't know, my friend? I'm not sure why you'd want to. I've made it clear that I don't like you. Why do you keep on trying?"

"You came out here. You intervened in that fight, and you're the one who offered me a bandage," I reminded him. "I'm not the only one who's trying here."

"Never mind. It was useless to ask you in the first place."

The bell couldn't have rung at a more awful time. I might've cried from frustration. What was with him? I was about to ask, but Dakota had other plans. Not looking back, he vanished into the crowd of emerging students. Dakota didn't notice the sketchbook that plonked down on the floor right before he shut the locker.

"Hey," I called out.

He was long gone, hidden in the masses of people.

I crouched, collecting the book from the ground. It opened on its own—honestly. If it hadn't been open and I hadn't see that first drawing, then maybe I wouldn't have felt obligated to look through the rest of the book. What I saw inside was more of a surprise than what Dakota had asked me before running away.

It was me.

In black and white, sketched to a tee. He'd taken the liberty of adding the freckles across my nose and the beauty mark over my eyebrow. One small note I would make, though, was that he drew my hair a little curlier than it was in actuality. I didn't mind it that much.

There I was.

Undoubtedly, he'd drawn me. And more than once.

At the corner of one, closer to the beginning of the sketchbook, "Sylvia" was written in his beautiful handwriting.

"He does know my name." The date written under my name said this drawing had been made before school had started. That meant it was drawn just after Beth's party.

Chapter Nineteen

Crave You

Dakota Ridgewood was the most confusing specimen on the planet. Time and time again, he called me "Sandra" without an ounce of hesitation in his cold-as-ice voice. He made it obvious that he didn't like me because I was the daughter of Elijah Ellington.

I tried to remind myself of that as I flipped through his sketchbook, discovering other sketches of me near the back. Toward the beginning, there were drawings of a girl with bleached-blond hair—he'd colored this one, unlike the sketches he had of me. The word "Diana" was written in the quick, swift strokes of a pen. I was pleasantly amazed to see there weren't any drawings of Carmen or other girls at school.

Other than the sketches of his sister and me, he had pictures of nature and cars. Trees, rivers, and clifftops dotted the pages of his sketchbook. Classic cars, futuristic vehicles without wheels, and cool concepts were scattered throughout.

My favorite drawings of me had a little sentence intertwining with the image.

I find my sin within her existence; I find my destruction within her persistence.

A few poems were written in the front, some on loose-leaf paper taped inside. But there was something intimate about going through his poems. I would've felt wrong reading them. I was invading his privacy enough by looking at these sketches.

After looking at the drawings for a fifth time, I still couldn't grasp why he made it seem like he hated me while behind my back, he drew me in his sketchbook. Why was that? Was this drama between our two families so deeply rooted in him that he couldn't show any form of kindness toward me?

● ● ●

Before the soccer tryouts, I sought out Beth before any of the boys could spot us. Doug, Pierson, Beth, and I had all agreed to meet up at the cafeteria before going out to the field where Coach Walker was holding the tryouts.

Beth and Doug were there earlier than everyone else, meaning I'd missed my shot at asking her alone. Stuffing the sketchbook into my backpack, I went up to them and sat next to Beth. I vaguely told her about the conversation I'd shared with Dakota, asking her about his past. I made sure not to bring up the drawings. Beth tried to ask about my forehead wound, but I just said I'd fallen.

Beth scrunched up her nose. "All I know is that Dakota went to juvie during the summer."

This wasn't news to me. The mystery, though, was what had gotten him in there to begin with.

"What was it for?" I asked.

"Do you always have to ask about that weirdo?" Pierson jumped in, taking the seat directly next to me. A deep frown settled on his face. "I feel like every time I see you, you're bringing him up."

"Are you jealous?" Doug teased. "Because you sound a little jealous."

"I am not jealous of that weasel," Pierson said, scoffing at the thought. "I just don't get why you're so adamant to learn more about him."

I shrugged. "I'm the new kid. I've got some catching up to do. There's a lot that's happened that I don't know about. I want to know the truth; I know it's out there."

"Sorry to break it to you, Agent Scully, but there are some things you shouldn't know about," Pierson joked. "It's best if you don't know."

"What's that supposed to mean?"

"Curiosity killed the cat," Doug mused.

"But satisfaction brought it back," I continued the saying, extending a finger at him. "Don't forget that part."

Pierson brought out a bottle of water and took a swig of it. "Well, since you're so intrigued, you could ask the guy himself and stop asking around like a nosy auntie."

I sank in my seat. He had a point there. "I don't want to ask Dakota."

"Then you should drop it. I swear, if he hadn't walked off so quickly that time in the front hall, I would've gladly kicked his arse for calling you the wrong name. I can't believe you care about getting to know a guy who can't stand you."

"I didn't need you to butt in like that," I stated. "I can handle myself."

"He doesn't know your name!" Doug said. "He kept calling you Sandra. He might as well have called you Petunia."

"I told you; you didn't have to get involved." I exhaled. "I can handle myself."

"I never said you couldn't handle yourself," Pierson replied. "I said I would've gladly kicked his arse. Free of charge. I would be doing a disservice to you and the rest of the community if I didn't. See it as me being a good friend."

"Ooh, right in the friend zone!" Doug shouted. He moved an imaginary microphone in front of my mouth. "How are you recovering from that devastating move, Ellington? What are you going to do next?"

"Nothing. No feelings were hurt in the making of this devastating move. It's mutual," I replied, pushing his hand back.

I couldn't stop thinking about Dakota and how he kept dismissing me but then had drawings of me in his sketchbook.

Pierson's voice yanked me out of my daydream, announcing it was time to get to tryouts. We gathered our things and started to leave the cafeteria. Since it had rained and was still raining, coach had said they'd split the tryouts into two different days. They were working in the gym for today.

A light conversation floated in the air between the four of us, nothing that involved Dakota . . . until Dakota came into view at the end of the hallway.

"I . . . I'll catch up with you guys," I said, drifting away from the others.

"You can't be serious, Sylvia." Beth sighed.

"I have something of his," I divulged. "I'm going to give it back to him."

"I don't see why you bother with him," Pierson groaned.

I ignored him. What was up with him?

Dakota was holding a set of keys, bouncing them from hand to hand. I tried to call out his name. He wouldn't respond to it. I moved a little faster, catching up with him, and tapped his shoulder. Dakota shot me a harsh look, although the pissed-off expression he wore was his default.

He had earphones in.

"What?" he asked while pulling out an earpiece as he went outside. He was making his way to the bike rack.

"You can't seriously be riding your bike in this kind of weather." I stuck my hand out into the rain, catching water droplets on my sleeves. "It's pouring out."

"I rode my bike to school this morning. I don't see why I can't do it again."

"You don't have a ride?"

He drove a Mustang to school. I'd seen him a few times, cruising with his windows down and blasting angry music. Some days, you could faintly hear him shouting along with the lyrics—muddled and mixed between the heavy drums. "What happened to your car?"

"You know why I don't have a car."

"No, I don't, or else I wouldn't be asking about it. Duh."

He leaned down to his bike. "I have to get it fixed because of the masterpiece your brothers did on it."

What did that entail?

I went to ask, but when I saw him finish unlocking his bike, I realized there was no way he could go out into the rain. Water was coming down hard, banging on the pavement and the rooftops of cars.

"You can't. You'll get sick."

He stifled a laugh, starting to roll out his bike.

"I don't need you to tell me what I can and can't do."

"I'll drive you." I brought out Tara's car keys from my pocket. The offer was made before I could stop myself. I stole a look to where my friends had been. Doug, Pierson, and Beth were nowhere in sight.

They would understand, right? Right.

"I can drop you off at your house."

Chapter Twenty

Cheater

Dakota stopped in his tracks. "Why?"

"Why what?" I shuffled in my shoes. "Am I not allowed to drop you off?"

"No, that's not what I said. I want to know why you'd want to. I'm not necessarily the nicest soul in town."

"You certainly aren't." I mustered the most innocent look I could plaster on without coming off as insincere, fluttering my lashes and refraining from rolling my eyes at him. "I'm doing what I would want someone to do for me on a rainy day."

He stepped up, studying me. His inky black hair stuck to his forehead, sleek and dampened from the rain. "Wouldn't your boyfriend be mad if you dropped me off?"

"I don't have a boyfriend."

"Hasn't Pierson claimed you yet?"

"I'm a person. Not a thing to claim. And he's my friend, not a werewolf."

"Pierson Bowen doesn't have girls as friends," he stated. "He simply has potential sexual partners. That's how all those guys work. Your twin brothers included."

"They've got girlfriends," I reminded him. "Faye's with Malik, and Carmen is with Hanan."

Dakota snickered. "Girlfriends have never stopped them in the past. I don't see why it would stop them now."

My teeth clenched. We'd been standing on the student porch for more than four minutes at this point, babbling about nonsense. "Do you want a ride or not, Ridgewood?"

"Ooh, we're calling each other by our last names now." He smirked, rolling his bike forward. "I'll take you up on that offer, Ellington."

Retrieving my small umbrella from my messenger bag, I led the way to Tara's car. I brought down the back seats so he could lift in his bicycle.

A second after I turned the car on, Dakota went for the radio, going straight for the alternative radio station and blaring it louder than ever.

I winced and reached to lower the volume. "Do you want to go deaf?"

"Sor-ry. Didn't know it was that loud, Grandma," he mused, landing his gaze on the glove compartment, popping it open and rummaging through the things inside without a care in the world. The way he searched through the car with such ease made the hair on the back of my neck rise. Driving him home was beginning to look like a bad idea.

"What are you doing now? Close that," I said, swatting at him.

We locked eyes, and he dug his hand in deeper.

"You can't go through people's stuff."

He shut it. "There's nothing interesting in there anyway."

"What were you expecting? Gold?"

He sighed. "Well, I was expecting at least napkins."

"Sorry to disappoint."

I drove the car out of the parking lot. Glancing at the campus,

I began to conjure up a lie. I needed a story to tell Pierson and Beth to explain my temporary disappearance. If I dropped off Dakota quickly, then maybe I'd have enough time to sneak back into school and act like I'd never left.

The only problem with that was I didn't want to rush while driving Dakota. It ached to admit it.

Simply because he's got drawings of you doesn't change the fact that he's a complete and utter jerk, my thoughts reminded me.

My thoughts were right. It didn't change how I felt about how he talked to me. He was out of line and rude. His snarky remarks didn't make me like him any more than I had the day before. Seeing those drawings had changed something in me, though; they'd changed how I saw him.

"Are we going to drive aimlessly, or are you going to tell me where you live?" I asked.

"Keep driving down this road and turn onto Hyde Drive. It's the only house on the street, and it's on a hill. You'll know it when you see it."

I nodded, letting the music in the car fill the space between us. From the corner of my eye, I saw him lift my backpack. My entire body stiffened. If he saw that sketchbook inside . . .

"Drop that or I'm going to have to kill you."

He smiled. "Doll, I'm already dead."

I faked a gagging noise. "Ohmigod, shut up, you overdramatic goth."

"Ouch." He flattened his hand to his chest. "That was rude."

"Yeah, so is everything you've ever said to me," I commented. His hold on my backpack was still firm, and he didn't appear to be letting it go. "Drop it now, Dakota, or I will kick you out of this car right now, right here, and make you walk."

"Okay, doll." He forced a sigh and rested it on the floor.

Smack.

The book was set free from my bag, hitting the floor.

"What the . . ." Dakota trailed off, collecting it off the ground. "This is mine. H-how do you have this?"

I laughed uncomfortably. Was it this warm before? Had the car gotten hotter? My skin certainly thought so. Maybe I had turned on the heater instead of lowering the volume earlier. "It's a funny story."

"Oh, really? Tell me then."

"You dropped it. I swear I didn't steal it," I explained. "Right when the bell rang and you stuffed the first aid kit into your locker, that little black book fell out. Out of the kindness of my heart, I picked it up and decided I'd give it back to you."

He scowled. "Did . . . did you open it?"

"Of course not," I fibbed. "I'm not like you. I don't go through people's stuff without them knowing. If you want to show me what's inside there, though—"

"I don't." His face became unreadable, looking at me closely. "Did you see my drawings?"

"I already told you."

"Tell me again, doll."

"Stop calling me doll," I commanded, despite loving the sound of it. "I don't want you to call me that."

"What do you want me to call you then, Sandra?"

"I'd like for you to call me by my name. Which isn't Sandra."

"I know it's not. It's Sylvia," he admitted. "But I like how you get so upset when I say it. It's cute to see you angry." He caught himself, but it was too late. "I mean, it's funny."

I tried not to grin like an idiot when he said that. I had to keep my composure: cool, calm, and collected. I was freaking Sylvia Ellington, Queen of Nonchalance.

Note to self: come up with a cooler nickname.

I veered away from the conversation about the sketchbook.

"So, I've got some theories about why Carmen attacked me."

"You don't need to think up theories. It's easy," he said. "She's a simple-minded girl. It's not that hard to figure out, Sylvia."

"You know?"

"Yeah, I do." He linked his fingers together on his lap. "I don't like keeping tabs on the gossip at school, but I happened to see her in first period, sobbing about how Hanan had broken up with her. All I was able to gather was that Hanan caught wind of how mean she's been toward you. Like after the Smell; apparently, she tried to fight you."

"And you didn't comfort her when she was crying like that?"

Dakota shrugged in response.

"That's rude. You guys dated."

"Yeah, we did date. We dated for nearly a year. And then she messed around with your stepbrother for an entire two months without breaking up with me first. I had to find out the old-fashioned way. I caught her in the act at a party."

"I didn't know any of those details. That's messed up."

"I have no sympathy for cheaters. It's simple. Don't have more than one girlfriend or boyfriend. If you want to have more than one, then tell them about it. Don't blindside them. People act like it's complex and hard to understand."

I inhaled sharply and nodded. We pulled up in front of a black gate enclosing a large estate atop a hill. Weeds that went up to my chest stretched across the front lawn. There was a backyard that seemed to go on forever.

Vines wrapped around the gate. A thickly wooded area curled around the back of the house about half a mile down, and the hedges desperately needed trimming. Where was Edward Scissorhands when you needed him?

"Is this your house?" I ducked my head down to get a better view. "It looks pretty vacant."

"Wanna come inside?"

I swallowed the bile forming in the back of my throat and stared at him, wide-eyed like a deer caught in the headlights. "Uh . . ."

"I'm kidding." He slapped his knee. It felt out of character. "God, you should've seen your face. It was priceless."

"You're not good at being nice."

He shrugged. "I wasn't manufactured to be nice."

After a brief wave in my direction, Dakota stepped out of the car and walked around to the back to retrieve his bicycle. It wasn't until he had gone through the gate that I noticed his backpack.

"What is with you and leaving crap?"

I got out my umbrella and shuddered at the gust of wind that hit me. After recovering from the blast and taking a second to catch my breath, I looked at the house. Somehow it looked even more intimidating from this angle.

I shut the car door and ran up to the gate Dakota had left ajar. Dakota was already at the front door. As he unlocked it, a dark shadow darted from under his legs and ran right for me.

Before I saw it, I heard the growling growing louder and louder. The weeds swayed as it came closer and closer to me.

It was a Great Dane and my greatest fear.

He bared his teeth at me, barking.

I was stuck in my tracks.

Chapter Twenty-One

Naive

Stumbling over tree roots, I raced back to the gate and ran for my life. Without thinking, I tossed Dakota's backpack to improve my speed. Still, I felt the dog coming for me, snapping at my ankles. Before I could stop myself from falling, my knees slammed against the cold, wet ground.

Tucking myself into a fetal position, I rushed my hands up around myself, blocking my face. If I was going to get attacked for the second time today, I wanted to at least be prepared for the impact.

I braced myself for the bite, but it never came.

There was a moment of strained silence. I relaxed my body out of its protective position and glanced toward the monstrosity of a dog. A few feet away, close to where I'd dropped Dakota's backpack, the dog had his head inside the bag.

Seconds later, he retrieved a sandwich.

Amazing! I wanted to cheer. I'm safe.

In the distance, Dakota was jogging to where the dog and I were.

"Did he bite you?" he asked, taking my hand and helping me to my feet. Once I was standing on my own, he released me.

"No, he didn't bite me."

I wiped my muddy hands on my wet jeans, smearing brown against the pale denim. I was a mess. The cover story I was working on for Beth and Pierson was getting less and less believable.

Dakota cupped my chin, forcing me to look at him. "Are you okay, though? You must be a little shaken up."

A fragment deep inside my heart told me the way he was holding my face meant he was asking me something different. His free hand grabbed mine, intertwining our fingers together. It felt right. I'd never felt this right before about anyone.

"Yes, I'm okay," I replied feebly. "I'll be fine."

Dakota's crystal-blue eyes shifted down to my filthy jeans and wet shirt. The rain that was pouring down now wasn't as hard as it had been earlier, but water was still collecting around my shoulders and in my hair.

"Aren't you cold?"

"Yes, I am."

He quirked his full lips into a smile. "If you want, I can go back inside and get you a towel to dry off."

"No, it's okay. I have to go back to school anyway. There's tryouts today—"

His hand dropped from mine. My heart did exactly what I'd feared it would do. "Soccer tryouts. Yeah, I know." He took an extra step back.

Dakota drifted away. Everything we'd said during the car ride here was thrown out the window. The same armored exterior was warning me to not come any closer.

Dakota began to retreat to the house. "In that case, I'm gonna head back. Thanks again for the ride."

I leaped, grabbing his wrist. "Actually, I'd like to take you up on that offer of a towel."

His exterior was unwavering as he gave me a hard time. "Aren't you worried that you'll be late to your boyfriend's tryouts?"

"Like I said earlier, he's not my boyfriend." I matched his glare. "Tryouts probably started by now."

There was a moment of silence.

"You want him to be your boyfriend," Dakota pressed on. "I know you do."

"Look. I want a lot of things, Dakota. And right now, a relationship is not one of the things on my list."

A playful smirk found its way onto his face. "Does your boyfriend, Pierson, know you feel this way about him? He'd be heartbroken if he knew."

I threw my hands in the air, nearly hitting him. "Can you drop it with that? I drove you to your house, and I nearly got killed by your dog. The least you can do is not annoy me for the next forty-eight hours."

"Forty-eight hours is a lot for me," he said. "But I'll try."

•••

Dakota put his demon dog on a leash and walked him through the house, leaving him in the backyard where they had a fence. My feet didn't go beyond the foyer, and no one could pay me to creep in any further. It was dead silent. Nothing was moving. Every thirty seconds, I swear, a small wheezing noise would shake the house, scaring me every time. It was like the house was breathing.

For the most part, the place was well put together—if you ignored the dust and cobwebs. I was expecting a rundown interior, but it was nothing like that. The couches were covered in plastic like at my grandmother's house, and the drapes were drawn, letting not a single ray of sunlight sneak in.

Dakota disappeared into a room upstairs.

There were a few soft-spoken words. I didn't catch much of it. A moment later, he emerged from upstairs holding a towel and some clothes in his hands.

"Here is the towel you requested." He flung it, and I grabbed the towel with one hand, shoving my hair into the fabric in an instant. He brought forth a faded maroon sweater with a name across the front: JIMI HENDRIX, LIVE AT BERKLEY, MAY 30TH 1970.

He handed me the sweater. I just knew it smelled like him.

He's giving me a sweater. He's giving me his sweater. I must never give it back to him. It is mine. I must claim it as my own. My thoughts were on overdrive, and I was having a little freak-out as I took the sweater from him.

"Your shirt's muddy and soaking wet," he explained, rubbing the back of his neck and not making direct eye contact with me. "Give it back to me whenever you get the chance."

Whenever?

Whenever had never in it.

You're never getting this back.

• • •

Driving back to school wasn't something I particularly wanted to do. But sometimes we must do the things we dislike the most. I'd learned that the hard way. During the drive back, I tried to create a lie to explain why I had Dakota's sweater if they asked.

Thankfully, when I got back to Beth and the guys, they only raised a brow at my outfit and kept their thoughts to themselves.

Beth asked why I had been gone for so long. No one else seemed to wonder.

At home, I found an issue.

Someone had snitched on me.

Tension consumed the room at dinnertime; I could tell by the way Tara was acting. Malik's attention was centered on his food as he chewed like a madman.

My father broke the awkward silence.

He flattened his napkin on the mahogany table, patting at it.

"How was your day, Sylvia?"

I slowed my chewing. "It was boring. I didn't do anything interesting."

"How did you like driving in Tara's car? It's nice driving, isn't it?"

"I guess."

"Let me ask you this one last question." He leaned in, letting out a deep breath. "I want to hear the truth, and I mean the complete truth. Did you let anyone ride in the car with you?"

"No, Dad. I didn't."

Malik's head bobbed up. "Bullsh—"

"Don't use that kind of language," Tara warned. "Especially at the table."

"What? I'm only trying to tell the truth," Malik said through a mouthful of food. He swallowed it all down. I was hoping he'd choke on it and die, but sadly, the world doesn't like me getting what I want, so he lived and went on to speak some more. "A friend of mine said they saw you drive Dakota home."

"I didn't think it was a big deal," I noted. "He was going to ride his bike in the rain if I didn't. I was only doing something I know you'd do, Dad."

"That's understandable, Sylvia, but you and I both know that you should've asked Tara. She doesn't even let the twins drive their friends home from school."

"They're seventeen," I replied. "I'm not. That rule doesn't apply to me."

"That rule applies in this house." Dad shook his finger at me. "Having a driver's license doesn't mean you can drive whoever you want in our cars. You need to let us know."

"Okay, Dad," I ended up saying. "I'm sorry."

"No, she's not," Malik sneered. "She'll do it again if you give her the chance. All she does is talk about him at school."

How would he know that?

He didn't sit next to me during lunch. We didn't have any classes together. I shifted in my seat, thinking of who'd ratted on me and my strange curiosity about the Ridgewood household.

There was only one possible culprit.

"I wasn't doing anything wrong." I stated. "I drove him home, and that was it."

"I heard you came back to school wearing his clothes," Malik disclosed. "I bet they were humping in your car, Mom."

"Hey now!" Tara warned him again. "Why must you be so vulgar?"

"It's true, though, Mom."

"No, it's not," I yelled, hitting the table with my open hand. "It's not true. I didn't do anything like that. It was raining! I was giving him a ride home. Is that illegal or something? I felt bad for him since Malik and his friends are why he doesn't have a car to begin with."

I wasn't a hundred percent sure if Malik was behind it, but Dakota had hinted that it was one of my stepbrothers.

After I said that, the adults' anger was redirected to Malik.

"Why would you do that, Malik?" Dad roared.

Malik waved it off. "She doesn't have proof. I didn't do a damn thing."

"I thought I told you that you can't talk to that boy." Tara sighed. "The last thing he needs is you and your pals tormenting him."

"I don't know what she's going on about. For all I know, whatever happened to him was well deserved. Time after time, he messes with the wrong people," Malik added, and finally he looked at me across the table. "You would be fine with what happened to him, too, if you had half a brain and weren't so obsessed with him."

"Bold coming from you," Hanan chirped, silencing both sides of the table.

Hanan and I exchanged grins, which only infuriated Malik. He flipped his drink while rushing to get out of his seat and at his twin brother. His flying fists were in the air.

My father got between them at breakneck speed, creating a barrier.

"It's time you excused yourself and went to your room," Tara instructed.

Malik left the dining room and went upstairs, no longer putting up a fight.

After dinner, I decided to help Tara wash the dishes. It was usually Hanan who helped, but he was preoccupied with a football game on TV.

My dad didn't bring up Dakota after Malik stormed off, so I assumed that was the end of the discussion. Once the dishes were cleaned, I went to my room and fell backward into the mattress.

Chapter Twenty-Two

Gasoline

Sleep didn't come easy. Restlessly, I tossed and turned.

When morning arrived, I dragged myself out of my bed and into the bathroom. I applied more makeup than I typically did, trying to hide the bags that had recently formed under my eyes. Hoping it would help my groggy appearance, I put on eyeliner.

Tara had taken her car into town earlier that morning. Hanan waited for me. Last night, he'd asked if I wanted to walk to school, and I'd agreed. With just the two of us, it was the perfect opportunity to find out who'd told Malik about me driving Dakota home. The twins hadn't been at school then. Malik's sources were limited to a handful of people whom I suspected could be the snitch.

"Do you think your mom's mad at me for what I did?"

"You mean about dropping off Dakota?" Hanan asked.

"Yeah, I'm curious if this might cause a rift between us. Like she can't trust me."

"That's the last thing that should be on your mind. My mom isn't like that," Hanan said without putting much thought into it. "Honestly, after Malik told your dad and my mom about what happened, they were pretty freaked out that you drove him home, but they were more worried for you. Malik kept spouting his own theory as to why you dropped him off, but your dad wanted to hear the story from you. After you told us why you did it, I didn't understand why Malik was so hell-bent on trying to get you in trouble."

"It's because he hates Dakota," I said. "He has a vendetta against him."

There was a pause before Hanan spoke, hinting at something more, but his face molded into an indecipherable state. "He's being Malik. No one knows what he's thinking," he admitted. "And to clarify, he doesn't hate Dakota. He's mad Dakota isn't his friend."

"You're not really clearing up the confusion here, Hanan."

"Listen to me when I say this: If you keep on trying to hang with Dakota, Malik will transfer the anger he has for Dakota toward you. It'll get worse—trust me."

"Why? What's his deal?"

"You don't want to know."

"No, I do. If I didn't want to know, then I wouldn't ask."

"That's not what I meant. I mean you'll wish you hadn't asked if you knew the reason behind it. It's too complicated."

"Try me," I challenged. "I like messy."

He let out a sigh. "You're not going to drop this, are you?"

"Nope. I'm pretty persistent."

"Fine." He caved. "There are some things I personally can't tell you, but what I can say is that Dakota and Malik's friendship kind of crumbled—or at least started to crumble—last year before second semester. It became a back-and-forth battle between the two of them. And then Diana . . . " Hanan trailed off. He shook his head halfway, recalling something he didn't feel comfortable speaking about.

I grabbed his hand. "You don't have to tell me. It's okay. I'm fine not knowing."

Telling him to stop wasn't necessarily what I wanted to do. I wanted to know badly. But I saw the pain hit his eyes. The last thing I wanted was to get him upset.

Hanan was right about one thing, though.

If I kept digging, I'd only uncover something I'd wish I never knew. I didn't want that kind of burden on my shoulders. For now, my Dakota investigation was going on the back burner.

My senior year was something I should be looking forward to. The most important thing for me, from this point on, was to finish my college applications and get good grades. October wasn't here yet. Students at Crescent were stressing about university and standardized testing. And here I was, trying to be like freaking Nancy Drew or one of the kids in Mystery Inc. No matter how hard I tried, I was no Velma from Scooby-Doo.

I needed to focus on college. That was my next stop after this train wreck. I needed to figure out where I wanted to go.

"Are you sure you don't want to know?" Hanan asked. We were in the school parking lot.

"I'm sure."

"All right."

"I do want to know one thing. Do you know who Malik was talking about at dinner? The supposed 'friend' who told him about where I was?"

Malik had never specified who his source was. I had the gut-wrenching feeling that it was Pierson. The raised brow he'd given me after I came back to the tryouts told me it had to be him.

"I don't know who it was," Hanan said unconvincingly. "You could ask around, but I doubt anyone will admit to it."

●●●

I was praying that someone would stab me in AP English class.

Repeatedly, I tried to understand what I'd been thinking when I'd agreed to take two AP classes. Dad had talked me into them. The counselor had recommended it first, saying it would be a piece of cake for me since I had taken AP classes the last three years.

"You look like you're about to faint," Ronnie said, nudging me. Her real name was Veronica Summers, but she went by Ronnie. After I'd seen her black lipstick and dark eyeshadow, we'd bonded over the type of products we bought. She sat next to me in Ms. Smith's English class. "Breathe, Sylvia. You remember how to breathe, right?"

I tried. "Thanks."

In the silence of my own mind, I thought of how much I wished Ronnie could sit with Xander, Beth, and me at lunch. She wouldn't, though. Ronnie had beef with Xander. One that ran deep. That was why we'd first hit it off so well. I'd sensed it was going to be a great friendship when I found out she didn't like Xander either.

"If you want, I wouldn't mind helping you," she offered. "I've got a good understanding of the material we've gone over."

I reached for her hands. "I would love you forever if you helped me. Are you serious?"

"Yeah, I am. I'm free after school tomorrow if that works for you."

"Yes, it does." I went to embrace her. "I could kiss you, Ronnie. Thank you, thank you, thank you."

"Hate to break it to you, kiddo, but I don't like you like that." She hugged me back and let out a low laugh. Pulling back, she tapped her finger on my nose. "I can see why Pierson can't stop talking about you, though. I'm not blind."

"Wait, what?" I tore away from her. "Pierson's been talking about me?"

This morning, he hadn't seemed any different. When Pierson had invited me to the celebration at his house this week, like Beth had said he would, he didn't seem to be acting nicer to me than he had before. What could he possibly have said about me that he couldn't say to my face?

Ronnie stared at me a little longer, piecing together her observations. "Why aren't you blushing like crazy? Had any of the girls in this class found out that Pierson Bowen was talking about them, they'd all be blushing and giggling. What gives? You don't want an Irish lover?"

"I don't want a lover. Period."

"I hear he's great in bed." She gave me a foxy grin. "And that he's got a really, really big—"

"I don't want to get involved with any guy this year. Pierson or anyone else."

Ronnie arched a knowing brow. "Now, that's not true. If I told you that Dakota wanted to do the frickle-frackle with you, you'd be jumping up the walls like Tigger on Ecstasy."

I squeezed my eyes shut. "Let's not talk about that person."

"Last week, you wouldn't stop asking me questions about him. What's changed?"

"What's changed is that I've realized high school doesn't continue after this year. This is it. I need to figure out my plans and basically beg a school to adopt me for the fall semester." I rested into my open hand and snuck a peek at her. "I want to focus on school and not boys."

She snorted. "Let's see how long that lasts, kiddo."

•••

The next day, when I entered Mr. Huang's class with a splitting headache, I had hopes of a freak accident causing every homeroom class to be cancelled today. I was greeted with disappointment. Our teacher was seated in his wooden chair, reading something on his dinosaur of a laptop, when I shuffled in.

A light whisper floated in the air as I went up the aisle, making my way to the back of the room. I looked around, wondering what the fuss was about. At last, my eyes hit the back of the classroom, and I noticed that Dakota was in Faye's seat, drawing in his sketchbook.

Refraining from grinning, I took my seat and pulled out a book to read.

"You look different," he pointed out, not looking up from his sketchbook.

I sat upright.

Was that a good different? I couldn't tell by his emotionless voice.

"Different how?"

"I don't know . . ." He inhaled deeply. "I'm not sure what it is. But something's different."

"Well." I swayed in my seat. "I'm wearing makeup."

Dakota lifted his captivating eyes off his sketchbook and fluttered them up to me, narrowing at the space below my own hazel eyes. Reaching out a hand, he brought his thumb to my cheek and then over the freckles on my nose, which were now covered in foundation and hidden from sight. He'd noticed, even though no one else had.

He dropped his hand, shaking his head. "You covered your beauty mark."

"I put on a bit of makeup."

"You look nice." He paused. "You looked good before too."

I faked a gasp. "Is that a compliment? Wow, I never knew this day would come. I'm going to have to mark it down. Make it a national holiday. I'll even tell my grandkids about this historic moment."

"See, this is why people aren't nice to you. No wonder Carmen fought you."

"And he's back to his rude ways," I mused, easing my back into the seat. "You should be nice more often."

"Nah, it's bad for my reputation."

"Why are you being nice now then?"

"I promised forty-eight hours of niceness—and that's all I'll do." He used his thumb to smudge the image. Dakota doodled a stream with a willow tree in the foreground. His talent astounded me. I couldn't draw anything other than stick figures, M-shaped birds, and suns with cool black sunglasses.

"So, tell me," I said.

"What?"

"Tell me how you're going to be nice to me today. Are you buying me lunch?"

"You forgot I only have a bike today, huh? There's no way I can get food and make it back in time for lunch. Let's be realistic."

"You should surprise me with a drawing."

"How would that be a surprise if you're asking for it?"

"Well, not insulting me isn't a form of being nice. You're just holding back what you want to say. That's hardly difficult."

"With someone like you, it's a real challenge."

"You're acting like you're not a pain in the ass."

"I'm not. I think I'm lovely."

"Prove it," I demanded. "I need evidence."

Looking to the left, Dakota checked the clock on the wall. "What are you doing after school today?"

I moved closer to him, resting my elbow on my desk. "I'm completely free."

"Not anymore," he said with a confident smile.

Chapter Twenty-Three

Snap Out of It

Dakota had a bike that made it possible to stand on the back while riding. I hadn't gotten on someone's bicycle like that since grade school, and I felt a familiar sense of excitement zip through me when I hopped on the pegs and placed my hands on his shoulders. For some reason, one I couldn't home in on, I was transported to summers back in Maine before the affair and my parents' divorce, long before I stopped thinking of them as superheroes.

I was going against Beth's instructions, Hanan's warning, and Xander's consistent nagging that Dakota was no good for me. Regardless of all of that, I didn't let any of it faze me as I held on to him for dear life.

"You have a good grip, right?" Dakota asked before pedaling. "I'm not picking you up off the ground if you happen to fall."

"Wow, such a gentleman." I flicked his ear.

"Ouch." He kicked off the curb. "I was totally kidding."

"You better be."

I shielded my nervousness with fake confidence, sounding braver than I was. Dakota wasn't talkative when it came to describing where we were going. He avoided every question I asked him with another question directed at me.

"Throw me a bone, a hint, anything," I pleaded.

"Why did you agree to come if you weren't ready to be surprised?"

"So, there's a need for me to be shocked? Is it a gift?"

He laughed. "Don't think so highly of me. I'm not that thoughtful."

"Aw, but I thought we were starting to get along."

"Why did that sound like a statement? It should be a question."

"It's more like a fact now." I touched his earlobe again, softly this time. He flinched all the same. "You gotta admit it, you're warming up to me like a stick of butter on a sunny day."

"Ew, no one has ever said that." He cringed. "Did you come up with that?"

"Yes."

"Of course, you did."

"I've been told that I have a wonderfully active imagination."

"Did anyone ever tell you to not speak unless spoken to?"

"No—that's rude as hell."

I tried flicking him again, but he must've seen me in his peripheral vision. Before I made contact, his hand wrapped around mine.

"Refrain from hitting my ear again," he said, "or else I'm going to make you walk the rest of the way alongside me. Understood?"

"I mean, I'm not opposed to that idea if you're going to hold my hand like this the whole way." He instantly dropped my fingers as if they were diseased.

"You're unbearable."

I laughed. "You say that like you're a joy to be around."

It was the same conversation we'd had in homeroom, but light this time. I could see Dakota smiling, laughing with me, too, as we continued to talk.

"What's that supposed to mean? I'm a dream."

"I think nightmare is the word you're looking for."

"Nightmare? Are you confusing me with your friend Pierson?"

"You've gotta be kidding."

"Actually, on second thought, I'm almost positive you were referring to your stepbrothers, Hanan and Malik."

No part of me could continue. It was like my body had a mind of its own, shifting the weight of the bike and making us come to a stop. We couldn't have been more than three minutes away from the school grounds. Behind us, I saw the outlines of the fence around the gymnasium peeking out in the distance and yellow school buses starting to file in.

"I'm not interested in seeing whatever it was you were planning on showing me," I said upfront, crossing my arms. "I'm going to head back."

Leaving with Dakota, wherever it was he had meant for us to go, had turned into something undesirable. My curiosity had gotten the best of me before, but not now. Standing on that hot asphalt, with one hand shielding my eyes from the sun, I began to realize that I didn't have the same impulse as I had this morning. No longer was there a drive to uncover the many layers that resided inside Dakota Ridgewood.

"What for?" he inquired. I could almost pinpoint the moment the look in his eyes altered. He was trying to piece together what had pushed me off his bike, working out the details.

"You can't insult my family like that and expect me not to react. I'm not going to mosey next to you like that's no big deal."

"I don't expect anything from you," he said, taking a step back and lowering his bike to the ground. "I do, however, expect you to use a word less embarrassing than mosey if you want me to take you seriously."

A smile was making its way onto his face, and I fought the urge to mirror it with my own, proving once more that I couldn't shake him off.

For a second, I'd been so certain that I'd washed my hands of anything related to him. But after one silent glance, one unrestrained smile, or the faint sound of his laughter, I fell back into the habit of wanting to see more of him.

It was a vicious cycle.

"I can understand why you have an issue with Malik. He got you stuck in juvie. But with Hanan, I can't sit here and listen to that. Honestly, I get that what Hanan did was wrong—"

"Wrong?" he cut in. "To simply write off what either of them did as wrong would be the biggest understatement of the century."

"I-I sympathize with you on the cheating thing—"

Once more, Dakota didn't let me finish. "It's more than that."

Lifting both my hands in the air, I said, "Well, how am I supposed to know that? I barely got here and somehow everyone expects me to know every family tree and timeline that ever existed in Harper Falls."

"If you need one that bad, I could map you out a few timelines so you're not lost at family dinners."

"That wasn't my point."

"Sorry." He chuckled, and part of me loosened up at the sound. We weren't walking on eggshells anymore, but with Dakota, you never knew when you were truly in the clear. He was as unpredictable as the weather on the East Coast.

"But on a serious note," Dakota said, "I don't think there's a way for me to see Pierson, Hanan, or Malik in any other way ever since . . . ever since my sister died."

"You don't think there's a chance for you to mend what's been broken?"

"Not everything that's been broken is meant to be fixed, Sylvia. I've learned to accept that the older I've gotten. It would be impossible to try."

"That doesn't mean you should give up on something because you see it as impossible." Out of nowhere, a thought came to me. "You know what would be a good way to start? Having someone in the middle. I can be like your liaison."

"This isn't a business venture, Sylvia. I hate those guys."

"You won't hate them after you hang out with them in a non-school setting," I offered. "What are you doing this Thursday?"

"I already know what you're going to say. I'm offended that you even want to ask me," Dakota grumbled, pushing his hair out of his face.

"You don't kn—"

"Oh, I know." Clearing his throat, he said, "To answer your question, I'll be nowhere near Pierson's house for his barbaric soccer extravaganza. I will most likely be doing something productive with my time and not getting drunk with those Neanderthals."

"You're so extra," I joked. "A simple no would've sufficed."

"I'd prefer to be extra than what you are. Which is insane. It's insane to want to hang out with that crowd of people."

"C'mon, they aren't that bad."

"Yeah, they are. If not worse."

"You're making it sound like I'm asking you to donate your liver."

"I'd happily volunteer to do that rather than be anywhere near them."

"Seriously?"

"Look, Sylvia. I'm the last person Pierson wants you taking to his house. Even if—by some strange twist of fate—I did agree to go to his stupid, idiotic party, there's no way he'd let me past the front door."

"Wanna bet that I can get you in?" I challenged.

"There's no way he would agree. He'll laugh in your face before saying okay to me coming with you."

"Then you shouldn't mind placing a bet on my ability to get you in."

He crept away from me. "You don't mean—"

"Just say yes already!" I yelled. "If you're so sure he'll say no, then why don't you put that theory to the test? If he says yes, you're going to that party, but if he says no, then I'll do your next set of notes. We're in the same AP History class."

He let out a loud, clear laugh. When he saw I wasn't laughing along, he stopped himself, catching his breath. "Wait. You're not kidding? Sylvia, you don't take proper notes, let alone finish a packet assignment without sneaking a glance at someone else's desk."

"That's not true. I take decent notes," I defended myself. "How would you know? We don't sit together."

"I have eyes. I can see you cheat," he confessed. "Compared to my notes, yours are below average."

"You're doing a great job at being nice. I thought you were meant to be nice for another day. What happened? All the niceness was used up, huh?"

"By being honest, I am being nice." He shrugged. "It's only the truth. If I must be one hundred percent honest, you do the bare minimum. On a good day."

"Oh, really? Well, if your notes are so perfect, then let me see them."

He whipped around his backpack so it was facing us. Snatching up his notebook before he objected, I studied the exquisite handwriting and lines of Roman numerals showing where he'd brought in a new topic. Each class had Cornell notes, divided by subject with colorful tabs.

He was right. His notes were better than mine. None of my notebooks were organized like that.

Silently passing Dakota back his notebook in defeat, I let his schedule slip out and onto to the dirt. He didn't stop me when I unfolded it.

"You have all AP classes for your academic classes." I darted a look up at him. "Are you deranged, or do you like being tortured?"

He smirked. "Is that a trick question? I thought it was clear. I'm very much deranged."

"No, seriously, though. How do you manage? I freak out from the workload I'm stuck with on any given day—you have it hard every day. And what's this?" I pointed down to his seventh and eighth periods. They had initials I'd never seen on a transcript.

"Oh, that? That basically says I go off campus."

"For two whole periods?"

"Well. Yeah." He stroked the top of his head, grinning. "Three times a week, I go over to the local community college and take some classes."

"Why?"

"You know how our birthday is in the summer," he said, and I nodded. "My mom enrolled me in school a year later than the kids I grew up with because I didn't meet the cut-off for preschool. The second I could, I started taking extra classes. That way, after I get my high school diploma, I'll get an associate degree at the same time."

"Why are you in school?" I asked, baffled. "You could've left."

"I'm obviously staying around 'cause the students are so nice to me."

"Of course." I played along. I didn't ask him why he'd been on campus yesterday after school, though. It was probably because of the rain stopping him from leaving. If I were him, I'd have waited for the rain to slow down or stop entirely.

"My brother, who was my full-time guardian, doesn't want me to miss out on the experience of going to high school. I would've left to take the GED exam a long time ago if it were up to me."

I squinted, thinking of a way that I could convince him other than doing his notes. That was a lost cause. "I'll wash your car."

"I don't need hired help." He motioned to his bike. "And as you can see, I'm without a car because of Malik."

There it was.

He'd admitted the one who'd damaged his shiny black Mustang. The mystery was solved.

"About this party thing, though . . ." I started.

"There's no way it'll work. As much as you want to try." He pressed on. "I know you'd like to think highly of these people. They aren't great to be around. You don't know them. You just met them."

"Oh, so you're afraid of them. I get it now."

He hissed, "I'm not scared of anyone."

"All right, then prove it."

"I—" He stopped, picking up his bike from the ground and hopping onto it. "I'm not invited to this party. I can't prove to you that I'm not afraid."

"I'll work on convincing Pierson. As long as you try to make it there."

That smile from earlier returned, subtle and small this time, but powerful enough to rumble a swarm of butterflies within me. "How about this? If for some unknown reason he's okay with me going, I'll . . . " He gulped. "I'll consider going. But since that's unlikely—"

I didn't let him finish his sentence. "Oh, trust me, I'll make it happen."

He rolled away from me. "I think you're a little too confident. You're scaring me."

I looked at the school behind us. "I'm going to go."

When I turned back around to Dakota, he was already pedaling down the road in the opposite direction, heading further away from school grounds.

Wherever he was going, he was pedaling fast and hard, making me wonder if he ran from his problems just as much as I did.

•••

A mission was brewing. I woke up motivated. Spanish class was the only class I shared with Pierson, but it was hardly the ideal place to drop a big question on him. For starters, Doug and Beth were there. They'd only influence his answer. After school, despite sounding more appealing, was off the table as well because that was when the second half of the soccer tryouts were being held. Pierson was helping the coach.

From what I'd seen the other day, his position as captain wasn't going to be taken from him. Beth had been right when she'd said he was the best. He left his opponents in the dust. Pierson was faster than any of them, making swift moves toward the goal. It was like watching him fight at the Smell all over again.

Thursday at lunch, I finally got up the courage to ask to speak to him alone. When I said, "I want to talk to you privately," nearly half the table made noises like middle schoolers, snickering and giggling at us. Beth frowned at me. I intentionally ignored it.

Pierson tried to hide his growing smile. We stood next to the soda machine, only two tables away from our usual spot in the cafeteria.

"What is it you want to talk about me?"

"I wanted to talk about that party you've got going on next week." Sucking in a dry breath, I balled my hands into fists. "Is it okay if I bring a plus-one?"

"Beth's invited."

"I mean someone else."

"You want to invite Alex? Sure, that's fine by me."

"No. I mean someone else." I emphasized my words more, hoping he'd catch on.

"Well, I don't know who else it could be. It's not like you'd bring Dakota with you."

He was laughing up a storm.

"Actually, I was hoping to."

"What?" he boomed. "I was joking, Sylvia. Have you lost your mind? You've gotta be joking."

"Well, I'm not joking."

"No. You must be."

"I'm not. I told him I'd ask if it was okay."

All evidence of that wonderful smile of Pierson's was gone. "You're wasting your breath. You should know the answer to that question. It doesn't need to be asked. There are people, not just one or two people but countless, who want to beat the living shit out of him. And all of them are going to be at that party. Ridgewood knows better than to think he can walk into my house and leave in one piece."

"Can't you keep your minions on a leash?" I mirrored his defensive stance and crossed my arms, standing my ground. "You can make them refrain from beating someone up for a few hours."

Pierson weighed his options.

"Maybe I don't want to stop them."

"Are you serious?" I scowled. "Then maybe I don't want to go."

Chapter Twenty-Four
Electric Love

Those words made Pierson backpedal, rethinking what he'd said.

"You don't need to start holding threats like that over my head."

"It's not a threat," I said, unfolding my crossed arms. "It's the truth. If you honestly don't want to stop your friends from beating someone to a pulp, then I don't want to be around those people. I've seen enough violence in the past few days. I don't need any more drama."

"What do you mean you've seen enough violence?" His concern shifted. "What happened?"

"It doesn't matter."

Pierson scanned my face in search of something to tell him what I was trying to hide. The damage Carmen had caused wasn't visible anymore with the amount of makeup I'd caked on. The only thing I had left from her ambush was a bump on the back of my head.

"I'll find out one way or another, Sylvia."

"No, you don't need to do that. There's no reason to run an investigation."

His answer surprised me. "I don't need to investigate. Carmen tried to fight you again."

"How did you know that?"

"She's the only one who's delusional enough to do it . . . And I caught wind of it before tryouts." He relaxed, easing against the side of the soda machine, skimming his eyes over me. I knew what he was doing. He was trying to read me. "I don't see why you'd want to defend her."

"I'm not defending her," I stated. "I know what you're trying to do. You're trying to divert the topic away from Dakota and the party. Nice try, but I haven't forgotten."

"Fair play; you've figured me out." He sported that loveable smile. "I'm not willing to let him go to the party unless I get something in return."

"I hope you're not asking for what I think you are," I fumed. "Because if you are—"

"Sylvia, I'm not enough of a dickhead to ask for a sexual favor from you. That's what you should expect from Franklin or one of his friends, those gobshites. But not from me," he snapped, clearly ticked off at what I'd insinuated. "I meant more in the line of helping me clean up the day after the party. It's usually a huge mess, and I hate doing it on my own."

"Oh, good. Because I would've slapped you if you'd meant something else." I felt like an idiot for thinking that was what he wanted from me. It was almost a habit of mine to think the worst of the straight male population.

"C'mon, I'm not that awful."

I pointed my finger at him. "No, you aren't. But you were awful enough to snitch about me to my stepbrother. You told Malik I drove Dakota home."

"What are you talking about? I didn't know you drove him home."

I almost fell. I braced myself against the wall.

"Well, someone told Malik that I drove Dakota home and that I came back to the tryouts wearing his sweater. I thought it was you."

"You assumed wrong, Sylvia," he said. "If there's anyone who would've told him, it would be Beth."

I stared at him before speaking. "Why would you say that?"

"You know how I drove her and Doug home after the tryouts?" I nodded. "On the way back, I heard her on the phone with Malik. I wasn't paying attention to the call. I heard her say his name, though. They kept talking even after she left my car."

"She isn't friends with Malik."

Or was she friends with him? I didn't know all her connections at school. If she was friends with him, it would make sense because her brother, Adam, was best pals with the twins and Pierson. They were always together. The main reason she couldn't imagine Pierson returning her love for him was because of Adam and Pierson's tight friendship. They were the closest out of the group. He didn't seem like the kind of friend who would go behind his best friend's back to be with Beth.

● ● ●

A problem I faced as a kid, and one I saw other kids struggle with, was asking for help. There was a short period of my life in Maine when I was a babysitter. While caring for youngsters when I was still very much a minor myself, I was reminded of the stubborn nature of children.

If we were making cookies together from scratch, the kid wouldn't admit when things were getting too difficult to mix with a whisk. When we read a book together, they'd refuse to accept help sounding out the word. Some kids were better at allowing assistance than others, but a lot dealt with a sense of pride.

Thankfully, I grew out of that as a kid—and I hoped many of the kids I'd taken care of had too. I wasn't afraid to ask when I needed assistance.

There was a thought brewing in my mind.

Pierson had planted a seed in me last week when he'd revealed that Beth was likely the snitch, and it had been growing over the past few days.

I deserved better friends.

In English, Ronnie told me she was invited to Pierson's soccer extravaganza because she was dating one of the players on the team. She wasn't too happy to hear what I had learned about Beth's disloyalty now that I was finally comfortable talking about it.

"Keep your friends close and your enemies closer," Ronnie offered. "When the time comes, use that knowledge against her. I'd say collect as much info as you can from her and dump it right over her head. For all she knows, you guys are friends still."

"I've been eating my lunch somewhere else for the last few days. She'll know something is up between us."

"Not if you lie and say you've been busy studying in a teacher's classroom during lunch."

"You're evil." I laughed. "I like that."

"Hey, I'm thinking ahead. I don't like Beth, to be honest, but I didn't want to say it out loud because you hung out with her. Anyone who associates with Xander is prone to be mean too."

"I thought we were close enough that she wouldn't go behind my back like that. I mean, what does she get out of telling Malik anything?" I asked, letting out a long breath. "She doesn't like Xander sometimes either. He constantly tries to tell her what to wear, say, and do in the hopes that it will make them popular."

She covered her mouth but then let her hand drop. "He's been like that for as long as I've known him. I'm not surprised that he's stuck on that. Same goes for Beth and her obsession with Pierson. You should've seen how she was as a sophomore. Someone apparently broke into his house and stole some of his cologne, his soccer jersey, and his boxers. Weirdest thing ever, but I think it was her."

"That's hilarious. Man, why couldn't I have been enrolled here when that happened?" I shook my fists in the air. "I think what's more hilarious is how he hasn't noticed her crush on him."

"I wish he'd wake up and smell the chloroform. He's got a stalker."

I laughed at her joke. But it didn't last very long. For a week now, since I'd found out about Beth, I'd eaten my packed meals in the library. "Is it okay if I eat with you and your friends tomorrow?"

Ronnie didn't think twice about it. "Yeah, of course. We eat in the drama teacher's classroom. Mrs. Duncan is the best." Collecting her things off the table, she went on to talk about what our plans would be after Pierson's party.

"Wanna go to an overlook after if it gets boring? There's a nice place I know near Pierson's house that gives you a perfect view of the valley. Super beautiful at night."

I smiled, nudging her with my shoulder. "Sure. I'd like that."

Doubt riddled my mind whenever I had a hard time adapting to the people around me here and trying to make sense of it all. Not an ounce of doubt, though, lingered in any corner of my heart when it came to Ronnie.

She was a true friend, breathing good intentions in each of her actions, living life in a way that for others would come off as an act.

•••

I left my AP History class annoyed with Dakota. For most of the week, I'd tried convincing Dakota to attend the party.

"Pierson may say he won't do anything. That's a lie," Dakota said. "The moment I walk in there, he'll find a way to piss me off and get me out of his house. I'm not going."

He was a lost cause by the time the bell rang. It didn't matter what I said, he just wouldn't budge. I had gotten him invited. That didn't mean he had to go. He'd only said he would "consider" it. That didn't mean he would follow through.

When the Thursday night of the party arrived, I spent too much time standing in front of my closet, thinking about what I should wear. There was a reliable outfit that I turned to whenever I didn't have anything better, but I didn't want to wear it tonight. Almost at random, I picked my cropped gray sweater and a black skirt. It was simple yet cute enough for the party.

Silently, I began tying the laces of my red boots. I stood up straight and flattened my palms against the fine material. My head whirled when I heard a honking noise outside my window. I raced to look and nearly had to pinch myself at what I saw.

Dakota's black Mustang was parked in the driveway. In my driveway.

Dakota exited his car and leaned against the hood, crossing his ankles and staring up at my window.

He was dressed in all black. Black fitted jeans, black T-shirt, and, to finish it off, a long, worn-out black jacket. I knew he had gotten his car fixed, but I hadn't expected him to show up.

I'd planned to drive to the party with Hanan, but that was forgotten when I saw Dakota. In a hurry, I grabbed my coat. I slipped my arms into the sleeves as I rushed down the stairs and to the front door.

Dad and Tara were pointing out the large window in the living room, gaping. I'd just opened the door when I heard my father's voice.

"You are not getting into that car, young lady." His voice was stern. "I don't want you going with him."

Tara gawked at my outfit. "Go back up and change. Do you see what she's wearing, Eli?"

"I'm wearing what you bought me." I shot them a glance over my shoulder. "I'll be back before midnight—maybe." Slamming the door shut, I ran to the passenger side and threw myself in. "Get in and drive."

"Well, hello to you, too," he said, leaping up from his car. The car was already on. I locked the doors once we were both inside. Dakota pulled out of the driveway as Tara and my dad bolted out the door.

"Oh, hi there, Mr. and Mrs. Ellington. Lovely weather we're having, huh?" he yelled out his window, giving a little salute as he sped off.

"Shut up." I suppressed a laugh. "What are you doing here? I thought you didn't want to go to the party."

"You ask that after you get into my car? This is the kind of conversation we have outside the car, not while we're already inside, driving away from your pissed-off dad and stepmom."

"My mind works in mysterious ways."

"I can see that."

"Why are you here, though?"

"I decided it wouldn't be so bad to get my head caved in by some jocks."

"Seriously, Kota."

"Whoa there, since when do you call me Kota? I'm not okay with this sudden desire to call me half of my name."

"It's actually three-fifths of your name."

He playfully prodded me with his finger. "Same thing."

"You don't like Kota?"

"I don't think anyone with any brains would like the nickname Kota."

"Kota has a nice ring to it," I said. "You're not supposed to like nicknames."

He waited a moment. "Are you trying to normalize bullying and name-calling?"

"No!"

"Sure, you're not, Livia."

"Ew, stop that. Stop that right now. This instant. Livia sounds like a type of medicine for stomach problems. I can see the commercials now, saying, 'Try Livia twice a day to improve your digestive tract.'"

I was waiting for the wonderful sound of his laughter, but it didn't come. "Most terms in the medical world are based off Latin words. That joke doesn't make sense."

"You're a real buzzkill."

"Or I'm not the kind of person who laughs at stupid jokes." He hit the brakes as we reached a stop sign. "I have a feeling you're one of those people who watch cartoons like South Park and Family Guy."

"Family Guy isn't the same as your typical Saturday morning cartoons. I'm not a kid. Adult animation is the correct word—smartass."

"Oh, aren't you mature?" he teased. "Do you drink coffee like the other grownups too?"

I exhaled. "Can we go one day without you being annoying?

Even when you did that forty-eight hours thing, you were still getting on my nerves."

"If you didn't annoy me first, then maybe we wouldn't have this issue," he replied. "Also, if I were nice to you, you'd treat me like Pierson."

"What's that supposed to mean?"

"You get whatever you want out of him and ignore the fact that he likes you. You're worse than him when it comes to that Beth girl."

"No, I don't." I sat up. "Wait, you know Beth likes him?"

"The whole freaking town knows she likes him," he said, turning onto a different street. "And yes, you do. You have him wrapped around your little finger. Him letting me go to this party makes it more obvious than ever."

Our conversation died down when his car cruised into a quiet neighborhood close to mine. We came to a stop before a large estate. Every single one of its lights was on, and loud music spilled outside. I could see Doug at the front of the house. His ginger hair was like a flame in the night, flickering with the wind. Malik was at his side.

The way everyone watched us as we got out of the car was like something out of a movie. Their attentive gazes moved with each step we took. I was almost afraid to get any closer to them, but a gentle hand at the small of my back ushered me forward.

"They're looking at us," I noted.

His hand snaked from my back to my hip, drawing me in. Electricity shot through me as his warm hand sent raging tidal waves through me, awakening my senses. "No, they're looking at you. I would be too if I were them."

Why did he have to say stuff like that? I didn't know how to respond. I would've stumbled with my next response had I parted my lips to speak. I was tongue-tied with the way his body felt so perfect alongside mine.

Dakota was so confusing. I could say that a million times, but the reality of it never seemed to click. One second, I thought he couldn't stand me, and then the next he'd do a one-eighty on me and show a different side that I wasn't aware existed. I decided I didn't mind being confused by him if it meant he would press me into his side as if the world wasn't watching, waiting for us to fall.

Chapter Twenty-Five
Drunk in Love

I'd lost Dakota.

The last time I'd seen him at the party was an hour ago. Soon after we'd walked in, he'd offered to get me a drink. He hadn't returned yet.

My nails and hair didn't see any rest during my nervous frenzy, as I stood biting my nails and running my fingers through my dark locks. Pierson had said there were people who would try to give Dakota trouble. I was hoping he at least had something to protect himself with if he got cornered.

"Don't freak out," Ronnie said smoothly, placing her hand on mine. "I'll drive you home if he doesn't show up."

"I don't care about getting a ride from him. Having someone drive me home is the least of my worries right now."

"If he doesn't show up in another thirty minutes, I'll look for him with you," she suggested. She nudged Finn, her boyfriend. "You'll help too. Right?"

"Oh, uh. Yeah, sure." He nodded, taking a sip of his drink. "I don't mind."

A thank you was on the tip of my tongue when I heard my name being called from behind me. I spun and saw Pierson approaching us with Doug and Adam.

"How are you enjoying the party?" Pierson asked after hugging me.

"I'm loving the music." I moved along to the beat of the song, "And I appreciate you being cool with me having a plus-one."

He waved it off as though we hadn't had a full-blown argument about it, curling his arm around my shoulder to bring me into another embrace. "If you're free later, come find me. I want to talk to you. I have to go to the store right now."

"What for?" I asked, but he must not have heard me because the question remained unanswered as he and his friends made their way around the room greeting his guests.

In the blink of an eye, new people were streaming into the room. Beth and Xander walked right up to us, pointing at me. I waved reluctantly.

Ronnie rolled her eyes and chugged down the rest of her drink. "I'm not drunk enough to interact with the Xan Man."

Finn grabbed her hip and held her close. "He's not stupid enough to say anything to you while I'm here."

Beth looked unrecognizable. Her trademark stick-straight hair had been curled into a frizzy mane, and she wore dark eye makeup just like me. Her skirt was practically identical to the one I'd worn yesterday, but I wouldn't mention that. When they came within arm's reach, Beth came for me and enveloped me in a tight hug. My arms were pinned to my sides as I endured it.

"It's like I haven't seen you in forever!" she gasped, pulling away from the hug but still holding my shoulders. I wished she'd stop trying. "Where do you go during lunch? You're never at our table anymore."

"Ronnie's been helping me with English. I've been busy with that for the most part."

"Is that what you're going by now, Veronica?" Xander asked with a scrunched-up nose. "I guess it fits the masculine attire you wear. By the way, how does your dad feel about that boyfriend of yours? Does he know about him? I'll gladly tell him for you when I see him."

Ronnie popped her knuckles. "I swear I'm gonna kill you if you do that."

Ronnie's parents were strict, not allowing her date until she graduated high school. There was no length Ronnie wouldn't go to to hide the fact that she was in a long-term relationship. Many times, when she was hanging out with Finn, she'd lie and say she was with me or one of her other friends.

Finn kept his hold on Ronnie, preventing her from lunging at Xander. Ronnie was quick on her feet, but Finn was quicker. "You don't need to start drama this early in the night, Alexander. Can't you find some lowlife to waste your time with?"

"Ooh, aren't you a sweet little thing?" Xander flashed his eyes to Ronnie. "I like your taste in men."

"Hate to break it to you, but you're not his type," she snapped.

"That's what you said about your last man. Maybe someone needs to knock on his closet door." He gave her a wink. It was all it took for her to go crazy. She reeled back and sailed a punch right into his nose. Xander's hand clasped his face, and he cried out in pain as rivers of blood seeped out from between his pale fingers.

Xander didn't try to stand his ground by swinging his own punch. Finn stood in front of Ronnie, blocking Xander's view of her. Beth grabbed the crook of Xander's elbow and guided him through the crowd and up the stairs.

"You've got real nice friends, Sylvia," Beth shouted over her shoulder.

"I only pick the best," I said with a smile. When they were gone, I turned to Ronnie. "Let me look at your hand." I held Ronnie's fingers up to my face. She was wearing bulky rings, and she winced in pain as I pulled them off her. "We need to get you some ice."

The three of us entered the kitchen and headed right for the refrigerator. After I applied ice directly to her knuckles, Finn asked if she wanted a cold beer, and she said yes. I got myself one as well.

•••

Time stopped while we were in the kitchen, drinking endless cans of something Finn handed me. With no luck, my eyes tried to focus on the time on my phone. It was just a blur. Ronnie, Finn, and I were laughing our asses off at nothing in particular. I held on to the walls to help me exit the kitchen, feeling lightheaded.

I was one step out of the kitchen when I saw a familiar, friendly face. If I hadn't been drunk, I might not have walked up to him.

"Piersy!" I slurred.

Pierson was sitting on the couch with a girl on his lap, shamelessly kissing her neck. Her cheeks were bright red. The sound of her giggling made me sick to my stomach. A flash of anger bubbled in my chest at the mere sight of them, and I didn't know why.

His green eyes found mine when he saw me stumbling toward him. He whispered into the girl's ear, causing her to get off his lap. "Sylvia. Glad I didn't lose track of you—I've been meaning to talk with you."

I exhaled. "Not as glad as you are to see her, huh? Huh?"

That amused him. I could tell by the big, goofy grin that went from ear to ear. "I never saw you as the jealous type."

"I'm not the jealous type." I collapsed beside him on the couch. "Can I call you Pier? I like Pier."

He smirked. "Sure."

"Okay, I have something I want to ask you, Pier." My voice fell to a whisper, or at least what I thought was a whisper. In reality, it was nowhere near. "You've gotta keep it hush-hush, though. You can't tell anyone I asked."

"I pinky promise." He stuck out his pinky, and I hooked mine with his. "What's the question?"

"Well, a little birdie told me you've got a huge private part. Like elephant trunk status."

"That's mighty bold of you to ask." His eyes widened, and a laugh exploded out of him. "Uh. I wouldn't call it huge. I'd say it's very above average."

I raised a brow. "Is this you trying to sound modest?"

"Maybe." He beamed, then crept closer to me. Our lips were startlingly close. I could see the glassy look in his eyes, probably similar to mine in my drunken state. "Do you want to find out how above average I am? My room's upstairs. There's no one in there. If you're interested—"

"She's not interested." Dakota barged in and took hold of my wrist, bringing me to my feet. He held my face in both of his hands and looked deep into my eyes. "Shit, you're wasted. You smell like a bar."

"She's having fun!" Pierson slurred. "Let her have fun. Maybe if you took that stick out of your arse, you could have fun too. Do you want to stay here with me, Sylvia?"

"She doesn't want to stay," Dakota answered for me.

"I was asking Sylvia. Not you." Pierson rose, holding on to the armrest to help himself up. "I don't want you to involve yourself, lad."

"I don't care about what you want, Bowen. She's not herself right now." Dakota tugged me away from the couch, leading me up the stairs and away from the party raging all around us.

I wiggled out of his hold and shoved him. "You didn't have to do that."

"Yes, the hell I did, and I'd do it again if I had to," he spat. "You don't know what the hell he would've done if he got you alone in his room. You don't know him, Sylvia."

"I know him well enough!" I shouted. He attempted to grab me again, but I pushed at his hands. "Get away from me! I don't need your help. Why does everyone think I need help? It's like Maine all over again. I don't need help. I don't want your help. I'm not going to screw up again." My back hit the wall, and an unwanted wave of emotion rammed into me. "I swear I'm not gonna screw up again, Mom," I croaked.

"How much have you had to drink tonight?"

"Why do you care? All you ever care about is pissing me off," I hissed. "You know, I lied that one time."

"What one time?"

"That time I found your sketchbook," I confessed. "I took some photos of them on my phone. You should apply for NYU. They've got moody, brooding people like you there. You'd fit right in."

"I figured you looked at them." He sighed. "I can explain—"

"No, you don't need to explain. I get it. You're obsessed with me."

"I really hope you don't remember any of this in the morning." He chuckled. "Obsessed isn't the word I'd go for. I just know how to admire art when I see it."

"That was the cheesiest shit I've ever heard come out of anyone's mouth," I said jokingly. "But I must admit, I'm flattered—or at least I think I am. Just don't go and slash my tires when your obsessive tendencies take over."

He buried his head in his hands. "I don't think I like drunk Sylvia."

Walking up to him, I grabbed his hands and pried them away from his face. "Hey, you don't like sober Sylvia either."

"I've grown to tolerate you."

"Aww, that must've taken a lot for you to say that. That was so thoughtful." I placed my hand over my heart. "You know, I tolerate you too.

"I should get you a cake with that written on top."

His hands were still in mine. They fit perfectly, with rough fingertips. He stepped in front of me, and in response, I moved my body against the wall. It was like we were dancing without music.

I looked at him carefully, observing his bright eyes flickering open and closed in amazement. I could see his eyes dart down to my lips. I knew what he was thinking; it was the same thing I was thinking. Craving closer contact, I stood up and strained my neck just enough to join our lips. He pulled his hands away to cup them around my face and kissed me back. I drank in the taste of his lips, getting drunk on the rush of emotions roaring inside me.

He kissed me slowly—too slowly. Almost like he was afraid to scare me off or hurt me. I raised my hands up to his broad shoulders, linking my fingers behind his neck. Heat swelled in my chest as I felt his hands slide down the small of my back, pressing me against his lean frame. I heard my heart hammering louder and louder inside my ribcage, fluttering like a restless bird.

A cold surface hit my back as he eased us against the wall, holding on to me a little tighter, as if loosening his grip would let me float away like a balloon disappearing into the cloudless blue sky.

My hand went to the front of his shirt, and I slipped it underneath, touching the ripples of his abs. Just as his lips opened, I took note of the tension building in his muscles. His body hardened against mine, drifting from me. He pushed my hand off him roughly. I couldn't read his expression. He broke the kiss and looked away, studying the floor with a blank expression.

Had I done something wrong? I wasn't sure. His face was like a suit of armor: guarded, empty. Unreadable.

I thought I was supposed to be the guarded one, hiding the most secrets.

Then, and only then, I saw it.

He wasn't as unreadable as I had first assumed. For the slightest of seconds, a grim expression crossed his face as he frowned down at the floor. I pressed my back against the wall again. The kiss had been heart-stopping. It would be all I'd be able to think of for the next few days. I didn't know why he had to end it like that.

His upset look deepened. "I shouldn't have done that."

"I kissed you."

"I mean I shouldn't have kissed you back."

"Why? Do you have a girlfriend?" It pained me to ask. I vaguely remembered Beth saying he was dating a girl at Boulder Valley High.

Dakota shook his head. "No, I don't have a girlfriend."

My body went rigid.

"Then why did you have to ruin it?"

"You're drunk, Sylvia. Of all the ways I've imagined kissing you for the first time, I didn't think you'd be half responsive in some hallway at Pierson's house."

My mind swam at what he'd disclosed. He'd thought about

kissing me, how it would play out. He wasn't drunk like I was. I knew he wasn't spewing random things.

He fished his phone from his pocket. His brows creased together at what he saw. "Would you want to get out of here?"

I hiccupped. "Depends on where we go."

"Anywhere besides here would be a million times better. Especially in a few minutes. Trust me," he hinted, but I had no clue what he meant. We interlocked our fingers, and he took us down the stairs and out the door.

Part II
The Bad

He came from a life completely different than mine,

But similar in a way.

Neither of us had a father.

At least not one to display.

The absence left my household dysfunctional and in disarray,

Thinking that the damage would always stay.

We longed for the father we never saw.

Disconnecting from life—and beginning to withdraw.

We were seeking something to drag us out of our self-inflicted darkness.

Little did I know,

That the one who'd pull me out would love me regardless.

Regardless of the sadness that resides in my heart.

Regardless of the way he left me with a mark.

—Sylvia Ellington

Chapter Twenty-Six

Teenage Dirtbag

The night faded into an array of exuberant colors and mismatched conversations. Dakota showed me more of his art, and I pointed out the ones I remembered and had taken photos of. When I woke up the next morning, I was in an unfamiliar location. I had only snippets of memories from our time together, recalling that I'd laughed so hard I'd snorted. Dakota had made sure to tease me about it.

An ache shuddered through my limbs. I tried to glance at my surroundings, seeing that I was lying in a bed and wrapped in black satin bedsheets.

To the left of me, there was a large rack of CDs with an acoustic guitar perched on it. The leather strap hooked onto it was worn out, and a few strings were missing.

"You're up sooner than I thought you'd be." Dakota strolled into the room and threw a water bottle onto the bed. I picked it up and drank out of it feverishly. "You're going to puke again if you drink that too fast."

I nearly choked. "I . . . I threw up?" The heel of my palm hit my temple, shooting another burst of pain through me like an earthquake. My head was throbbing, punishing me for last night.

I grimaced. "Please tell me I didn't throw up in your car."

"No." Dakota shook his head, sitting on the edge of the bed. "You threw up on me. My shoes, to be exact. You didn't seem sick during the drive. The moment you stepped out, though, you threw up right on me. I stopped at the dollar store around the corner and got you a toothbrush. You kept singing while brushing your teeth. It was some made-up song about how much you loved the color of my eyes. It was pretty funny." He laughed to himself.

"Oh no." I could feel myself crumbling back into the sheets, wanting the earth to open up and swallow me whole. "I'm sorry."

He shrugged nonchalantly. "I needed to replace the shoes anyway."

"I'm so sorry."

"It's okay, Sylvia. You already said sorry. You sent me thirty-five bucks through Apple Pay. Even after I said you didn't need to. You also said sorry about a million other times last night, so you don't need to tell me again."

Wait . . . was I hearing him right? Where was the Dakota I knew? This wasn't the same person who had insulted me countless times without an ounce of regret. This couldn't be the same guy who'd refused to sit next to me in homeroom.

I groaned into a sitting position. "Where am I now? Your house?"

"We're at my brother's apartment. This is the room I sleep in when I stay here sometimes for the weekends."

"And where did you sleep?"

"On the couch in the living room." He gestured at the door, which was ajar. "Do you remember much of last night?"

"I was about to ask you. I don't remember that much after we left Pierson's house."

"Not much happened. I wanted to go to a Boulder Valley party, but you didn't feel well, so I drove around for a while, and then we grabbed something to eat, hoping it would sober you up. It didn't." He smiled, shifting his gaze to me. "Then I drove here, since it was the closest place I could get to. You were out of it, and with how we'd stormed off from your dad's place, I figured it would be a bad idea if I dropped you off at home."

"That's all that happened, right? We didn't ... do anything else?"

"No, we didn't sleep together, if that's what I think you're asking." He looked at me, visibly upset with me for what I'd insinuated. "Give me some freaking credit, Sylvia. I may be a jerk sometimes, but I'm not a complete dirtbag. I'd never take advantage of someone in that state."

I slouched my shoulders. "Don't take it personally. I expect the worst of everyone I meet."

"I know what you mean. I can relate to that." He patted the bed, smoothing down the fabric with his fingers. "I understand it's basically every other guy's plan to get laid when they go to a party. But my intentions weren't to sleep with you when I picked you up. I'm not the kind of guy who scopes out a party for a potential drunk girl to screw. I think that's pathetic."

"You've got standards."

"No. It's called not being a terrible person. I shouldn't be rewarded for bare minimum behavior."

In vivid detail, I recalled the kiss we'd shared in Pierson's house. It had felt like the world was melting around us when I was in his arms. The only thing in focus was us. Everything else was static, unimportant, and irrelevant to the connection we'd made.

Using my thumbnail, I traced where he had kissed me only hours before. A flash of heat fogged my senses, causing me to shudder as I remembered how he'd made me feel, and then how he'd stolen it all away without a care in the world.

"I don't know why you have to be so confusing," I said feebly.

His eyes shot up to mine. "I'm not trying to be confusing now."

"You always are, though. You do one thing, and then you do the opposite. I don't understand you, Dakota. Can you just decide if you hate me or not?"

He didn't scowl. Instead, a smile was making its way onto his face. "Where is this suddenly coming from?"

I cleared my throat, stirring in my spot on the bed. "I mean, with what happened . . . at Pierson's house . . . before we left."

He inched closer to me on the bed. I raised my legs. They were the only barrier between us. He was directly in front of me, leaning on both of his hands, crouching forward. "You mean how you kissed me."

"Well . . ." I trailed off. "More how you ended it. And how you said it wasn't how you'd imagined it playing out."

"To tell you the truth, right now is pretty close to how I've imagined it." He moved in closer. My heart clenched at our proximity. I was on edge, wondering what he'd do next. His hands were on either side of my bent legs.

"How did you see it playing out?" I asked.

"I knew I wanted you to be able to feel each painstaking detail. I wanted it to be so good that simply thinking back to it would turn you on."

"That's a tall order."

He popped up a brow. "You're questioning my capability."

"No, it's just that I'm a hard person to convince and—"

He lifted my chin and crushed my lips against his, stopping my response dead in its tracks. Like I remembered, the sweet scent of his cologne was drowned deep in his clothes, crowding my senses. I circled my legs around his hips, holding his shirt by its collar. It was as if I was trying to bring him even closer to me, but it was useless.

Dakota pushed his body into me, grinding his hips into mine. My fingers got lost in his hair, combing through his dark locks. I brought one hand down and ran it under his black T-shirt, loving the feel of his flexed abdomen. When I snuck my hand into his shirt, he took that as a sign that I wanted it off. I sat under him as he discarded it, letting it hit the carpeted floor beside the bed.

I had been right with my earlier assumption. Dakota definitely looked better in less clothing.

He lowered himself back on top, rekindling the kiss between us and the raging fire burning within. I opened my mouth more and tilted my head, deepening the kiss. Every fiber of my being was aflame, and the fire was only growing hotter when his kisses went down to the hollow of my neck, sucking my skin and teasing it with his teeth.

I felt his hands roaming the insides of my thighs, pushing back the fabric of my skirt and venturing underneath. My body jolted upward at the thought of him going any further.

Humming against his lips, I tamed my restless thoughts as he brushed his thumb against the length of my underwear, putting a little more pressure between my legs each time.

"We're home alone, right?" I asked, out of breath.

"Yeah, my brother's not here," he said after pulling away for a short moment. "It's Friday, so he's got work today."

Friday . . . was a school day.

I settled my palms on his chest. "Oh, no. We have school."

Dakota peered at his clock. When he saw we were already an hour late, he went back to kissing my neck. "Attendance was taken in homeroom by now. Guess we're not going to school."

I shoved him again, but more playfully this time. "You can ditch if you want, but I'm going to school."

"How are you going to go to school if I ditch? I'm the one with the car."

"More of a reason why you shouldn't ditch." I smiled and got off the bed, looking for my shoes. Dakota got up as well, focusing my eyes on the material of his fitted jeans. They were more stretched in the front than they'd been before. He grabbed one of the pillows and held it in front of him when he caught me staring.

I raked my hand through my hair in distress. "How am I supposed to go to school wearing what I wore last night?"

"You can borrow some clothes." He cleared his throat. "Dion's got lots of clothes in the spare room that are pretty unisex."

I was still perplexed.

"Dion likes designing clothes. Put on one of the fits and we can go to class, you nerd."

I rolled my eyes. "Yeah, says the guy who takes extra classes at the local community college. I'm such a nerd compared to you."

"You will not and cannot call me a nerd."

I laughed. "Nerd."

"Stop that."

"Geek."

"Sylvia."

"I can see it now, actually. Kota the Poindexter. You could have your own cartoon," I teased. "Maybe even your own cereal."

"This is my last warning. If you say anything nerd-related again, I'll throw you back on this bed."

"Is that a threat?" I waited before adding. "Or is that a promise . . . nerd?"

All I saw next was a blur as he leaped at me, snatching me by the waist and pushing me back onto the bed. I fell, giggling until my sides hurt. I could tell we were going to be later than we already were.

Chapter Twenty-Seven

Rebound

After Dakota led me to the room that held Dion's clothes, I locked the door behind me because the look on his face told me he still didn't have any intention of going to school.

I walked to the pile of clothes Dakota had motioned to before I closed the door, lifting some of them up off the floor and onto a bare bed, stripped of any covers or pillows.

Most of them were either too tight or too large for me to put on without a belt. I saw a box to the left of me near the tall, dusty lamp. I picked it up and searched through the clothes inside it, quite liking the choices inside. There was a cute pink-and-black floral dress with a sweetheart neckline. Slipping it on, I was beyond satisfied to see that it fit like a glove. I twirled in front of the long mirror, inspecting the detailing and the way it wrapped around my body.

As I watched my reflection, I saw something unusual. My hand flew to the red patch on my neck, grumbling when I realized, "Great. A hickey."

I rummaged through the box and found a scarf. It was late September. Wearing a scarf in sunny California was idiotic. I had no choice. I didn't have any of my makeup on me to conceal the mark. Swinging the scarf around my neck, I secured it tight enough that the hickey was covered.

Smoothing my hands one last time over the front of the dress, I unlocked the door and stepped out. Dakota was sitting on the couch. There were pillows and a large duvet crumpled up on the floor to show that he had indeed slept there.

"What do you think?" I spun. "It's a lot nicer than what I expected to find in there. It kind of has a vintage touch to it."

"Yeah, 'cause that's my mom's dress. She wore it back in high school." Dakota stood, digging his hands in his pockets. He wasn't looking me in the eyes, only at the dress itself. "There's so many photos of my mom wearing it at Crescent."

"She went there?"

"Yeah, she did. She was in the same graduating class as your dad," he added. "My sister found the dress about a year ago in the attic and did some work on it. She wore it a lot; it was one of her favorites. It was kind of her thing to sew and design clothes too. Diana and Dion did that together. You know, before she . . . " He swallowed loudly.

Dakota still hadn't quite looked at me. The playful grin on his lips was wiped clean. A bleak expression made its way onto his face.

"Oh. Uh, I'll wear something else then." I reached for the doorknob. He held on to my hand, stopping me.

"No, it's okay. You look good in it."

"I'll go change, Kota," I insisted.

"We're already late. You don't have to," he said firmly. He stalked to the couch, slung his backpack over his shoulder, and grabbed the car keys off the coffee table. "We should get going."

● ● ●

For most of the drive, I felt a tension growing in the car. I wrapped my coat around my body, hoping that if he saw only half of the dress it would be less of a burden.

Dakota turned onto a more familiar road. A sign to the left of us read: "Harper Falls Next Two Miles."

He took a slight turn, and he placed his hand on my knee. It was what I needed to confirm that we were okay. Reading Dakota was a challenge, so I needed to rely on his small movements to understand where we stood. It was a bit exhausting. I wished he would talk about what he was thinking.

When we got to the school parking lot and got out of the car, I could already feel myself getting annoyed with the scarf around my neck. The shining sun above my head wasn't making the fabric feel any less awful.

Dakota hooked his finger into the scarf and tugged, revealing the bright hickey. He chuckled. The jerk was chuckling. "Is that my fault? It's some nice work."

I shoved him. "This isn't funny."

"Oh, really? Then why am I laughing? I think it's funny." He pulled at the scarf again, getting a second look. "Aw, you've got two hickeys. They're twins."

I swatted at his hands. "Stop that."

"You weren't telling me to stop earlier." He smirked, opening the school doors wide. The hallways were vacant. Despite the fact that we were alone, I was still nervous with the way he was talking. "If anything, I have a feeling you were close to begging for more . . . maybe begging for me to bring my head down between your—"

"Please stop." My eyes nearly fell out of their sockets. I didn't know what else to say, so I kept it at that, hoping he would drop it.

He laughed even louder at my silence. "I love how that makes you feel uncomfortable."

"Shut up, or I'm going to give you a hickey. Let's see how cute you look with a scarf around your neck in the September heat."

"I'm sure I could pull it off. I've been told I look great in winter wear."

"Yeah, only 'cause that's the one season you can hide this entire mess"— I motioned at his whole body—"from the public eye."

He rolled his eyes. "Hey, you like this mess."

"Nah. I don't like you. I'm just using you for your body."

In one swift motion, he pulled me to the side and pushed me up against the school walls. I strained my neck to look up at him. His arms were firmly circled around me, and his chest was pressed to my chest. "Take that back."

"Or what?"

He flashed his eyes up at the clock across from us. We were only a foot away from the cafeteria. "Well, in about five minutes, the bell for Lunch A will ring. Freshmen will be having lunch. A bunch of students will walk in here and see me, standing here with you. Pressed up against a wall."

I narrowed my eyes at him. "You wouldn't."

"Oh, you should know by now that I don't have much of a reputation to tarnish."

A rebuttal was forming when I heard someone clear their throat. Dakota and I looked at the same time, both seeming displeased at who we saw.

"You better have something important to say, Betty." Dakota stepped back.

I knew, for a fact, that Dakota was aware of who he was talking to and that her name wasn't Betty but rather Beth Greer. He'd said her name in the car while driving to Pierson's house yesterday. Pissing people off was like a full-time job to Dakota.

"It's Bethany," she corrected him. "We've had the same classes since the second grade."

"You look more like a Betty." Dakota sighed and then turned to me. "I'm going to sign myself in. I'll see you later."

He didn't go for a kiss, a peck on the cheek, or a hug. Rather than doing any of those things to show affection, Dakota patted me on the back. He wandered down the hall without looking back. He'd had me pressed up to a wall seconds ago, and all he could give me before leaving was a pat. On the back.

When Dakota was far enough away, Beth started to talk. "So, you guys are dating, huh?"

"I wouldn't really call it dating. I do hate him a little less."

"Sounds like dating to me."

No one asked.

"What is it you want to talk about?" I asked, irritated.

"I just wanted to tell you that . . . " She paused, closed her eyes, and took an extra step in my direction. After she fluttered her eyes open, she dropped a bombshell. "I slept with Pierson last night."

"This is something you should be telling your doctor. I don't need to know if you had sex." I raised an eyebrow. "But other than the randomness of that, congrats, I guess."

She exhaled. "You're not mad?"

"Beth, you've been in love with him for ages. Of course I'm not mad. I was never interested in him," I admitted. It wasn't a lie either. Sure, I thought Pierson was attractive, but I wasn't drawn to him like the other girls on campus. "How did that work out, though? At the party, he was pretty drunk by the time I saw him."

"I wasn't in my right mind either," she confessed. "Frankly, it wasn't how I'd pictured being with him. It was different. He kind of . . . said some off things, but I tried to go with it."

"What do you mean?"

She shook her head. "It doesn't matter. I'm glad my first time was with him."

"Wait, what?" I faltered out of my relaxed stance. "You lost your virginity while you were both drunk? Are you stupid?"

She stepped back. "Why does that suddenly change things?"

"It changes everything. Your first time shouldn't be at some party, half-numb with toxins in your blood. It should be special."

"It's not like he was some stranger I met the other day, Sylvia. I've known him for years."

"I wouldn't necessarily call you guys best pals, though."

The bell rang overhead.

"See, this is why I didn't want to tell anyone in the first place," she snarled. "You're so judgmental. Can't you be happy for me?"

"Beth, I didn't mean for you to take it the wrong way," I began to say, but I lost her in the rush of kids filling the hallways.

•••

It was very much established that simply because I'd kissed Dakota, not just once but twice, it didn't change how he acted around me at school. As a matter of fact, if anything, he was worse. He didn't say anything to me. At least before the kiss, he'd try to publicly annoy me.

"I'm not shocked. I never expected Dakota to be the kind of guy to hold hands with a girl in the hallway or share a short moment under the stairwell. But God, is it too much to ask for a hello?" I ranted to Ronnie at lunch. We were in Mrs. Duncan's classroom.

She faced Finn. "If you did that with me when we started dating, what do you think I would've done?"

"You would've neutered me," he said without a pause. "Then and there."

"You know me too well," she said and pecked his cheek. Ronnie faced me again but stopped her next words. "There's someone behind you."

Hoping it was Dakota, I turned but saw Pierson at the drama room door, waiting for me. He rubbed the back of his neck, avoiding my gaze. "Can I talk to you?"

I got up from my seat and followed him into the hallway. Without him saying a word, I had a hunch he wanted to talk about his rebound sex with Beth after Dakota had dragged me out of the party.

"Are you okay?" He placed his hand on my shoulder. "You know, with what happened last night."

I flinched from his touch. "I don't know what you're talking about. I left with Dakota a few hours into the party. I only saw you twice before I left."

"No, you didn't." He tilted his head, observing me. "We had sex last night."

At that point, I was positive I had died. I died and returned from the dead by the time I found words to speak. "You didn't have sex with me, Pierson. You had sex with Beth."

"No, it was you. You left your skirt in my room."

I went and grabbed the backpack Dakota was letting me borrow. I fished out what he was talking about. "You mean this skirt? Yeah. I was wearing it when I woke up this morning."

He shook his head. "But . . . but you were responding to your name when I said it."

Chapter Twenty-Eight
Fade into You

My mind wasn't in the right place to comprehend the words that had fallen out of Pierson's mouth and entered my ears. The hangover I'd woken up with was making everything ten times more intense. Sounds and light made me cringe. I genuinely didn't have time to process what Pierson had told me.

He reminded me that I'd promised to help him with the cleanup job after school. I said I'd meet up with him after the last bell. That was when he added that he would try to clarify what had happened the previous night. I went back to Mrs. Duncan's classroom, rethinking my friendship with Beth and whether I should be afraid of her or not.

What kind of sick person would pretend to be someone else and lure their crush in simply so they could sleep with them? Was her obsession that deep? I knew she'd said she hadn't been in the right headspace either, but I was questioning that part of her story. She'd gone to the party with her hair styled the way I did mine and worn a skirt identical to one of my own. Something about that made me think she'd had this all planned out beforehand.

I collected my things after Spanish class, mulling over everything. Beth hadn't shown up to class, which was strange because she'd been at school this morning. Carmen was missing too. Pierson followed me to my locker, trailing behind me. Ronnie's locker was next to mine. I greeted her with a small smile.

"I'm glad Beth didn't show up." Pierson spoke for the first time since we'd left Spanish. "I've never done anything wrong to her. Why would she do that to me?"

Ronnie slammed her locker shut. "Are you seriously asking that, or are you playing dumb for the cameras? Open your eyes. She loves you, bonehead. She's Macbeth crazy for you."

"Don't." I shot her a warning look.

"Don't be ridiculous. I would know if she had feelings for me. I'm good at spotting those kinds of things," Pierson assured Ronnie. "I've known Beth for a long time. If that was the case, then why couldn't she tell me?"

I tried to refrain from glaring at him with no luck. My glare was forming faster than I could stop it. "What alternative universe are you living in where telling your crush about how you feel is an everyday thing? That's not how things work here."

"You're best friends with her brother," Ronnie replied. "If I were her, I know I wouldn't tell you. It would only screw up your friendship with Adam."

"That doesn't matter," I whispered, messing with the lock on my locker. "We can't gloss over what she did. She assaulted him for twisted reasons, and I can't get over that. I don't see how either of you can. She doesn't love him at all. This isn't love."

"It's obsession," Ronnie continued. "I don't think you could arrest her for that—"

"I'm not pressing charges," Pierson cut in. "I want to forget it happened."

Ronnie shut her locker and angled her body. "What happened the other night?"

Pierson gave her a cautious look.

"I already know half of it, kiddo," Ronnie said. "Apparently Beth came into your room and pretended to be Sylvia."

Pierson stopped squinting. "That's not exactly what happened. I'm a little shaky on the details because I was wrecked. I went upstairs. There was only a little light in the room, so I could only really see the outline of a body. I thought it was Sylvia."

"Do you do that a lot when you drink? Hallucinate that it's Sylvia? If so, I think you're the one with the problem, not Beth," Ronnie teased.

I nudged her. "You should leave."

"Sorry. I'll go," she said and walked off down the nearly empty hallway.

"Like I was saying," Pierson went on, "I couldn't tell who it was, but I figured it was you. I was so drunk. I didn't try that hard to figure out who it was. I said your name once, and you—or the person I thought was you—responded. That's how it was every time I said your name or asked you something. Whoever it was never corrected me." He leaned against the lockers, lifting his hand to his face. "I can't believe she would do that. She took advantage of me. That's a crime."

A hand wrapped around my waist, coming from behind. "Just like how you tried to take advantage of Sylvia?"

I turned my head an inch, and my forehead hit Dakota's chin. For most of the day, he'd avoided me, but now he decided to put his arm around me. I fought against the butterflies in my stomach. I hated the feelings he caused in me more than I hated his confusing nature.

It was 3:30. What was he doing here? Didn't he have off-campus classes?

Pierson's entire stance shifted when he laid eyes on Dakota. He rose off the lockers and balled his hands into fists. "You're brave showing your face here after last night. I know you were a part of it."

A part of what?

"I've got no clue what you're talking about," Dakota said coolly. "I left with Sylvia long before anything happened."

"What are you two going on about?" I became a barrier, hands hovering in front of both of their chests. There was a clear tension—more than there usually was—between them. Nothing they had said made sense.

"A bunch of Boulder Valley kids crashed the party last night. We were able to kick them out, but they didn't leave quietly. I think it's strange how you conveniently left before they came."

I did remember Dakota talking about leaving last night, but I hadn't been in the right mindset to question him or understand what he meant.

"I didn't know they were going to be there," Dakota said. "The only reason I dragged Sylvia out of the place is because you kept trying to make sexual advances on her like some pervert in an after-school special warning kids about the dangers of high school parties and underage drinking."

"I wasn't myself the other night. My memory is blanked out in spots. I didn't know Sylvia wasn't there the whole time until she told me during lunch. You should know better than me, Dakota, that alcohol can make people do strange things," Pierson said, causing Dakota to harden against me, frowning even more. Pierson had struck a chord. "Anyway, are you ready to leave, Sylvia?"

"Where are you going?" Dakota asked, looking down at me.

"I'm going to his house to help clean up," I replied. "I promised I'd help him out."

"You're rich enough to pay someone to do that for you, Pierson. Your parents have cleaners," Dakota stated loudly. "You don't need her to be your little personal maid. Admit it, you want some lame excuse to get another chance to get in her pants. Good try, but it doesn't matter if she's drunk or sober—she doesn't like you."

Unknowingly, purely from the anxiety this conversation was giving me, I dug my nails into the back of Dakota's hand.

He flinched but didn't move his hand away. "It's not like I'm lying."

Pierson's eyes shot down at the Dakota's hand on my hip. His upset look didn't fade when he saw that I wasn't telling Dakota to move it.

Pierson zeroed in on me—and only me—when he spoke. "I was wrong about you, Sylvia. I would've never pinned you as the type of girl who gravitates toward lowlifes like him. If it wasn't clear enough before that he isn't a good guy, then it'll become more obvious. I guess you want to get hurt by him. He's a waste of time."

Dakota pouted playfully, not taking any of this seriously.

Pierson brushed past us, purposely hitting Dakota's shoulder.

"It's not worth it." I got a good hold of Dakota's arm before he could go after Pierson. "Can you try to not fight everyone at the drop of a hat? You'll get yourself arrested again with those instincts."

Dakota shook me off. "At least this time I wouldn't mind getting arrested."

"It doesn't matter, Kota. Let's get out of here. I've got my dad to go home to. I bet he's itching to scream at me and ground me until I graduate."

"I'd love to get front-row tickets to see that." His frown melted only slightly. "I'll drive you home. C'mon."

A little part of me wondered if he'd stayed behind longer than he typically did just so he could take me home. I smiled at that thought. Even if it turned out to be false.

We went through the empty hallways with his hand planted on my waist. Dakota had worked hard to not show me any attention during school. It was only when Pierson was nearby that he'd put his arm around me. At the party, he'd held me like this after we'd stepped out of the car. Why was it such an issue now that we were in school? Was he embarrassed of me? If he kept this up any longer, I knew he would cause me more heartaches than headaches.

What if Pierson was right? What if he did hurt me?

As intriguing and confusing as Dakota was, I didn't like the thought of him hurting me in any way, shape, or form. He'd never given me a reason to think he was like the dangerous guys my mom had associated with when I was growing up. Dakota wasn't a bad guy. His harsh attitude always contradicted his actions and made people think he was awful.

I didn't know if there was a word for what we were or what we were doing. It was only the first day of this so-called arrangement, and I didn't feel closer to Dakota than I had yesterday.

Sliding into his car, I shut the door and put on the seat belt. He didn't turn on the radio. We drove quietly for a few minutes, letting the noise of the tires driving along pavement fill the air. Deafening silence was eating at me, begging for some type of conversation.

"Do you know what we're doing." My voice didn't rise at the end like it should've for a question.

"We're driving to your house," he said. "Do you want me to drive you somewhere else?"

"No, that's not what I'm talking about."

"What is it you're talking about then?"

I sighed, gazing out the window. "It doesn't matter anyway."

"Can you not be so cryptic and tell me what you mean?"

"I mean, do you have any idea what we're doing here? Tell me what you're planning on doing, what your intentions are or aren't. Because if this is some kind of joke, a sadistic joke to mess with me, then tell me now so you can spare me. I've gone through enough problems in my life. I don't need you to be another addition to the already long list."

He swerved off the road into a wooded region. The car came to halt, mixed in with the trees and their swaying branches. "This is about what Pierson said, isn't it?" He didn't wait for my response. "Look, Sylvia. Last time I checked, I don't need to tell you what my intentions are when it comes to you. Because truth be told, I have no clue what I'm doing."

"You can't possibly think I'll believe that you woke up yesterday morning suddenly not hating me anymore. People don't change that easily. Not that long ago, you were calling me Sandra and cursing me out. I thought for sure, after we kissed, you'd act different. You're the same. No, you're worse! You ignore me!" I shouted. "I'm not buying it. I'm not that gullible."

"I'm not asking you to buy any of this, Sylvia. So stop freaking yelling at me like I betrayed you before I've done anything to piss you off."

I crossed my arms over my chest. "You could already have something planned out."

"Have I given you any reasons to not trust me?"

"No, but you haven't given me any reasons to trust you either."

"You're out of your mind," he seethed, huffing loudly.

"Maybe I'm thinking ahead."

"You're so paranoid. And for what? Nothing. Is it the fact that

I don't know where this is going or the fact that there will be people like Pierson saying I'm up to no good that's really bothering you?"

I bit my bottom lip, answering with my silence. Dakota saw that as enough evidence to confirm his second assumption was dead right.

He unbuckled his seat belt and twisted toward me. "I didn't say anything to you because I knew what people were going to do. Beth would've told the entire grade before lunch if I did anything different. I've had to deal with the constant burden of the entire school despising me for the last year. I don't want that happening to you, too, simply because you associate with me."

I opened my mouth.

"Let me finish," he requested. "I enjoy that I don't know what I'm doing with you. Isn't that how this is supposed to work? It's supposed to be scary and spontaneous with no designated direction or map laid out for us to follow."

I shrugged. "I wouldn't know. I've never done this before."

I wasn't being completely honest. Dakota didn't need to know that I had "done this," or at least something close to it.

"Well, first lesson is you don't yell at people when they haven't messed up." His full lips pulled into a soft smile as he brought his hand up to my cheek. "At least let me mess up a little before you get that scowl going on your face. Trust me, I'm going to mess up, but I haven't done anything this early on in this . . . whatever this is."

"I'll try to remember that." I returned his smile.

Dakota Ridgewood was a lot of things compiled into one, too complex for most to want to bother with. He was a puzzle. I wasn't the first to be drawn in by him, but I wanted to be the first to disarm his barriers and unlock the person he was keeping behind those defensive walls. I'd seen glimpses of the person he kept locked away, but only for brief moments.

Cupping my face, he lifted it up an inch, matching our lips together. Every doubt I had in my mind vanished with that one simple kiss. The argument we'd had was completely forgotten as I tilted my head, giving him more access to slide his tongue along mine.

We are going to be okay, I thought blissfully.

We are going to be okay.

Hopefully.

For the first time in a long time, I give myself to another person in a way that I've only done a handful of times. I dive deep between his arms, and he enters and exited my world in a way that can only be describe as breathless.

We're going to be fine.

He would never hurt me.

Right?

Chapter Twenty-Nine

Not

In kindergarten, my best friend didn't become my friend solely based on their niceness. You could say that was the first example of me accepting inadequate companionship.

In Mrs. Williams's class, on most Fridays, she handed out goodies to her students. The catch was we had to be on our best behavior. Without fail, we got our stickers or candies. We'd only recently moved to this new school district in the inland Maine area so that my dad could go back to school for a law degree.

"What do you have in your bag?"

The voice made me look around, left and right, to see who was speaking to me. A girl with circular glasses, pigtails, and a dress dotted with pink butterflies blinked her big eyes at me.

"Do you have any Jolly Ranchers?" she asked. "I only got chocolate."

Her tongue poked out of her mouth in disgust.

I checked the plastic bag Mrs. Williams had placed on my desk. "I have lollipops."

"Oh, give me one!"

"No, let's trade."

"Nah, my mom likes chocolate. I want to give it to her." She pushed her glasses up her nose. "I'll be your friend if you give me a lollipop."

"How about my best friend?"

Her hair swayed in the act of agreeing. "Deal."

We pinky promised, and that was as serious as things could get as a kid. My word was my bond. Any time I had lollipops, I gave them to her. We sat next to each other on the bus. She promised to hang out with me at lunch, and when she forgot, I would try to find her and plop beside her. Her last name was close to mine, making me think it was kismet that we were seated near each other.

Our similarities ended there. She was shorter than me, but most girls in my grade—for years—would be shorter than me. I could thank my mother for that. Ciara was her first name, and her hair was sleek and smooth. Her eyes were as big as her mouth—and I meant that in the meanest possible sense. Candy couldn't buy her friendship for very long.

"Are you adopted?"

That was what she asked me.

"You don't look like your dad."

That was what caused me to knock her to the ground.

Chapter Thirty

Ours

Dakota dropped me off at my house, driving slowly into the quiet neighborhood. Right when my hand touched the door handle, he told me to check the glove compartment. I popped it open and found my phone tucked inside.

"You left it in my car last night," he said. "It's kind of weird how you don't have any phone numbers in there from Maine."

I retrieved my phone. "You went through my contacts? How the hell did you get inside?"

"You went through my sketchbook," he replied pointedly. "It's only logical that I go through your phone."

"That still doesn't explain how you were able to solve my passcode."

He winked. "That's a secret I'll keep to myself."

"That's an invasion of privacy."

"So what? You invaded my personal property, snooping through my drawings without permission. Now, you can say we're even."

"In what world would looking at some drawings be equivalent to hacking into my phone?" I unbuckled my seat belt and opened the door. Going through my contacts, I saw there was a new number added in the R category: Dakota Ridgewood.

Fighting against the expression growing on my face, I tried to look unfazed that I now had the ability to annoy him at any hour of the day.

"Are you going to answer my question?" He arched a brow. "Actually, I have another one. Why don't you have that many phone numbers saved? Is this your burner? Are you hiding your real one somewhere else?"

"That's three questions, not one."

"Sylvia. Please."

With the window still open, I said, "I can't answer any of them. Or I'd have to kill you."

"Bull."

"Look behind you," I whispered. And I swear, for a moment, Dakota looked pale.

The sight of that alone made me laugh, destroying my air of mystery.

•••

I was expecting a long lecture and an even longer verdict on what my punishment would be for going to a party and staying out all night. When I got home, I got none of that.

Partly, that had to do with the fact that neither of the adults were home when Dakota dropped me off. I stayed in my room for rest of the day, doing my homework. There was a practice exam coming up in Spanish class. I was midway through testing myself when I heard the gravel crunching from the driveway outside. My knees jolted, kicking me off the bed in one leap toward the door. I waited, counting the seconds between the sounds of car doors opening and closing, keys shaking up and down, footsteps, and then, finally, the undoubtable grumble of my father's bellowing voice.

"Hello!"

From the muffled reply, I could tell someone was downstairs. I'd missed my chance to be the first person to greet him. At that point, I decided it would be smart to stay in my room. I hated confrontation with him. Oddly enough, I wanted Tara to join him to speak with me about how I should be reprimanded. Maybe then I could advert any real punishment.

"You went to school today?" was the first question my dad asked.

He was the one who came to me, entering my room thirty minutes after coming home. He was still in what I was sure he'd worn to his office. A red tie was loosely pulled from his shirt collar, already in the stages of being undone and tucked away into the closet.

There was no point in lying to him, so I admitted where I'd been.

"Yeah, I did go to school," I said, hastily tucking a piece of hair behind my ear and avoiding any eye contact as I shut my notebook. "I got a ride from Dakota."

"You weren't wearing that when you left yesterday," noted Tara, appearing in the doorway with her hand on Dad's shoulder. "I remember what you had on when you left and—"

"It's Dakota's mom's dress," I interrupted, darting my gaze directly at my father. "If I'm not mistaken, you knew her well, Dad, didn't you?"

His eyes narrowed, sharp as a knife. "I don't know what you're talking about."

"Obviously, I'm talking about Dona Ridgewood. You went to high school with her."

He remained silent, but the sight of his hands tightening at his sides was a clear enough answer. I was beginning to sail on unsafe waters, watching the storm brewing behind his glasses.

"You're having dinner in your room tonight."

The order came from Tara, not my father.

"You heard her," Dad added. "And that'll remain until further notice. No after-school activities either. And your phone?" His gaze zoomed around the room like a hawk. "Where is your phone?"

"Dad—"

"No."

"I think that's excessive, Elijah," Tara chimed in. "What if we need to contact her at school? She'll need it then."

"Fine. If she's heading to school, she can have it," he explained, snatching the cell off my desk. "But the second you're in my house, that phone goes right into my hands."

"Till when?" I moped. "I have group projects coming up. I'm going to need that at home."

"And when that time comes, we'll discuss your new terms and conditions."

The door slammed shut, ruffling a few pages off my lap.

My father wasn't the type of parent who held back how he felt. He was never a violent man, but he let his temper take hold of him, dominating how he reacted to certain things. I had predicted that he would yell at the top of his lungs. But I hadn't predicted that.

Later that night, I ate my dinner in my room, feeling like the unwanted stepchild with each step I took upstairs.

School wasn't any better. A towering wall had formed, with me on one side and Pierson on the other. As the month changed from September to October, the divide became clearer. Dakota and Pierson had switched places. Pierson was the one dismissing my existence at every corner. I pretended I didn't mind.

Even if he had crossed the line by questioning Dakota's intentions, I still wanted Pierson around. Believe it or not, I cared for that egotistical brat. He had his faults and flaws like we all do, but I liked the confident way he spoke his mind. He didn't keep things to himself.

Being with Dakota had its drawbacks because Pierson wasn't the only one inching away from me. Dakota had been right about how the school would react. The alliance against me was so bad that I had to move seats in Spanish class. Carmen cried out in victory, joking about how everyone treated me. "One small step for mankind, and one big step closer to becoming a shut-in like her future mother-in-law."

I wanted to remind her that she'd dated Dakota in the past, but I was too mad to find the right words.

Xander and Beth no longer sat with Pierson, for obvious reasons. Pierson couldn't stand Beth for what she'd done. I knew if either Xander or Beth had a say in it, they would've sided with Pierson and his desire to exile me. Ronnie, Finn, and Finn's junior friend Gabriel—who also sat in the drama classroom at lunch—sided with me.

In a different scenario, or perhaps in another life, I could have continued the school year with the same two friends I'd made at the beginning of the year.

This wasn't that story.

My mismatched posse of pals suited me better anyhow.

Dakota didn't like Gabriel very much, though, because he blatantly tried to hit on me in front of him. Gabriel was either very bold or very stupid. I didn't mind Gabriel as long as he kept it to harmless comments that wouldn't tick Dakota off.

No one knew what Dakota might do if Gabriel tried anything more. The way Dakota leaned into me, curling his arm around my hip and glaring, told me that he wasn't taking any of Gabriel's flirting lightly.

The upside to this alliance was that Dakota had slightly stopped pretending I didn't exist on school grounds. Gradually, he caved in and became a regular for lunch in Mrs. Duncan's room.

"I couldn't care less who you befriend, Sylvia. I'm not judgy," Ronnie said one Friday. She was devouring a fruit cup. "I think what Pierson's doing is childish. He'll come to regret it."

I stabbed my fork into my chicken salad. "Yeah, I hope. I thought we were friends. Everything is awkward now."

"Is that why you didn't go to cross-country tryouts last month?" Ronnie asked.

My face dropped.

"Well, it's half the reason."

"Do you miss Pierson?" Finn asked.

Dakota noisily cleared his throat. "If you don't mind, I'd rather we talked about something else. Anything else."

"Yeah, we can." I dropped my utensil and tried to swallow my bite. "What do you guys want to talk about?"

"Let's talk about Halloween!" Gabriel shouted.

"Oh, right, I forgot Halloween was coming up," Finn noted. "Is it next weekend?"

"Yeah, it is, but I haven't given any thought to Halloween since I was a kid," Ronnie said, looking over at Gabriel. "You still give a shit about that holiday?"

"You guys asked for a subject change, and I gave it to you. Stop questioning it," Gabriel grumbled and faced me. "What are you planning on doing for Halloween, Sylvia?"

I shrugged my shoulders. "I haven't thought that far ahead. I'm not that into Halloween. How about you, Gabe?"

"I'll be here at school. We have rehearsals for the play. I do the lighting and sound. I'm also going to the Halloween dance, helping them out with the music and whatnot. I'm basically booked until winter break," he blurted out, then suddenly he began to beam. "I love that you call me Gabe. You've got a little nickname for me."

"Don't feel too special," Dakota snickered.

I poked Dakota. Wanting to keep the conversation away from Pierson, I asked Gabriel another question. "What are you planning on being for Halloween this year?"

He gave me a devilish grin before answering. "I was hoping to be your boyfriend." He winked.

My back stiffened, waiting and watching for Dakota's reaction to Gabriel's confident statement.

"I think that position is taken," Ronnie said, picking up her spoon and digging into her yogurt.

"By whom?" Dakota asked with a blank face. "If you're implying me, you're very wrong. I'm not involved with anyone."

I shoved his arm off me and stared at him. It had been approximately a month since we'd kissed for the first time. Since then, I'd lost count of how many times he'd tried to steal a kiss from me—yesterday, we'd cut class to make out in the janitor's closet. Though we hadn't confirmed what "this" was, we hadn't gone as far as saying there was nothing there either.

Dakota's voice had been strong when he'd said he wasn't involved with anyone. Was I not someone? Was I not involved with him? Or did he have his way with every girl? These questions went straight to my heart, causing me to inch away from him.

"Oh, you aren't involved with anyone?" Gabriel sat up, smirking. "Well, in that case, Sylvia—"

"Don't think about finishing that question. She doesn't want to go out with you. She's not interested." Dakota jumped in.

Gabe scoffed. "And how would you know that she's not interested in me?"

"Because she doesn't go for geeks like you. You've only seen women undress on the Internet or in your imagination." Dakota brought his hand to my waist. I knocked my shoulder into him, hard. "What? What did I say?"

"You're so . . . so . . . "

"I'm so what? C'mon, now. Use your words."

"Infuriating." I half laughed, half snarled and got to my feet, collecting my bag and my lunch tray. "Why don't you stop talking and keep your lips sealed? Every time you open your mouth, you piss me off."

After dumping the remainder of my lunch into a trash can, I left the tray and headed to the hallway. Hiking up my backpack strap, I quickened my step when I heard Dakota coming after me, running at a much faster rate.

"Sylvia, wait up."

"Leave me alone," I said, glaring over my shoulder.

He got a hold of my elbow. "At least give me a chance to speak."

"You've said enough."

I came to a stop.

There weren't that many people in the hallway, only a few kids scattered here and there, but they were seated further down the hall. I eased against the metal lockers and held my glare.

"Why did you have to run off like that?"

I struggled to keep my cool.

"Oh, I'm sorry. I thought the whole 'I'm not her boyfriend, but you can't go to the dance with her' was my cue to leave the scene.

You can be confusing sometimes. I don't think you see it." I took a step forward. "How can you be so smart but so stupid at the same time?"

"Yeah, says the girl who's practically failing most of her classes."

I narrowed my eyes. "You looked at my progress report."

In homeroom, I'd left the report in my binder because I hadn't taken it to my locker yet. I had a feeling he'd peeked at it when I went to the restroom.

"I didn't look at it exactly. I skimmed it," he clarified. "I didn't follow you into this hallway so we could talk about your laughable grades. Unless the grades are the reason you're being so snappy all of a sudden."

"So snappy all of a sudden?" I repeated his exact words, full-on scolding him this time. He was unbelievable. "If you're so smart, then why can't you figure out why I'm so exasperated?"

"Ooh. Exasperated. Someone's reading their SAT prep book. Personally, I would've used the word vexed. But that's just me."

I threw my hands up into air. "I'm done! It's like I'm talking to a wall."

"You must know some very good-looking walls."

He was at my heels. I couldn't shake him off.

I never knew what kind of day I would have with Dakota. One moment I thought I was getting closer to him, and then the next, I'd get hit with another hurdle to jump over.

I pushed through the glass doors leading to the grassy field. There were fewer students here. It was a sunny day in Harper Falls. Not a single cloud was in the sky.

"Sylvia, I was joking. Lighten up," Dakota said from behind me. "Talk to me."

"I'm done talking." I turned and started walking backward.

"Maybe you should go find someone else to not be involved with."

I spun a little too quickly, snagging my foot on the curb. I was falling, and I was falling fast. I waited for the impact of the ground to my face. Hands coiled around my hips, grabbing me in midair.

Realizing who it was, I elbowed Dakota's chest.

He unwrapped his hands from around me and winced.

"You're welcome." He coughed, rubbing his chest. "Ouch, that really hurt."

I sat down cross-legged on the grass. "Great. Now we feel the same."

"You can't seriously be hurt by me saying I'm not in a relationship with you."

"So, are you saying you wouldn't mind if I started dating Gabriel?"

His raised his shoulder. "You're not dating him."

"See. This is what I don't get. You didn't tell Ronnie, 'No, I'm not her boyfriend.' You said, 'I'm not involved with anyone.' And then you have the audacity to threaten Gabriel for being interested in me." I sighed. "Kota, pick a mood and stick with it."

He joined me on the ground, combing through the blades of grass as if he were looking for an answer hidden there. "You're not going to the Halloween dance with Gabriel. If I can speak frankly, I'd prefer if you didn't go anywhere with him."

"Are you going to take me to the dance then?"

I had no interest in going, but I wanted to know what he'd say.

"I don't go to dances. It's not my kind of scene." He peered up at the sun. "Also, Jiménez probably has us booked that night, so I'm not going to be free."

"Booked for what?" I was a bit intrigued. "Are you going to do lap dances and a striptease for some middle-aged women? If so, I'd love an invite. Plus a bucket I can throw up in after."

"I will not be doing any lap dances for anyone." He chuckled. "We're in a band."

"Of course you are." I rolled my eyes. "Let me guess, you guys play heavy metal music."

"No, it's mostly our attempt at recreating punk rock music with a math rock and new wave sound to it. New wave is already associated with punk rock, but we're doing more experimental things with it. Jiménez wants to go for more of a Joy Division feel, whereas I'm going for a Sex Pistols and the Undertones vibe."

I nodded as if I knew who those bands were. "That's interesting. Do you sing backup?"

He snorted. "I don't do backup. I sing lead."

"Sing for me," I insisted. "So that I can be distracted from the fact that you're by far the most confusing person I know."

"I'm confusing?"

"Don't ask that like you didn't just whip my head through a loop for the last five minutes about how you can't date me but don't want me to date other people."

He sighed deeply. "Sylvia."

The way he said my name felt like a song in my ears, adding a new bounce and vibrancy to the syllables.

"Would you believe me if I told you that I was scared?"

"Scared of what?"

"You."

I laughed, truly laughed through my nose, and slapped his knee. "You're lying."

"Why would I lie about that? I think about how easily I could mess this up every day."

"You can't possibly be that stressed."

He moved his hair out of his eyes. "I wouldn't use the word stressed."

"How could you be scared? You're acting like I'm an eight-eyed, supersized tarantula. There's nothing scary about me. I don't bite."

"I'm not scared of you—that would be ridiculous. I said that wrong the first time. I'm scared that I might do something that would eventually make you not like me."

"You say that like I already like you."

"Ooh, that hurt more than the actual blow to my chest."

I cracked a smile, and so did he.

"You can't put that much strain on the future. If you want me to be completely honest, being standoffish is going to only make me want to stay away from you—not come toward you," I told him.

His smile widened. "But it has been working so well so far. You can't get enough of me, admit it."

"Trust me, I'm close to having had enough of you."

"Okay, okay, I'll compromise," he said at last, raising both his hands. "How about you come to our next performance? It's tomorrow. We can get dinner afterward."

He moved his hand into mine, and I nodded.

"I'd like that." A rush of realization came over me, and I shook my head. "I can't. I'm grounded."

"Till when?"

"Till the foreseeable future." I grimaced. "I don't see how you could get me out of it—you're the reason I'm grounded in the first place. They don't trust me anymore."

"Were there any exceptions?"

"Only related to school," I disclosed. "I could pretend I joined a club."

"No, that's too simple." He leaned in more. "And hardly believable . . . I thought you wanted to convince them you weren't lying."

For the rest of lunch, we stayed outside, and I tried brainstorming ideas on how I could escape for the night. Truth be told, for the most part, I was just begging Dakota to sing for me, but with no luck.

Chapter Thirty-One

Oh Well

After Tara picked me up from school, I sensed something more off about her than usual.

When we got home, Tara unlocked the front door, pushing it open. "Make sure you pack your bags when you get up to your room."

I gripped the strap of my backpack. A gut-wrenching pain quaked into me. "What for?"

"Your father will tell you when he comes back from work."

I didn't go upstairs. "Why can't you tell me now? I want to know."

"It's your grandmother," she announced. "We wanted it to be a surprise—"

"She's back from her trip already?" I rushed to ask, looking around the room with wonder, almost as if I was hoping she was nearby. "I thought she wouldn't be back for another week. I hope nothing's wrong."

"She's fine. She misses you, from the sound of it." Tara darted into the kitchen, turning on the sink. She said something else, but I couldn't understand her over the water gushing out of the faucet. Heading upstairs, I kicked my shoes off into the corner of my room. The door creaked closed behind me. I threw my backpack ahead of me and took out the paper Dakota and I had been writing on during lunch.

We'd ranked excuses that could get me out the house for a few hours from "Most Believable" to "Unbelievable." None of those plans, though, had taken into account the chance my grandmother would be back in town. Her visit threw our entire vision of sneaking out for Dakota's gig out of whack.

My phone buzzed with a new text from Dakota. I was torn, feeling the pull from two different directions at the same time.

It had been approximately four years, three months, and a few odd weeks since the last time I'd seen my grandmother. Last I'd heard, she'd taken a trip to Zanzibar with her husband, Frederick.

I loved my grandmother. There was one issue, though. She had no filter. She was a very elegant lady who came from a well-off family, but if you pressed the wrong button, she could change in an instant. With Tara nearby, I knew there was going to be a problem.

When she'd seen me four years ago, she'd had only dreadful things to say about Tara. Even though it was a year after the finalization of my parents' divorce, my grandma had still hoped my father would reconcile with my mom. She preferred my mother, with her laugh and her loving presence. That was one of the many ways Grandma and I differed. The woman Grandma had met was long gone by the time I could form my own opinions.

Grandma came from a long line of businesspeople, mainly in hotels and real estate in cities across the nation. My grandmother was the first woman in our family who didn't get married after high school. She went to college like her brothers and got herself a degree, not knowing she'd take over the family hotel business. She was also the first woman in our family to not change her last name to her husband's when she finally did tie the knot. It was a good idea because she eventually got remarried five years after my father was born.

• • •

Grandma stood on the threshold of Dad's front door, hesitating. She had on a large hat in a vivid red that matched her flamboyant clothing. Removing the hat, she took her first step inside and went for a hug.

"My my, you look like your mother. More and more each day." She beamed, holding me close. "You could be twins if she were standing beside you."

"Thank you." I grinned with tight lips.

Holding my shoulders, she continued smiling at me. "Have you finished packing?"

"No, I've hardly started. I only just got home from school."

"Take your time, and bring as many things as you want to put in your room at my house. It'll be you, Hanan, and me for the weekend." She released me, and I stepped closer to the stairs. "Frederick is still out of town. It'll just be the three of us. If we have time, we can go to the lake or the beach. Whichever one you like."

"Why is Hanan coming with us?"

"He wanted to work out at the country club," she answered. "It's such a long drive on his own, so he figured he'd come with us."

"Sounds like a lovely weekend, huh?" Tara chimed in.

I merely smiled, knowing damn well I had no say in this whatsoever. It was better than being grounded, I supposed. Deep down, I wondered if this was simply my dad's idea to get me away from Dakota over the weekend and involve a parental figure I saw as an authority.

I still didn't know why Hanan would want to go with my grandmother and me. We weren't the kind of people he hung out with on weekends. There were parties he could attend and Boulder Valley kids to mess with. I tried not to think too much about it as I went upstairs to finish packing.

•••

The drive up took longer than I'd thought it would. No one told me why I was suddenly going to stay with my grandma, but I hoped it would be revealed at some point during the stay. It was so random that I had a feeling this wasn't well thought out.

Grandma's house had been in our family for over a century. It was originally a mayor's mansion, standing tall on an inclined road leading up only to it. In the early 1900s, it had been expanded upon, and we'd almost lost it before the Second World War. I knew this from memory because Grandma had never let me forget it.

She only referred to Frederick, her fifth husband, by his name or as "my partner." She never called him her husband. I knew, long before she was with her new man, that she didn't like titles. She was happy, and that was all that mattered. Grandma and Dakota could relate in that one way.

Dakota.

I sucked in a dry breath, trying to not think about him. The second we'd gotten into the car, Grandma had warned us she wanted us to have what she called "an old-fashioned trip to Grandma's house." Which meant no technology, like when she'd visited her own grandmother all those years ago.

Grandma showed me up to the room I'd be sleeping in. She said I could leave a few things in the dresser and have this room as my own whenever I stayed here. I nodded and walked around the spacious room, brushing my fingertips over the blue walls.

"I want to ask you something," I said, so softly she asked me to repeat it.

She sat down next to me on the comfortable window seat. "What do you want to ask, dear?"

"It's nothing you should take personally."

She only smiled back at me, putting her thin hands on mine and squeezing them. "Ask me anyway. I won't be mad."

"I'm happy for what you did for me when my parents got divorced." I swallowed dryly. "You did a lot for me."

"I would do it all over again too." She'd made sure I knew that. "I used everything in my power to get you out of the foster system. Your father cared so much—"

"He left me there."

"Sylvia, that's not entirely true." She sat on the edge of the bed. "What do you remember?"

There was a drop in my tone. "Did you think I was too young to recall?"

Chapter Thirty-Two

Years Prior

Mom is hardly awake when I come home from school. Her boyfriend is sprawled out on the couch next to her, facing the ceiling with his eyes shut. A bottle is sitting on the coffee table, bundled in a crumpled-up paper bag.

She's done it again.

I've seen her like this before. She was worse after Dad left, doing it nearly every other week. But she's been sober for so long. I could see the life coming back to her eyes and the color coming back to her face, the woman that my father had fallen in love with. The woman who was my mother. This carcass of a mess lying on our couch half alive isn't my mother. She's a hollowed-out casket of skin and bones. Too fragile and thin to be considered human. Too broken and heartless to be my mother.

I check her pulse, which is faint, and feel her face. Her skin is still warm to the touch. Grabbing the house phone, I call for an ambulance.

I take the seat beside my mother and push her hair back. It's wet and smells like cigarettes and loneliness. "It's okay. You'll be okay. I'm here for you." It's what she should be saying to me. Not the other way around. "They're coming. They said they'd be here any minute." I rush to wipe the tear racing down my cheek. As many times as I have seen this, I still find myself upset at the sight. She always says the last time will be the last. But it never is.

I should be upstairs, doing my homework. I should be outside, playing with the other kids. I shouldn't be in here, hoping my mother is still alive.

Her boyfriend stirs out of his sleep at the sound of the sirens. He's infuriated. He hides something under the couch and stumbles his way down the hall into Mom's room. He stays there until the ambulance takes Mom.

• • •

Mom got in trouble for leaving me alone with her in the condition that she was in, drunk and nowhere near responsive. Dad was in California. Grandma was in New York. That left me in the foster system, waiting to see what the state of Maine would do with me.

Grandma rushed to Maine. Dad stayed.

I couldn't hate Dakota for disliking my father.

The man who gave me life didn't want me anywhere in his own when he got a new wife, new kids, and a new reality to subscribe to.

Grandma got in touch with the right lawyers to help my mother. Grandma didn't lose hope for my mother.

She'd repeatedly say: "A daughter needs her mother."

She couldn't, though, convince my father to step up to be a parent and take care of me. I temporarily lived with my grandmother, staying in one of her walk-ups in New York while my mother was in rehab.

It mostly worked.

Mom was able to subdue her addiction to the point that she

no longer raised any red alarms. Late-night cocktails became the norm. Day drinking was a rare affair.

Pushing me back into my mother's custody, forcefully, made me struggle to let my dad or his family come back into my world. In a sense, it gave me the belief that I was never truly their blood. Did they care for me? Did they see how much I suffered in my mother's care? Did they see no worth in saving me from her?

Was there no worth in me at all?

• • •

Turning to my grandma, holding back the tears, I asked, "Why the sudden urge to see me now?"

"That's not true." Her smile faltered. "I called every birthday. Every holiday. I even sent money a week in advance of your birthday and for every holiday."

"I never saw any of that money." I dropped her hand and got to my feet. I needed to breathe. This was news to me. I began pacing. "Either you're lying to me or—"

"Your mother could've hidden it from you," she filled in for me. "It's no surprise. Who do you think paid for her rehab? I nearly killed your father for not taking you out of there any sooner. He tried, but with no luck. Your mother convinced him against it. She said he'd ruined their marriage. She didn't want him to ruin her kid and desert her like he'd deserted your mom."

My feet froze, nailed to the ground when she said that. A lot of my hate for my father came from the fact that he'd left me with my mother when she was in no way fit to be a parent.

"He tried to send letters and money to you, along with clothes and school supplies, but the gifts were always sent back," Grandma went on to say. "The pair of us tried so hard for so many years. I was close to getting some lawyers on my team to take you from her. She couldn't deny us time with you. Before I could do it, your father stopped me. He didn't want to make this a big battle. I can't believe she allowed you to come now after all those failed attempts."

I snorted. "She's always been stubborn."

I recalled the times when we didn't have enough to survive, the days when we didn't have running water or food. Conversations stamped into me, by my mom, to show that my father didn't care about me.

As I sat there, letting my thoughts destroy me in silence, I wondered what else she'd lied about.

Chapter Thirty-Three

Anti Anti

After what I'd learned, engaging in any sort of conversation with my grandmother became a challenge. I had no actual hate toward her whatsoever. She had been unaware of what my mother was hiding from me, and she wasn't the cause of my shift in mood.

I kept reflecting that had they been more forceful in getting me away from my mother, what happened in Maine last year would've never occurred.

The next morning, I was having breakfast with Grandma, pretending not to think about our talk the day before. Hanan was still in bed upstairs.

I pushed the food around on my plate and sighed.

"You haven't eaten any of your breakfast," Grandma noted, motioning to my plate.

I threw the napkin down. "I ate the toast."

"Hardly. You didn't really eat your dinner either. Is something wrong?"

"My entire life with my mother is currently being questioned." I rose from my seat. "Please excuse me so I can go back to listening to music in my room."

"You keep playing Fiona Apple's music like you're trapped in the nineties."

"I'm a sullen girl."

"Please, stop being so melodramatic, Sylvia," Grandma pleaded. "I know what will cheer you up."

"A new mother? I think it's a little too late for that."

"I was thinking more along the lines of you, Hanan, and me going to the country club this afternoon. It's sunny out. There are a lot of people your age there."

"Yeah, lots of people who go to my school. I see them enough. I don't want to see them on my weekends."

"Is there someone at school who's bothering you?" Grandma asked, looking at me with a new expression on her face. I hadn't even opened my mouth to answer her when she began to speak again. "I want to know who. If it's a Ridgewood, I can most definitely handle it."

That caught me off guard. "Why is a Ridgewood family member your first guess?"

"Because our families have had issues since the dawn of time," she said effortlessly. "It's my first guess because there's no one else who has such an established hatred for us. Don't you already know that?"

"I mean, I know there was a problem back when my dad was in school."

"I wouldn't say that. Are you talking about what your father did to Dona Ridgewood?"

I pretended like I knew what she meant and nodded.

"Oh no, you mustn't be."

"She used to be Dad's friend or something, right?" I said, just to get a reaction.

Grandma flinched at that. "She was never his friend. That poor girl almost got him arrested."

"You're telling me . . . Dad got in trouble before graduating high school? I would've never thought that in a million years. I thought he always lived life on the straight and narrow."

She refrained from laughing. "He's like that now, but when he was your age, I had to keep him out of everyone's hair. If he wasn't vandalizing one place, he was terrorizing another group of people. He and his friends were mean."

Mean felt like a lighter variation of what she really wanted to say. If he weren't her only living son, perhaps she would have found herself cursing in vain. My dad said the death of his brother had changed the family. I was too young to sense any real shift. But with the way she stared into the distance, holding on to her next words, I could hear the unsaid complaints she had pent up about my dad.

Why cry? The thoughts must've echoed. Why fight when he's all you've got left?

"Were they ever mean to Dona?" I asked out of nowhere.

"They were only boys." Her red-rimmed eyes opened. "Boys will be boys."

Chapter Thirty-Four

Jet-Black Heart

On Sunday, Grandma gave us our phones on the drive back to the house. But she wouldn't let us turn them back on. She asked us to wait until we were in the comfort of our own rooms before rejoining the internet. Her words, not mine.

I had my phone in my lap, feeling its heat on my bare thigh. It had been forty-eight hours, but it felt like weeks since I had last talked to Dakota. Before handing my phone to Grandma on Friday, I'd sent a text to Dakota talking about the trip I was going on and how I wouldn't be able to go to his gig. I never saw a reply, even after checking right before handing off my cell.

Going upstairs, I began the process of turning on my phone. Once inside my room, I dropped my overnight bag next to my bed. Like an unwanted storm, new messages and voicemails begin hitting my phone. I skimmed through the text messages, but they were practically identical. Repeatedly, Dakota asked if I hated him, if I was okay, and if I could forgive him.

Scrolling back up to the last thing I'd sent him, I saw that my messages from Friday had never sent. The whole weekend had gone by, and he'd assumed I never got back to him about his gig.

I called Dakota, and someone picked up after the first ring.

"Sylvia, is that you?" Dakota slurred. "I kept calling and calling and calling, but that stupid lady in your phone told me to leave a message after the beep. I didn't want to talk with her. She's not very nice. She wouldn't let me talk to you. And I need to talk to you."

I shouldn't have seen this as amusing, but a smile crossed my face no matter how hard I tried to hold it back. He was clearly drunk. "I'm here right now, Kota. You can talk to me."

"But you aren't here. You're in a phone."

I only smiled even harder. "I can come over."

"Yeah, you can." His voice lightened up. "Oh, no, you can't. I got you in trouble, didn't I? That's why you haven't responded to my messages."

"No, I'm—"

"You must hate me right now." He cut me off, louder this time. "You're gone. You're never coming back. I can't get you back, can I? It's too late. I spent so much time making you mad when I should've been making you happy. Making you mine."

The call dropped.

Stunned, I attempted to call him back. His line was busy.

I texted Ronnie, telling her about the call I'd had with Dakota and my need for a ride. I knew I had to see what was up with him. He'd stopped responding to my calls or texts. My mind recklessly thought of the worst-case scenarios, fearing that he was wandering the lonely streets—or even worse, he had gotten into a car in his inebriated state.

Around four o'clock, my phone began to ring. It was Ronnie.

"Are you a hundred percent sure he was wasted?" she asked, skipping a greeting. "And that he seemed like he was off to do something crazy?"

"Yes, I am."

"Sylvia. Sometimes you get things wrong."

"I'm never wrong."

"That's a lie," she said. "You thought Algeria was in South America last week."

"Okay, I'm not the best when it comes to geography. I'll admit that. I'm not wrong about this, though."

"You better not be. I'm outside. I got up and drove here on a weekend when I should be sleeping until an hour before my shift. But instead, I'm here. If that doesn't show what a good friend I am, then I don't know what will. I sacrificed sleep for you."

I jumped off the edge of my bed. "You're kidding me. You're here?"

"I mean, you did text me begging for a car."

"Sorry, was that overkill?"

"Obsessive, to say the least." She paused before adding, "I can see how much this matters to you, and that means it matters to me too."

Sprinting to the window, I saw her car parked outside. Her black Jeep was turned off. I could somewhat make out her figure inside. Quickly, I put my shoes on, pulled my hair back into a tight ponytail, and slipped on a jacket. Ronnie would meet me outside, hoping that we could convince my parents together that we had a group project due.

Dad was baffled at first by the suddenness, and he asked why I hadn't mentioned it sooner. "I've been at Grandma's place all weekend with no phone," I explained. "I would've said something sooner, but you weren't home when I left on Friday."

He stuffed his hands into his pockets. "You'll be back at what time?"

Ronnie grabbed my arm before I could speak. "I wanted her to sleep over."

"I'm sorry, but she's grounded for the next three weeks."

Three more weeks? That's brutal.

"I get that, sir." Ronnie mirrored his nodding, loosening her hold on my arm. "The problem is, though, we were supposed to work on it all weekend. And it's already four o'clock. I don't see how I could promise you a reasonable time. It's better she stays over than dropping her off late. I live kind of far, and with traffic—"

"I think that's a good idea," Tara interjected. "Let her go, Eli. It's for school."

That finally did it. Dad agreed, letting us go on our way. Sighing in relief, once we were in the Jeep, I turned to Ronnie and gave her a hug.

"Brilliant," I whispered. "You're brilliant."

"He better be worth it."

•••

"I haven't been up here for a long time," Ronnie said when we pulled up to Dakota's house. "I think it's been at least four or five years."

"Why were you up here?"

"Well, a long time ago, I was friends with Beth—shocker, I know." She dropped a smile to the floor. "Beth and her brother had this thing where they would get as close as possible to the house to get a good look at Dakota's mom, Dona Ridgewood. Half our class was a part of it."

"Oh, yeah. I think Beth told me about that once. You guys got a dollar if you got a good look at her, right? Did you ever get a good look?"

"No. None of us did. The purpose behind it was less whether

we saw her or not and more if we could invent the scariest story about what we'd seen. It was a bunch of bullshit. I only did it once or twice, then my mom found out what we were doing and told me how messed up I was to do that to Dakota's mom. It was at that point I knew Beth wasn't the kind of person I wanted to hang out with. I mean, if she could do that to some poor lady who did literally nothing to her, then imagine what she could do to someone who pissed her off."

"I don't want to think about that." I shook my head and unbuckled my seat belt. "What do you know about Dakota's mom?"

"I don't know much. The trial that put Dakota's dad in jail happened when I was twelve or thirteen. Most of it went right over my head because I was a kid," she said. Oddly, the time lined up with when my parents had gotten a divorce and my father went back to Harper Falls. "Anyhow, do you want me to stay?"

"I'd really appreciate if you could stay in your car."

"Sure thing. I'm going to go down the road and find a parking spot. If you want to head back home, just text me. I'll leave you two hormonal lovebirds alone."

"We are not going to be doing anything." I grinned at her. "Thank you, though. Honestly. For driving me here on such short notice."

"It's no problem."

I leaped out of her tall car and hit the ground, landing on my feet. Carefully, I searched the untrimmed grass for Dakota's demonic dog. I made it to the front porch alive and went to knock on the door.

But it was open.

This was the part of the movie where most people would start telling the protagonist to turn back and not enter the house.

Everything about the scene matched what you might see in a scary movie. It was almost too perfect, with the low-hanging clouds, slight wind that rushed through the trees, and creepy house that was conveniently left unlocked.

Like in horror films, I stepped into the house. I moved with hesitation in my step, questioning my own choices. My foot kicked the side of a doll, causing it to roll over to the fireplace.

"I'm done, Dakota," someone said from upstairs. The stairs cried out as the guy's weight shifted down the steps. "You guys can deal with him, but I can't do this anymore."

With fearful eyes, I hid behind the long drapes, waiting for the guy to pass by and reach the front door. He slammed it behind him. Breathing a sigh of relief, I left my hiding position and went in the direction of the stairs.

"You're going to wake up the baby if you keep up this bitching and moaning," someone else said from one of the rooms.

I walked along the wall, pressing close against it. I got a view of the person speaking through the crack between the door and its frame. He looked very similar to Dakota.

His nose, sharp cheekbones, and lips mirrored Dakota's, but they had different eye colors. Where Dakota's were bright blue, this other person's were gray. I decided that he must be Dion. He was the more responsible, more likable Ridgewood from what I'd heard.

"I want to see Sylvia."

Dakota's words were crammed together, connecting as one. I figured he was still drunk from the sound of it.

"I told you already," Dion said. "I don't know who Sylvia is."

"We can get you a new Sylvia," a different voice said. "A hot one."

I strained my neck a little and saw Jiménez perched on a

dresser with a toothpick in his mouth. Typical. "I know ten girls like Sylvia who'll be a hell of a lot more fun."

Something went crashing down, breaking as it hit the wooden floor.

"I swear if you wake up that baby, you'll have another thing coming for you," Dion went on to say.

"Why do you care so much? It's not your kid. You're not her father—I don't even know who the father is," Dakota slurred. "Diana didn't want to take care of her, and she's her goddamn mother."

Had I heard him correctly?

Diana had a kid . . . a kid Dion was taking care of.

Was that why Ronnie had said Diana had been missing classes? I was still reeling over the fact that she was a mother. Dakota didn't know the father. I wondered who the father was and if he was someone I knew.

"What if it's Malik's . . . " I trailed off, not able to finish my thought. It would make sense if Malik was the father. He'd only just started dating Faye this summer. Dakota had a deep hatred for him, a hatred I didn't quite understand.

Who knew? Maybe that was Malik's kid.

"Who's there?" a new voice called out. The door opened, shining light in my face.

Chapter Thirty-Five

Somebody That I Used to Know

Lifting my hands up to shield my eyes from the light, I flashed an insincere smile. Nervousness bubbled up as three sets of eyes peered at me, frowning. I suddenly wished I were back in Maine with my mother. Being with her was a challenge, but I longed for it now. Wanting to be with her was something I hadn't felt since I was child, running from the thunder and lightning outside my bedroom window.

"Who the hell are you?" Dion asked.

"Um, uh, I am—" I began to say.

"Sylvia!" a voice yelled. "You're back!"

I didn't need to move my hands away from my face to know who that was. Quite the opposite, actually. I raised both of my arms up more when I saw Dakota rushing right for me. I got my very first bear hug from Dakota.

"Sorry about him. He's rarely like this when he's sober," Dion sighed, prying him off me.

"Oh, trust me, I know," I assured him.

"He's a happy drunk."

"Sometimes a violent drunk," Jiménez added, motioning to the space behind him. There was a tall CD rack on the floor with the contents spilled out. The bed was unmade, but other than that, the room looked spotless. Dakota had similar bedsheets to the black satin ones at his brother's apartment.

"Don't say that with her standing right there!" Dakota stage-whispered and straightened the front of his shirt. "He's lying. I'm not that bad, Sylvia."

Dion stopped rolling his eyes and looked at me again, differently than when they'd discovered me in the hallway. "Wait, are you Sylvia Ellington? I heard about the new Ellington family member, but I didn't think it was true. I thought it was only a rumor."

"Yes, she is Sylvia Ellington." Dakota took the words out of my mouth. "She's related to the same Ellington that Mom keeps talking about, the lawyer that put Dad in the slammer."

Dion slapped the back of Dakota's head. "I'm going to have to sew your mouth shut." He narrowed his eyes on me, pulling his lip ring between his teeth in thought. "How long have you been standing in the hallway?"

"Yeah, what did you hear?" Jiménez asked.

"Not much," I lied. "I got here two minutes ago. I only came so I could see how Dakota was doing. He sent me a lot of texts and voicemails, and I got worried. What happened?"

I attempted to shift the conversation away from me to Dakota, who was the real problem.

Dakota hiccupped and rubbed the back of his head, where his brother had hit him. He pouted. "Ouch."

"Don't worry about this guy. He'll be fine," Jiménez said, putting a heavy hand on Dakota's back.

"Maybe if he didn't go to that stupid gig, he wouldn't be like this," Dion scolded.

"Nah, I would've found booze one way or another." Dakota winked. "I've got my ways."

Dion crumbled to the ground, holding his head. "See what you did!"

Jiménez matched his energy. "I did nothing! He's the one who decided to drink after our gig last night."

"Then I kept drinking after we left," Dakota filled in. "And then when I got home, and then when I woke up . . ."

"How are you still walking?" I inquired, cocking a brow. "You should be on the floor right now. Blacked out and in need of a stomach pump."

Dakota patted his chest. "I've got an iron liver."

Jiménez lowered Dakota's hand from his chest. "That's not where your liver is. But okay."

The anger directed at Dakota turned into pure laughter. Only after did Dion remember there was a sleeping baby in the room adjacent to Dakota's. He told us to hush. A door at the end of the hall slowly opened with a creak that echoed throughout the house.

"What's with all the commotion?"

The laughter died altogether, along with our smiles and the lighthearted energy in the air. A shadow moved through the unlit hallway. I could make out a white nightgown and long, slender legs coming our way.

Dakota's mother, Dona Ridgewood, stood at the door.

The infamous woman who hadn't left her house in years.

And now I knew why.

At first, my eyes focused on her unreal sapphire eyes, shimmering under the warm room lights. It was like the entire ocean was captured in her irises, from the roaring deep blues to the tranquil light blues. Long auburn hair fell over her thin, bony shoulders. It was when she turned to the side, looking at me even harder, that I saw the burns starting at her left wrist and stretching down to her toes. Just on that side. Her right side didn't have any scars. The left side was entirely engulfed by bright, discolored flesh.

She shuffled back into the shadows. "Who is that? Dion, you said only Jiménez and Paul were coming."

"She's here for me, too, Mom." Dakota looped his arm with mine. "She's my g—good friend."

Perfect. I'm friend-zoned even by drunk Dakota.

"I don't care if she's your . . . wait." She stopped. I could feel her eyes on me again. "You look familiar. Do I know you?"

"Of course you don't, Mom," Dakota snapped, getting a little too loud. "You haven't left your house since my fifth-grade graduation."

I wanted to say something to Dona, but I didn't know what I could possibly tell her. She'd said the exact same thing Beth had said to me when we'd first met. Why did people keep thinking they knew me? I didn't have that familiar of a face.

She touched her chin. "You look a lot like someone I knew . . ."

"She's an Ellington," Dakota said with a smile. "You know her dad."

I had to stop Dion from slapping Dakota in the back of the head again.

Instead of rushing to kick me out, the unthinkable occurred.

"Is that so? Hmm. I'll be downstairs in a moment. Where I hope you all are by the time I come back out." She turned back toward her bedroom. "Dion, start up the kettle."

Of all people, I didn't understand why she would want to sit down with me.

•••

While waiting for Dakota's mom, I shot a text to Ronnie that I wouldn't need her to stay. There was so much more I wanted to know, and I didn't know for sure how long this conversation with Dana would last. Dion offered me the spare room they had upstairs if I needed a place to stay tonight. Drunk Dakota assured me he'd even go as far as checking under my bed for any monsters if I was still scared.

Gracefully, Dona walked down the stairs. "So, you're Eli's daughter? I didn't know he had children."

"Yeah, I lived on the East Coast for most of my life. This is my first time in California."

"You were born there?"

"Born and raised."

She waited before adding, "Hmm. Did your father tell you about his glory days at Crescent High?"

"Mom, stop," Dion pleaded, setting down the a pot of tea just like she had asked him to do. "I doubt she knows any of what you keep talking about."

Dona's body practically floated onto the coach across from me. "We can always ask. Did you father ever happen to tell you? Yes or no?"

"Stop living in the past, Mom," Dion sighed. "Let it go."

"It's a harmless question," she insisted. "I want to know if your father ever told you about his contribution to the legendary tradition for all the senior boys at Crescent."

Dakota gulped. "I don't like where this is going."

"No, it's okay. I don't mind answering." I patted his hand on my knee. "I'm not all that close with my father, so he never told me about that."

She sat there observing me, periodically glancing down at the hand on my knee. Dakota had no intention of moving it anytime soon. "I swear, you remind me so much of someone I knew."

"You keep saying that, but you haven't said who."

She picked up the teapot and poured herself a cup. "I doubt you'd know who Layla Jama is."

I sat up straight. "Layla Jama is my mother. How would you know her? She's lived on the East Coast for most of her life."

She laughed. "No, she hasn't. She lived in Harper Falls until she was old enough to drive. That's when she drove right out of this town and to New York to pursue some childish modeling career."

Chapter Thirty-Six

Ophelia

"Hold on." I gripped the armrest, shutting my eyes and trying to digest the tidal wave of information that had hit the shoreline of my awareness. "You're saying that you knew her when she was a kid? She used to live here?"

"She was in my graduating class."

I was left speechless. There was nothing I could contribute to this conversation besides silence. I was still trying to deal with what my grandma had told me yesterday. Now I knew there was more to what my mother hadn't told me—like where she was from and how she'd met my father. Who lied about that kind of stuff?

"I don't believe you," I whispered.

Dona set down her cup and got up from her seat. "I know where you're coming from. I would have a hard time believing me too. Smart of you to be skeptical." She walked to the bookshelf and retrieved a slender book, handing it over to me. "Go through that all you want. Your mother is all over it. She was in nearly every club back in high school. You father was on the track and the football teams. Check the senior superlatives."

"My dad did sports?" I asked, a bit surprised.

Dad had this strange limp that only came out when he ran, and I couldn't imagine him playing any sports.

"Well, he used to," Dona answered. "When he still could."

My fingers flipped through the yellowed pages. I went to the front of the yearbook and saw the countless things my mother had been involved in. Her eyes were bright with life—just like how she'd looked before the affair and the divorce that had destroyed her.

A lump formed in my throat when I saw how happy she seemed, making things in a pottery class, sitting with her friends on a field. She had been the president of the speech and debate team and captain of the volleyball team. I reached the senior superlatives and saw my parents in the largest photo as Biggest Pranksters.

In bold, swirling red letters, there were my parents' names: "Elijah Ellington and Layla Jama." I was expecting "Biggest Flirt" or "Cutest Couple" . . . I wouldn't have thought they'd end up in that category.

I darted my eyes up at Dona. "What made them get this title?"

Dakota snatched the yearbook out of my hands and slammed it shut. "I think that's enough. I don't want to talk about this anymore."

"Honey," Dona started to say. Dakota wouldn't let her finish.

"No," he boomed and got to his feet, grabbing my arm and pulling me up. "I'm not interested in this. You're probably giddy as hell to tell someone who isn't Dion or me for the first time in years, but I'm not. This was years ago, Mom. Get over it. She's not her parents. What happened shouldn't affect how you feel about her."

"You're still drunk," his mom concluded.

"Things may be a bit foggy, but that doesn't mean I'm clueless about what you're doing." He dragged us out of the living room and up the stairs. I could hear his mother muttering and trying to say something to Dion, but he only told her that Dakota had a good point.

Unlike Dakota, I was on his mother's side.

I wanted to look at that yearbook.

One more time.

• • •

I was gifted with a dreamless night. There was no activity behind my shut eyelids, my favorite kind of sleep.

Wiping a hand across my groggy eyes on Monday morning, I let out a long yawn. At some point last night, I'd allowed Dakota to sneak into the spare room with me. I didn't know if he was still wasted, but I doubted it. We'd talked about our parents, and I felt relieved to share how I felt about my mother.

I twisted my body. I was in front of Dakota. His left hand somehow remained on my hip despite all the movement.

Before getting into bed with me, he'd discarded his shirt and jeans. They were on the bedroom floor with my shoes and clothes. I wasn't naked. Dakota had lent me some of his clothes to sleep in. I wore his oversized gray sweater and some basketball shorts.

He looked so peaceful asleep. The crinkles between his brows were gone. I was certain this was the first time his permanent scowl had completely dissolved off of his face. I brought the tip of my index finger over a birthmark on his shoulder, outlining it.

"Stop that," he grumbled.

I continued to do it anyway.

Dakota sighed. "I said stop that. I'm trying to sleep."

"But I have a question."

"Okay."

"Who did your tattoo?" I motioned to the one that said his sister's name. "It's nice."

"Thanks. Dion did it." He rolled onto his back. "You know what I just realized?"

"What?"

"Your parents might be worse than mine."

Covering my face, I begged, "Don't remind me. I was hoping that was a fever dream."

Dakota strained his neck to look at me, lowering his head a bit so we were eye to eye. "Hey, your secret is safe with me."

"Thank you," I said, nuzzling closer into his chest. "Wild to think my mom grew up here. She never told me about it."

"I would lie about that, too, if I were her."

I snorted a laugh. "If you were her, then that wouldn't be the only thing you would be lying about . . . God, it makes me hate her so much."

"My sister lied."

It came out of nowhere.

"Diana lied so much, and so well, when she was alive that I never caught on to any of it," he said. "It took me a while to realize that it didn't matter what I did or didn't do. She'd only ever make her own choices. I had no power to change that. And the same goes for your mother. We all have choices, Sylvia. Don't let her choices, be they good or bad, dictate your happiness."

I had never seen Dakota speak so freely about his sister without freezing up and frowning at the sound of her name. My hand floated up to his cheek, and I brushed the pad of my thumb over his cheekbone.

We talked endlessly for the next hour and a half. Nothing serious was brought up. We just enjoyed each other's company, kissing in between laughter. I kept teasing Dakota about the drunk him I'd seen a peek of last night, and he reminded me of the drunk Sylvia he'd seen at Pierson's house.

"You were more of a mess than I ever was," I noted.

"No way. Maybe I said a lot of things I probably shouldn't have said, but at least I didn't go as far as making a move on you. You were all over me after a few drinks. I had to be the gentleman in the equation and rip you off me. You're lucky I never pressed charges."

"That's a lie. You did not rip me off you!"

"Yes, I did. You were very handsy. Do you know you've got this tendency to touch my stomach any time we make out?"

"I do not!"

"No need to be shy. I think it's funny. Especially with how pissed you were at how I ended the kiss."

I shrugged. "I will admit I am a talkative, hormonal drunk. But I'd rather be that than go off spilling secrets like you."

"Secrets?"

"You talked about how Diana le—" I cut myself off. "Loved dancing . . . while sewing those dresses she liked fixing."

"That's not a secret I even knew," he said. "I feel like you're not telling me something."

"Pshaw. I've already told you everything I know."

He got up onto his elbows, gazing down at me. "Sylvia. Be honest with me. That's all I'm asking from you."

Dakota's eyes were so much bluer with him this close, the color of a thousand seas crashing behind his half-slit eyelids. He looked at me with the utmost sincerity. He had no clue what I'd almost hinted at.

I understood that, sooner or later, I'd slip up with my knowledge about Diana's child.

"When I was coming up here, I might have . . . slightly . . . overheard you confessing that Diana left a kid and that you didn't even know the father."

He rubbed his eyes with the heel of his hands, letting a loud breath out. "I can't believe I said that. That conversation didn't cross my mind." Dakota sat upright, bringing me along with him and forcing me to sit up as well. He held both hands on my arms, his expression hard. "Sylvia, you have to promise me you won't tell anyone about that. The ultra-religious people of this town already talk bad about Diana for killing herself—saying it's a sin. If they knew she left a child, they'd insult and disrespect her more in death than they did while she was alive."

"I would never tell anyone." I collected his hands into mine, squeezing them. I hoped that cleared up any doubt he had in his mind. "It's not my secret to share."

"Good."

"Can I ask one thing, though?"

"Yes."

"The school isn't that big. Are you positive you don't know who the father is?"

"It's not that easy to figure out. I love her, but she led a double life. She was not open about who she dated. There are a lot of missing puzzle pieces about what she did before she died. I've tried to narrow it down by using diaries she left behind. She talked about her experiences, the guys she messed with, but she never wrote down names. She just wrote what she did with them or where they hung out. She'd add one small quality about the guy, but that's all.

"I even tried going to some parties to see if I could figure out who they were," he continued. "If she was around, she'd want the dad to be involved in the kid's life. That's what she was trying to do before she died."

That explained why Dakota had gone to Beth and Adam Greer's party. He already didn't like being associated with them. It made sense that he'd snuck into the party just to get a lead on who the father was, talking with Diana's old crew.

"The closer I got, though, the more Malik and Pierson shut me out. They obviously didn't want me anywhere near their friends." Dakota rested his arm on the headboard, relaxing his shoulders. His eyes were fixed on some point above my head, but he never looked directly at me when he spoke. "No matter what I tried, I couldn't get any solid clues."

It pained me to see him like this. The defeat and internal turmoil shone clear in his eyes. It was hurting him to not know what she'd done during that year. There were obvious gaps in the story that still confused me, but I kept them to myself.

"Dakota, if there's anything I can do to help, I will," I said and tangled our fingers together on the bedsheets. "It doesn't matter what it is, I'll try to help."

He smiled weakly. It was a half-smile, but it was a hell of a lot better than the frown he'd been showing off moments ago.

There was hope.

•••

Around 7:00 a.m., Dion called us downstairs for breakfast. Dona hadn't kicked me into the street yet or cursed me because of my parents. Color me shocked. She was quite kind, talking to me as she handed me my plate of steaming food.

Jiménez had stayed over, too, in another room on the first floor. There were four of us sitting around the table when Dion appeared at the entrance of the kitchen with a child in his arms. He placed her in the high chair at the head of the table.

I tried not to make eye contact with the baby. Children always made me nervous. They cried and cried, and I got more stressed out with every passing second. I applauded any parent out there who could handle children without losing their minds.

"Do you remember much of what you did last night, Dakota?" Jiménez asked while walking to the coffee pot. He poured himself a cup and sat back at the table.

Dakota winced. "I wasn't blacked out. I remember."

Smiling, I said, "You said some . . . interesting things."

"Can we pretend none of that happened?" Dakota groaned and turned to the infant, letting her wrap her tiny fingers around his thumb. "Don't you agree with me, Ophelia? We should drop it and talk about something else."

Dona left after she finished her meal, so it was just the four of us plus Ophelia at the table. The conversation felt forced at times, but Jiménez aided the cause by talking about their gig the other night. Dakota had apparently jumped into the crowd, swinging like a madman, and tried to encourage a mosh pit.

"With that kind of attitude, you'll get us kicked out of every appearance we make," Jiménez said. "You need to calm down on the craziness. Focus on the music."

"No one takes us seriously. We might as well have fun," Dakota said.

"Well, yeah," Dion agreed. "With the kind of band name you guys have, no one will ever take you seriously. What kind of name is Dakota and the Pull-Out Methods anyhow?"

"It's an amazing name. It won't change," Dakota protested. "Every single one of our band members were unexpected pregnancies."

I let out a loud, clear laugh. "That's ridiculous. You need to change that—pronto."

He faced Ophelia again. "You like that name, don't you? Your momma liked it and thought it was funny."

"Hey," Dion barked and gestured to me.

"She already knows." Dakota went back to playing with Ophelia.

"I knew it!" Jiménez exclaimed. "Great, now we're ultimately screwed."

Dakota waved him off. "She's not going to tell anyone."

"Yes, she will. You said she's friends with Pierson and his friends. I know she'll tell people," Jiménez sneered, putting a toothpick between his lips. "It's a waiting game now to see when she'll spill the beans."

"First of all, I will not be telling anyone Ophelia is Diana's daughter," I began. "Second of all, stop acting like Sylvester Stallone from the movie Cobra and take that toothpick out of your mouth. You look weird. You've only had coffee for breakfast. What can you possibly be picking at?"

This remark was only for Jiménez.

Everyone was silent for a heartbeat, then they erupted into laughter. Jiménez even laughed along, and it sounded genuine. However, he didn't take the toothpick out of his mouth.

Once everyone settled down again, Jiménez started talking. "Dakota, why don't you have her fill in for the plan?"

"What? No. I'd never get her involved in that," Dakota snapped. "Besides, she's not even on speaking terms with Pierson or his friends."

Jiménez shrugged his shoulders. "That can be changed."

"I don't want him anywhere near her," Dakota argued. "How many times do I have to tell you guys this? I feel like I've said it a million times."

"She can be our key inside."

"What plan are you talking about?" I asked.

I wished later I hadn't.

Chapter Thirty-Seven

Control

"Dakota has this idea. He wants to get back at Pierson," Jiménez announced.

"Oh, don't give me all the credit. It's more your idea," Dakota replied.

"Can someone tell me what the idea is already? I can't tolerate this whole back-and-forth thing much longer," I blurted. "It's getting annoying."

It was too early in the morning. I hadn't consumed any caffeine. I'd only pushed around the food on my plate, hardly eating. I wasn't in the mood for the lack of answers I was getting.

Jiménez sat up with his elbows propped on the table. "We've been trying to brainstorm ways to crack that cult of theirs at Crescent Hart Academy. I can't put my finger on what's going on, but a few of my buddies have our suspicions. We need someone to get close enough to the group."

"And what?" I stared at them, stunned. "Get myself killed while trying? No, thank you. I'm not interested in being your little spy."

"There's no risk of you getting killed. They aren't involved in anything illegal," Dakota said. "There are a few strange incidents we want explanations for. Some of it links back to what Diana was getting herself involved in."

"What was Diana involved in?"

"Your guess is as good as mine, Sylvia." He fell back in his seat. "We think Pierson and his friends know what Diana's last few days consisted of. And who the father of her kid might be."

I rushed to ask, "If I did agree to help . . . not saying that I do . . . but if I did, what is it you'd want me to do?"

"I think we should use you as the seductive bait to get closer to Pierson. We believe he's the ringleader, the main guy holding the answers to our questions."

"No," Dakota protested. "Not happening. He's not getting anywhere near her."

"It's harmless flirting, my guy. Chill out," Jiménez said. "They can both keep their clothes on. You won't have to sacrifice much."

"I said no," Dakota snapped, wrapping a hand around my waist. "I don't like the sound of this idea."

"I agree with Dakota," I added. "I don't have any interest in flirting with Pierson."

"I'm not asking you to give him a lap dance, princess," Jiménez explained. "I'm only saying entertain the guy enough so you can search his room and bug his laptop."

"What do you know about bugging a laptop?"

Jiménez lowered his brows at me, amused. "Sylvia, when I was in junior high, I broke down firewalls for websites for fun. I can bug an electronic device without breaking a sweat."

"What's the purpose behind bugging his laptop?"

"By doing that, I can access his activities, maybe look at old emails to see if there are clues or hints, and I can also activate the webcam."

"Ew, you want to watch him? That's creepy."

He calmed my nerves by shaking his head. "Not in a sexual,

Peeping Tom kind of way. It's turned on, recording him, whenever the camera is being used. If he's going on a video call, then so are we."

"I don't know," I admitted. "I feel kind of wrong invading his privacy."

"This is our only way in."

"There's gotta be something else you could do," I said, shaking my head. "Can't you just hack his email or something like that?"

Jiménez ran his hands through his hair, sighing deeply.

"I could try—emphasis on the word try—to limit it to having my computer screen mirror his."

"That doesn't sound as bad."

I was mostly trying to convince myself. Taking in a slow breath, I said, "If you're able to do that, then I think I'll be okay with it."

"They didn't exactly paint out the entire picture for you." Dion shook his head and took his plate to the sink. "The plan these two constructed requires the bait to interact with Pierson for a long period of time, slowly uncovering information. It's a full-time job. It doesn't just stop after one meeting."

"Also, you'd have to break off whatever you and Dakota are doing," Jiménez added, winning a glare from Dakota. "It's nothing personal, man. I'm just saying keep it on the down-low and don't let Pierson know about it. Maybe make it seem like you guys aren't cool with each other anymore when you're on school grounds."

Dion snapped his fingers, nodding in agreement. "That's a good idea."

Why was Dion involved in this? Wasn't he supposed to be the mature one in the equation? Why wasn't he telling them to not bug some jock's laptop?

Dion really sucked at being the adult here.

"You don't have to do it," Dakota reminded me. "No one is pressuring you."

"But it would be very, very helpful if you did this," Dion added. "It's been eating me alive not knowing what happened to Diana."

"Diana's dead," Dakota boomed. "Get over it."

Three sets of eyes were staring back at me, not including Ophelia. She was currently knocked out in her high chair, with saliva dribbling down her tiny chin. I wished I were her right about now. She didn't have the same problems I was being faced with.

"I'll help." I tapped Dakota's knee, hoping he'd respond, but he pushed me off. "What's wrong?"

"I didn't ask you to do that for me." He walked out of the room. Everyone looked at him as he stormed out of the house. Reluctantly, I trailed after him.

"A thank you would've been nice," I said, hugging myself against the cold morning air. "You know, this is partly for you too. Don't you want to know what happened to Diana?"

"Of course I do. That's not up for debate." He stopped a few feet ahead of me on the dirt path toward the black, creaking gate. "Simply because I want to know doesn't mean I want to deal with seeing you walking around with Pierson like . . ."

"Like what? Like I'm dating him? Why would you care, Kota? You're not involved with me. You're not involved with anyone from what you keep telling people."

"I don't want you being a part of this plan."

"They do, though."

"You're not flirting with Pierson or dating him."

"Or what?" I challenged, pouting my lips in a mocking way. In a teasing voice, I taunted him for what he was telling me. "Are you going to get mad? Are you going to beat him up if I flirt with him?

Guess what? You don't own me, and if I want to be a part of this plan, then I'm going to be. I'm not yours to control. I'm not even your girlfriend. Your opinion doesn't hold value for me in the way you think it does."

"You... you're right. You're not my girlfriend," he repeated. His shoulders relaxed, and he took a step closer to me. "But you are the first girl I've cared about in a long time. Isn't that enough for you? It's going to kill me inside if I see you with him. We started figuring out what... this is only recently."

I shivered, enveloping myself in his words like an embrace. A cure to my thirst, and possibly the start of my own fall. I decided to believe him.

My eyes closed. "You don't need to feel threatened by him."

"I'm not in the least bit threatened."

It was clear that he was. Just to be safe, I added, "I'm not into Pierson."

"Do you find him attractive?"

I didn't speak.

Dakota shut his eyes. "Answer the question, Sylvia."

"Why does it matter if I find him attractive or not? It doesn't change how I feel about you."

His eyes stabbed into me. He was yelling. "Answer the damn question, Sylvia! Stop avoiding the question!"

"I'm not avoiding it!" I matched his scream. "I don't find him attractive."

"You're lying. Be honest, Sylvia."

"Are you kidding me? I am being honest."

"No, you aren't."

"Yes, I am. I have feelings for you, Kota. I want to be with you. Only you."

"Why can't you just be honest with me?"

"You know what? I don't need this. I don't need you!" I forced a laugh and turned back to the house. "I was kind enough to offer my help, but you always find a way to piss me off in the end. Despite me being on your side, you're too stubborn to see that."

I managed to get upstairs and back to the spare room without him saying anything to me. I started picking my things up off the floor and throwing them onto the bed. The bedroom door shut behind me.

I heard the clicking of the lock.

"Get out, Dakota. I need to get dressed."

He pressed his back against the doorframe. Something about his still stance told me he wasn't going to move anytime soon. "We should talk about this before you run off."

"That's what we were doing on your front lawn. We were talking."

"No, we were arguing."

"Same thing," I grumbled.

"Sylvia . . ." He expelled a tired breath. I should be the tired one. "That wasn't healthy."

"You know what was more unhealthy? You not listening to me."

"I'll listen now."

I paused. "Give up, Dakota. I mean, who are we fooling? I don't think I can do this much longer."

"What are you talking about now?" He peeled himself off the doorframe and walked to my side, sitting down on the unmade bed.

I stopped reaching for my clothes, knowing what I was about to say was going to hurt me more than it was going to hurt him. "I'm talking about us."

Chapter Thirty-Eight
Pillow Talk

"You're not saying what I think you're saying."

It was all Dakota said, sitting so calmly on the bed with his eyes on me. I wasn't looking at him anymore. I just couldn't. But I could feel his eyes boring holes in the back of my head.

I swallowed a dry breath. "I think it's for the best."

"Is that what you honestly think or do you know? Because there's a huge difference."

"You don't need to get loud with me." I was still not looking at him. "Take a moment and listen to me. We're always fighting. Give me a day where we aren't at each other's throats."

"This morning."

I scoffed. "I said give me a day. That's only a few hours."

"Well, it was going fine until you started this."

"Of course it's my fault. It's always my fault, isn't it?"

"I'm sorry. That was wrong—"

"Don't you see it? It's right in your face. Normal people don't fight like this."

"Yes, they do. They do it behind closed doors so no one can see them," he elaborated. "Everyone gets into arguments."

"I wasn't trying to say they don't. But this isn't the same. I can't think back on one entire day where you didn't tick me off or where I didn't make you mad. That's not normal."

"No one is normal," he stated. "That's such a subjective thing to argue about. What one person finds normal may be abnormal to someone else. There is no single definition of normality. It's different for all of us, depending on our culture, our upbringing, and lots of other variables."

"You know what I mean. It's not productive. It's abusive."

"I'm not continuing this conversation until you look at me."

"No."

"Sylvia, turn around. If you want to stop arguing and have an actual conversation, you're going to have to look at me."

I didn't look at him.

"I said turn around!"

I threw the shirt I had in my hands down onto the floor and finally faced him. "Are you always so controlling? Is this how you were with Carmen? No wonder she ran off with Hanan."

His eyes squeezed shut, and he took in a strained breath. "You did not just say that."

My hand flew to my mouth. "I'm so sorry—"

"You basically said I deserved to be cheated on."

"I don't know where that came from." I shook my head and stepped away from him. The words had catapulted out of me before I could stop them. I was angry; he was angry. My mind was never in the right place when I was with him. "You pissed me off."

That was all it took to light to the fuse. Suddenly, Dakota's eyes fluttered open, and he was back on his feet again. "You're blaming me? You're unbelievable. Since we're taking low blows, I might as well do the same."

I stumbled back. "What are you talking about?"

"You've been here long enough. Word spreads. I don't know the details, but apparently you didn't move to California to get close with your dad. You were expelled from your old school. You had some issues with students, and especially some parents. It isn't clear why, but I must say, I am impressed." He began to clap slowly. "It makes sense why you've already got a long, long list of enemies at Crescent Hart. It's like you have a talent for making people hate you. Tell me, Sylvia. What's your secret? I want to know how you do what you do."

"Nice try, but I'm not offended by that comment. Mainly because it's coming from someone like you. You've got a larger hate club than me. It's so massive it fills up this entire county."

He snickered. "I'd take that any day rather than a father who can't keep his junk in his pants. I'm sure you've got little half-siblings running around this whole state. You're an idiot if you think Tara was the first and only mistress."

"I already knew that. My dad's a gigolo."

It felt so wrong to laugh, but I did.

Dakota wasn't expecting that.

His silence only made me laugh even more.

The laughter spread uncontrollably. I hadn't realized what I was doing until I felt tears running down my cheeks. And they weren't from laughing so hard.

I slid my back against the wall and crumpled to the floor. My hands shielded my face, waiting for his menacing laughter to begin. Dakota seemed like the kind of jerk who laughed at emotional people. I was merely waiting for the inevitable.

"Are you . . . crying?"

He lowered himself to the floor and went to touch my face.

"Are you really crying from what I said?"

I slapped his hand.

"Sylvia . . . " His voice grew quiet as he glided his thumb over my fallen tears. "I didn't mean to make you cry. I'm sorry, doll."

"No, you aren't." I hadn't looked at him yet. I knew he had a smug look on his stupid face. I just knew it. "Why aren't you laughing? It's hysterical, isn't it?"

I looked up at him. What I saw wasn't what I was expecting. Concern washed over his features. The scowl I knew from memory was nowhere to be seen.

"I would never laugh at you for crying," he promised. "I think you make me out to be worse than I actually am."

"I could say the same to you." I sniffled. "I've been trying to convince you to like me since day one."

"Hey now." Dakota caught another tear with the pad of his thumb, quirking a smile. Placing a hand over his heart, he said, "I'm a changed man."

I returned the smile.

I didn't know how we had gotten to this moment. It was obvious that the storm had passed, and we were left with the aftermath of its damage. I had to find the willpower in me to want to pick up the pieces.

He moved from his crouched position in front of me on the floor and sat down. By bending his legs and planting them at my side, he made a sort of bridge over my extended legs.

Dakota wiped off the last of my tears. He didn't move away, instead holding my face in his hands. "We're going to need to talk. Why were you crying?"

"You'll think it's stupid."

"No, I won't."

I sucked in a breath. "With all of the shouting, it ... it reminded me of my parents. I thought of how scared I am that I'll end up like them. I'm practically destined to be in a messed-up relationship like theirs."

"That's not going to happen. Your parents' mistakes won't be your own. You're an individual separate from them."

"You don't get it, Kota. There was zero trust by the end of their marriage. What really messed my mom up wasn't the fact that he was cheating. I think she'd be a lot better if that was all. He'd cheated before Tara when I was a kid. I didn't see it then—I was only nine. But now, looking back, I can tell that it wasn't the first time with that woman either. But what was so different with Tara was that my mom could see my dad changing, becoming more responsive, listening to her. At first, she thought it was her doing, but after we found out about Tara, Mom knew it wasn't because of her at all. He was changing for another woman. She'd tried so hard to tame him, I guess, but with no luck. Dad didn't like going on family outings, but he does now. He didn't like taking vacations, but now he flies Tara to all sorts of different countries and states. I know I'd be crushed if I found out someone was changing for another person after all my failed attempts."

Dakota refused to accept this. "People don't change for others. You can only change for yourself. I know that for a fact. You can try all you want, but people won't see the benefit of doing something different unless they're willing to do it for themselves."

"No, I think our actions can help open their eyes to what they're doing."

"How long will that work?" He didn't wait for me to respond. "Hours? Days? Weeks? However long it might be, that influence will fade, and old habits will come back."

"That's so pessimistic."

"So are the rest of my beliefs." He reached over and smoothed his finger across my jawline. "But with you around, I'm starting to feel optimistic about the future. About myself. Perhaps I'm partly wrong. People can change. But only if their heart is open to it."

I shuddered at his warm, assuring touch, full of longing and loneliness. Moving my head into his hand, I plopped a kiss in the center of his palm. I lifted my eyes up to his. It took everything in me to not close that distance, meet our lips, and seal the day with a kiss. I knew I wasn't the only one who thought that, because he cupped my face and kissed me.

He didn't rush to take off my clothes, and I didn't race for the buckle of his belt. It wasn't like what you'd expect with us both so close to each other. It was a slow-burning kiss, sweet and hot, breathtaking enough that it almost hurt when it ended. There was an unattainable part of Dakota still shut off. It was like no matter what I did, there would always be a portion of him that wasn't up for grabs.

That was the day I officially saw Dakota as a challenge. Desperately, I needed to know what made him so guarded and closed off from everyone who tried to care for him. I wanted to disarm him.

●●●

The rest of the week passed uneventfully. Other than Monday, Tara drove me to school most days. When she didn't, I walked to campus with Hanan. Malik remained a pain in my ass. Finn and I got a bit closer after the three of us—Ronnie, me, and her boyfriend—studied for a chemistry test together. I still had iffy feelings about him. Men with nice, thick eyebrows are usually questionable.

Jiménez relentlessly tried to convince Dakota to let me into their plan. It took time, but Dakota finally caved to the idea.

But today was different than any other day this semester.

On November 5th, going into the winter season, we conjured up a scenario that would fool Pierson into thinking I hated Dakota.

Today was vital.

Nothing could go wrong.

"I don't like this plan," Dakota said outside the cafeteria. He had pushed back this little scene we had planned out for as long as he could manage. "I think we should do this at lunch tomorrow."

"Tomorrow's Saturday, doofus," Ronnie reminded him. "It's a good plan. Don't sweat it."

"You think it's a good plan because you thought of it," Dakota countered. "It's so overdramatic and unrealistic. I doubt anyone will believe us."

"Yes, they will," I said, patting his back. "We've got this."

He glared at me. "I don't know why you had to bring Ronnie into all of this, Sylvia."

"I'm her best friend. I'm involved in anything she's involved in," she answered for me.

"I wasn't aware you guys were a package deal." He fixed the collar of his shirt. "Are you ready to do this?"

"I've been ready since last week," I said with a shot of excitement. "You're the one who's been backing out each time we try to start."

Dakota raised his hands. "All right, all right. Relax. I'm ready."

He took another set of deep breaths, and we walked into the cafeteria. Ronnie stayed back at the entrance. Once we got closer to the first row of tables, I made my first move and grabbed Dakota's hand. Like we'd planned, he shook me off.

"Don't touch me. I'm still not okay with what you did the other night—"

"Louder," I whispered from the side of my mouth. There was

no way people would be able to hear him. No one would notice us with how he was practically mumbling his lines. "And more ticked off."

Dakota grumbled softly.

I went to grab his hand for a second time, and like before, he shoved it.

"Don't you dare touch me, Sylvia. I'm still not okay with what you did the other night."

I faked a whining noise. "I'm sorry."

To give it an extra touch, I forced my eyes to water. All it took was a few sad thoughts regarding middle school. Soon enough, I was bawling.

"Wow, you're crying. How pathetic. You aren't allowed to do that, Sylvia."

"I never wanted to hurt you," I said, wiping my cheeks. "It was never my intention to—"

"Save it!" Dakota shouted. "Save it for someone who cares about your pathetic self. And guess what? You won't find that sympathy from me. I'm done with you."

A row of students at the nearest table started staring at us, tuning in on the show unfolding before them. Perfect. The rest of Ronnie's script wasn't any kinder.

Dakota took a step closer, pointing his finger at me. "I have no clue what I saw in you in the first place. Maybe I was just hoping you'd be easy."

"Please, I genuinely doubt anyone here wants to sleep with the knockoff version of Eli Goldsworthy from Degrassi."

"You're lucky I don't get that reference."

"I wouldn't expect someone as dumb as you to know anything about good TV."

"Leave me alone!"

Dakota walked off as more people started watching us.

"No, you're not going to just run away like that!" I chased after him and grabbed for his arm. Just like how we'd rehearsed, he held on to my shoulders.

"What don't you get? You mean nothing to me. You look stupid running after me like this." He shook my shoulders. "Wh—"

"Step away from her," someone said from the left of us. We both turned—and just as we'd hoped, there was Pierson. His hands were balled up in fists at his sides. I spotted his usual entourage, Doug and Hanan, a step behind him. "I'm warning you, Ridgewood."

"Stay out of this, Pierson! It doesn't involve you," Dakota shouted.

"You're making me get involved in this. Now, before you do anything you regret, get your hands off of her."

Dakota scoffed. "Or what?"

"Do what he says," Doug replied. "No one needs to get hurt."

"I'm not taking orders," Dakota said, and he looked back at Pierson. A glimmer of something new sprang into his eyes. His hands dropped from me, like they were supposed to. But what he did next wasn't part of the script.

Dakota spat. Right into Pierson's left eye.

That wasn't supposed to happen.

"Ooh, looks like you've got a wee bit of spit on your eye, lad." Dakota mocked Pierson's accent. That was all he said before Pierson's fist met Dakota's face, hitting him square in the jaw.

Abort mission. I repeat, abort mission.

My mind went into overdrive.

Chapter Thirty-Nine

Just Saying

Dakota lost his balance for a moment. Once he regained it, he looked at how many people he was up against, measuring up his competition. It was three against one: he was outnumbered. Even so, he tried to take a swing at Pierson, but Doug jumped into the fight and pushed him right in the chest. The blow caused him to tumble to the floor. They loomed closer to him—like a pack of hungry wolves going in for the kill—as Dakota struggled back onto his feet.

"Stop it!" I shouted and practically threw myself onto Dakota. "Stop, please!"

A teacher who was supervising the cafeteria caught on to what was going on. Pierson and his friends stepped back from Dakota as she approached us.

"What's going on here?" the teacher asked, lowering her glasses to look at Dakota and me. We were still on the floor. Under her hard gaze, Dakota and I rushed back to our feet and stood before her. No one spoke at first. "I hope you can all explain what's going on."

"Nothing to worry about, Mrs. Logan," Pierson said. "Dakota slipped."

"Yeah, slipped on your fist," I stated. "Be honest."

"What was that?" Mrs. Logan asked, clearly having missed what I'd said. "Can you repeat that? I didn't hear you."

"Nothing," Dakota filled in for me. "I fell. Sylvia was helping me up, but then she fell as well. We're just clumsy."

"Yes. Very clumsy, I see," Mrs. Logan added, examining both of us one last time before facing Pierson and his friends. "I want you to get back to your lunch. It'll be over in fifteen minutes."

"Yes, ma'am," Pierson chimed, linking his arm with mine. "We'll be going. I'll get you away from him." He said those last words softly.

I pulled away from Pierson's touch. Dakota shook his head.

Go with him, he mouthed.

I hated this plan more than he did. I didn't want to be near someone who'd hurt my Kota—

I meant Dakota.

He wasn't mine. What was going on with me?

I followed Pierson and the others. From the looks of it, they were heading to the gymnasium. All the boys had on their athletic wear. My guess was proven right when we took a left in the hallway. Seated against the lockers outside of the gym doors were two very familiar faces: Beth and Xander.

For weeks, I'd averted my eyes and pretended like I didn't see her down the hall. My chest ached, thinking of how the person I used to look forward to talking to had transformed back into a stranger.

The look on Beth's face told me she wasn't surprised to see Pierson showing up at the gym. She was surprised that I was there. I could see the frown on her face consuming the smile that had been there before.

"Hey, Beth," Doug said. His tone was a lot less enthusiastic than

I remembered. I had a hunch that he knew about what she'd done to Pierson at his party. Poor guy. He hadn't realized that he was in love with a psycho.

I had a few questions for her. Most of those questions started with "why," and they were quite repetitive. They all revolved around how she'd pretended to be me. She'd said she was drunk, but the more I thought about it, the more I doubted it. It was both sick and vile, not to mention twisted and extremely wrong.

"Hi, Doug," Beth said meekly. "Hey, Pierson. How ar—"

"Don't bother asking how I'm doing because then I'll feel obligated to ask you the same in return. And frankly, I don't care how you are." Pierson opened the heavy metal gym doors, letting them creak and squeak. "Let's go, guys."

The doors banged shut behind us. There were a handful of other students in the gym, playing basketball on half of the court. Coach Walker was on his phone near the entrance, occasionally looking up to make sure no one went under the bleachers. Hanan and Doug left to pass around a soccer ball in the other half of the gym, leaving me alone with Pierson.

A gnawing feeling started in my stomach. I was hyperaware of the distance between our bodies and the direction Pierson's hands fell when he sat down.

He was smiling. "How have you been? I haven't seen you for ages."

"Are you serious?" I made a face. "You've chosen not to acknowledge me. I'm here every day of the school week."

"Dakota said not to talk to you. And with you guys dating, I didn't want to get in the middle of that."

What? That didn't make sense.

"When I saw that fight at lunch just now," Pierson continued, "I knew I had to step in."

I crossed my arms. Pierson had another think coming if he thought I'd believe that lie. "Dakota did not tell you that."

"Yes, he did. Why would I lie about that?" He pulled out his phone. "I thought I blocked him. But I guess he got a new number. He started texting me like crazy after my party."

I glanced down at his phone, and like Pierson had said, I saw Dakota's number at the top. Pierson hadn't gone as far as saving it in his phone, but I knew the number well enough. The text messages made it clear that he didn't want Pierson anywhere near me.

All this time, Dakota had acted like he didn't understand why Pierson was ignoring me. Now I had proof Dakota had had a part in it. But it still didn't explain why Pierson had made an alliance of people against me. A part of me—quite honestly a silly part of me—wished he would've ignored Dakota's threats and come to me directly about the messages.

"It boggles my mind how you can hang around him without losing your mind. He's a complete and utter waste of space." Pierson stuffed his phone into his pocket. "He's got a few screws missing if he sends messages like that."

I darted him a dark look.

For a second, I forgot the whole plan.

Letting out a low yawn, he asked, "Can I ask you an honest question?"

"Yeah, go for it."

"Is that how you guys act daily? Do you scream at each other, ignoring the fact that you're in public, all the time?"

"No."

"Has he ever done anything more than . . . scream at you? Has he ever done anything violent?"

"Are you asking me if he's hit me?"

"Yes."

"I can assure you that he's never laid a hand on me."

"Well, if there's no physical abuse, then I guess it's emotional abuse."

I unintentionally found myself glaring at him. "Abuse is a heavy word that shouldn't be thrown around. I don't have the most picture-perfect relationship with Dakota, but it isn't emotional abuse."

"That's exactly what someone who has been emotionally abused would say. Denial is the first stage. It's okay. I'm here for you whenever you're ready to admit it." He rested his hand on my shoulder and pulled me into his chest. "I'm here for you, Sylvia. We can get through this together."

"I'm not in an emotionally abusive relationship," I stated louder. I eased backward. "What would make you think that? All because of one argument?"

"There are a lot of things that contributed to me asking what I did and saying what I said. Dakota's dad was known for treating his wife like shit. John Ridgewood only got worse once he found out about the other guys she was getting involved with . . . and then there was the fire. People say he was getting back at her for infidelity."

"Wait. Slow down." I gaped at him, wide-eyed. "You're going to have to rewind a bit and tell me what the hell you're talking about because I didn't understand most of what you said. Her husband abused her?"

"Dakota never told you?"

That didn't answer my concerns at all.

"Mostly what I've heard is that it could've been a setup," I said.

"That's a conspiracy theory." He whistled. "There's a lot you don't know, then, and I don't think I'm the right person to tell you."

"Don't be silly." I touched his arm. "You can tell me."

"No, honestly, Sylvia, it's best if you ask someone else … I don't know, maybe your father."

"Why the hell would I ask my dad?"

"He was one of the people involved in the affairs, from what I know."

I refrained the urge to gag. I didn't want to show Pierson my disgust, though. "When exactly did this all happen?"

"I'm not positive. But Dakota's dad lit that big fire six years ago, and he went to prison about five years ago. Do the math."

That lined up perfectly—almost too perfectly—with the window of time when my father separated from my mother.

"My dad is the last person who'd tell me anything."

He shrugged innocently. "Never hurts to try."

"If I ask him, I'm accusing him of cheating on his current wife."

"Ooh, sounds fun. Can I be an audience member?"

"I'll promise you front row seats," I swore, nudging him with my elbow.

Once the bell rang, I left the gym. Pierson, Doug, and Hanan had PE next, so they stayed. I waved goodbye to Pierson and made my way to my next class.

After I turned the corner, I stopped walking.

My ears, nosy as ever, picked up on a plan brewing.

Xander and Beth were at their lockers, talking too loudly for me to not notice. Beth looked sad while rummaging through her open locker, searching for a textbook.

"I don't want to go, Alex."

"I didn't ask you if you wanted to go," he countered. "Franklin invited you."

"That doesn't mean I'll say yes."

"I said yes for you. You can thank me later at your wedding."

She slammed her locker shut. "I'm not interested. He's only going to push my limits and ask for more. I know I don't have any evidence that he's a part of the Senior Salute, but I have a feeling that he is."

"Who cares if he's a part of it? Most guys our age are. Trust me, you'll like him a lot more once you get to know him."

"He's not my type. You know that, Alex."

"Oh, I'm sorry I couldn't get Pierson for you. The only time he'll give you the time of day is if he's half responsive and thinks you're Sylvia. I must admit, that was a wild plan."

She hushed him. "Shh. People are still around. Can you be quiet?"

They wandered off down the hall, away from where I was standing. I hit my back against the wall, trying to digest what they had said. The only useful information I had gotten from them was that there was some kind of group called Senior Salute.

After last period, I met up with Dakota and Jiménez, and we all walked over to a pizza place close to the school so I could tell them what I'd learned. I had lied to Tara and told her I had a study session at the library and that she should wait about an hour and a half before picking me up.

We settled into a vacant booth with red leather cushions and checkered detailing on the tabletop. Other than the tacky wallpaper and the obnoxious pop music playing over the loudspeakers, I didn't mind this place all that much. By the time our food arrived, I'd told the entire story to Jiménez, along with the eavesdropping I'd done at Beth's locker.

"Are you a thousand percent sure they said Senior Salute?" Jiménez asked, his mouth full of cheese pizza.

"I'm more than a thousand percent sure," I answered. "They said something about how Franklin might be a part of it. But then Xander said most guys our age are a part of it anyway. What's Senior Salute?"

"Senior Salute is something that hasn't been done at our school since my mom went there," Dakota explained. "It was a group of senior boys who challenged each other when it came to the dating scene. There was this abhorrent system based on how many points you earned for each thing you did with a girl. At the end of the term, there was a jackpot someone won. When you joined Senior Salute, you added to the pot. Whenever you put a new name down, you added a small monetary contribution. Your dad is the reason they had to stop it. Something happened during our parents' senior year that made them ban the tradition."

"A little sick to call it a tradition." I cringed. "I can't imagine that flying today."

"If it's really back, then we're all screwed," Jiménez announced. "It's a secret who's involved. And not every member knows who's all a part of it unless they're the leader. They do it to make sure there won't be lots of names a snitch can give out."

I set down my pizza down. "What did my dad do back in high school?"

"He took a complete nobody to prom," Dakota said, twirling his empty spoon against the table. "Convinced a girl he was in love with her, slept with her that very same night, and then dumped her in front of everyone in the most humiliating way possible."

"She had to drop out because she got pregnant," Jiménez filled in.

"Do you guys know the woman this happened to?" I asked.

"It was my mother," Dakota said. "And the kid she had was my brother, Dion."

My skin chilled as the realization hit me, putting the puzzle pieces together and realizing that Dakota and I shared a sibling—an older brother I didn't know I had up until this very moment.

"How do you know that's true?" I rushed to ask, choking on air. "Since I got here, all I've heard is rumors on top of rumors—"

"You can ask Dakota's dad in person," Jiménez offered. "Who wants to visit the state penitentiary?"

He must be joking.

My back went straight up like an arrow.

"Shut up." Dakota slapped his hand flat on the table. "I should've never told you."

"Dakota's dad called him the other day from prison," Jiménez filled in, speaking over Dakota's constant attempts to shut him up. "He wants to see him. They're reopening the case."

Chapter Forty

You Don't Know Me

Most of me didn't want to know how far my father had gone making Dona Ridgewood think he was in love with her. If I uncovered the truth on my own, I'd digest it better—or at least that was what I would like to think. I was reeling at everything that had come to light since I'd come to this horrible town.

I was developing a deep dislike for this place—along with the people who polluted these streets. Still, I knew I wouldn't trade this life for what I'd endured in Maine anytime soon. The drama here was at least bearable.

I choked on my pizza. "I don't want to go to jail."

"I wouldn't blame you. I don't want to see that guy either." Dakota snorted.

Swallowing my food, I asked, "Wait. If Beth and Xander were talking about there being a Senior Salute this year, then who's to say there wasn't one last year? The senior boys could've been involved in Diana's last days. It all connects."

"That could be possible."

"How could we know for sure, though?"

I was stumped.

"That Irish guy might know." Jiménez wiped his mouth with the back of his hand. "When's the next time you'll see Pierson outside of school?"

"In Spanish class today, we agreed to be partners on this project. So, I'll see him at some point over the weekend. I haven't asked my dad for permission to go over there, but I think they'll be okay with it since it's school related."

"You're planning on being alone . . . with Pierson . . . in his house." Dakota took a long, drawn-out pause in between each set of words. "Is his mom going to be there?"

"I don't know. I didn't ask him if she'd be there or not. I mean, she should be there." I shrugged. "I was going to suggest my place. He insisted that we use his place."

"I don't like the sound of any of this." Dakota slammed down his drink.

"You're not okay with anything that has to do with Pierson," I said, growing impatient. "You're at like a ten on the overprotective-o-meter. We need you at like a five."

"She's got a point," Jiménez added. "The fact that you spat in his eye is a sign that you are taking this a little too personally. Anything Sylvia does while she's with him isn't real. You need to relax for a bit."

"Fine." Dakota grimaced. "I'll be cool."

"We should take advantage of the fact that you get to be in his house. It's a perfect opportunity," Jiménez said. "We need to plant the bug in his computer."

Dakota shifted in his seat at Jiménez's suggestion. It involved me getting access to Pierson's laptop and cell phone. I didn't know why Dakota was so against the plan. He was even more against it than I was.

I agreed with his friend. "I'll do it."

"Enjoy having control of someone else," Dakota said out of nowhere. "I'm not that easy to control."

"What are you going on about?" Jiménez asked.

"I'm not seeing my dad," he announced. "I don't care how many times you ask me."

This was clearly a conversation I hadn't been part of from the beginning.

Jiménez snapped his fingers, inching closer to him. "Give me a month."

"No. Not happening. Not in a million years."

They got closer in the middle of the table.

"How about in a year?"

They were staring each other down.

"I'll give you a minute—to get a mint," Dakota barked. "You stink. Pay more attention to your dental hygiene or you'll end up dying from gum disease before you can convince anyone to do anything else."

I laughed, looking at the two of them. I allowed the sensation to move in like a low tide and settle in my bones. I would miss this—their faces, their harsh demeanors— if I ever lost it.

Despite the encounters I'd had early on, burning my fingers on pretty flames, I was beginning to find my footing in these streets.

To calm the growing power of the waves inside me, rumbling on about the unknown, I reminded myself that I had no real relation to the Ridgewoods.

Writing it off as fiction, I blocked out the information like words on a page, dismissing their existence as an editorial error.

Rather than the cruelest joke of all time.

•••

After we polished off our drinks and devoured our pizza slices, Dakota took me back to school. Jiménez hopped in his car, planning on meeting up with me before I went to Pierson's house. He needed to give me the equipment. Then, and only then, could I become fully transformed into a super-secret double agent.

By mistake, I'd left one of my textbooks in my locker. To do my homework this weekend, I had to get it. Dakota and I snuck back on campus to retrieve it. When I opened my locker door, Dakota began clear his throat.

"You know, you can back out whenever you want to."

"I'm aware," I said, pushing some things in my locker. "I know what I'm getting myself into. It's you who doesn't like the sound of it. You'll have to get used to it."

"I don't want to get used to it."

"You're going to have to. It's only the first day."

"That should be a red flag that we shouldn't be doing this." He stroked his hand to my face, trailing his fingers over my cheek. Catching loose strands of hair, he softly pulled back. "How about instead of going to his place on the weekend, you come over to mine? Dion is going to San Fran to visit his old college friends. I'll be alone at his apartment."

Lugging out my math book, I shut my locker. "Keep talking. You've got my attention."

"Saturday night is taken up by this gig Jiménez signed us up for. But I could pick you up during the day. We could drive over to Dion's before the show." He snaked his hands around my waist and drew me in, pressing his lips to the hollow of my neck. I knotted my fingers around the nape of his neck. Out of habit, I bit the inside of my cheek. He swiped his lip up to my face and started a path of sweet, soft kisses across my jaw. "We can entertain ourselves."

"How are we supposed to get away with that? It's not like you can drive up to my house and pick me up."

"Why not?"

It took every ounce of strength to pull back and look at him. "You can't be serious. Don't you remember the last time you picked me up? If you came by, my dad would see your car pull up, and he'd bolt the doors shut. Also, as much as I like this bright idea of yours, my grades are more important."

He took this to heart. "You're ditching me for homework?"

I started to make my way to the student porch. "I'm passing my Spanish class with a B. I'd like to maintain that grade for as long as I can manage. First-semester grades are important when I apply to colleges."

"I'm a hundred percent certain that you'll have a lot more fun with me than learning about how to conjugate verbs with Pierson." Dakota set his hand on the small of my back and pecked my cheek. He didn't move right away. "I'm in a very giving mood. If you know what I mean."

I brought my hand up and moved his big head away from my ear. "You're trying a little too hard to persuade me . . . It's not working."

"Maybe I can change your mind before your group project."

"We'll see about that," I said, pushing the main doors open. Tara was pulling into the lot. I noticed Dakota step behind me and stay inside the school as I hurried down the steps toward the car.

The moment I got into the car, I wanted to get off my chest the plans I had for the weekend. I mentioned the study session with Pierson. Adding Ronnie's name into the mix, I embellished more in the hopes that I could get another sleepover out of them.

Tara pushed her black-tinted glasses up the bridge of her nose, blocking out the strong sun. "I'll talk to your father about it."

• • •

Just as she had promised, Tara relayed my plans to my father. He was okay with me hanging out with Ronnie for the weekend, stating that he wanted a call or text from me that night.

Before I headed out on Saturday, I stuffed a change of clothes into a bag alongside my schoolwork.

Pierson's home wasn't far from mine.

When I got to his house, I knocked three times. I counted. After fifteen seconds, the door was yanked open. A slender woman wearing loose-fitting jeans and a flowy blouse greeted me at the door.

"You must be Sylvia." Pierson's mom stretched out her hand and took mine, firmly shaking it. "I'm Siobhan. Come on in. We were about to have some lunch. Do you like tuna? I made tuna melts for you kids."

I followed her into the dining area. "I'd love some. Thank you."

My bag was left on the tiled floor, leaning against a wall.

Without a large cluster of teenagers roaming around the house, I could appreciate the beauty of the place more.

A picture near the dining table caught my full attention. It was a sports outing. From the equipment they had, I could tell they were members of the lacrosse team. I got up from my seat and grabbed it off the shelf.

"How old is this photo?" I asked.

"It's from the end of sophomore year," Pierson said, coming up behind me. He took the picture from me to look at it. "The members have mostly stayed the same. Except for the ones who graduated. It was back when Dakota was still playing."

"Oh, I haven't heard you say Dakota's name in so long. Dakota... Dakota Ridgewood, wasn't it?" his mother chimed. "Aren't you friends with him? You never have him around anymore. You should invite him more often."

"Mum, I told you why he hasn't been around in a long time." Pierson returned the photo to the shelf. "I'm not friends with Dakota. He quit the team and got all melodramatic after his sister died. He turned into a complete prick."

"That's no way to speak about a friend." His mother shook her finger at him. "You should ring him up."

"No, Mum. I will not." Pierson grabbed the photo and moved it into the small wastebasket near the entrance to the kitchen.

His mother shrieked at the cruel act. "Oh, but I thought that was such a nice photo."

"It's better in the trash." To me, Pierson asked, "Did you know he was on the lacrosse team?"

"No," I said feebly. "I didn't know you guys were friends either."

"You must not know a lot about him, then. He was my first friend when I moved here."

Part III
The Ugly

How foolish was I . . .

To say I couldn't live without your attention?

I used to write about us with so much affection.

The anchor of my heart sinks into your shore,

Basking in your glorious glow.

I find myself swinging in your water,

Getting lost in your sea.

The ocean is a metaphor,

For your longing for me.

Oh, look at how fast we have fallen.

Far

Far

From where I am recalling.

I see the errors in my ways,

For placing such pressure on you.

Because in the end,

The greatest lesson you taught me,

Has left an everlasting impression on thee.

The only one who will save me,

Love me,

Cherish me,

Will always be . . .

Me.

—Sylvia Ellington

Chapter Forty-One
Friend Crush

I wasn't in the mood to argue with Pierson. Even though Dakota had his guard up at times, I still felt like I knew him better than any other kid at school. I wouldn't quite say I knew everything there was to know about him, but he wasn't a stranger to me. Knowing that he had been on the lacrosse team seemed like such a trivial fact, like what his favorite pizza topping was or which hand he wrote with. It didn't have much significance to me.

For the most part, I didn't vocalize any of my thoughts to Pierson. Whenever he said Dakota was a lowlife, I remained unfazed. Any time he told me I was better off without Dakota, I tried to bite my tongue. My energy was getting depleted toward the end. I knew if it wasn't for the plan, I would've gone off on him.

Pierson was easily distracted, so I fed into his ego when I knew it could benefit me. For the plan to run smoothly, I needed Pierson to trust me.

Selflessness became my only form of conversational currency. I asked about his other likes and hobbies but never followed up with my own. I insisted he tell me what he missed from back home in Ireland. When it came to Maine and my own homesickness, however, I shrugged it off and rushed to my next question.

About two hours in, we'd finished a good three-quarters of the project for Spanish class. We needed to write a comedy sketch in Spanish about us doing any interesting task.

By the time we wrapped up our project, it was three o'clock, and Jiménez was asking if I had finished my job yet. I needed some space away from Pierson. He and I were working in the living room. It wasn't like I could easily slip out of sight without him knowing.

I texted Jiménez, informing him that I would get to it as soon as possible. Since it was time for me to leave, I told my ride to drive toward Pierson's house. I also reminded Jiménez we needed to pick up Ronnie for the gig later tonight.

When I got a text saying he was five minutes away, I turned to Pierson and set down my textbook. "I need to use the restroom."

"It's up the stairs and to your left," he instructed, pointing in the general direction of the staircase. "When you get back, I want to pick your brain on an idea I have."

"Yeah, definitely."

I got up from the couch, making the short journey up the stairs to the restroom. Peeking over my shoulder to check if the coast was clear, I went cautiously into his bedroom. My heart was pounding in my ears when I shut the door, taking what might well be my last breath.

Guilt was floating through me, intensifying with each agonizing step to his laptop. I turned it on. Following the short steps Jiménez had given me, I put in the flash drive he'd handed me the night before and moved the file saved on it onto Pierson's computer. There was an email Jiménez had sent Pierson as well, but Pierson hadn't opened it.

Luckily, Pierson was logged into his email when I checked. The email Jiménez had sent was spam riddled with bogus information, asking him to open an attachment and fill out a fake form.

Opening the attachment would spread a virus to the computer. Jiménez had said something else would happen that would let him crack into the laptop, something important, but I'd been too bored by the nonsensical lingo he was spewing to really listen to him.

After I was done, I shut down the laptop and exited the room.

I nearly dropped the flash drive when I saw who was across from me, pressed against the wall with his hands deep in his jeans pockets.

Pierson's face tightened. "What were you doing in my bedroom?"

Swiftly, I stuffed the flash drive into my back pocket.

"I . . . uh . . . got lost."

"You were lost for a very long time." He eased off the sky-blue walls and inched forward, towering menacingly in front of me. "Either you tell me the truth or I'm going to take whatever it was you stuffed into your pocket just now."

Okay, so maybe I wasn't all that swift.

Shutting my eyes, I sighed in defeat. My mind buzzed for a lie—any lie. "All right, I'll tell you. I wanted to see the ideas you were talking about downstairs."

While playing twenty questions with Pierson, grilling him about everything under the sun, I'd learned that he wanted to be on the show Shark Tank. In great detail, he'd described a cherished notebook that had all of his concepts and creations inside.

"I doubt that."

Great, he isn't falling for my BS.

I didn't blame him. My lie wasn't convincing.

"No, really, Pierson. I wanted to see if you had a sketch for that . . . that . . . what was that fry idea again?"

"The ketchup Twinkie." He grinned at me, lighting up. "I actually do have a drawing. Wanna see?"

"I do. I can't picture it in my head—so I want to see it."

Pierson bolted to his room, and I went after him. "I don't have a name figured out yet."

"That's always the hard part." I pretended like I understood, making up a question on the spot. "How did you come up with it?"

He was flipping through his cabinets, throwing things out left and right.

"I love Twinkies. It's my favorite American snack."

"Understandable."

"Well, I was at this burger spot near school. You know, Fatburger?" I nodded, and he went on. "When I was eating their huge steak fries, I thought to myself, wouldn't it be nice if there was ketchup syringed into the middle? My plan is, essentially"—he flipped open his red notebook, showing me the prototype—"why not have a hybrid between a Twinkie and a French fry? So then you never have to dip your fry."

I snapped my fingers, hoping he assumed I liked the concept.

After one glance, I fought against the impulse to compare it to Dakota's art. There was no room for comparison. I'd seen children draw better than Pierson. He was waiting with bated breath, though, wanting to know my every thought.

"Do you have questions?"

"I do. If you're deep-frying it," I began, thinking out loud, "wouldn't there be a problem? The ketchup could start leaking out."

"I haven't thought out all the kinks."

His knuckles ever so slightly brushed mine when he dropped his hand to his side. Gradually, his eyes moved up, pausing on my lips. Pierson's gaze stayed there as if he was refraining from doing anything more. Holding back, perhaps, on his impulses.

There was a shift in the atmosphere, and I wasn't all too sure if I liked it or not. The sway in his walk and the movement of his hands as he walked toward his bed were different. When he gestured for me to take the empty seat next to him on the bed, I sat down.

Dakota wouldn't be okay with this.

Dakota would probably lose his s—

It didn't matter how Dakota felt about this. His thoughts should not be the ones worrying me right now. Jiménez had said to him, loud and clear, that whatever I did with Pierson wasn't real. I had no intention of kissing Pierson, so that was off the table. But just enough flirting to get him off my back would help keep this plan from falling apart.

Jiménez and Dakota hadn't voiced their own opinions on who the possible father of Ophelia might be. I had a hunch that it was someone Pierson knew.

The room fell silent. I wanted to kick myself for getting in this kind of situation.

"Can I kiss you?"

It came out of nowhere, completely out of left field and out of the blue. Whatever phrase you can imagine, place it there. I was lost on how we had gotten to this destination.

"You want to kiss me?" I squinted. "Why don't you just kiss me?"

"I want to ask if you would be okay with it."

Is it weird no one has ever asked?

Okay, so maybe one time in middle school.

But each smooch after that (and there weren't many), the guys hadn't asked me before deciding to go in for the kill. I'd been on this earth for eighteen years, and most of my first kisses had been without warning.

With Dakota, there hadn't been a pause for questioning either the first or second time we'd kissed. Did I mind it then? Was I aware of it? I didn't get to think about it much further than that. My heart hurt. I was messing with Pierson, and here he was, treating me better than I was treating him.

"Yes," came out of my mouth. I added, "You can kiss me."

Pierson's focus was now on my body, and his hand moved from behind me to my knee. His face was getting close to mine. I watched with open eyes as he joined our lips.

Pierson held my head in place, attempting to deepen the kiss with his tongue. I shook him off before he could succeed.

"I can't."

I could still taste him on my tongue, and I could see him start to complain. I quickly stated, "I just got out of a relationship, Pierson. I don't want to start anything new. It was wrong of me to say that you could kiss me when my mind is thinking about someone else."

"I wouldn't care . . . as long as you eventually start to forget about him."

I refused to accept his response. "I hardly know you. You should be with someone you know well."

He scoffed. "We know each other."

I entertained the idea.

"If you know me so well, then what's my middle name?"

"Doesn't it start with an E?"

I blinked, genuinely shocked that he knew that. "How did you know that?"

"You told me in Spanish class."

"I did?"

"I'm sorry I don't remember the name. It's Arabic, isn't it?"

"Yeah," my throat tightened. "It is."

Does he know me better than Dakota?

I didn't like the trajectory of this talk. We needed to change it up.

The previous sexual tension was still there, lingering in the air, but I was doing a good job of ignoring it. I hadn't yet processed the fact that he'd kissed me. I needed something to distract me. "If you don't mind me asking, why is your name Pierson?"

"It's my dad's and granddad's name," he replied in a soft tone. "They both ended up being failures in life, so I guess my mum thought it would be a brilliant idea to keep that running in our family by naming me after them."

"Can we switch? I'd rather have failures than cheaters."

"Sure, we can switch. My mum and dad unfortunately never were cheaters."

"Unfortunately?" I echoed.

He smirked. "It's kind of funny thinking back on it now, but when I was a kid I would hope—pray, really—that my mother had cheated on my dad. Because then maybe there was a sliver of a chance that he wasn't my real dad and that there was a cooler dad out there in the world just waiting for me to meet him."

I rested my hand on his broad shoulder. "I know the feeling. I thought the exact same thing whenever I was with my mom. I told myself that I wasn't her kid. The only problem with that idea is I look way too much like her. It's freaky."

He brought his hand up to rest on mine. "Eh, I doubt she was that bad, though. You guys are closer now, right?"

I kept my reply short. My mother was more of a mystery to me than anyone else.

"We're the closest," I lied.

Not very well.

Pierson didn't bother doubting me about that, though.

Chapter Forty-Two

At My Worst

I don't like talking about it.

Not talking about it is the easiest way to pretend it never happened.

Mom's officially home from rehab.

Her fourteen-year-old daughter is back in her life—and she couldn't care less.

"I need some water. Go get me some," Mom orders. "I have to take my medication."

Despite my anger toward her, I reluctantly get up and get her a glass of water. She takes the cup and thanks me, gulping down the pill in her hand and then some water.

The smell of booze is sealed on her lips. She's wearing the clothes she had on the other night, only now there are new stains on the fringe. I wonder how long it will take her to notice that there isn't any food in the fridge and that I haven't eaten since the lunch I got at school yesterday afternoon. I asked my friend Emma to let me have her leftover fruit.

The kids around the table always look at me funny when I ask for food. They make up their own assumptions about why my mom can't pack me a lunch or give me money.

Other kids, like Lola and her gang of friends, tease me about it.

∙∙∙

"You shouldn't let Lola talk to you like that," one of my friends tells me. His name's Ian, and he wears these multicolored suspenders that Lola makes fun of all the time. I think they're cool. The other kids tag team with the name-calling.

As all great rivalries begin, Ian used to be friends with Lola. The tides shifted after summer.

"It's not like I can do anything about it," Ian says. "Four against one isn't a fair fight. The second I walk up to her, her hounds will have their own insults to throw at me before I even get the first word out."

"That's not true." I poke him. "I'll be there. Two against four isn't all that bad."

He nudges me. "I'll have your back. You take on two and I'll take on two."

I shake my head. "Thanks but no thanks. I would like to live to the age of fifty, and if I try to confront her, there's no way I'll live to see the tenth grade."

He chuckles. It's a nice kind of chuckle, the kind that makes you want to laugh along. "Maybe some other time then."

∙∙∙

From that day onward, my friendship with Ian only grows. For the most part, after school, we just hang out at his place or over at the nearby city library.

I'm comfortable with Ian. We can talk about anything and everything under the sun, and we laugh at the same kinds of jokes. Whenever someone tries to corner him at school, I always have his back. He does the same for me whenever I'm in the same kind of situation. He doesn't know what I've gone through, especially when it comes to Mom's problem with sobriety, but he's good at sympathizing and making sure to let me talk when I need it. And with what's going on at home, I need someone like him to talk to.

The good thing about Ian is that he doesn't judge me, no matter what I say to him. He doesn't look at me with disgust, and he never tells me to shut up like my mom does.

That's why, when it feels right, I tell him what really happened that afternoon I found Mom unresponsive.

He doesn't scream.

He doesn't swear.

He's calm.

He places his hand on my shoulder and tells me that everything will be okay.

Right now, it's what I need to hear. What I need to feel. I've been starving for affection for so long that my heart almost bursts when he moves to hug me. I don't want to release him. I hold on to him in fear that he will fade out of existence if I let go.

●●●

There's something off about the gossip that's polluting the halls when I walk into school on Monday. I spot Ian, but he's not standing next to my locker like he usually does most mornings.

He's standing next to Lola and her friends.

His back is to me. He can't see me when I walk up to him.

"... her mom's such a whore. Always out, drinking and doing drugs. Sleeping with anything with a pulse," Ian says, using that laugh of his that I used to like to hear.

"I bet she ends up being an alcoholic like her mom," Lola chimes in. "I wouldn't be surprised if she's already had a taste herself."

"She's like a broken record," Ian complains even further. "Whine, whine, whine. 'I'm so poor.'"

Lola is about to speak, but she stops, finally realizing that I'm standing there with my hands in fists.

The hours we spent together amounted to nothing. Drinking soda until our heads hurt at the local Burger King. Having his mom pick us both up from the one-dollar movie theater. Planning out the life we would have in high school together. Thinking of where in the city we'd live together as newly college-graduated adults.

All those memories crumble into dust at my feet.

Was he ever my friend, or has he been Lola's little spy, leaching information out of me? I don't know, and right at this moment, that is the least of my worries.

Ian's eyes widen when sees me. He tries to explain, but my fist goes for his mouth before he can muster up a lame excuse.

His glasses fall to the floor.

His body follows with a thud.

A teacher witnesses the entire thing.

It isn't long until I'm sent to the principal's office.

I don't care. I don't.

Oh, God. I care so much.

He's the first friend I've had in so long.

The first person I've trusted since my father up and left us for his perfect family in California.

I hope they expel me. They probably won't.

But my stupid, naive, gullible little heart can only pray for it anyway.

Chapter Forty-Three

A Lovely Mess

"How are you feeling?" Jiménez asked me the second I entered the car, a few blocks away from Pierson's house. It was far enough away that he wouldn't be able to see me getting into Jiménez's rust bucket of a vehicle. "You were in there longer than I thought. I've been waiting for you for the last twenty minutes."

I hid my expression by not meeting his gaze and staring down at my phone. "I apologize. I got caught up with installing the flash drive thing."

My hand fished the drive out of my back pocket, and I gave it back.

"Everything synced up right. Don't worry. It worked. I've got full access to his laptop. What took so long, though? You didn't answer me the first time."

"Nothing. Can you drop it?"

"Why?"

Avoiding his question, I pretended to be fascinated by the radio and began fiddling with it. I couldn't see myself telling anyone about kissing Pierson.

Partly because it had felt good.

I was still grappling with what that meant. What exactly had changed? The more I thought about it, the more I kept telling myself I'd enjoyed it to satisfy the lack of attention I was getting from Dakota. Half of me was certain it was the excitement of it all, whereas another part thought I was simply in a temporary drought, clinging to any semblance of affection to quench my thirst.

If I didn't tell Dakota, and he found out some other way, it would backfire, especially with how things had ended with him and Carmen. I needed to be honest.

To help ease my anxiety, I gave Jiménez Ronnie's address. It was in a rough part of town, a bit further away from Harper Falls and near South Emerson. From what she'd said to me, no one at our school really knew where she lived.

On weekends, it was hard to catch Ronnie free because she was usually working over at the supermarket in Boulder Valley. She loved that job as much as she loved Xander. Recently, she'd been trying to keep herself busy since she and Finn had broken things off the week before. She hadn't specified why they'd ended. Ronnie was taking it fine from what I'd seen. I had gone to visit her the day after it happened. Ronnie wasn't the kind of person who would tremble in front of people. She buried her emotions deep inside. I knew she loved Finn, but Ronnie was too headstrong to beg for him back. I hoped they could work out whatever problem they had.

After Ronnie got into the car, we made the long drive down to the venue. I hadn't gone to the city since I'd come to Harper Falls, and I was excited. Considering how tight we were on time, I knew I'd have to do an outfit change once we arrived at our destination.

Jiménez's car made it through the rough terrain, with roads curving between steep, dusty mountains and rolling hills. A train disappeared in and out of the rocky slopes and above treetops. I saw the people inside bustling with blank, emotionless faces, ignoring their surroundings. Ronnie and Jiménez were unaffected by the life blossoming outside their windows, but I was entranced. I didn't know where it came from, but I loved people watching. I adored it even more at this distance, where I could get away with it.

Once we got closer to the city, the hills were replaced by tall skyscrapers and sidewalks that stretched out for miles. I saw the faint outline of the mountains in the background, hidden behind the obstructive buildings.

As we neared the venue, I brought my bag up to my lap. We used the back entrance to skip the long line outside. One of the band members let us in. Jiménez and Ronnie turned one way as we went into the building, going to the dressing room, whereas I was heading toward the restrooms. I already had my ticket, and Dakota had told me they would have my name if I needed to go backstage for any reason.

I didn't know how Jiménez had managed to book them in this place, but that guy seriously had some tricks up his sleeve. The seating area had at least two different levels facing the oval-shaped stage. Dakota's band was in the greenroom, waiting for the show to start. There were only a few people seated or walking around the venue.

I had a hard time finding the restroom. When I finally did, I quickly went into a stall and swapped outfits. After I changed into my red halter top and short skirt, I retrieved my makeup pouch and exited the dingy stall. Once my makeup was applied, I gave myself one final look in the scratched-up restroom mirror.

"Perfect," I said, flattening my hands over my top.

"Sylvia, is that you?"

I turned and saw someone exit a stall and walk to the sink. I wished it was just a rude stranger. But unfortunately, I knew her.

"Leave me alone, Carmen."

I wasn't in the mood.

Carmen turned the sink on and ran her fingers through the water. "I think that top would look better if you lost a little bit of belly fat. By a little bit, I mean a lot. You look three months pregnant."

Gripping the sides of the white sink, I took deep breaths.

I will not let her piss me off. I will not let her win.

I counted up to fifteen. My lucky number. I counted down from fifteen.

"Why are you here?" I asked in a smooth voice. "There's a sign out front that says no animals inside. Did you sneak inside in someone's bag like the bitch you are?"

"Aw, I was almost offended by that comment. Nice try." She squinted at me in the mirror. "Why are you here? Ah, right. You're here because you're dating Dakota . . . oh wait, I mean not dating. I forgot. You guys broke up. Right?"

"Seriously, tell me, why the hell are you here? Are you one of his groupies?"

"Oh, please. If I wanted Dakota back, I could take him away from you. Just. Like. That." She snapped her fingers. "I'm letting you have him. That's my gift to you," she said with a smirk. "Isn't it sad?"

"What?"

"I doubt he ever said you were his girlfriend even in private when you were together." She went for the paper towel dispenser. "When we were together, he always called me his girlfriend in front of friends and family and said, 'I love you.'"

I felt my eye twitch.

"Aww, has he not even said that to you? Poor thing."

"Save your breath for someone who cares."

She took a step toward me, eye to eye.

"Take another step and see what'll happen," I warned. "My bag isn't just full of clothing."

"In all seriousness, though, maybe it's a good thing that he's not with you. Aren't your families supposed to hate each other? You're weird for trying with him. If I were you—"

"I'm not you. Thankfully," I supplied.

"Whatever. I think I've done enough charity work for today by talking to you, Canada."

She crumpled her paper towel and tossed it into my sink. The restroom door swung closed behind her.

My hands were still clinging to the edges of the sink, waiting for my anger to cool.

I counted down and then up again.

It took a while, but I finally calmed down after my tango with the Devil of Crescent Hart Academy.

•••

I didn't have much trouble getting to the greenroom. Once I told them who I was, security pointed me the right way. I thanked them sincerely.

"You're back! Took you long enough," Ronnie teased. We were in a massive room without any windows. Mirrors covered the walls, making the place look larger than it really was. "I thought you were lost for a second there. They were trying to convince me to go and look for you in the crowd as if you were Waldo."

"Sorry about that." I dropped the bag I'd been carrying. "It took me a while to find the restroom. Where's Dakota?"

I didn't feel confident enough to use his nickname around others. As an unspoken rule, using "Kota" was reserved for when we were alone.

Jiménez, Paul, and two of the other band members were here,

but I didn't see Dakota. There was a different group near the door, and a third band sat on the couches in the corner.

"He's talking to someone in the band Bedhead," Jiménez answered, motioning to the group lounging on the furniture.

Jiménez got to his feet and cupped his hands around his mouth. "Hey, Dakota!"

Dakota emerged from the group and came to a halt when our eyes locked, raking his gaze down my outfit. "What are you wearing?"

"Clothes. Like everyone else in this room," I snapped, looking down. "What's wrong with what I have on?"

He walked up to me, still scanning me. "You're not wearing that out there."

"It's a lot better than what she had on before," Jiménez said. "Trust me, Dakota. The getup she had on before looked like she just came back from going door-to-door selling life insurance policies to the elderly."

"Shut up," I hissed. "That's an exaggeration."

"I didn't ask you to join in, man. Stay out of it." Dakota faced me again. "Honestly. What were you thinking? You're going to have to change or wear my jacket over that."

I was laughing—genuinely laughing in his face. "Who do you think you are to say something like that to me? I don't even listen to my parents when they tell me to change out of an outfit. What makes you think I'll listen to you?"

"Ooh. She told you," Jiménez chimed in and snapped his fingers in a Z formation. "She don't need no man bossing her around."

I turned to Ronnie, and she gave me a high five.

Dakota knew there was no way he'd win this argument. "Can we talk about this in the hallway? In private?"

"Sure, but it won't change my mind."

I followed him. When the door closed behind us, I didn't waste any time. "I don't know why you care, Kota. Last time I checked, you're not my boyfriend."

"Stop throwing that in my face. It's only a word. An overused word. What effect does a word have over what I've done or said?"

"Oh, please. You said 'girlfriend' to Carmen when you were together. I bet you used titles all the time."

"How would you know . . ." His head snapped around the hallway. "Is she here?"

"Yes, she's here. Why do you care? Do you wanna meet up with her and have a reunion or something? Rekindle that relationship and tell her you love her again?"

"Wait, what?" He shook his head repeatedly. "Is that what she told you? She's pulling lies out of thin air if that came out of her mouth. I never said I loved her. Half of the reason why we never worked out is because she wanted to push our relationship further and further, when I wasn't ready for it."

My shoulders relaxed. "You never said it to her?"

"No. Never. I've never said 'I love you' to anyone. Well, other than my own family. And I rarely used the boyfriend/girlfriend title with her. Only time I did use it was when she practically forced it out of me in front of others," he revealed. "Look, Sylvia. Whatever she told you, can you forget it and listen to what I'm trying to say? I thought we at least knew each other well enough to not let an ex get between us. All she wants, and all she'll ever want to accomplish by talking to you, is to separate us."

"There's an 'us'?"

I hated how my voice wobbled and almost cracked.

Dakota tucked his finger under my chin. "There's always been an us."

I felt my breathing go heavy when he let the space between us decrease. His lips found mine without much effort. It was the first time we'd kissed in days. After ignoring each other in the hallway, it felt good to have him so close, his hands venturing up and down the sides of my body.

"That was cheesy," I said after I broke the kiss. I moved in again to peck his cheek. "But only a little cheesy."

He wrinkled his nose. "Bad kind of cheesy?"

"There's only one kind." I snorted. "It's okay, though. I won't tell anyone you said that. Your manhood will stay intact."

"About your clothes, though . . ."

I arched a brow.

"Never mind," Dakota admitted at last. "I'll drop it."

"And . . . ?" I waited.

"Sorry. I'm sorry."

•••

Unsurprisingly, Dakota had given Ronnie and me some great seats for the show. We screamed our lungs out when they introduced his band. There were a few funny faces at the sound of his band name. I made a mental note to try to convince him to change it after the show.

Dakota told the crowd who he was and the title of their first song. I wasn't a huge music fan, but I saw the appeal in his singing. It had a good hook, and that was all I paid attention to. Ronnie and I made fools of ourselves, dancing to the music and jumping around without a care in the world. We pretended to sing along to a song we didn't know.

Once they were done with the second tune, Dakota moved his

electric guitar away and pressed his lips back to the mic. "Okay, so we weren't planning on performing these two covers today. Last minute, I decided we should." He swung the guitar back around, and as if he'd known where I was all along, his eyes zeroed in on me, and he strummed the chords. "This is for my doll. I hope the words in these songs better explain things than I ever have. I hope they fit our ever-changing hurricane of a love affair."

Ronnie slapped my arm repeatedly. "I think he's talking about you! He calls you doll? Why didn't you tell me that? I'm offended that I didn't know about this little nickname thing you two have for each other. Can you believe he said that out loud in front of at least two hundred people?"

I hushed her, telling her that I wanted to listen to the song. A big, goofy smile made its way onto my face. The beat was a bit more up-tempo than their other stuff. It was more pop than anything. The lyrics snagged at my heart, describing Dakota in every way. I couldn't have agreed more with the cover.

It was perfect.

We definitely were a lovely mess.

As much as I hated to admit it, that was the day I fell in love with Dakota Ridgewood. I could see myself falling for this confusing boy a hundred times throughout the decades to come, having him learn new ways to make me laugh or piss me off. The scary part, though, was that I couldn't see him ever loving me back as much as I wanted him to.

I would eventually become that woman who gave all of her love to a man who didn't give a damn. The girl who poured her soul out for a boy who hardly cared. The one who never walked away from what was hurting her because she thought it would change and that the boy, sooner or later, would open his eyes, finally realizing how important she was to him. I would be that girl, and I already knew it as if my fate was carved out in front of me.

A tear trailed down my cheek.

"Aw, don't cry." Ronnie moved in beside me and pulled me into a hug. "I'd get emotional too."

She thought I was crying for an entirely different reason.

Chapter Forty-Four

Sullen Girl

It was dark when we left the venue. I hadn't spoken much, keeping to myself as the gig came to an end. Ronnie was aware of my sudden mood change. She suggested going to the overlook she'd talked about before, hoping it would cheer me up. I shook my head and told her I didn't want to go.

In the back of the car as we drove over to Dion's apartment, Dakota tried to start a conversation with me and placed his hand on my leg. I merely shrugged him off and continued to stare out the window. Instead of engaging, I continued watching the trees blur past us and the pedestrians walk by.

"Sylvia?" Dakota sat back. "What's wrong with you?"

"Nothing's wrong with me."

I left it at that, not wanting to start something I couldn't finish.

"Are you mad about something that happened at the gig?" Dakota asked, tilting his head to get a glimpse of my expression. But it was blank, emotionless. A gut-wrenching pain was growing in the pit of my stomach, processing the sad reality that I loved him but couldn't even get him to define us. "Are you mad about what I said on stage?"

"I'm not mad about that."

"Then what is it?"

"Let it go. I'm okay."

Dakota started to say something, but Ronnie stepped in. Turning around in the passenger seat, she said, "Stop pestering her, Dakota. If she doesn't want to talk, then respect that choice. You being a jerk won't get her to speak."

"I wasn't being a jerk." Dakota dismissed her with a wave of his hand. "Why don't you butt out of our conversation? I wasn't talking to you, Ronnie. I was talking to Sylvia."

"You're talking at her." Jiménez joined in. "She hasn't responded to half the stuff you've been saying to her. Give the girl a break."

The rest of the ride to Dion's apartment was awkward, to say the least. Dakota scooted away from me, and I didn't protest. I was glad that I could have more breathing room. A thick fog always formed when he was alarmingly close to me. I never thought straight. There was no way I could concentrate with his body that near.

I was grateful when we finally got to the apartment complex. The argument hadn't resumed. Grabbing my bag of clothing and other essentials, I exited the car. Dakota was outside before me. Once I was standing outside, I regretted my decision to spend some time alone with him.

The short trek to the correct building and then up the steps felt like I was walking for an eternity. My mind played out how I imagined the following few hours. I was praying that morning would come soon. Maybe I could pretend that I was tired and wanted to go to sleep.

Dakota opened the front door with his free hand. The other held his coat, hanging off two of his fingers over his shoulder. "What do you want to do?"

"Sleep."

He glanced at me with an arched brow. "Sleep?"

"Yes. Sleep. I'm tired."

"It's not that late."

"I'm aware of that." I threw down my bag and sat on the lumpy tan couch, beginning to remove my shoes and peeling off my socks. "Who cares what time it is? It doesn't change the fact that I'm tired."

Dakota rested his guitar case against the wall connected to the kitchen before turning toward me. "What's the matter, Sylvia? You can't pretend there's nothing wrong because I know there's something you're not telling me."

"I'm sleepy."

"You aren't sleepy." He stepped in closer. "Say you're mad, you're pissed, you're annoyed, even yell or scream at me—do anything. Be honest. Something is running through your mind. I'm tired of trying to decode what you mean, Sylvia."

"You're the one who's making my words cryptic. I'm exhausted. There's nothing for you to decode."

"Yes, there is."

At once, I got up from my seat.

"What do you want me to say? That I'm angry with you?"

"I'd take that any day instead of you lying to my face."

"I risked getting caught by my father and getting grounded—and for what? This idiotic cycle of arguing? Why the hell do I put up with this?"

"That's a good question. Why do you?"

"You know what a better question would be? Why do you want me here to begin with? What's your ulterior motive?"

His hand flew to the bridge of his nose, pinching it. "You can't honestly be bringing this up again at a time like this. We've had this argument. I don't want to waste the first real time alone we've had in a long time fighting."

"We never came to a conclusion on that argument."

"Yes, yes, we did. I said that I didn't need to tell you what my intentions were since I didn't know what I wanted either. All I know is that I want you for as long as I can have you. Is the fact that I want you around not a good enough reason?" He didn't wait for my response. Taking another step, he erased the remaining space between us. The frown on his face had partially melted, but there was a stern, serious gleam in his eyes when he put his hands on my back. "Why is it so hard for you to accept the fact that I'm not going anywhere?"

"Maybe because the last person I let in did a lot of damage once they got the chance to. I thought he was a friend. It ended up messy. I almost had to move schools because of it. I don't want to trust the wrong person and get myself back in the same situation."

"Give me the address of whoever did that, and I'll pay them a visit."

I laughed. "You shouldn't resort to violence."

"This time I would be using violence for a noble cause," he mused, swiping his thumb over my cheek and holding my face in his left hand. "No one hurts my doll."

"Don't use the word my like that. You don't own me."

"Sylvia. You know what I mean. I don't mean that as if you're my property. You take shit too seriously. Stop being difficult." He rolled his eyes playfully and smiled. "What was it that caused you to almost change schools? Does it have anything to do with why you're in California now?"

I sat back down on the couch. He followed me and took the empty seat beside me, resting his arm around my shoulder. "The reason I left Maine was completely different. I was talking about this friend I had back in middle school. We were close. I told him everything because there was no one else I could talk to. But right after I opened up to him, he went behind my back and told the whole school what I was going through at home."

"That's awful. Is that what you're afraid of with me? That I'll tell people if you start opening up with me?"

"I don't know what you'll do . . ."

"Hey." He angled my body so I was in front of him, cupping my face in his hands. "I'm not like that person. I will never, ever do that to you. No matter what. I'd rather I got hurt than see you in any kind of pain. You can trust me."

"I do trust you . . . sometimes," I tacked on, moving away from his touch. I relaxed into the couch and folded my hands onto my lap. I needed composure. Sobbing in front of Dakota wasn't an option. "I don't know where to start, though. There's a lot."

"Whatever you feel comfortable talking about. If that's what you want. And if you don't want to tell me at all, I'm perfectly fine with that as well. We can watch TV and laugh until we forget about this conversation."

I smiled at his answer.

Easing back into his arms, I rested my back against his chest. I couldn't look at him while I told him. It would make everything a lot harder to talk about. Things were better this way, not seeing his reaction.

"I got bullied a lot growing up."

"I can relate to that."

"You probably can." I grabbed both his hands, laying them flat on my lap as I interlocked our fingers while I spoke. "There was this one kid, though, named Ian. I thought he was my friend—my best friend, even. We did everything together. I told him all my secrets and hopes and dreams. He told me his too."

"What was one of the secrets?"

"I talked about my mother's problem with drinking."

"I'm sorry to hear about that."

"She's alright now. Most days," I added. "But that's not what I wanted to tell you. Do you want to know why I ended up moving to California?"

He nodded.

"I got expelled from my last school."

"That's badass."

"I didn't intend for that to happen. I just wanted to be left alone."

"By who? That old friend of yours, Ian?" Without me saying a word, he knew the answers. "He did something to you, didn't he?"

"He went behind my back and told everyone about my mom's previous addiction, and . . . I snapped. I couldn't take that abuse from someone I once cared for."

"What did you do?"

"I waited."

"You waited?"

"I waited until I had something. Something heavy to hurt him as much as he'd hurt me," I divulged. "In April this year, I found out that Ian's father—who was the vice-principal at our school—was cheating on his wife. I stayed behind really late at school one day and saw something I shouldn't have in the parking lot."

"What did you do?"

"I-I . . . " I stuttered. "I took photos of them. That next day, I woke up extra early to make printed copies of those images. I then plastered them all over Ian's house and all over campus. I didn't do a good job disguising who I was, though, and the school was able to find out it was me. They called it vandalizing school property."

"But they were just pictures ... weren't they?"

I cracked a smile. "They were framed and then hot glued onto the lockers. Inside of classrooms. Some on ceilings too. I'm pretty sure they had to hire help to get them removed."

"Wow, I never thought of you as a troublemaker."

"I never told anyone why I left Maine." I moved in to touch his knee. "Until now."

"I'm the first person you've told, ever?"

"Yeah." I nodded. "I'd appreciate it if we start watching something funny to distract me."

Dakota snatched up the TV remote and flipped it on, quickly pausing to kiss my cheek. "At your request. If you want to talk about it more, I'm here for you."

I brought our interlocked fingers up to my lips and kissed the back of his hand. "I know."

Chapter Forty-Five

Back and Forth

"I don't want to, Dakota," I said, going into his room. But he wouldn't take no for an answer. He wanted to cheer me up. I had lost a lot of energy telling him about what had happened in Maine. It had drained my mood and the will to hold a decent conversation. "I don't want to listen to music. My head still hurts from the live performance."

"Just hear me out," he pleaded. "I want to show you something."

"I saw your vinyl collection the other day. It's impressive. Happy now?"

"I don't need you to stroke my ego by telling me I have an impressive vinyl collection. I'm aware of that," he stated smugly. "I have something I want to show you. I was planning on giving this to you for Christmas—to make sure I got everything right. But I think it would be better if I gave it to you tonight."

"What is it?"

"It wouldn't be a surprise if I tell you." He shut the door after I stepped inside. I made myself comfortable by sitting down on the bed. "Close your eyes."

"No," I protested. "I won't."

"Please, close your eyes."

"Do you have any reptiles you plan on throwing on me?"

"No. I don't. Now close your eyes."

"How about rodents?"

"Sylvia. Shut your eyes."

I groaned but eventually did as he asked and sealed my eyes closed. He ordered me to stretch out my palms, and even though it took me a second, I did that as well. Dakota placed something solid in my hands. It was in the shape of a small rectangle.

"You can open them now."

I fluttered my eyes open and saw a cassette tape in the center of my palm and a Walkman in his hands. Dakota handed that to me as well. "Remember last week when you said you haven't been getting much sleep?"

"Yeah." I remembered telling Dakota about the annoying construction work that was going on over in my neighbor's backyard. They were extending the back portion of their house to add a gazebo plus a spacious pool. "What's this for?"

"Well, since you said music tends to help you go to sleep, I decided to make a mixtape of some songs that usually help me. A lot of it's jazz music, like Miles Davis and Duke Ellington's stuff. I've got some doo-wop music and some Nina Simone, too," he explained. Right before I was going to thank him for his sweet gesture, he had to ruin the moment by saying, "Also, I think your taste in music is quite awful. I thought I'd enlighten you."

"Your music taste is nowhere near as good as mine."

"I'm the more musically inclined one between the two of us. Hello, I'm in a band."

"Yes, you are in a band. That doesn't mean your taste is better than mine. I used to play an instrument. I was a musician once."

"Are you honestly pulling that card out again?"

"What? It's a good point."

"We've been over this, Sylvia. Playing the oboe for one year in the sixth grade does not make you a musician."

"I was the best oboe player Lincoln Junior High had seen in years. I could make a comeback."

He forced a laugh. "I'm sure you will."

This infuriated me. I thought I had decent taste in music. Simply because I didn't listen to jazz or blues songs didn't mean I had awful taste. I pushed myself off of his bed and headed to his collection of vinyls, CDs, and cassette tapes. Grabbing a cassette tape that had been set on its side, I pulled it out of its case. The title scribbled on the thin white strip intrigued me.

Dakota came up from behind me and snatched it out of my hand. "What are you doing?"

"I want to listen to whatever's on that cassette tape. It has my name on it."

He stuck it into his back pocket. "That doesn't mean you're allowed to listen to it."

"It clearly has 'Sylvia' written in black ink. It's for me."

"I'm talking about a different Sylvia. A Sylvia with an I in her name and not a Y."

"Nice try, but you spelled it how I spell my name."

"I'll need to fix that then. It's a typo."

No part of me believed him when he said that.

"You don't know any other girls named Sylvia."

"You don't know that for a fact. I know loads of girls named Sylvia." Dakota took the tape and the Walkman back and intertwined our fingers. "Let's do something else. Something that doesn't involve you going through my things."

● ● ●

"It's a cult classic," I proclaimed in defense. We were back in the living room, tucked under a blanket and arguing about what we should watch next. There was no way I was backing down. "No movie tops it."

"We're not going to watch that. I've spent years avoiding eighties teen movies, and I will spend the rest of my life avoiding them even more."

"Oh, c'mon," I snapped. "Some of my favorite movies are from the eighties."

"I like classic movies. Saw Night of the Living Dead the other day, and that was great. The more that I think about it, though, I'd say I'm a huge art house film fan. The weirder the better. I've seen a few good action movies this year—"

I pretended to snore. "Bo-ring. You're way less cool than I thought you were."

He turned down the volume on the TV. "Maybe if I were left with no options, I'd watch it, but I'm not in the mood to watch a movie where the most popular girls in school are all named Heather."

"One is named Veronica."

"So?"

"It's hilarious."

"I'd rather watch Iron Chef," he said with a slight yawn.

"We just watched an entire hour of Iron Chef. There's only so much dicing and sautéing I can take for one night."

"How about we watch—"

"Please. Let's watch Heathers."

"Or we could—"

"Kota! Please. Just one movie."

"Ugh, fine." He folded, switching the cable over to the Blu-ray.

He put on a streaming service that had the movie. "If I don't like the first fifteen minutes, we're watching Wait Until Dark."

I scooted away from him. "Isn't that an old film with Audrey Hepburn in it?"

"Yes, it is." He paused and flashed a look at me. "Stop judging me. I know that look. You're judging me. What's wrong with watching an Audrey Hepburn movie? It's got a good plot. She's home alone, and she's blind. Three robbers sneak into her apartment after having gone into the one next to hers the day before and killing the woman inside of it. Now that movie is an actual classic. It has all the elements thrillers these days are lacking. It does a good job of keeping the audience on the edge of their seats without using big explosions or gun fights."

"Hmm. Maybe we can watch it another weekend. It sounds interesting," I admitted. I curled up next to him on the couch and pulled up the blanket, relaxing into Dakota's body and waiting for the movie to start.

Everything from our last conversation had been pushed to the back of my mind. Dakota had done a good job keeping me distracted, either watching cooking shows or making caramel-covered popcorn in his kitchen. We'd laughed at the first batch we'd burned by accident, cheering once we got it right the second time around.

If I could capture this memory, pause our relationship right in this moment, I would. I wouldn't want to push further into the future to see what life held for us. I didn't want to be anywhere else but here, with him.

• • •

The movie ended, and even though Dakota didn't admit it right away, I knew he'd enjoyed every minute of it. He did, however, rush to talk about what he'd hated in the movie before giving it a compliment.

"You can't convince me that J.D. was ever supposed to be the love interest," Dakota said, refusing to comprehend the choices in the film. "He's terrible."

"You don't think girls date terrible guys?"

"I'd hope she'd see the value in leaving him. He dressed funny too."

"You can't hate eighties clothes," I said, throwing the blanket down to my feet. I stretched my limbs and gave my leg a shake, feeling it slowly wake up. "That's unacceptable."

"The colors are loud and annoying, and the hairstyles were almost laughable. And what was with the oversized fits? Did people in the eighties not know how to get the right measurements on their clothing?"

"You're looking too closely at frivolous details." I strained my neck toward him and pecked his cheek. "That's okay, though, because it's probably one of the many things I love about you."

I hadn't just said that.

There was no way those last words had left my mouth.

Perhaps Dakota didn't hear me say it, my thoughts offered. Strangely, I was hoping that he had noticed what I'd said.

He flinched away from me and pulled himself off the couch. "I'm going to get some more popcorn. Do want something from the kitchen?"

My dignity. If you can find it.

"No," I said timidly. "I'm okay."

Dakota returned only minutes later, carrying more caramel

popcorn and a new glass of Dr. Pepper Cherry. "You left your phone on the microwave. It was buzzing like crazy."

"Thanks," I said and took it. I checked my notifications and found multiple missed calls from Jiménez and Ronnie. I had a few text messages from a private number, but I ignored them.

We silently watched Food Network for fifteen minutes until annoyance was literally eating me alive. Was he going to dismiss what I'd said entirely, as if I hadn't said anything at all? He was evil for that.

"Can you drive me home?" I asked out of nowhere.

"What for?" He rested his bowl of popcorn on the coffee table. "It's late."

"I don't want to be here anymore. If you won't drive me home, at least walk me to the nearest bus stop."

"Are you insane? You're not taking a bus at this hour."

"I have pepper spray in my bag. I'll live." I reached over for my socks and started to put them back on. "I want to go home."

"Sylvia, hold on." He gently took one of my socks out of my hands. "Where is this coming from? I thought we were fine."

"Yeah, we were fine until you started to ignore the big elephant in the room."

"What?"

"The very obvious issue that both of us are aware of but will not acknowledge. That's what ignoring the elephant me—"

"I know what the metaphor means. What is the elephant in the room in this situation, though?"

I sprang to my feet.

"It doesn't matter anymore. I don't want to be somewhere I'm not wanted. I've dealt with neglect my whole life. I'm not going to take a second of it any longer."

Dakota took both of my shoulders and held them firmly. "I've told you, more times than I can count, how much I want you, how much I care for you. I've shown you more than once. What more do you want from me?"

For you to love me.

But those words never left my lips. I wasn't brave enough to utter such words for a second time today. He'd ignored them so easily when they'd first come out of my mouth. Nothing would get me to say it again.

An angrier, darker part of my heart wanted to hurt him in any way possible. To make Dakota unhappy, just like how I felt for not receiving the words I craved hearing.

"Pierson kissed me today," I confessed. "I didn't kiss him back. Now that I think about it, maybe I should have. He smelled so good, and he had me in his room, sitting on his bed. We could've done a lot more than kiss—"

"Stop, just stop it." Dakota hands dropped from my shoulder and flew to his ears. "I know what you're doing. It's not going to work."

Dakota quickly went to his room and stepped back out with his shoes on and one of his jean jackets fitting tightly around his broad shoulders. His car keys jingled in his hand.

I walked beside him to the exit. "Where are you going?"

"Getting some fresh air," he replied and opened the door. "Don't leave and take a bus home. Please, Sylvia. I'll be back soon."

The front door slammed shut, and soon after, the loud noise of his Mustang rang in the air. I knew where he was going. It was no mystery. Franklin was having a party at his place this weekend. No doubt, Pierson and his friends would be there as well. Beth had been invited by Franklin, so she'd be there too.

I instantly regretted starting an argument with Dakota. It had felt purposeful in the heat of the moment. All I wanted was to get him mad and have him admit that he cared for me more than he was letting on. I didn't want him to run off and try to start a fight with Pierson.

Three times, I tried to call Dakota, but he wouldn't answer. To keep my mind occupied, I played a few games on my phone, wishing it would deflect my real thoughts long enough.

Once that started to bore me, I went over to the new text messages I had received. I had no interest in replying to any of the ones sent by the private number . . . until I saw what they had written.

> **UNKNOWN**: *I wonder what Elijah Ellington will think of his daughter when he finds out what she really does on the weekend.*
> **UNKNOWN**: *You don't look like you're studying at Dion Ridgewood's apartment.*

Underneath the text message, there was a photo—taken outside of the apartment. The picture was a little blurry, but you could see that it was Dakota and me lying on the couch. There was a time stamp at the bottom right corner. It had been taken tonight.

I walked to the blinds and closed them, shaking at the realization that we'd been watched. My stomach was in knots, and my mind began to wander, wondering who the hell had sent these texts. It felt like something out of a horror movie—or a plot twist straight out of a melodramatic teen drama.

The sound of my phone on the coffee table caught me off guard, scaring me to death. I brought it up and read the new message I'd received.

UNKNOWN: *You don't need to worry after seeing that. It's nothing compared to everything else we have on you. By the way, congrats. You've been chosen this year.*
ME: *Chosen for what?*
UNKNOWN: *One or more members within Senior Salute have pledged donations in your name.*

"What the fuck does that even mean?" I muttered.

Moments after that text, a picture was sent. I had to download it for the image to properly load. While my mind registered what I was looking at, seeing each pixel come into focus, my mouth fell agape. It was a photo of Dakota's car. The windows were somewhat tinted, and swaying trees could be seen in the background. It was undoubtedly us in the back of his car ... getting more familiar with our bodies. Everything from my waist down was exposed. Not a minute after I had gotten the picture, a short clip of the event was sent. There was video proof. It was half a minute long and had no audio of the intimate time with Dakota in between my thighs. You couldn't hear the wind from outside the car, and you couldn't hear the breathing of the person who filmed it.

Another text arrived, telling me good luck. There was a winking smiley face attached, taunting me to act.

Was Dakota behind this?

• • •

"That's great!" Ronnie said from the other end of the phone. "I'm happy that you were able to tell him where your heart stands."

"Yes, it was great . . . until he didn't say anything back. Wait.

No, he did. He asked me if I wanted something from the kitchen."

I had counted the number of CDs, tapes, and vinyl records Dakota owned. I'd re-counted them backward, thinking that would help. Counting was usually my favorite form of relaxation, but it wasn't doing anything for me now.

I'd then organized Dakota's book collection, first by name then by color, and washed all the dishes in the sink. My mind was going on overdrive, pretending I hadn't gotten that text message.

My anxiety was through the roof. I was scared, so scared that I couldn't tell Ronnie what had happened. When she'd called me fifteen minutes ago, I'd hurried to tell her why Dakota had left in the hopes that would occupy me.

"I cannot believe you had the courage to say that to him."

"I can't either," I said. "It wasn't like I had it planned out or anything. It . . . it just came out. He was running away from me before I could say anything. I couldn't simply take it back after that."

"That's not my motto. Deny, deny, deny. Deny until he can't even remember what you were talking about."

I couldn't see her, but I could picture her squinting at me, ready to laugh. I was going to miss her after senior year. That was a fact. Once college came around, I would be miles away from here. I'd started applications for Syracuse and a few other New York universities. I was desperate to go back to the East Coast. The toxicity here was sucking me dry of any joy or happiness.

Where was Dakota going to college? Was he staying in California, or was he planning on going out of state, like me? We hadn't talked much about it, but I knew it would come up sooner or later.

I didn't expect him to follow me to college, but I would be lying if I said I wouldn't mind if he went to school hundreds of miles away from me. Long distance wasn't my thing, and I didn't know if this connection we had could last. With the obstacle of getting a plane ticket every time we wanted to see each other, one of us would eventually grow tired.

Not wanting to upset myself more than I already was, I asked Ronnie, "Why was it you called earlier? I'm sorry I missed your call from before."

"After we dropped you guys off, Jiménez and I started talking. I ended up going over to his place to review some things he had picked up from Pierson's laptop. He keeps all of his passwords inside a note on his computer. It's way too easy to get in. Not long after, we were able to get into all of his social media accounts."

"Let me guess, you started reading one of his messages, and you found out he's a part of Senior Salute?"

Pierson was among the people I'd have bet my money on being part of the Senior Salute when we'd first started this operation.

"We don't have any solid evidence to back that up," Ronnie said. "We did uncover that he's been talking with Franklin about Senior Salute. Franklin is definitely a part of Senior Salute, and he was trying to convince Pierson to join this year. That's what we got from the conversation. Franklin was boasting about deflowering three freshman and two juniors. I guess deflowering is one of the competitions they have. Franklin suggested that Pierson try to bag you, get your virginity and all."

"Well, there's nothing they can deflower from me. That ship has sailed." I shivered. "What was Pierson's response?"

"You don't want to know."

"I do want to know if I'm asking."

"You need to read the whole conversation, Sylvia. Before you jump to any conclusions—"

"Tell me, Ronnie."

She took a sharp intake of air. "He said he'd think about joining. Franklin said he'd check to see if anyone had donated in your name already. It's like a rule or something that more than one thing can't be done on one person. About a day after that was sent, Franklin told him that there was already someone who had won the bidding on you."

"There was a bidding match on who goes for me?" I seethed. "That's disgusting. Did they say who?"

"The name didn't come up in their conversation ," she informed me. "Don't sweat it, Sylvia, we'll get on it before the end of the weekend. I haven't scratched the surface when it comes to Pierson's direct messages."

My words were muffled by pounding on the front door. It was brutal, urgent. I brought the phone down to my side and went to the living room. I wasn't ready to face Dakota yet, but I had to eventually.

Despite how strongly I felt about Dakota, I should've given him more time to process this relationship before throwing the "L" word into the mix. I was in the wrong. I unknowingly wore my heart on my sleeve, manipulating the situation to benefit me. Whereas he had his heart hidden, locked up away from sight.

"I'm sorry for saying that about kissing—"

I began to apologize, opening the door, but I stopped short. The person in front of me wasn't Dakota at all. He was the last person on earth I wanted to see on Dion's doorstep. "Xander?"

"I kn-know. I should've called or s-s-s-something," he stuttered, rainwater dripping down his face. At some point, it had started to shower outside. I'd been far too consumed by cleaning the house and distracting myself to notice that small change in the weather. "But I figured you would be here with Dakota. This is the only place close enough to Franklin's house. I didn't know where else I could've gone. I knew I needed to leave."

He let himself in uninvited and wiped his boots on the mat. He rubbed his hands together as if he had just survived the biggest torrential downpour known to man.

I hadn't closed the door. He was out of his psychotic mind if he thought I was going to let him stay. "How did you know I was here? I didn't tell anyone I was going to be here."

He fished out his phone. "You posted a photo of your caramel popcorn on your socials. It had Boulder Valley as your location. I figured that you'd be at Dion's apartment."

Now I really didn't want him here. Beth's stalker tendencies must've rubbed off on him.

"This is bad timing for us," I said. "I don't want to come off rude, but you can't be here unannounced. Dakota only stepped out a moment ago to take a walk. He'll be back any second."

"His car wasn't in the parking lot."

"Weirdo."

"I'm observant."

"You say observant; I say stalkerish."

"Potato, potahto."

"What is it that you want? If you want a place to crash, this isn't it. Dakota wouldn't let you sleep here."

He came around to the couch and sat down.

This guy was getting a little too comfortable.

He hugged himself. "I can't go home."

"Yes, you can." I gestured to the door. "It's only a few miles away. You can make it; I believe in you."

He buried his face in his hands, frowning and sighing into his palms. I was about to snap at him again, but I stopped myself when I heard the soft sound of him beginning to cry.

This Saturday wasn't going the way I'd wanted it to.

"I can't go home. Not at this hour."

"You can take the bus."

"I wouldn't know where to get off. Not only that, but my parents wouldn't let me in at this hour. I tried to call Beth—since she was at the party before me—but she wouldn't answer. She ditched me at the start of the party. She walked off with Franklin. When I confronted her about it, she blew me off in front of everyone and humiliated me. I started walking to the bus stop, but then my phone died. And then"—he paused to breathe in deeply—"I remembered seeing your post and thought, 'Hey, you're not far.' I just need a place to stay until the rain stops so I can charge my phone. Once that's done, I'm going to order a ride out of here. Promise."

"Why won't your parents let you in?"

"My dad's probably passed out drunk. Not even an earthquake could get him out of his sleep. He's been a mess since my mom dropped him." Xander's soft voice cracked. "Sorry for the trauma dump."

Like it or not, those words struck a chord inside me.

I shut the door. I remembered that I still had my phone on a call.

"I'll get back to you later," I told Ronnie.

"Is Xander there with you? I could've sworn that I heard his voice." I didn't say anything. "Oh my God, he is there! You let him inside! Tell him to go home! This is a trick!"

"He needs somewhere to stay while it rains."

"This is exactly like a scary movie. You're letting the psycho killer into your house. Right now, the audience is most likely screaming at the screen and telling you that you're an idiot. That is the biggest bad move ever. You're walking right into his trap. He has to be part of Senior Salute or something."

My attention went to Xander. He was dabbing a napkin to his cheek, crying into it.

"I don't think so."

"Stop being so gullible! Don't believe anything he tells you."

"I won't."

"I know you, Sylvia."

"I'll call you tomorrow."

"We need to meet up and talk about this Pierson thing, though."

"How about before school on Monday?"

Pierson and I had plans to meet up before breakfast was served at school to do a run-through of our Spanish project and figure out who would do what section when we presented.

"Works for me," Ronnie agreed. "Seriously, Sylvia. Be safe. He's crazy, and he will do anything to be accepted by others. Don't assume he's being honest with you."

Ronnie was nothing but right. Despite agreeing with her, I knew I needed to be there for Xander. There was something I had only ever seen in myself glimmering in his eyes now.

•••

Before daybreak, Xander was long gone, and Dakota wasn't back yet. I called Ronnie, and she drove me home. I apologized for constantly asking for a ride. She shrugged it off and said she didn't care all that much, enjoying any excuse to get out the house. I tried to give her gas money, but she refused to take it from me.

For the rest of the weekend, I didn't get a single text or call from Dakota. It was obvious that what I'd said had caused this entire relationship to crumble.

Who knew three words could do so much damage?

Chapter Forty-Six

Smother

I was sleep deprived, just like the night I'd spent alone at Dion's apartment. My restless mind wouldn't let me stop thinking. I was too busy wondering about the anonymous texts and worrying about Dakota's whereabouts. All my calls remained unanswered, and eventually they started to go straight to voicemail. Either his phone had died or he'd purposely turned it off to avoid me.

Considering I had to see Ronnie before seeing Pierson, I woke up earlier than I did most school days. I checked my phone one last time before I headed for the bedroom door, closing it behind me. I was getting used to the lack of activity on my phone.

Putting on my backpack, I went quietly down the stairs. Everyone else was still sleeping, except for my father. He was up at 4:00 a.m. every day. Watching the news took up an hour of his morning routine, then drinking coffee in the living room alone, and then reading the same current events on his phone, scrolling past digital articles.

After he was satisfied, he ate a bagel or a banana, then wrote that day's installment of his weekly newsletter that he emailed out to his college friends and family. The newsletter never consisted of anything you couldn't find on your own but rather centered on topics that had interested him long enough to pose a question or create a passage on its importance. Afternoons were exclusively left for work. He liked that time of day to concentrate on the cases he was working on.

"Bye, Dad. I'm going to school a little early to work on my project," I explained, going up to the door. "I'll be back the same time after school."

"Wait." He sat down his mug. "I'll drive you to school."

I waved him off. "No, you don't have to. I can bike it there."

"Don't be silly. I'll drive you," he insisted and flipped off the TV. "I was going to head toward the office in fifteen minutes anyway. It's in the same part of town."

I didn't fight.

"Do you want to grab something to eat before we go? Since I'm driving you, you have more time."

"I'll be fine."

He looked at me with a sideways expression but left it at that. I hadn't eaten my dinner last night, and I hadn't left my room for the most part except for brief bathroom breaks. It was hard to eat when my thoughts were somewhere else.

I would've liked it to be a silent drive to school, but my father found it a great time to talk about college and how my admission process was going. I told him I had started about six applications.

"That's wonderful." He patted my shoulder. "What do you plan on majoring in?"

"I listed myself as undecided."

"Well, do you at least know what topics you might want to study?"

I stared out the window. This wasn't what I wanted to talk about. All his life, he'd known what he wanted to do. Even before he was a lawyer, he had drive and passion in every job he had. For me, I couldn't make choices, even small choices regarding what I wanted to eat for lunch. How was I supposed to choose a subject—at the age of eighteen—that would lead to my future career? I had no direction in life.

Simply to get Dad off my back about it, I said, "I was thinking about anthropology and psychology."

He was impressed by my response, smiling and nodding with pure delight. "That's good. Have you thought of any Ivy Leagues?"

"They'd laugh at my application." I snorted. "Just because you got your law degree at Harvard doesn't mean I want to go to some Ivy League. I'm perfectly content going to a public university or a state college."

The car pulled into the school parking lot. I was glad we'd arrived. Any more of this conversation and Dad would've tried to convince me to apply to Dartmouth or something. We both knew that was unlikely. With my track record, I was more likely to get into San Quentin than Stanford.

I went for the door handle. Dad's voice stopped me.

"I called Pierson's house on Saturday night. He said you weren't over there working on the project. He also said that you had left hours earlier. I don't need to ask who you could've been with. I can make an educated guess." He lowered the volume of his classical music radio station and cleared his throat. "Do you want to know why I'm disappointed in you?"

Great. He's already on the "I'm disappointed" part of his speech. I'm doomed.

"Dad, I can explain—"

"You don't need to. I understand. You want to be with Dakota. He wants to be with you. I was a teenager once; I know how it works. I also know how easy it is for people to get pressured into doing things they don't want to do. You can be with Dakota, but I'd rather if you didn't sneak off to his house. Are you at least being safe?"

"Please, Dad, stop."

He shook his head. "I want you to invite Dakota over for Thanksgiving dinner."

"What?"

Had I heard him right? Was I making this all up? There was no way my father, Elijah Ellington, had said those exact words.

"I would prefer if you were open with your relationship with that boy rather than sneaking off with him to God knows where. If he matters to you, then I want to meet him properly. He can bring his brother if he wants."

"You don't think that's a bad idea?"

"Bad idea? What for? He's his family."

"Dakota said..."

I couldn't spit out the words completing the thought forming in my head.

"What are you going on about?" Dad was perplexed, waiting. "What did he tell you?"

"I've been hearing a lot of things since I got to town."

"Like what?"

"Rumors that I don't know if I should believe."

He flashed a look at the clock in the car, reading the time. "We should have this conversation at home. I'm running late. Is it okay if we do it then? You can tell me anything then."

I couldn't dismiss his offer. It was too good to be true.

Or a total nightmare waiting to happen.

"I can hold off."

"And can you ask Dakota about his Thanksgiving plans?"

"Yes, I can. I'm sure he'll be free."

• • •

Ronnie and Jiménez were sitting on the bleachers.

"Why do you have that camera around your neck?" I asked Ronnie when I got to where they were sitting, high up on the top row. "Is that for your film class?"

After the art teacher had quit her job last month, the teacher who replaced her had turned the class into a film course. Ronnie, Pierson, Dakota, and Carmen were all in that class—so was Ronnie's ex, Finn.

"Yeah, it's for film class." Ronnie held the lens with both hands. "I have to choose a topic that fascinates me and make a film about it for three to seven minutes and then show it to the entire school. Mr. Omar somehow got permission to premiere our little films in front of the school on the last day before Christmas break. Even though he would've graded them by that time, he still wants to torture us by showing our peers."

"It's okay. I'll clap so loud for your short film."

She wiped away a fake tear and patted my shoulder. "You're a true friend."

"Speaking of friends..." I shot a knowing look at Jiménez. "Where's Dakota? I figured you would have invited him to this meetup."

"It would be best if Dakota wasn't here," Jiménez said earnestly. "I'm not all that sure where he is, though. Have you contacted him?"

"Yes, I have." I refrained from checking my phone again. "He hasn't been responding to any of my texts or calls."

"He's missed all of my calls, too," Jiménez admitted. I was glad to hear that this wasn't only happening to me. "I haven't heard back from him since I dropped you guys off on Saturday. Did something happen that night?"

Ronnie and I exchanged looks.

"Nothing out of the ordinary," I replied. "We had a bit of an argument, but he didn't have the reaction I was looking for."

"You wanted a reaction out of him? That's weird," Jiménez mused. "And extremely stupid. Why are you so backward? Just talk to the guy."

"Enough about Dakota. Let's get to why we're here," Ronnie announced. "Jiménez, show her the printouts."

He swung his messenger bag to his lap and handed me a packet of papers—conversations between Pierson and lots of other people. Emails. Private messages. Notes saved from himself. It was a treasure trove of the innermost aspects of Pierson's life.

Jiménez pointed at the first sheet. "The one thing I noticed is that the bid on you had an outsourced component to it."

"What does that mean?" I inquired.

"We think a girl has joined Senior Salute. And that she's using a new method they call outsourcing. Someone is paying someone else to act on deviant behavior."

"This is getting worse the more you tell me about it," I grumbled, pressing my water bottle to my forehead in the hopes of cooling me down. "What else did you find?"

"No solid evidence yet—but we think Beth seems like a suspect," Jiménez concluded. "She's super rich. And she hates you for being close with Pierson."

"Who's to say she didn't pay Dakota so that she was free to go back to gawking at Pierson unbothered?" Ronnie suggested

"Beth isn't going to do anything to me," I assured them. The talk I'd had with Xander had made me form different beliefs. "She's into Franklin."

"I had a feeling you'd say that." Jiménez shook his finger at me and brought out his laptop. "Ronnie told me you let Xander into Dion's apartment on Saturday."

"Ronnie!"

"I'm sorry!" she shouted with her hands in the air. "I didn't know who else to call. I was worried for your life. I'm sorry."

"She's not lying. I had to reassure her on the phone that Xander wouldn't kill or kidnap you. Ronnie was legit hyperventilating. I swear, she thinks she's in a Lifetime movie," Jiménez said, smirking at his computer screen. "After she told me about Xander being there, though, and how she overheard you guys talking about him being at Franklin's party, I thought I'd do some snooping." He turned the screen so it was facing Ronnie and me. "I couldn't access the private security system, but I was able to access street security footage. There are some doorbell cameras and traffic cameras that face in the direction of his house."

I was a little baffled at how he could've done this all on his own. "Isn't it illegal to access that stuff?"

"Cocaine and meth are illegal, but people still get a hold of them somehow," he retorted. "I don't have much time in Harper Falls. School's gonna start soon. Do you want to ask more questions, or do you want to see what I found?"

"No need to get sassy," Ronnie joked. "Play the footage you found."

He pressed Play and showed us the file he had on his computer. "I looked at stuff from the start of the party to the end of the party. I didn't see Xander's car pull up after watching the tapes the first time. I had to rewatch them at least twice. I couldn't spot his car at all." He paused the video. "Until about ten o'clock, when he finally does show." He pointed at the red vehicle in the third frame. "Look at this."

The video was kind of fuzzy. Jiménez refreshed it to make it clearer. Someone else had stepped out of Xander's car.

"Dakota," I breathed. "Or at least someone who looks like him."

"Sylvia." Ronnie sighed. "That's him."

"I know what he's capable of. He wouldn't go off and hang out with Xander. That has to be someone else."

"Sylvia, if I wasn't one hundred percent sure myself, I wouldn't suggest this to you. He's my best friend," Jiménez said. "But after I saw that, I knew I had to check some other things. I found footage of Dakota entering Franklin's house at the end of August and the beginning of September. After what I've collected this weekend, I think there may be a chance that he could've been the bidder against you—"

"I don't want to hear it." I held my palms to my ears, blocking his words out. "That's not true. That can't be true. You said it was a girl who had bid on me."

"No one can honestly know who has bid on who," Ronnie reminded me. "The only person who can say is the leader of Senior Salute. And that person isn't Franklin. He's nowhere near the top. We're only guessing based on who openly hates you. Dakota isn't off the table. In August, he did still hate you."

"How would you know Franklin isn't near the top?"

"Because Finn is the head of Senior Salute. He has access to that kind of information." Ronnie exhaled painfully slowly. She didn't look at me when she let that secret slip about her ex. "The main reason we broke up is because I found out about him being in Senior Salute. I'd gone through his phone out of curiosity one night and found loads of message about operations against students. They kept calling him Maestro, which is the title they use for the leader. He keeps the money, says what is acceptable and what isn't. Knows who's involved and who isn't. Organizes it so nothing gets messy and keeps it under wraps. People think it's Malik or Hanan who runs it. They're too popular. They want to participate, not play adult. Also, they're not as smart as Finn. They wouldn't know how to keep their mouths shut or how to keep everyone's identity hidden."

I couldn't believe she hadn't told me this until now. "Did you see Dakota's name in the text messages?"

"I don't recall. If Dakota is a part of Senior Salute, I would have to check Finn's planner. It would be there."

My mood changed. "Why don't you do what they made me do with Pierson? Get with Finn and try to get information out of him. I want to show you guys that you've got the wrong person."

Dakota couldn't be the person behind the text messages I'd gotten. There was someone else, and they were using Dakota as a scapegoat. Dakota was in those photos too. Why would he sabotage himself?

Ronnie shook her head. "Finn and I are different from Pierson and you. I loved him—and I still do. I can't look at him without wanting to scream. I couldn't put on a fake face and pretend to care for him when I can't help but crumble at the thought of what he's done."

As much as I wanted to get answers, I knew I couldn't put Ronnie through that. Dion and Jiménez might've convinced me to get close to Pierson, but Ronnie wasn't the kind of person who could pretend.

"I think it's time I leave," Jiménez said and shut down his computer. "I don't want to overstay my welcome."

When Jiménez was gone, I grabbed my backpack and waited for Ronnie at the bottom of the bleachers. Counting until my emotions could subside wasn't an option at the moment. I needed to blabber about anything—anything other than what they'd told me.

The ringing coming from my backpack cut into the conversation I was having with Ronnie. I retrieved it and pressed Talk. It wasn't a number I was familiar with. "Hello?"

"Sylvia? It's Dakota."

I wasn't as happy as I'd thought I would be, partly because what Jiménez had showed me had left a sour taste in my mouth. I was still struggling to grasp it.

"Where have you been?" I asked.

"Looking for my phone, my laptop, and a freak-load of other things. I came home on Sunday morning to find my stuff was gone. It's not funny, Sylvia. You're the only one who was there. I had to wait until Dion came home this morning to finally use a phone. Where's my stuff?"

Chapter Forty-Seven

Strawberry Letter 23

"I didn't steal . . . " I trailed off, gradually making the connection. "Xander."

"You let him into Dion's apartment? What the hell were you thinking?" Dakota seethed. There was a hint of uneasiness behind his words. "Oh, right, you weren't thinking. That was the problem."

"Hey, you don't get to be angry."

"Yes, the hell I do. You let Alexander—the part-time snake and full-time best friend of a stalker—into my brother's home without even asking for my permission."

"He said he needed a place to stay dry."

"And you didn't shoo him away?"

"I told her to kick him out!" Ronnie shouted into the phone.

I cupped the phone, brought it away from my ear, and set my eyes on her. "You're not helping. I'd like it if you didn't side against me right now."

"Sorry," she murmured sheepishly.

"You don't get it, Sylvia," Dakota said with no rage. "A lot of my belongings are at Dion's. Along with my sister's. You gave him complete access to a lot of our things. Including the diaries Diana left behind. I can't believe you would be that careless and let him in without thinking twice about it."

"I—"

"You know what? I don't want to hear your excuse or the sappy sad story he gave you to let him in Dion's apartment."

"I think you're blowing this a little out of proportion."

The phone went dead.

Here I was, waiting desperately for some form of communication from Dakota. I wasn't expecting a bitter phone call with so much hate wrapped around each word. Had I messed up? Most definitely. But that didn't mean I'd done it intentionally.

Once I'd told Dakota what had happened in Maine, my barriers had been down for the first time in four years. I was open. I was accepting. Xander had caught me at the perfect time to swoop in and send a dagger into my heart. I was easy prey at that point.

I shoved my phone back into my bag.

"That didn't seem like a good conversation," Ronnie said. She flinched at my cold expression. "I'll shut my mouth from now on."

The parking lot was starting to fill up. Students had begun to file into school, chattering away about their weekend. I would give anything to trade my weekend for someone else's. Anyone else's.

I checked the time, not seeing until then that I had missed the meeting with Pierson at the cafeteria. There were about ten minutes until the first warning bell. I started to walk toward the glass doors of the entrance. Someone stopped me in my tracks.

Dakota.

He was standing near one of the white columns, leaning his shoulder against the large mass to stay balanced. "I saw Jiménez. He told me what he said to you."

"That doesn't sound like a straight denial."

"Can we go?" He motioned to the parking lot. "Can we talk somewhere private?"

"We have class."

"I'd only make you miss homeroom. One period at most."

Without protesting any longer, I got into his car. I hadn't raised my guard up against him until we were almost off school grounds.

I smoothed my hand over the leather interior of his car, loving how lush it felt on my fingertips. In a way, it helped me not look at Dakota while I spoke.

"I . . ." I began.

"What is it?"

"I don't trust you," I breathed. There were two ways I could continue this conversation. I could start with a question and see where it led us. Or I could state what I knew and make him spill the truth. "I know where you were the other night. Jiménez showed me some videos. Still, I don't know if I can believe it. I think you need to start answering some questions."

He slowed the car at the parking lot exit. "I told you. I went to get some fresh air."

"And you had to take your car?"

"I needed to get out of the apartment."

"You're going to have to give me better answers than that," I ordered. "That, or I'm going to step out of this car and start walking in the opposite direction."

"Right now isn't the best time to give me an ultimatum." His hands gripped the steering wheel until his knuckles paled.

"Where were you?"

Dakota fell quiet, holding on to the steering wheel even harder. Raising a hand off the wheel, he ruffled his fingers through his hair. "I went to a lake."

I arched my brows. "You didn't."

"I did."

He took the first left on Fillmore Road, cruising past a graveyard adjacent to a gas station. A little bit further, I saw a man-made lake in the distance, glistening with specks of light caught on the waves.

"Out of all the places you could've gone, you decided to go to a lake." I wore a questioning face, doubting his earlier response. "Why a lake?"

Twisting the steering wheel to the right, he drove the car in the direction of the lake. The waterfront was free of any cars. Besides the occasional buzzing insect, there wasn't much movement. Dakota's hand found the keys, and he turned the car off. The rumbling noise faded, leaving us in silence.

"Tomorrow will be the one-year anniversary of when Erick Thompson almost died. I was going to go visit him but decided it would be best if I didn't." He hesitated, allowing his words to hang in the air as I went for the door handle and pushed it open. He followed suit, rushing to my side once I emerged.

"Is he a friend of yours?" I asked.

"Hardly." He kicked his shoe against the dirt. "He went to Boulder Valley. Malik had this thing about treating those kids like garbage for no reason besides the fact that they were our rivals in every sport."

"This was back when you were friends with Malik and Pierson, right?"

He narrowed his eyes. "How did you know we were friends?"

"Pierson told me. I didn't really think it was true."

He forced a laugh. "Yeah, it's true. I used to be on the lacrosse team and the basketball team. We got to be friends that way. I thought they were my best friends and that we'd know each other for years after we graduated."

"I know what you mean by that." I exhaled. "Friends can change."

He leaped onto the boardwalk that stretched over the water. "No, it wasn't like what happened with you and your friend in Maine. We never had issues with secrets or trust. I honestly thought of them as my family at one point. If there was some kind of problem in the group, we solved it before the end of the day. That was how we were.

"Things were fine until I caught Hanan with Carmen. It went downhill after that. I should've left the friend group once I caught her cheating. I could see there was division in the crew. It was like they were on Hanan's side. Saying that I wasn't a good enough boyfriend and that it was about time someone stole her from me. Stupid stuff like that. Things only got worse after Erick came into the picture. Malik had a hobby of messing with Boulder Valley kids. One of his favorites to torment was Erick Thompson. The guy was already getting picked on at his own school because he was poor. Malik and Pierson rubbed it in his face. Malik slept with his sister to piss him off and got his own blood to not stick up for him."

"That's awful." I frowned. "I don't know how he could possibly do that."

"Malik can do some horrible things without thinking twice about it." Dakota settled down at the edge of the boardwalk. He sat far back enough that his shoes didn't touch the water. "Anyway, the fall of junior year, I agreed to go with Malik, Hanan, and Pierson to the beach. Something didn't feel right when we ended up here instead. I wasn't sure why Malik had pulled up to a lake and not the beach . . . until I saw Erick's car parked here. Malik had convinced everyone else that we should push it into the water. May I remind you that we were under the influence, except for Malik. Malik was just mad. He was the only sober one. He had this whole plan of how he would get back at Erick. Apparently, Erick's sister was fed up with the bullying and broke off things with Malik. Malik didn't like that. It humiliated him. I tried to say we shouldn't do anything to Erick anymore, but three against one wasn't a fair argument. I watched the street for incoming cars, and the three of them pushed the car into the water. It wasn't until the car was entirely engulfed in water that we started to hear the screaming."

"Erick was in the car." The end of my sentence didn't rise like a question should. It was flat.

He nodded, averting his gaze. "Afterward, I learned that Erick had been kicked out of his house and that he'd started to live in his car. It was the only home he had . . . and we had pushed it into the water. Of course, after I heard the screaming, I had to dive in. I took off my shoes, and I got him out. The other guys stayed behind."

I squeezed his hand, reminding him that I was there for him. The waver in his voice caught my heartstrings, telling me he was still beating himself up for what they had done. "Did you call the police?"

"Yes, I did once I pulled Erick out of the water. He wasn't really responding at first. Hanan called for an ambulance, and we waited for them."

"How did Erick end up?"

"He's alive, but he isn't the same person anymore. Once he woke up fully, he pressed charges." Dakota drew in a slow breath. "It was the first time any of us had been arrested. I could sense that division in the group more when the trial happened. There wasn't a jury since we were all minors. Our final punishment was up to a judge. I was appointed a public defender, and your father supported Malik and Hanan—he also agreed to work for Pierson.

They put all the blame on me. Your father used everything he knew about my family to argue that because my father was a violent man, I was following in his footsteps. He marked me as a bad seed and the mastermind behind the attack. He made a decent case, I must admit."

He laughed without any humor.

"The entire town thought badly of my family and dismissed my parents as lunatics. My punishment was decided before I even walked into that courtroom. It was all based on prejudice because of my last name. The judge sided with the rich kids. They were given community service while I was sentenced to three months inside a juvenile hall."

"Does this by any chance have anything to do with that whole rule against being in Boulder Valley and the Smell?" I asked.

"In a sense." Dakota shrugged. "There was an unwritten rule before about not going to Boulder Valley High in large groups. After Erick's accident, there was kind of an agreement that we wouldn't cross paths and cause trouble like we did before. Boulder Valley High students didn't go to our campus or our hangout spots, and we didn't go to theirs. Then Jiménez and a bunch of our friends started crashing more of Pierson's parties. That's why Pierson stormed into the Smell that night. He was getting sick and tired of the party crashers."

I leaned into his shoulder, moving his hands into mine and knitting our fingers together. "You went to this lake because of Erick. You didn't go to Franklin's party?"

"I didn't go to that party," he said after a beat. "Why do you think I would be at that party?"

I released a heavy sigh. "You can't ask me questions. I have too many of my own."

"Fair."

He held on to me as if he were going to lose me. We relaxed onto our backs, lying flat on the boardwalk, facing the cloudless California sky. We stayed like that for a long while.

I could feel the outline of his lips kiss my forehead. My eyes were closed, and I was lightly dozing off while blissful silence floated in the air. A good five minutes had gone by when Dakota spoke again, softly, into my ear.

"Sylvia?"

I didn't respond.

"Sylvia?" Yet again, I kept silent. "I guess you're asleep."

He chuckled.

"Sylvia . . . I love you, Sylvia. And I'm so sorry. I wish I were better. Not for me—but for you. You deserve something special, something more than me."

He kept going.

"You don't understand it when I say you're mine. I've never had anything of my own. I've never had anything that was mine. My sister was never truly my sister. She was wrapped up in her desire to be among the popular kids. My mother was never mine either. She was too hung up on what happened years ago to even remember that she was alive. You're the first person I've ever had as my own. My doll, my Sylvia . . . I'm so sorry, though. I'm sorry."

Chapter Forty-Eight
This Is What Makes Us Girls

Pretending to be asleep is much easier than you'd think. Despite the urge to stop that person and talk to them, you hesitate. There isn't much skill behind remaining silent.

I had rested my head against Dakota for only a few moments when my eyes began to grow heavy. I was going to tell him that I didn't want to talk, but then he said something that nearly stopped my heart.

I'm so sorry...

Sorry for what?

There was so much sadness in his voice, something that sounded foreign to him. Dakota seldom showed any emotion. The way his words were beginning to wobble near the end told me this wasn't a declaration of his love for me. It was him confessing to something bigger and darker.

I let out a fake yawn a couple minutes later, acting unfazed by what I'd heard. When we left the lake, I was more convinced than ever that Dakota was hiding something. I could see it in the way he looked at me. There was no sign of the mischievous grin that I loved so much. He pressed his lips together, creating a thin line, holding back unsaid words.

"My dad wants you to come to our Thanksgiving dinner."

I said this so that I could hold on to him for a moment longer. Just a few days more, I thought, was all I needed if his last words to me at the lake had been meant as a farewell speech.

"Uh. I can't do Thanksgiving. I have something planned."

"It took a lot out of my dad to consider letting you come to the dinner."

"Good for him. What do you want me to do? Give him a cookie?"

"Dakota . . ."

"I genuinely don't want to have to endure multiple hours with that man. What am I supposed to say to him when I walk up to your house? 'Hey, remember me? I'm the guy you put into juvie and the son of a man you put into jail . . . So where's the food at, fam?'" He stifled his mirth. "Not happening, Sylvia."

"Oh, please, Dakota. It's one day." I pressed on. "I'd like for you to at least tolerate him. I'm sure you feel the same way about your mom and me. She hates me, but I'm willing to work something out."

"She doesn't hate you. She hates your parents. There's a difference," he corrected me. "And you can't blame her. You hate your parents too."

I stared out my window. We weren't driving back to school. "Well, she doesn't like me."

"She doesn't like most people—hence why she doesn't leave the house. People judge. People spread lies and gossip. She's quite content not dealing with people at all."

"That's depressing."

"You'll get used to it. I know I eventually did."

There was no way I was going to win this argument from the looks of it. "Can you do this one thing . . . for me? Look at it as an early Christmas present."

He made a pained expression.

"You do have a present for me, right? I have something for you. You should have something for me."

He was at a loss for words.

"Ugh. Drop me off at school. I'd rather go to class than be stuck in this car with you for another ten seconds," I grumbled and fell back in my seat. I couldn't handle him anymore. Maybe him ignoring me was better than this. He didn't respond right away. "I said take me back to school, Dakota."

"I heard you the first time." He blew out a soft breath. "You're pissed. I don't know why. But I can tell that you are."

"I'm not pissed."

"Yes, you are. I know you, Sylvia."

"You don't know me that well." I crossed my arms over my chest. Dakota shook his head and did a sharp U-turn. I was sure that was an illegal move. I searched at my surroundings, trying to figure out where we were off to. The puzzle pieces finally came together.

"I said I want to go back to school. Not your brother's apartment."

Despite my words, his car pulled into the apartment complex. "How long have we known each other, Sylvia?" He didn't wait to get my answer. "After all that time, do you think I wouldn't get you something for the holidays?"

"After you made that stupid face, I thought you didn't get me anything."

"What face? This is just my face."

"You know what I'm talking about! That face that basically said, 'Aw, snap. I forgot about that. Dang it.'"

He muffled his laughter, putting the car in park. "First of all, I don't say 'dang it' or 'aw, snap.' Ever. It's not in my vocabulary."

"Well, the Dakota in my head does. He's a lot nicer too. Maybe you should take pointers from him."

"The Sylvia in my head is a lot more fun—and quieter." He caught himself. "Actually, I take that last part back. She's not quiet at all. She's quite loud. Especially because of what I'm doing to her. Maybe you should be more like her."

I flicked his ear. "I shouldn't have invited you to Thanksgiving dinner. I bet you'd say that kind of stuff with my dad there."

He winced, rubbing his ear. "I have manners. I wasn't raised by wolves."

"That's debatable with the way you treat people." I clicked off my seat belt. "Why are we here?"

"You asked about your present." He unbuckled his seat belt and ducked out of the car. He continued to talk while walking to the stairway that led to his brother's apartment. I tried my best to keep up. "I decided to divide it into three different things. Only one of those three things is ready. It's also part of my project for film class."

"I don't want to know about it," I rushed to say. "I can wait until December. You don't need to tell me now."

He peered at me over his shoulder. It was that same look, with his lips pressed together. What wasn't he telling me? We were going to be together in December, weren't we?

"I want to give this to you now. Or at least get your approval." He took out his keys and unlocked the door. Dion was at work, so we had the place to ourselves. I locked the door behind me. Dakota walked to the desktop computer in the living room.

"I'm glad I put it on the laptop and my desktop." He groaned. "Even though I wish I had my laptop instead because it has certain edits in it that this version doesn't."

"Why do you think Xander took it?"

"I'll find a way to get it back," was all he said, not answering my question. "I don't have a plan right now, but I know by the end of the day I'll come up with something. Most likely something that involves Jiménez as my getaway driver."

"Tell me about your project."

"We were given this assignment to make a short film about something we're passionate about or that inspires us."

"Ronnie told me about that part. What's yours about, though?"

"Well, I'm not that good at film. No surprise there. I had this whole concept in mind that just didn't work on film. First, I had to get it approved by my film teacher. Instead of making a short film, I told him I wanted to make a short animation since drawing is my strong point. He saw some of the storyboards I had in my sketchbook and he said he loved the concept."

Dakota pulled out an extra chair for me.

I squirmed in my seat. "What's your topic?"

"You," he said in a soft voice. "I titled it waan ka xumahay. It means 'sweetie' in Somali."

No, it didn't. Macaanto would be the word he needed. Waan ka xumahay meant "I messed up." But I wasn't about to tell him that. Had he purposely used the wrong translation so he could slip in a deeper meaning? Or was I interpreting it wrong?

I opened my mouth to speak. "I—"

"Before you say anything, let me show you what it is."

"Okay. Uh, play it then."

Dakota logged on to the desktop and searched for the file. I folded my hands in my lap, waiting for him to start the short animation. Nerves were eating at my insides.

What was there for him to be sorry about?

I hushed my thoughts and watched the images on the screen come to life. The first shot was a re-creation of the party at Beth's house where we'd met. It was in black and white. The scene changed, moving to our next interaction. The only thing in the background was gentle, angelic music until we got to the moment when we were standing in the rain in front of his house. In the narration, I heard the start of a poem.

We're avoiding it, of course we are.
Who would want to be so bare?
Bare.
Nothing.
I yearn to scream my nothing.
What words could be right enough
Or golds shrine bright enough?
Not enough
for the feelings that stir inside of us
Chivalrously, we're avoiding it
Maybe. Maybe we is just me.
A crash from this would be deadly
Although this high is amidst clouds
The fall too is thunderous
The tranquil comfort could soon be struck by rumbling pain.
Of course we're avoiding it; floating brings comfort and safety.
Maybe. Maybe it's just me
Who's breathless at the sound of your name
Perhaps it's only my lips that curl at just the thought of you
Your smile, I mimic
Your soul, I envy
Your mind, I lust
My mind, is lost.

We're avoiding it, the words on my tongue
I bite as they catapult from every vein and every vessel they travel with such speed
I chew, avoiding it.
Maybe it's just me.
Maybe, maybe I should shout it out
Shout loud enough from over here
Loud enough for you to hear
But loud is not loud enough
Amplify will not apply
For the root of the chord in my words
The grain behind the grumble
The umph behind the urge
Each time I think to let it out?
We're avoiding it. (Silently)
Of course we are, muddled in our affection
Afflicted by the absence
And adhered by adoration
I'm stuck
By only sticking to you
Maybe it is just me
Avoiding every impulse
Of course we are, to speak.
Or maybe it's just me who craves the freedom of honesty
I beg you take my body
But it's all already yours
My stomachs knots
My blushing cheeks
My jaw dropped on the floor
Avoiding it, of course we are

The rhythm with which we fall
Maybe it's just me
It's just the way I am.
My heart is weak to beauty
My mind is overthrown
And all the time the demons I wished would dance with yours
Instead
Are tamed and soothed
By your sorcerous self, smoothed
Soft
Gentle, by fire
While your flames flicker freely
We're avoiding it, of course we are.
Who would want to be so burned?
Maybe it's just me.
Trample me, I will not bend
To keep your step in time.
Any ache, I will take
So long as you will smile
We're avoiding it.
Of course we are.
Maybe, maybe it's just me.
Of course! We are avoiding it
At best reason to dodge
Not because our hearts are scared of ending only scarred.
With sacredness we scarcely scream.
But leave it live untouched.
Maybe, we're avoiding it.
As three words are not enough.

∙ ∙ ∙

The film faded into black, leaving me bare to what it had shown me. At some point during the film—I wasn't sure when—I had started to cry. Quickly, I tried to wipe away the fallen tears, but a hand caught mine.

Dakota lifted his hand to my face, swiping his thumb under my eye. "I didn't mean to make you sad, doll. I don't like seeing you cry."

A breath rumbled out of me as I rose out of my seat, turning away from the computer. "What was the point of that poem, then? It didn't sound like a happy one."

"I'm not always a happy person," he replied, rising out of his seat and moving toward me. "But I am happiest when I'm with you. Why aren't you satisfied with just that?"

"Because I can't just be satisfied with that when you don't acknowledge me as your girlfriend. I can't just be satisfied with that when you won't even do one dinner with my father. Now, simply because you've made this video, you think that will change things? You won't say my name and say I was the inspiration behind this. At your presentation, you'll probably lie and make up a different muse," I shouted, flailing my arms around. "You try your best to show me that you care, but you never show it in the ways I want you to."

"Why do you care what others think about us? Are you dating everyone at Crescent Hart Academy, or are you dating me, Sylvia?"

"Dating," I echoed, a bit relieved. "We're dating now? Okay. Well, that's one step in the right direction."

"You skipped over everything I said in the poem."

"I'm a selective listener," I said shamelessly. "I hear what I want."

He touched his temple, muttering to himself. "Why do I put up with this? You're lucky I love you."

I leaped forward, pointing my finger in his face—despite knowing he hated that kind of stuff. "You said it again."

"Again . . . " His brows knitted together. "You heard me at the lake?"

"I didn't say again. I said . . . ahhh. Amsterdam."

Dakota wasn't buying it. "You're not a good liar. We need to fix that. I need you to be able to lie for me if I ever need an alibi."

"Do you plan on committing a crime anytime soon? If so, I plead the fifth," I said with a hand up high. "And don't try and slide past what you said, Ridgewood."

He took another step forward, bringing us chest to chest. "I have no clue what you're talking about, Ellington. No clue at all."

"Oh, come on. You can say it. I'll even start it for you. 'I love . . .'"

"Watching you undress," he finished, wiggling his brows. "What? You set yourself up for that one."

Without hesitating, I slapped his arm.

"Ouch!" he yelped. "You're so abusive."

"Seriously."

Dakota cupped my face and held me there, looking into my eyes and not saying a word. "I love you, Sylvia. The sad part about that, though, is that I think I've loved you for a lot longer than I let on—"

"Shut up." I cut him off, connecting our lips together and forgetting about what he had said at the lake. "I forgive you for playing hard to get."

● ● ●

Dakota drove me home after we realized it was too late to go back to school. I kept to myself for most of the ride. When Dakota pulled into my driveway, Tara was standing outside next to her car. I stepped out of Dakota's car and walked slowly up to the house.

"I was about to drive up to the school." Tara didn't appear to be angry from the looks of it. "I got a call about you not being in your classes."

"I wasn't feeling good. I threw up, so Dakota took me home. He doesn't feel good either."

"So sorry to hear about that. That's nice of him, though, to bring you back home." She walked beside me into the house. "Your friend came over about fifteen minutes ago. The one who came over a few times before for study sessions."

Ronnie? Why was she here? She hadn't told me she was coming over.

Tara pushed the door open. My eyes immediately turned to where Ronnie was sitting on the couch. The loud noise of the door swinging shut caused her to look at us.

Something was off about the way she greeted me, like she was afraid someone down the hall could hear us. I'd never seen this much concern in Ronnie's face . . . ever. She always tried to crack a joke or laugh about something inappropriate. Whatever news she had for me, it couldn't be good. Regardless of the sickening feeling washing over my entire body, I guided her up to my bedroom and told her we could talk privately there.

I took the edge of my bed, and she sat at my desk, swinging around in the chair.

"I saw Dakota's car pull out of the driveway," she admitted and set her phone on the desk beside her. "You still trust him?"

"We talked a lot at this lake after we left school. He said he didn't go to the party."

"And you believe him?"

'Yes.'

"Sylvia. You can't believe everything he tells you. He could be lying. Did he give you actual proof that he wasn't at the party?"

"I know he's not lying. I have a gut feeling."

"I'm sure you also had a 'gut feeling' when Xander went to Dion's apartment." She whispered, "Pretty dumb."

"Hey, that's not kind to say."

"I'm sorry, Sylvia. You're my best friend. I love you and all, but you honestly have the worst judgment. You forgive so easily. I don't understand why, but it's getting a little annoying. I keep witnessing it again and again. I feel like you're letting these people walk all over you."

Her phone began to buzz. Finn's name flashed on the screen. It was a new text message.

I arched my brow. "I'm the one who forgives people too easily, huh? How about you? That's Finn texting you right now, isn't it? I bet you're taking him back."

Ronnie snatched up her phone and threw it into her bag. "I haven't taken him back. You know I wouldn't after what I found out. I can't trust him."

I brought my legs up and tucked my knees under my chin, watching her carefully. A new thought suddenly occurred to me. "Should I trust you?"

She flinched at my words. "Why the hell shouldn't you trust me?"

"Well, I don't know. Maybe because when I was at Dion's apartment, you and Jiménez were the only ones who knew where I was.

You dropped us off. If anyone had snitched about our location to the members of Senior Salute, it would be you. You've been with Finn for how many years? Two, right? And in all that time, you're expecting me to believe that you've only recently learned about him being the Maestro of Senior Salute?"

"I can't believe how easily you can throw me under the bus, but you can't consider— not even for a moment—the idea of Dakota being behind this." She forced an airy laugh and got to her feet. "You try so hard to defend Dakota that you've become blind to what he's capable of."

"I know him, Ronnie," I said without any uncertainty. "He wouldn't hurt me."

"But you think I would!?"

"You're the one who threw him under the bus."

"With evidence! We have actual footage of him entering that party with Xander."

"You have footage of someone you think is him."

"God, you're so damn stubborn! I can't win with you, Sylvia." She threw her hands up. "Do you want to know why I'm here in the first place? I came here to tell you that I'm willing to pretend to be with Finn so you can get some information out of him. I've been texting him since third period to see if I can meet up with him on the weekend and get some information out of him. But after this conversation, it's clear that you wouldn't even trust anything I told you."

I rushed to my feet and tried to stop her. "Ronnie, that's not what I s—"

"I don't want to hear it," she snapped, throwing her backpack over her shoulder. "You know, I've spent so many years not really having a friend in this town. And the second I get one, she turns on me for some guy."

Ronnie let out one last exasperated sigh then shut the door. Just like that, I had lost my best friend.

•••

Dakota didn't show up to school for two weeks. On the last day before Thanksgiving break, he was still a no-show. My father pestered me about Dakota, asking if he was coming and if I had told him what time he should show up.

The day after the lake, I'd lost any courage to talk to my dad about any of the rumors that kept me up at night. After today, once the visitors were gone, I wanted to finally have that conversation with him.

One hour before Thanksgiving dinner was supposed to start, I broke it to Tara and my dad that Dakota wasn't going to make it.

"Oh, that's okay," Tara said while setting the table.

Hanan came in from the kitchen, asking. "Mom, who did you invite?"

"I invited the Wallenbergs, and Faye and her father," she replied. "And I believe your father invited a family over who only recently moved to Boulder Valley."

"Ah, right." Dad snapped his fingers. "I don't think they'll be able to come. They're still unpacking and figuring out the town. The family has two kids. If you don't mind, I'd love for you to show them around, Sylvia, since they'll be attending Crescent Hart Academy."

"Shouldn't Hanan and Malik do it instead?" I suggested. "They know the town better than I do."

"He's already asked us," Malik chimed in. "I have too much of a social life to be stuck with some new kids."

"Fine," I agreed. "I won't mind showing them around for the second semester. Is there anyone else coming, Tara?"

She paused to think. "Oh, right. I completely forgot. I invited your friend Pierson and his mother over. At least you'll have them here."

"Great." I met the heel of my palm to my forehead.

Pierson, for most of the week, was taking advantage of the fact Dakota wasn't around. Whenever we started a conversation, he somehow always hinted at wanting to hang out with me again. Any chance he could, he offered to get me tickets to something. A movie. A concert. An art show in the city. A play going on in the town over. There was every public outing you could think of running through that boy's mind, thinking of how he could touch his lips to mine. To him, choosing the stage for our next kiss occupied the conversation anytime we sat together in class.

When the doorbell rang, I told everyone I would get it. I was praying it was Pierson so I could at least have someone who didn't hate me in the room. Twisting the doorknob, I began to yank the door open.

To say I was shocked would be the biggest understatement of the year.

It was Dakota. He was dressed in a crisp button-up shirt with a black sweater over it. He'd paired that with black slacks and dress shoes. Dakota had even gone as far as to slick back his hair in way that I rather liked. It was possibly the first time I had seen him without a leather or jean jacket. There was a premade pie in his hands and an uncomfortable smile on his face.

I bit my lip, stopping the impulse to fully form a proper smile.

As much as I was glad to have Dakota here, a stab of fear hit me when it dawned on me who else would be attending the dinner. Pierson thought I had broken up with Dakota. If he saw him at dinner, he would know we were definitely still together.

Chapter Forty-Nine

Too Young

Dakota's eyes looked spaced-out when I asked him if he wanted to go back inside. We were in the backyard, waiting for Tara to finish setting out Thanksgiving dinner. We'd snuck out here to get some privacy, hiding away from the twins.

His mind was somewhere else, so I asked him a second time. Waving my hand in front of his face, I jarred him out of his thoughts. "Anyone home there?" I chuckled. "What was it you were thinking of?"

Dakota shook his head and brought a hand up to his face, pinching the bridge of his nose. He laughed into his hand. Bright sapphire irises hit me, looking at me a little differently than he had before. "It's nothing. Just spacing out. Let's get back inside."

He curled his arm around my body, leaning me into him with each step toward the house. I wondered what it was he was pondering so deeply. "I didn't tell you about this one other guest we're having over."

"Like I said, as long as it's not Betty, I'm okay with whoever it is."

"Tara invited Xander's family and Malik's girlfriend."

Dakota flashed a look down at a watch that wasn't there. "Wow, time flies. Looks like it's already time to leave."

He walked ahead of me, but I grabbed his arm. "You're leaving?"

"There's no way I'm staying."

"You can't leave me with the wolves."

I hadn't yet revealed that Pierson would also be joining us. At first, I'd been worried that having Pierson and Dakota in the same room would be mayhem. However, the longer I thought about it, the more appealing the idea seemed. With all of my enemies in the same house, Dakota could hopefully keep me sane.

"I'll stay. But once the food part is over, I'm out," he declared. "Why didn't you invite Ronnie? You could've had more people on your side."

My head dipped. "We're not friends anymore."

"Since when?" He took my chin gently and lifted my head up. "I thought you guys were best friends."

"We were until I accused her of being a part of Senior Salute."

Dakota lowered his hand from my face. "She couldn't be part of Senior Salute."

"She was dating Finn, though. He's the maestro."

"Maestros aren't allowed to involve their girlfriends. Even if Finn wanted to, he couldn't tell Ronnie. He'd be stripped of his position and wouldn't be able to conduct the second-semester jackpot. Finn loves power too much to put that at risk."

I wondered how he knew this much about Senior Salute. I didn't bother to ask him.

"There's another semester I need to be cautious about?! Perfect. I thought everything was done this semester."

I realized that there was a lot of apologizing I needed to do to Ronnie. I was an awful friend for having jumped to conclusions so quickly. I had been betrayed by a best friend in the past. It was a feeling I was used to.

Dakota pulled the back door open, and I walked inside, thinking of ways I could apologize to Ronnie. I knew I needed to do it as soon as possible.

The front door was wide open. My father was letting someone in. I couldn't see who it was past my dad's back. "I wasn't told that you wanted to come for dinner," he was saying. "I would've set an extra plate if I knew you were coming."

"Oh, I'm not staying for dinner. I just came to drop by and say hello." My father sidestepped, revealing who was at the door.

Finn, Ronnie's ex-boyfriend, stood on the doorstep, grinning up at my father, and then he looked at me. "There she is. The girl I wanted to talk to."

"Sylvia?" Dad turned around. "A friend of yours is here to speak with you."

Words could not describe how taken aback I was.

What was with all of these unwanted guests?

My feet were bolted to the floor.

"I'm here for you," Dakota whispered into my ear. "I'll be there."

"I was hoping for a one-on-one conversation with her," Finn said, knitting his hands in front of him. "If you don't mind."

The two guys stared each other down. Dakota leaned in a little closer, glaring daggers into Finn. "I think it would be best if she had someone with her."

"I won't be long," Finn promised. "It's quite important. I'll be fast."

Dakota held his stance, but not for long. I hated Dakota for not putting up more of a fight. I hated my father for letting the Devil himself walk into our home. Above all, I hated how I wanted to step outside that door and walk to my own funeral.

Funnily enough, Finn was dressed in two different shades of red.

How fitting.

I'd only taken a few steps outside the front door before Finn started speaking. He didn't ask me how I was doing or if I was having a nice holiday—he just cut to the chase. He really was planning on making this as quick as possible.

"I've been hearing you have some questions regarding Senior Salute."

"I don't want to join."

"There aren't any spots open," he replied. "But I do know you've been asking a hell of a lot of questions you know you shouldn't. I don't know exactly what you've discovered, but I want to warn you that if you tell any outsiders anything, then you'll be facing some ugly consequences."

He wasn't scaring me.

"If you're trying to blackmail me with that photo and video you sent, then you honestly must not be as smart as Ronnie said you are. Revenge porn is illegal. You'd be arrested for filming and distributing that. You're already eighteen, so the law won't be all that kind to you. You honestly think my dad wouldn't sue you for everything you've got? He's a lawyer, Finn."

"You think that's all I have on you?" He hooted a laugh. "That's not even the beginning. That message you received was only a warning. It's a hint about what they have in store for you." He wiped the corner of his eye from laughing so hard. "I didn't come here to be amused by your cluelessness, though. I'm here to make a deal."

"I'm not interested."

"You haven't heard what it is yet."

"It involves you. I don't want to be a part of it."

Finn lifted his hands up, seeing that he wasn't winning with me and calling some kind of truce. "Listen. It's clear that Ronnie doesn't want to end this break. She's officially made it a real breakup."

I pointed under my eye and drew down the path a tear would've fallen if I gave two shits about his failed attempts. My lips pouted. "Aw, poor baby. Get to the point."

"I know you're friends with her. You're closer with her than anyone else. She'll listen to you if you tell her that I want her back. All I need you to do is convince her to take me back. If you can get her back with me, then I'll make your name unlisted. First- and second-semester jackpots."

"Unlisted?"

"It means people can't use you for donations or bids."

"That's all?"

Finn drew in a long, strained breath. "I'll also answer one of your questions. One."

"Who's behind the video? Who filmed it?"

"I can't release that kind of information to just anyone. I'll give you a hint, though. They are someone who once cared about you or still cares about you. They were once your friend or are your friend now."

"That's the stupidest hint ever. You covered so many people with those two sentences. That's a fucking riddle."

"It's the best I can give you," he offered. "Now you have to do your part. Get me back with Ronnie."

I didn't feel right about this. I would never set Ronnie up with someone who was this hungry for power over the weak. "How do I know I can trust that you'll take me off the list?"

"You can trust me. You know how much I love Ronnie. I'll do whatever it takes to get her back. She won't speak to me anymore. I thought I had her back for a second, but she was gone before I knew it."

He must've been talking about the time she was texting him in the hopes of getting information out of him.

"Please, Sylvia. I wouldn't ask for help if I could do it myself."

His voice wavered, losing its authority. Just saying her name caused him to frown. He buried his head in his hands when I remained silent.

I cleared my throat. "No."

Finn's eyes shot up to mine. "What?"

"I said no. I'm not helping you."

Finn stepped back, looking at me. "You're making a big mistake, Sylvia. I'll give you until December tenth to get me back with her."

"That's two days before school ends."

"I'm aware of that. That's more than enough time for you to convince her to come back to me." Finn went down the front steps toward the driveway where his car was parked. "I hope you don't disappoint me, Sylvia."

Chapter Fifty

Suddenly I See

Only a few minutes had passed since Finn's car had driven away from my house. I'd taken a seat on the front porch, not quite ready to go back inside. Not quite ready to do anything at all besides look at my options. There was no way I could go to Ronnie, ask for her friendship, and then turn around and demand she take back her ex.

It was clear that Ronnie still had feelings for him, but she'd been strong enough to leave. I was a bit envious of that quality. She didn't like taking crap from anyone. She was self-aware to the point where she knew when to leave a bad situation. I, on the other hand, was enticed by a dangerous fire.

"Hey."

I hadn't noticed that the front door had opened. I spotted Hanan poking his head out.

"Are you okay? You've been out here for a while."

"I needed some time to think."

Pushing strands of hair behind my ear, I looked away to hide my red eyes. After learning about Finn being a part of Senior Salute, I couldn't trust anyone else who might be involved. It seemed like any guy at our school was a possible suspect. For all I knew, Hanan could be in Senior Salute too. Regardless of how kind he'd been to me, I still couldn't help but feel cautious around him now.

"I'll be back inside in a second," I announced, tugging at the fabric of my black dress. "I just want some more time alone."

Hanan took the empty space next to me on the steps. "Getting a visit from Finn is never a good thing. I'm assuming he talked to you about Senior Salute."

I shot a look in his direction. "You're part of Senior Salute?"

"Not necessarily."

My eyes sharpened on him, unsure if it was the truth.

"The club is hard to avoid. But I'm not tempted to join," he explained. "I think preying on people the way they do makes you a disgusting person. There's nothing powerful about what they're doing."

I recalled the first day I'd met Hanan. He had told me how he was tired of the kind of people he hung out with. He was tired of the boring cycle. I thought back to that night before we'd left for the party. Would I have ever befriended Beth if I'd never gone that night? Would I have been so tempted to pursue Dakota? Where would I be if I hadn't attended that party at all? Where would I be if I'd never left Maine?

I quickly decided that my life was better off the way it was. Despite the obstacles I had faced—including the fake friends and the unnecessary drama that polluted my daily routine—I wouldn't want to go back. For my entire life, I'd only ever been floating, letting the tidal waves of bad news crash into me without much care. I couldn't have imagined that I could find happiness and peace in Dakota.

I turned to Hanan. "I couldn't agree more. It's cowardly. Adding money into the mix makes it seem like some sick sport. Human interactions aren't a game."

"They're too stupid to see that, though."

I flattened my hands on my lap. "I know there's a chance that you aren't a part of Senior Salute ... but right now, I can't really take anyone's word."

He laughed to himself.

"What's so funny?"

He laughed even more. "You."

I squinted at him, bemused. "I don't understand what you mean."

"I find it funny that you're only now starting to not trust people. I know about a fraction of what happened in Maine. I would've expected you to be more standoffish. You're the opposite, though."

"I guess I am. But I wasn't so open when I first came here."

"Oh, really? Is that what you think?" He smirked. "Tell me then. What is it that made you change? And don't give me that 'I fell in love so now my barriers are gone' answer. Because I know you're not in love."

I puffed out a breath. "I am. I love Dakota."

"No, you're not. You hardly know Dakota. I feel like he knows more about your past than you know about his. I bet I know more about him than you do. I'll put money down right now, right here, just to prove I do."

I closed my hands, gripping the step. "I know a lot about his past."

"All right. Do you at least know why his dad is in jail? The real reason? Or why Malik and Dakota used to be best friends but now can't stand to be in the same room together?"

"I do know," I answered feebly. "And simply because you know more about him than I do doesn't mean I'll trust you."

"I don't blame you. I didn't come out here to tell you to trust me. Who you do or don't trust is up to you," he said. "But I do ask you to be cautious about who you decide to trust. From what your dad has told us, I know this isn't like what happened in Maine a few months ago. That doesn't mean you should take this matter any less seriously."

I inched away from him. "How do you know that?"

"Your father told Malik and me about what happened not too long before you got here. I get why you had to leave and why you did what you did. I wish they could've done something about the bullying at your school."

I bit the inside of my cheek, remembering the nightmare that was my life a few months ago. The bullying hadn't been so bad. It was when people had started making death threats, slashing my mom's car tires, and throwing rocks at our house that things went from bad to awful.

"Malik was against the idea of you moving in with us, and I guess for the longest time he thought you weren't coming," Hanan went on to say. "I wouldn't be surprised if he outsourced someone to take an interest in you."

I sighed. "Do you know who else has pledged in my name for Senior Salute?"

"You don't want to know who I think it is."

"No, tell me. Who is it?"

He drew in a long breath, staring out toward the streets. "Either Xander ... or Dakota."

I got up from my spot on the steps. "I don't want to hear it."

"Hear me out first."

Slowly, I returned to my sitting position. "Talk."

"Think about it. I'm sure you already know that his sister and his mother were victims of a Senior Salute. It's clear Dakota didn't like you before. Why wouldn't he want to go after you given what happened in the past? He has a motive to hurt you and the perfect opportunity since you two are close."

"I've had enough people say he's behind—"

"Wait. I'm not the first person who's suggested Dakota could be in Senior Salute? What the hell, Sylvia? Isn't that a big enough sign on its own?"

I was moments away from telling him that I knew Dakota well enough, but my words were interrupted by the familiar white Audi that pulled up.

Siobhan exited the passenger seat, carrying a bottle of red wine in one hand. Pierson trailed after his mother, keeping his head down.

"I hope we're not late." Siobhan grinned and pulled me into a hug.

"You're right on time. Everyone's already inside. We're just waiting for a few more people." I returned the smile. She walked past me to say hello to Hanan and enter the house. Pierson stayed in front of me with his head still facing the gravel. "Hey," I said.

Pierson grumbled something incoherent while staring at my feet.

"Huh? I didn't catch that."

"I said I got you a gift. I know it's too early for Christmas, but I wanted to give it to you now." He reached into his back pocket.

Hanan snickered when Pierson retrieved a small box. "Of course," he grumbled to himself and went inside the house.

With Hanan and Siobhan gone, I faced Pierson again. His eyes were still glued to the ground.

I refused to look at the box. "You didn't need to get me anything."

"Think of it as an early Christmas gift."

"It's not even December."

"Please."

Reluctantly, I nodded my head.

"Take it."

At first, I hesitated, but then I grabbed it from him. I opened the gift slowly, not wanting to mess up the gold-and-blue wrapping.

That was another strange habit of mine—preserving pretty wrapping paper.

Inside, a velvet jewelry box held a ring with a pair of hands holding a heart with a crown above it. Squinting at it, I noticed that there was a diamond in the middle of the heart, shimmering bright under the November sun.

"It's called a claddagh ring. I had it made for you," Pierson informed me. He had a matching ring on his own finger, minus the gemstone. "It's a traditional Irish ring. It symbolizes love, friendship, and loyalty."

I was speechless. Partly because it was the exact same gift Angel had given to Buffy on Buffy the Vampire Slayer. They were in a relationship, though. And it didn't seem odd to give such a meaningful ring to Buffy.

I handed the ring and the jewelry box back to Pierson. "I can't accept this."

"I want you to take it, Sylvia. I went through a hell of a lot of trouble just to pay for it."

I couldn't win with him. He obstinate determination wouldn't take no for an answer. I thanked him.

We headed toward the house.

"Not everyone's here yet," I said. "We're still waiting for people to show up."

"Who else is here?"

"Well, my dad, Tara, Hanan, Malik, the spawn of Satan . . . and Dakota."

Pierson hesitated a step away from the front door. I could sense profanity ready to spew at me. I raised my hand at him.

"I don't want to hear whatever nasty remark you're about to say. My patience is wearing thin, and I can only take so much today before blowing a fuse."

Pierson murmured again, but I was quick to shut him up.

"Thanksgiving is the one time when I can stuff my face and slip into a peaceful, food-induced coma. No one will mess this up for me. Not you, not Malik, and not even Xander. You better not start any fights."

"Yes, ma'am." He saluted. "I won't start anything if I don't get provoked."

I narrowed my eyes at him.

"Fine." He sighed. "I'll try my hardest to not start any problems."

• • •

The dinner wasn't as chaotic as I'd thought it would be. I did have to moderate the conversation a few times, but that was to be expected. My shoulders didn't relax until Xander's and Pierson's families left. My eyes followed Xander's every move, making sure he didn't sneak off and head to my bedroom. I wasn't planning on getting my laptop stolen.

I didn't have much time to speak with Dakota after dinner was over. However, with my father's permission, he drove me to Ronnie's apartment complex. Dakota offered to go in with me, but I refused. This was something I needed to do on my own.

It was hard to find parking, so he eventually stopped on the street. I figured she should be at home with her two younger siblings. Hopefully. She could also be at her part-time job. But since I wanted this to be a surprise, I hadn't texted her. Knowing Ronnie, she wouldn't reply to any of my texts anyway.

Finding the apartment she lived in wasn't hard. I knocked on the door until I heard someone approaching. The chain was still on when Ronnie opened the door, cracking it ajar.

She slammed it shut right away. "No one's home."

"Ronnie." I sighed. "I just saw you."

"Go away, Sylvia."

"No. I'm not leaving. I want to talk."

"I can't talk. I'm too busy being a bad friend who believes my boyfriend before I believe my own best friend . . . Oh, wait. No, that's you."

"C'mon, Ronnie. I really do want to talk."

"Last time we talked, you didn't want to listen," she said from behind the door. "I don't want to talk to you."

"I'm sorry!" I shouted. "I shouldn't have jumped to that conclusion. I was wrong."

The door opened again. "Say that again."

"Say what again?"

"Say that you were wrong." Her face poked out.

"I was wrong."

"Say you were wrong, I was right, and I'm not a two-faced friend," she added. "Also, say that you're an idiot."

"Ronnie! I'm not saying that!"

"I'm hurt, Sylvia. You need to regain my trust. Now go on and say it."

I groaned. "I was wrong. You were right. You're not a two-faced friend. I'm an idiot."

"Perfect!" She beamed and pulled out her phone. "Now I want you to say it into the camera. I need to capture this moment. Say it with more pep, though."

I slapped her hand away and frowned. "I'm not doing that."

She shrugged. "It was worth a shot."

The door closed again, and she unhooked the chain, then opened it wide enough for me to step inside. I walked past the coffee table and sat down on the couch.

"My little sister is asleep, so don't talk too loud," Ronnie said as she walked to the kitchen, returning with two bottles of water. "We're the only ones home."

She set the water bottles on the coffee table. "I'm glad you came to your senses sooner than later. It's kinda hard to get a refund on most of the gifts I got."

Our friend group had discussed doing a white elephant gift exchange for the kids who ate in the drama room. News spread, and I'd told Pierson about it. Some of the jocks were participating since they thought it was a cool idea.

"I don't want to hear what you got me!" I plugged my ears. "Dakota already showed me one of my gifts. I don't want to see what you got. I can wait."

She slumped into the seat beside me. "He gave you your gift? Ahead of time? That's a little weird."

"So did Pierson."

"The only reason I would give someone an early Christmas gift is if I knew I wouldn't see them for a while."

I shook my head and picked up the water bottle, twisting the top. "No, Dakota's not going anywhere. It's because I made a crack about him forgetting about gifts."

With Pierson, I wasn't sure.

"Okay. If that's what you say." Ronnie took a sip, eyeing me the entire time. "What was it exactly that made you realize I wasn't lying?"

"I learned a few rules about Senior Salute leaders."

She shook her head, lowering her bottle. "I don't want to hear anything about Senior Salute or Senior Salute leaders. I told Jiménez I want out of that plan of yours. I don't want to be involved in this anymore. I was quite content with my life before all this started."

"I wish I had the option to walk away from this."

"If you want me to, I could speak to Finn."

"No. It's okay. If you start talking to him, he'll only get the wrong idea. He'll think you're taking him back."

"He's real cute if he thinks I'd take him back. Besides, it's not like I can."

"Why do you say that?"

Almost as if on cue, one of the bedroom doors opened and closed. A shadow fell across the wall, getting closer to us. "Hey, do you know where I left my toothbrush?"

Twisting around to face the hallway, I saw something I wasn't expecting. Jiménez tried to duck away. It was too late. I'd already seen him. He was stripped down to nothing but a towel around his waist.

I cocked a brow at Ronnie, who was now shrinking down in her seat, avoiding eye contact. "You said your sister was asleep. That's not your sister."

"No one's here besides me." Jiménez laughed, giving me a little wave. "Hey, Sylvia."

"I didn't know you were here either." I cleared my throat. "When did you and Jiménez become an item? And why was I not notified about this?"

"We're not an item," Ronnie corrected me. "He came over to study."

I scoffed. "He's here to study with a towel on? He doesn't even go to the same school as us. Tell me how that even makes sense?"

"No, she's telling the truth." Jiménez defended her. "We were studying for Sex Ed."

Ronnie slapped her hand to her forehead. "Jiménez! Did you have to say that? Really? Right now?"

"It wasn't like she was going to believe your studying lie anyway." He walked over to the kitchen, getting himself a cup. "Be glad that I had the decency to put on a towel."

Ronnie only exhaled into her hands. "I'm so sorry about him."

"No, it's okay." I closed the water bottle and got to my feet. "I think that's a sign I should leave."

Ronnie grabbed my hand. "You don't have to go."

"No, I think I do," I said, going to the door. I told them goodbye and headed down the stairs, laughing to myself at the fact that Jiménez and Ronnie were together.

"How did it go?" Dakota asked when I got in the car.

"It went well, actually. Jiménez was there."

"Jiménez? That's interesting." He smiled. "Are you ready to go?"

"Yeah." I patted my pockets. "Wait, no, I think I left my phone."

"Maybe you left it in the car."

I looked around and patted the floor of the car, but I came up empty-handed. Grabbing the handle of the glove compartment, I yanked it open and searched it just in case I'd thrown it in there before leaving. My phone, along with some papers, fell out, landing on my lap. I would've shoved them back into the glove compartment if it weren't for the words written on the very top.

"Transfer papers to . . . Boulder Valley High? Why do you have these?"

Dakota smacked his lips shut, flashing his eyes between me and the papers.

"Tell me the truth."

"Put those back where you found them."

"You're transferring to Boulder Valley High." My voice cracked. "Is . . . is this why you gave me my present early? How long have you been planning on leaving?"

"A little over two weeks." Dakota pulled out of his parking spot. "I was going to tell you."

"When? The day before winter break?" I knew I was right from the way he nervously threw me a look. I flung the papers at him. "Oh, wow. You were going to wait until the last moment! That's real brave of you. You didn't want to ask me to see how I felt about it."

"Last time I checked, the transfer forms don't ask me to get consent from my girlfriend," he admitted harshly. "Sylvia, I'm going to a different school. Not a different country."

"You could've at least told me in advance."

Dakota attempted to speak, but I told him to stop and drive me home. There was no way he could redeem himself after this. As his car pulled in alongside my house, I threw the door open.

"Sylvia."

"What?" I shouted.

"I think . . . it would be best if we stopped seeing each other."

His expression told me a completely different story. He looked pained at the thought, frowning to himself.

I gripped the door handle. "If that's what you want."

Slowly, he nodded his head.

Before I slammed the door shut, I could've sworn that I heard him whisper, "Sorry."

But for what?

Chapter Fifty-One

Lovers to Strangers

Dad was sitting on the porch when Dakota dropped me off, doing something I'd only seen my mother do: smoking a cigarette. The biggest difference was that you could still see the tan filter—fully intact. Dad didn't have the same habit.

My head hug low as I scurried to the door without making direct eye contact. Dad was more observant than I gave him credit for because the first thing he said was, "What's wrong, Sylvia?"

I flinched away from his words like a burn.

"Nothing is wrong."

"You look upset."

"Dakota broke up with me."

Dad flicked the cigarette to the ground, stomping it out. "You want to talk about it? I'm here if you need someone."

"There's nothing to talk about."

"Actually," he said while getting to his feet, "I have something I want to tell you. Can we go inside?"

Trailing into the house with Dad, I thought of what he could possibly have been waiting to tell me. When my mind settled on the most plausible, I felt fearful. Was he itching to kick me out? Was this going to be his warning speech? Would he tell me that there was a ticking clock waiting to go off on the eve of my graduation from high school? Would I be forced to find a new home when college came knocking on the door?

Dad walked us into his study. It looked like a room straight out of the seventies: the walls were wood-paneled, and the floor was carpeted. What this space desperately needed was a better window. It was unbelievably stuffy.

"Take a seat."

I felt like one of Dad's clients.

"Am I in trouble?"

"Heavens no."

"Then what is this about?"

Dad sat down in front of me, linking his fingers together. "It's about your birthday."

"It's not for another six months."

He went into his drawers, retrieving a manila folder. "No, it's about the one that already passed. Your eighteenth birthday." Dad slid the folder across the desk, tapping the top of it. "These are your adoption papers.

"My what?" I froze. "I'm adopted?"

"Layla is your aunt," he explained. "She was your mother's sister. When you were almost four years old, you were placed into the foster system after both your parents died."

"You adopted me?"

He nodded. "Layla and I both agreed that we would tell you when you turned eighteen . . . but I didn't realize you were already eighteen when I picked you up at the airport."

I flipped the folder open, seeing my birth certificate and two names I'd never seen before in the spot for my parents. "What happened to them?"

"You father had extreme anger issues," Elijah detailed, taking off his glasses. "He had an obsessive, jealous personality, and he couldn't handle his own emotions."

Sounds a lot like someone I know.

"He was upset over the people your mother talked to. He didn't like seeing her in revealing clothes. I remember getting calls from her about how much he scared her."

"You knew her?"

"Yes, I did. Your mother and Layla were both raised in this town. We went to high school together," he stated. "And we headed to the East Coast together—the three of us. My mother loved your mother too. When she heard you were in the system again after Layla got in trouble with the law, my mom flew there on a red-eye. She saw you as her only grandchild since I've had fertility issues for as long as I can remember."

"I don't understand . . ."

He reached over to touch my knuckles. "Which part?"

"Everything."

"You need to elaborate, sweetie," he smiled. "Can you tell me what confuses you?"

"Dakota told me that you had an affair with his mother."

Dad's mouth fell open, and he waited a beat. "I dated her in high school—"

"He didn't say dated."

Elijah coughed like he'd swallowed a fly. "I don't know what you're accusing me of."

"Did you purposely frame Dakota and his father?"

"Of course not! I can't believe that's what he's been telling you. I can't believe I let him into my house!"

"He has every right to think that since you put him in juvie for almost drowning someone when he wasn't a part of it at all!"

"Sylvia . . ." He held on to his chest, stunned. "What did he tell you? That's not why he went to juvie."

"Then what was it?"

"He was arrested for selling tobacco to minors."

•••

Dakota was dead to me. Putting distance between Dakota and me wasn't as difficult as I'd thought it would be. We had only two classes together. The seat next to me in homeroom remained empty for the rest of the semester. He spent his lunchbreak in his car and rarely made an appearance near my locker or in the cafeteria. In his absence, Pierson, unsurprisingly, took my side. It took a lot of convincing, but I told him not to give Dakota a hard time.

Finals came and went without much excitement. Pierson and Ronnie planned to throw me a big bash a week after the last day of school. Everyone had been way too stressed out about exams and were planning on going simply to let off some steam. People who didn't even like Pierson were asking for details about the party.

I'd told Ronnie about the deal Finn had offered me. And even though she'd said she would talk some sense into him, I knew it was no use. He wanted one thing, and that was Ronnie. There was no in between. There was no way I could negotiate myself out of this.

"This is ridiculous," Ronnie said on the last day of school. Winter break was only a few hours away, and I couldn't wait. "You can still see each other if he starts going to Boulder Valley High. How do you think Jiménez and I are working it out? Dakota has a car. You guys could've made something work."

I sighed, picking at the sticker on my textbook. "He didn't care enough to tell me he wanted to leave. It came out of nowhere. I thought we were okay. But I feel like it's something more than just moving schools."

"Give me the okay and I'll gladly run him over with my car. I'll even pretend like it was an accident."

Covering my mouth, I refrained from chuckling. "There's no need to get violent. What's done is done."

I had cried about it after it happened, screaming into my pillow, but I eventually had to stop myself. He didn't deserve my tears. I swallowed my anger whenever I saw him at school, pretending that it didn't hurt. I was starting to like the idea of him leaving for Boulder Valley High. Things would be easier that way.

•••

Ronnie and I made our way to the auditorium for the end-of-semester assembly. Film class would be presenting their short films. I had seen a bit of Ronnie's, and I thought it was a very interesting concept. She had chosen to base her film on the misrepresentation of women and people of color in the media and how it can affect our self-esteem.

We took our seats and waited for the room to fill up. It was 11:00 a.m. when the film teacher walked onstage. He introduced himself and explained what his class had been told to do. I was happy that I had Ronnie to sit through it with. When Dakota's film came up, Ronnie began to boo at the screen.

I hushed her, but I was laughing between breaths. Ronnie held off. The film began just how I remembered. There was a re-creation of the night we'd met. Everything was exactly the same ... up until the part where the poem was meant to start.

The film cut to black.

A few students chattered amongst themselves, wondering what had happened. It wasn't long until the screen lit up again, but on a new image. It captured the outside of a familiar building. It took me a second, but I recognized it as the venue where Dakota and his band had performed, the gig where he'd dedicated two songs to me.

"What the..?" I gazed up at the shaky video.

The shot cut to the interior. Loud footsteps echoed down a lonely hallway. A figure walked past the camera. She turned around, showing us who she was. She was aware of the camera and winked at it. The video was even date-stamped. It was the same day we were there.

"I didn't know Carmen was there that day," Ronnie admitted.

"Yeah, she was. I ran into her in the restroom," I informed. "I didn't know that she went backstage."

The next shot wasn't as shaky, but the quality was poor, something you'd expect to see from a security camera at a liquor store. The film was grainy. You could see Carmen walk into the greenroom. A guy was seated on one of the couches. He looked too much like Dakota for me to ignore it.

Carmen strutted up to the guy, resting her hand on his shoulder. There wasn't any sound. It wasn't necessary. It was clear what was going on. I bit the inside of my cheek when he pulled her in closer, causing a metallic taste to dance on my tongue. My body went rigid when their lips met and his hands slid down to her hips.

The audience roared, speaking loudly and laughing. I flew out of my seat, covering my mouth with my hand and sprinting for the exit. I fought back the tears, but they were already pouring out by the time I was in the aisle. I was only a step outside when someone grabbed my arm.

I was forced to look at her. The satisfied look on Carmen's face told me she had waited for this moment far too long. "I told you I was only letting you have him."

I shook her off. Words fought their way to the surface, but I forced them down and moved toward the exit. Someone shouted my name just as I left the building. I froze at the sound of his voice. I hated that I stopped. I hated the way my stupid heart still skipped a beat at the sight of him.

"None of that's real." Dakota stopped at my side. He reached for my hand, but I slapped it away from me. "I didn't do that. Senior Salute has to be behind this. You couldn't even see a clear shot of my face. You know—"

"I don't know anything. This wouldn't be the first time you lied." I cut him off. "I do know what I saw. It all makes sense. Why you kept on saying sorry, over and over again."

"I would never hurt you like that. I've told you countless times how disgusting I think cheating is—why would I do that to you? Why would I do that to you with someone who had cheated on me?"

A good quarter of the auditorium had followed us out, witnessing the worst day I'd had in a long time. There were a few people shouting at us, begging for a physical fight. I wasn't going to let them have what they wanted. Punching Dakota wasn't enough to mend the hole forming in my heart.

"It didn't look like me." Dakota tried to defend himself. "Sylvia, listen to me."

"No! I know what I saw!"

My tears were coming down faster.

A hand grabbed my shoulder. "You don't need to listen to him."

I looked back, relieved to see Pierson.

"Leave before I regret letting you leave," Pierson warned.

Dakota hesitated, but he walked off, returning to the auditorium.

"All of you leave!" Pierson shouted to the swarm of teenagers. "The show's over."

Burying my face in his shoulder, I wished I could fade out of this world—out of this dreadful, dreadful place. I wanted to be transported to a better time when there wasn't so much heartache and deception in my life. A time when Dakota wasn't the villain in the story but rather the hero who swept me up in his arms.

I had left Maine to leave my problems behind, thinking it would be safer in a new location where I didn't know a soul. But California had worse demons lurking in its alleyways, masked as lovers and friends. I'd been lied to and played as if it were some kind of game.

This wasn't how we were supposed to end.

This wasn't how we were supposed to end.

Repeating it had been meant to make it less painful, but it wasn't working. My tears only fell faster, harder. My cries grew louder, muffled by Pierson's bulky red sweater. He held me, firm hands circled around my waist.

We didn't say anything in that moment. No one bothered us as I felt myself wither away in his arms. Every now and then, he would tell me, "It's going to be okay" and "We'll get through this."

It was the way he said "we" that carved out the slightest bit of hope that this could've been worse. But that small moment was gone when the soul-crushing memory flooded back.

All this time, I had been so hung up on disarming Dakota, I had lost sight of the dangers of doing so. In a land where dreams came to die, I was another dreamer who had found my own dream crushed by reality.

Chapter Fifty-Two
Don't Let Me Go

Dad thought I needed a real routine, one that was outside the constant cycle of thinking about Dakota, not eating because of Dakota, and avoiding sleep because of Dakota.

Any time I talked, or even opened my mouth to say anything at all, his name came to mind in the worst possible way. Each thought was separated by memories of Dakota. Dad suggested I should join the track team and finally take up that poetry class.

This time, I took his advice to heart and signed up for the spring poetry class at the community center.

Christmas break was nothing but constant visits to Ronnie's apartment, crashing in her spare room, dodging calls from Dakota, and pretending like my life wasn't over. When her mom was fast asleep, she would text to see if I needed anything, and I'd always ask for her to sleep in the bed with me.

Tonight, though, was different.

She hadn't showed up when I texted her. I stretched my limbs and didn't find her at my side. I heard voices down the hall. I knew for certain that she wasn't talking to her dad. He was long gone, headed in for his graveyard shift.

Letting out a long yawn, I slipped on my sandals—the only shoes I'd brought with me—and went down the hall.

I made sure my hand was firmly on the hall doorframe when I saw who was at the front door.

"She doesn't want to see you. Now leave before I call the cops."

"Please let me speak to her. Please," Dakota begged. Dakota never begged. His hands were wrapped around a box. "I need just one minute—"

"I won't let you say a word to her." She cut him off. "Leave, Dakota. You've been stringing her along this entire time and fucking with her head when we both know you still love Carmen. The last thing she wants right now is your half-assed apology."

"I wasn't cheating," he snapped. "You know none of that's true. That video is beyond fake."

She shook his head. "She doesn't want to talk to you."

"I'll talk to him," I said, holding the wall harder when I said it.

Ronnie turned around. "You don't need to talk to him."

"I know I don't need to do anything," I told her, heading to the front door. "Go back to bed. I'll be fine."

Simply seeing him standing there at the front door hurt me more than I'd thought it would. I swallowed the vile words I wanted to throw at him.

Dakota had dark circles, proof that he'd lost almost as much sleep as I had. His shirt was half tucked in, half out. There were stains on his jeans. Everything about his appearance looked off. He was a mess. Oddly, that made me feel better.

Good, I thought. I hope he's gone through hell.

Ronnie hesitated in the hall but eventually headed to her room. Dakota raked a hand through his greasy hair. I wondered when he'd washed it last.

His eyes scanned my body. When they reached my face, a pained expression shot into his eyes. "Sylvia." He sighed. "I miss you so much. I haven't slept in what feels like days. I haven't been able to eat. My thoughts are completely off the rails."

"I don't care."

"I shouldn't have just broken it off."

"Once again, I—"

"Are you even listening to me?" He shook his head. "I didn't do any of that stuff you saw on the last day of school. You have to believe me; it was a setup."

"I don't have to believe you, Dakota. I don't have to do anything for you. I know what I saw during that presentation. You've been stringing me along. You knew it would hurt me if I found out. Well, guess what? You've succeeded." My voice cracked. I couldn't hold myself together anymore. A tear rolled down my cheek. "Aren't you happy now?"

"God, no." He frowned, stepping forward to catch my falling tear, but I slapped his hand away.

"Don't you dare touch me. You've lost that right," I growled. "Why did you come here anyway?"

With a shaky hand, he handed me a small, beat-up cardboard box. I flipped open the top and found three cassette tapes, each one with a different label. A vintage Walkman was tucked in the side with one tape already inside. Each cassette had my name written on it in his beautiful handwriting.

"I told you it took a lot longer than I thought it would to get you this gift. It's one of the three parts of your gift. I made these"—he shook the box—"back in November."

"Is there another part?"

He nodded. "The third gift is at the corner of Fifth and Ninth streets. If you want, I can drive you there."

"I'm not getting in your car."

There were too many memories in that car, trapped inside the leather seats and tinted black windows. I had loved him in that car; our relationship was sealed in there like a vault. There was no way I'd get back in there after everything that had happened.

"I understand," he said meekly and walked backward away from the door.

I shut the door and went to the living room, lifting the Walkman out. I pulled out the only empty cassette tape case in the box and found a small note written quickly on a piece of paper.

My Doll,

A while ago, a much more awful version of me told you that I would never sing for you. I've evolved, believe it or not (with help from you). And I've taken the time to make a set of cassette tapes written out to align with our roller coaster of a relationship.

I've added a few original works that I created. At the bottom of this box, you'll find another one of my gifts to you.

I know I can't buy you a customized claddagh ring, tickets to our favorite show, or a shiny new car, but that doesn't mean I love you any less. You don't understand how much it tears me apart inside that I can't spoil you like you damn well deserve. I've given you all that I can, and even though you've never asked for more, I hate that I can't shower you.

Just wait. I'll get famous and make up for it all. ;)

— Your Kota

Bringing up the index card for the cassette tape already inside the Walkman, I read it in a shaky, wobbly voice. Then I went through all the index cards for the cassette tapes and read them.

Side A: For When You're Missing Me

"Thank God for Girls" by Weezer
"I Miss You" by Blink-182
"505" by Arctic Monkeys
"I Want to Hold Your Hand" by the Beatles
"Sunshine Superman" by Donovan
"Knowing You" by Dakota Ridgewood
"She's a Genius" by Jet

Side B: For When We Aren't Together (Short-term, Of Course)

"I Wanna Get Better" by Bleachers
"Too Late to Turn Back Now " by Cornelius Brothers & Sister Rose
"Love Will Tear Us Apart" by Joy Division
"What We Had" by the Drums
"My Doll" by Dakota Ridgewood
"Too Late to Say Goodbye" by Cage the Elephant
"I'm Not Gonna Teach Your Boyfriend How to Dance with You" by Black Kids
"If I Ever Fall in Love" by Shai

Side A: For When I'm Confusing

"Hard to Love" by the Drums
"Friday I'm in Love" by the Cure
"Cold Cold Man" by Saint Motel
"I Don't Know How to Love" by the Drums
"When You Sleep" by My Bloody Valentine
"Enough" by Dakota Ridgewood
"Island of the Misfit Boy" by Front Porch Step

Side B: For When You're On Your Period & You Want to Kill Me

"Janie's Got a Gun" by Aerosmith

"Bloodstream" by Ed Sheeran

"Bloodstream" by Stateless

"Flow" by Cage the Elephant

"And It Hurts" by Junica

Side A: For When I've Messed Up (Hopefully Not a Bad Mess-up)

"All Apologies" by Nirvana

"How Soon Is Now?" by the Smiths

"Gone" by JR JR

"Sweetie Little Jean" by Cage the Elephant

"She Loves You" by the Beatles

"How It Ended" by the Drums

Message from me

Side B: For When You Forget How Much I Love You

"R U Mine? by Arctic Monkeys

"Baby I'm Yours" by Arctic Monkeys

"Money" by the Drums

"Flawless" by the Neighbourhood

"Afraid" by the Neighbourhood

"I'll Be Your Mirror" by the Velvet Underground and Nico

"Rollercoaster" by Bleachers

"If I Tremble" by Front Porch Step

"Aware" by Front Porch Step

Epilogue

Pierson's party was the last place Hanan Pejman thought he would be on a cold December night. He'd promised to go only because Sylvia had asked, begging and pleading all day. It was awfully hard to say no to the saddest girl in town.

He was getting a headache from all the screaming and loud music inside the house. Then Carmen tried to approach him, and that was his cue to step out for fresh air. After that big stunt in front of the whole school, there was no way he'd take her back. The only reason she had temporarily been nice to Sylvia was because of him. He'd asked for her to not give Sylvia a tough time. Carmen had promised she wouldn't start any trouble. But all that had changed after that night at the Smell when Hanan had gotten hurt. Vengeance had sparked in her eyes, and Hanan had seen it right away. He'd broken it off, thinking it would make her less destructive. It had done the opposite, though.

Hanan eased his back against the side of the house and fished out his phone, checking his notifications. The back door opened. He poked his head around the corner and saw Pierson walking out, grinning like a fool.

"You look happy," Hanan pointed out. "Did you get someone's number?"

"Nah." Pierson bit the corner of his lip. "But I think I'm really close to getting with Sylvia."

Hanan snorted a laugh and stuffed his phone back into his pocket. "I have a feeling that you'll be losing her trust pretty soon."

"What are you talking about?" Pierson growled. "You're delusional if you think I had anything to do with what happened on the last day of school."

"Oh, am I?" Hanan mused. "Because the only one I can see benefiting from this is you. At first, I thought it was just Carmen behind it, but then it hit me. If Sylvia never gets back with Dakota, then who would be the winner? Ah, right. Pierson. It's the perfect opportunity for you to swoop in, steal the girl, and look like the hero." Hanan began to slow clap. "Bravo. You're a class-A manipulator."

Pierson rushed up to him. "I didn't do this."

"Then why are you trembling?" Hanan observed. "You and I both know that Dakota is the last person to do something like that. The way he was with Sylvia was different from how he was with Carmen. Somehow, you managed to always be at the right place at the right time. You're slick for pulling that off, that's for sure."

"Sylvia doesn't think that."

"So, you agree that Dakota wasn't the one in the video kissing Carmen?"

"I didn't say that."

Hanan found himself laughing in amazement. "You're really something else, Pierson, if you're the one behind all this. I might not like the guy, but I at least have the decency to not ruin Sylvia's image of him."

"I swear I wasn't behind it."

Hanan took a step forward and grabbed Pierson by his collar. "You better pray I don't find out you were. Because if I find out you were involved in even a small fraction of it, I'll make sure next semester at Crescent Hart Academy is hell. And you know I'm fucking capable of ruining your life."

"W-why do you even care so much?" Pierson stammered.

Hanan dropped him, causing him to stumble back a few steps. He refrained from punching Pierson square in the jaw for even asking that. "I know what she's been through, and I know that she doesn't need you or your stupid friends to mess with her. Do you know she recently found out she's adopted?"

"She told me."

"Did you bother to ask what happened to her parents?"

Pierson fell silent.

"Her dad killed her mother. He was an abusive maniac and took his own life after taking hers," Hanan hissed. "She doesn't need a stupid friend like you taking advantage of her when she's at her lowest."

"Hey, I'm one of your so-called stupid friends."

"Yeah, don't remind me," Hanan huffed, smoothing out the wrinkles from his polo shirt. "I'm serious about what I said, though. I'm hoping you aren't a part of this."

Pierson shifted nervously in his shoes. "You . . . you can't tell her that I did it. She won't ever look at me if she knew I set that entire thing up. I wasn't going to do it, originally; honestly, I wasn't going to. I was set on never doing a Senior Salute thing. But when Finn practically gave the chance to me, I knew I had to take it. Dakota's spot was open—"

"Wait. You can't do a Senior Salute on a member. That's against the rules. Don't you mean you set a bet on Sylvia?"

"Dakota is an ex–Senior Salute member. Finn cut him off after he found out that he wasn't doing the tasks anymore and that he wanted to protect Sylvia."

"Anymore?"

"Yeah, he . . . he did a lot before he finally cracked and stopped taking orders. He switched the script and refused to go ahead and do what the other Senior Salute members wanted. This all started because someone in Crescent Hart Academy wants Sylvia gone, and gone for good," Pierson informed him. "Finn offered her spot to the second-highest bidder."

"I don't get it. You're telling me that you targeted Dakota and not Sylvia?"

"Exactly."

"So, who's the one going after Sylvia?"

Pierson shrugged. "Apparently, it's a pretty big deal. Something huge. I tried to tell Finn to go easy on her, but he said that he wouldn't. Supposedly, she wouldn't make some kind of deal with him."

This book has a playlist matching a song to each chapter title.

You can find it on Spotify, titled *Disarming Dakota Playlist*.

Acknowledgements

I would like to thank my mother, first and foremost, for getting me interested in reading in the first place. I want to thank my Wattpad readers, as well, for being there every step of the way as I wrote this book. I was about eighteen when I finished the first draft to this story. I'm now turning twenty-seven and I finally get to see this book in print. I want to also thank my editor, Fiona Simpson, for helping craft this story. Lastly, I would like to thank my husband, Troy Daniels, for being the amazing support system that he has always been for me.

About the Author

At the young age of eleven years old, Sumeya Abdi Ali began writing comic books in her bedroom to cure her boredom. Slowly, that love for storytelling grew into writing short stories in magical settings. By the time she was seventeen, she started her Wattpad account and began posting on the site to share stories with the world. In 2015, Ali won a Watty Award for Ditching Greek in the New Adult Genre category.